Acclaim for *The Letter Opener*

"Maclear is a novelist of promise. She has a way of drawing characters and drawing readers to them." —*The Hamilton Spectator*

"In this unusual, cerebral tale, Maclear shows her young narrator striving—successfully at last—to connect the missing pieces in the great puzzle that is the world." —*Toronto Star*

"Maclear does have a very felicitous way with words that makes the book a compelling read.... There is resonance and thoughtfulness to [her] writing, and in her visceral championing of the lost, the forgotten, the quiet and even the shabby." —*Quill & Quire*

"Kyo Maclear's humanity is an indispensable part of everything she writes. It's the basis of her commitment to history's forgotten people and its undelivered stories. Her voice is exquisite and incisive." —Joy Kogawa

"An ingenious work of fiction that combines rich, intimate characters with a narrative that unfolds like a puzzle box. *The Letter Opener* is that rare book that nourishes both the mind and the heart, at once wise and tender." —Naomi Klein

"This is an extraordinarily thou   e diaspora of lost souls who hav   s. It all feels so tranquil, so exact,   scien- tifically organized way, the repor   , observant and honest witness." —Elisabeth Har

The Letter Opener

The Letter Opener

Kyo Maclear

HARPER **PERENNIAL**

A Phyllis Bruce Book

The Letter Opener
© 2007 by Kyo Maclear.
P.S. section © 2007 by Kyo Maclear.
All rights reserved.

A Phyllis Bruce Book, published by Harper Perennial, an imprint of
HarperCollins Publishers Ltd.

First published in hardcover by HarperCollins Publishers Ltd: 2007
This Harper Perennial edition: 2008

HARPER ● PERENNIAL®
is a registered trademark of HarperCollins Publishers Ltd.

Excerpt from *The Waves*, by Virginia Woolf, reprinted with
permission from The Society of Authors as the Literary
Representative of the Estate of Virginia Woolf.

From "Stoned Gloves" in *Pacific Windows: Collected Poems
of Roy K. Kiyooka*, © 1997, Talon Books Ltd., Vancouver, BC.
Reprinted with permission of the publisher.

HarperCollins books may be purchased for educational, business,
or sales promotional use through our Special Markets Department.

HarperCollins Publishers Ltd
2 Bloor Street East, 20th Floor
Toronto, Ontario, Canada
M4W 1A8

www.harpercollins.ca

Library and Archives Canada Cataloguing in Publication

ISBN-13: 978-0-00-200894-5   ISBN-10: 0-00-200894-7

Photograph on page ix by Sami Suni; page 173 by Johnny Lye;
page 237 by Mark Roeper/all iStockphoto
Design by Sharon Kish

Printed and bound in Canada

For my parents, Mariko and Michael

the way they fell
the way they lay there

the dust sifting down,
hiding all the clues

From "Stoned Gloves," by Roy Kiyooka

Part One

A pair of leather shoes (dark grape colour)
An LP by the Mamas and the Papas (slightly scratched)
A pack of cigarettes (Player's, unopened)
A silver ball made of the foil from cigarette packages
    (8 centimetres in diameter)
A small potted houseplant (philodendron)
A notebook of inventions (spiral bound, slight tear on
    back cover)
A navy blue sweater
A brass belt buckle (second-hand)
A digital watch
A canvas shoulder bag (olive, messenger-style)
A silver chain necklace
A portable chess set (wood)
A pair of eyeglasses (steel framed)

One

Andrei vanished a year ago, during a snowy week at the beginning of December 1989. Here is what I remember of our last moments together.

A face peeking through the furry oval of a hooded parka. Blowaway snow sparkling in the air. Grey slush on the tops of our boots. As we walked to the bus stop after leaving the mail office, we were discussing Communist soft drinks. Vita Cola, Top Topic, Traubisoda, Polo Cockta, dark, sweet-sour beverages in thick bottles, a world of fizzy substitutes I had never imagined.

"Kofola! A delicious blend of coffee beans, herbs and squash!" he said, in his best announcer's voice.

"Squash? That doesn't sound right," I protested.

He had been especially talkative all day, full of nervous non-stop banter. We ran to catch the bus together, and when we arrived at the subway station, we went our separate ways, with him rushing down the long flight of stairs to catch the southbound train, and me pushing hip-first through the narrow exit turnstile, off to do some Christmas shopping. Without a word of warning or farewell, he was gone from my life.

The words *vanished without a trace* have always seemed fateful, conjuring up images of jets sucked into a swirl of ocean, mountain climbers swallowed by sudden clouds or the deserted, gritty alleys of film noir. But Andrei did vanish without a trace, and I immediately entered the surreal territory inhabited by family and friends of the disappeared. A place of trails winding into mystery, of dead ends.

Andrei's desk area at the mail office where we worked soon became a museum tableau. Everything was just as he had left it—the dented cushion he'd rested against, the crumpled coffee cup in his wastebasket—but the alchemy of loss was already at work. A banana ripened on his desk. Burnt-brown spots spread with each passing day, the air carrying its moist, oversweet odour. All my senses were strangely heightened and the smell became emblematic of his absence.

I didn't know whether to worry or be angry or sad. Often, I just felt numb. I kept calling his apartment, hoping he would answer, but the phone just rang and rang, echoing the hollowness I was feeling. By the fourth day, his workstation was stacked with unopened packages, a row of yellow buckets piled half a metre high with parcels waiting to be sorted. I began to avert my eyes, lurching my desk away from his, closing off my sightlines by rearranging my shelves. My co-worker Baba was convinced that Andrei would return. "Give him a few more days," he said. But my mind was not so easily reassured. I kept inventing reasons to get out of my chair and wander around the office.

On the fifth day, I arrived at my desk earlier than usual and spent a few minutes scanning the local newspaper. I played a game of "what if," randomly placing myself and people I knew into certain stories.

A live-in nanny from Manila had defied a deportation order.

A mother in Utah had lost her baby down a well.

Two children in Windsor had tied a third child to the railway tracks.

It was a kind of emotional litmus test. To see if I could bear life's daggers. I made the substitutions—imagining myself as the brave nanny and the grieving mother—then became aware of what I was doing and folded the paper in half.

I looked over at Doreen, the office receptionist, eating a Chelsea bun at her desk. Doreen was a thin, nervous bottle blonde who tied her hair up like a ballet dancer's. Today she wore a light-pink blouse, a blouse so pale it blended with the tone of her skin, producing the brief illusion that she was wearing nothing at all. I considered asking her if she had anything new to report, but she was focused entirely on the pastry in front of her. She uncoiled it delicately, licking the icing off her fingers, taking small savouring pecks. Her nonchalance both fascinated and appalled me.

Off in the distance, I heard the first mail truck pull up at the unloading dock of the Undeliverable Mail Office, then a second and a third, until I knew a fleet of red and blue trucks was parked expectantly outside the concrete building. I sat back in my chair, arms folded, and waited.

The mail arrived promptly at 8 a.m. (as it did every morning), with the thunderous clatter of doors opening, the clacking of plastic tubs moving across metal belts and rollers. The wind rushed in, too, and a few stray leaves fluttered to the floor. The first buckets to be unloaded at the dock contained misdirected and miscarried paper mail. Packages and parcels came after. Finally, a bucket arrived containing the rubble, the items that had come loose in the mail: contents that had sprung from burst envelopes and overloaded boxes; things that didn't yield well to friction belts, flat sorters and mechanized claspers; rebel objects that had bobbed away from the mail stream and now required human hands. All of this was set into a hamper for special attention, then wheeled to my workstation in the corner of the room.

On that Friday after Andrei disappeared, I was counting on my job to get me through the day. I listened for the last loading door to clang shut.

Marvin, one of the dock workers, was rolling a hamper toward me, creating a blunt drumming sound on the side with his palm. When he arrived at my desk his face was flushed and shiny, accentuating the small pits in his skin. He took a long, deep breath, removed his toque and unzipped his parka, exposing a T-shirt that said *Brains and Brawn*. Delicately, he pulled off a delivery slip attached to his clipboard and handed it to me to sign. As he waited, he raked his hands through the container, letting the smaller objects slip through his fingers.

He picked up a child's geometry set, opened the lid and tilted the metal box toward me. "Brings back memories."

I glanced up and wrinkled my nose. He smiled, flicked the lid closed and started picking up objects at random, turning them over in his hands. From across the room came the grunts of three workers who were attempting to move a mountain of misdirected magazines onto a larger pallet.

Marvin turned around and gestured toward Andrei's desk: "Still no word?"

"No, not yet. I'm hoping he'll be in later today."

"He'd better be."

Marvin tore off a copy of the delivery slip and said goodbye. To my right I could see Baba preparing a cup of coffee in the staff kitchen. (To make his Nabob taste "Lebanese," Baba always added several heaping teaspoons of sugar and a sprinkle of cardamom from a small envelope he carried in his pocket.) I watched him carefully stir and taste his drink. Below his dark moustache, his lips curved downward in a faint frown.

"Have you heard anything?" he said, crossing the floor toward me, cradling the steaming cup in both hands.

"No, I was hoping you had."

Baba stood for a moment looking me over. I glanced down but I could feel his eyes running down my flat hair, under the square of my chin, up my pale cheeks to the bags under my eyes.

"You didn't sleep again," he concluded.

"I stayed up late watching a movie."

He shook his head. "I'm starting to worry about you."

"Don't. Honestly, I got a few hours of sleep."

And then, perhaps to prove that I had slept, or perhaps because it was preying on my mind, I told him about my dream.

It was a lucid dream, the kind of dream where you are aware that you are dreaming but remain helpless in determining the outcome. It was about Andrei and his pigeons. The pigeons were swishing around Andrei's head, cawing—rapid, high-pitched cries—more like crows than pigeons. I couldn't make out the setting, but I think it was a park because there was a rustle of wind. I was afraid for him.

I remember calling to him—loudly, I thought—but there was no sound. My mouth wasn't moving. A few seconds later my alarm clock went off. Then the phone began to ring, and the moment I picked up the receiver and heard Paolo's voice, Andrei was gone, leaving only a strange afterimage of a man wrapped in a rippling cloak of bird wings, lifting away.

"Naiko, my dear, what you need is a good, long rest." Baba was speaking in the voice he used to reassure frantic postal customers.

"Andrei will be back. I guarantee you. He's done this kind of thing before. When we worked together at the hotel, he disappeared once for three days. Maybe he was drinking, I didn't ask. We've called everyone there is to call. Trust me. He'll turn up eventually."

"Yes." I nodded. "You're right." But my words were forced. All the random tragedies I had ever read about in the newspaper or seen on the news—the multi-car pileups, subway suicides, house infernos, muggings and murders—flashed through my mind. All those calls to the police, the hospitals, immigration had yielded nothing. There was no one who matched the description we had provided: *Romanian, 33, white male, curly brown hair, pale brown eyes, 5'11", 155 pounds.*

"Was he erratic or depressed?"

"A drinker? A drug user?"

"Was there anything in particular that might have driven him away?"

Perhaps I had omitted something crucial in our report. Maybe there was a scar or birthmark I could have mentioned or a nickname or alias I had never learned that would have made the profile more complete. What were the truly distinguishing parts of a person? Foot size? Ear shape? Teeth condition? The information I had about Andrei suddenly seemed so paltry. For that matter, how would I draw a composite picture of myself: *Japanese Scottish Canadian, 29, female . . . mud-brown hair, medium-to-robust build, dimpled arms, small bust . . . ?*

Police APBs. Personal ads. The idiom of want.

After Baba left, I sat chewing my nails, feeling shaky. I became aware of the room's ventilating flues, the lights buzzing overhead, the water pipes clanging as hot water travelled from the basement heater to faucets throughout the building. I could feel the building's substance seeping into my pores.

Outside, morning traffic clogged up Ellesmere Road; cars honked in the distance. Every time the door swung open, I expected it to be Andrei.

(Maybe Baba was right. There was a precedent. He had vanished, he had reappeared, he had vanished . . . he would reappear.) I kept picturing him walking through the door and cracking a joke about his absence.

Perhaps it was the steady rhythm of a conveyor belt across the room that finally soothed me. My mind focused on the clacking of the plastic containers as they moved across the metal rollers. A draft travelled up my pant legs. I popped a vitamin and slipped on a pair of cotton dust gloves. For a moment, I forgot about Andrei.

By the time the clock struck 9 a.m. I was immersed in my work, matching objects to customer claims letters. The entire room had settled into a hum of efficiency. For the first time since Andrei's disappearance, I allowed myself to sink into its particular oblivion. As I worked, I settled into my chair, my thighs softened and spread against the stiff cushion. I embraced the tedium.

The Undeliverable Mail Office employs a staff of twenty-two people. It is the only mail recovery facility in the country and is housed in a suburban building known as the General Post Office. The open space in which we work is as big as an airport hangar, a warehouse that resembles a giant pawnshop. Over five million pieces of mail pass through its doors every year.

I have been in mail recovery for over eight years. I started working for Canada Post as a summer-jobber during university, a temporary postal clerk selling stamps, weighing packages and so forth. Just as I was about to enter my final year of university, I took a chance and applied for a permanent position. To my surprise I was offered a full-time spot at the Undeliverable Mail Office.

At the UMO, I store routine in my muscles and bones like a precious fuel, finding gratification in the simple reunion of people and their possessions. Others might see me as unambitious or incomplete, but not so. I love my job because most days it requires attentiveness and intuition, and I have these qualities.

As much as I try to persuade my father and my older sister, Kana, otherwise, they behave as though I lead a tragically narrow existence. I tell them it's certainly more gratifying than selling car insurance or writing advertising copy. (They overestimate the value of a liberal arts degree in today's world.)

When I wrote to my father in England to announce that I had accepted a permanent position in mail recovery, he made no attempt to hide his dismay. ("Forgive me if I'm sermonizing; but sometimes I worry, not that I'm always right, that your intelligence is being squandered, that you are giving up opportunities to express your creative aspects.") It's a terrible thing when people think they're safeguarding your dignity by putting down what you love to do.

Thank goodness for my mother, who supports my choices. She's the only one who doesn't seem to think that the start of my real life still awaits me. She knows better.

She knows that some things only appear dull from the outside; if you approach anything with a restless or impatient attitude, you will get bored or irritated. Once you get inside the work, it is infinitely rewarding. Ask a Zen monk. Or a psychiatrist.

In any given week I might see twenty primary school photographs. Some arrive unmounted. Others are inserted into cardboard frames that have been printed to resemble wood. On the surface, they might all appear the same, but on closer inspection, there are always shades of difference. Hands resting in laps. Hands clasped together. Feet crossed. Feet spread. Hair long or short, tied up or loose. Shoulders hunched or pinched back. Eyes focused or drifting. Mouths grinning or not. Most people would readily agree with the verdict that no two children are alike. What's harder is to get them to extrapolate to the inanimate world: no two clock radios, no two rubber duckies, no two lace doilies . . .

That is my experience with my flock of objects. There are always subtle distinctions. A nick, a scratch, a tear, a blot, a blemish, a loose or tight part, a missing widget. Every object carries its own genetic code.

To my surprise, the last time my sister was in town she came by to see where I worked and to take me out for lunch. Andrei was away having a tooth fixed. I was standing with Baba by the staff kitchen when Kana arrived at reception. I saw Doreen point toward my desk.

"She looks like you," Baba said. "Same features." He indicated his nose and chin.

"Except she's prettier," I said.

"Only if you like—" He made a gesture signalling *very tall*. I gave him a friendly jab.

I am not unattractive, but beside Kana I feel plain and squat. She's willowy and sleek and wears her long hair loose but perfectly combed. Mine is short and parted on the side in a stylish but sensible bob. But it isn't just the way she looks that attracts attention, it's the way she acts. She fills space more purposefully than most people. You get the sense that she is going places even when she is sitting in a chair.

After a few quick introductions, Kana and I left the office and walked through the parking lot and toward the street. She was wearing a belted beige coat and a pair of brown leather boots that grazed her knees. Her hair had grown several inches since I had last seen her. I was wearing a dark green Paddington coat that suddenly felt several sizes too large. Even though I was leading the way, she walked briskly, her hair whipping lightly in the breeze, and I soon found myself rushing to keep up. By the time we sat down in the restaurant, I was winded.

"Well, then," she said, after we had placed our orders. "Before I forget, I have something for you." She dug around in her bag and brought out a package wrapped in tissue. "I met up with Dad during my layover at Heathrow. It's from him. Burberry."

"Thanks," I said, staring dumbly at the plaid scarf I had unwrapped. I was still taking in all the information I had just been given. "I didn't realize you've been keeping in regular touch with him."

"Off and on. Lately more on," she said, trying to sound indifferent. She stood up and draped the scarf around my neck. "Well?"

"Very nice." I took it off and laid it carefully across my lap. "It must have been expensive."

She shrugged. "He can afford it. Which reminds me," she said, leaning forward, "we were talking and guess what? He wants to help pay for you to finish your degree."

I leaned back. "No way. Forget it."

"Think about it."

"No," I said.

I folded up the scarf and shoved it in my coat pocket. By now, I understood that my sister was on an errand. I had become a "cause" uniting my sister and my father. They were both devious.

"How's Paolo?" she asked, changing the subject.

"Fine. Busy. He's been doing a lot of weddings lately. You should see some of the arrangements they ask him to make. They're hideous. And they all have these epic names like Love's Jubilant Glory—"

"He's *still* at the flower shop?" She narrowed her eyes. "Isn't it time you both had a fresh start?"

"Don't, Kana."

"Are you living together yet?" She inspected a fingernail.

I shook my head.

"At least he's better than that last guy you dated."

"Eric."

"Paolo's sweet. He just needs someone to work on his fashion sense. Those flannel shirts and ratty cords . . ." She shuddered.

"I like the way he dresses." I took a deep breath. "What about you? Are you still with Daniel?"

"John. When we find the time. He's been assigned to the Jerusalem bureau. But I think it's starting to get to him. He keeps sending me cards signed 'Flak Jack.' Hey,"—she fished through her bag again—"did you bring any cigarettes?"

"Uh-uh. I quit."

"Wish I could," she said, tossing her bag onto the empty chair beside her and gesturing to the waiter. "You know, there are career counsellors."

I scowled at her. "I like my job."

"You're a glorified clerk."

"I'm not a clerk. I'm a mail recovery employee." No matter what anyone says, there *is* a hierarchy. People in mail recovery feel superior to window clerks, who, in turn, feel superior to letter carriers, who, in turn, feel superior to the machine operators in Primary Sort.

"You're almost thirty, Naiko, for chrissakes."

Kana is a journalist with *The Independent*. In any given week she'll hop between England and France, or wherever, covering stories on soccer riots, immigration reform and government corruption.

Kana has her suitcase. Her days zip by. My days come and go with an almost liturgical consistency.

She's the daughter my father wanted.

Every morning, I ride to work on the bus, a twenty-minute journey past landscaped factories and new subdivisions rising from muddy plots. Every day, I scan the billboards from my window seat as we pass car dealerships with their plastic flags flying and Asian grocers with their crowded storefronts. I hold my takeout coffee, taking small sips until I feel the bitter sediment on my tongue. The doors wheeze open and shut. It is not until I experience the hiss of the brakes, so loud it sends a shiver up and down my spine, that I feel fully alert.

I am at ease among the familiar crowd. The man leaning against the silver pole, the smell of wet smoke on his clothing and hair. The university student, about my age, very pale and thin, even in her puffy down jacket. (Lately she has been reading *Ulysses*, which I've started a couple of times and never finished.) The harried young woman, also about my age but eight months pregnant, with her singing toddler and "family-size" box of Tide.

Of course, there are days when the journey is unpleasant, mornings when I witness school kids bullying one another or find myself sitting beside someone with a severe cough. I don't mind the mutterers but I do my best to avoid those passengers who, without provocation, erupt into abusive rants or sexually explicit monologues. My boyfriend, Paolo, detests public transit. For the most part, I find that riding on the bus gives me a feeling of contentment. For a short, suspended time, I am in harmony with others.

That Friday morning I remember watching the toddler bouncing on his seat while his mother struggled to undo his scarf. As I smiled in sympathy, I instinctively raised my hand and felt for the scarf my father had sent me. Andrei had been gone for almost a week. I turned back toward the window and watched the freezing rain splash across the glass.

"Some people would rather not be found."

That's what the police officer said, explaining the protocol around missing persons. "A child's disappearance is an immediate Amber Alert. But with capable adults, things can get muddy."

Of course, I was upset by his words. I thought I knew Andrei well. I couldn't imagine that he wouldn't want to be found. What I have learned since is that men, the ones who are not obviously endangered or victims of foul play, seldom disappear in any passive sense of the term. Men run. They escape, they bolt, they hide, they pursue. They start new lives, with new names, in new places. They feel no need to explain.

Two

Pens in a glass jar, flower-print calendar, ledger book, a pair of cotton dust gloves. Such small anchors are my bearings. Every morning when the mail trucks arrive and the doors clatter open, I pull out the drawer and fish out a pair of fleece socks. I layer them over my regular socks so that my feet do not get prickly from the cold. After that, I grope in the drawer for my vitamins. I take one from the bottle and lean back against the chair, chewing it slowly, watching as Marvin makes his way across the floor.

If you repeat particular actions over and over, you can feel them creating a protective force field around you, dissolving your worries, making you feel safe. When something unexpected happens, you can feel that force field being broken. Andrei's arrival in my life was like that. It broke me open.

Andrei started working at the Undeliverable Mail Office just ten months ago. When he first sauntered in, a confused expression on his face, he seemed like someone who had taken a wrong turn. (I later learned that he had misplaced his only pair of glasses, which explained his exaggerated squint that first day.) Everyone focused on him: a compact and attractive young man, with a disorderly head of light brown hair and a prominent, almost Roman nose. Doreen, seated at her reception desk, seemed particularly enthralled, and I am quite sure I saw her glance at his hand to see if he wore a wedding band.

It was Baba, however, who made the first move. He stood to welcome his old friend. (When Andrei first arrived in Canada, they had worked together as waiters at a hotel near the airport. Baba, in fact, had recommended him for this job.) Andrei squinted and smiled, perceptibly relieved to see Baba approaching from across the room: Baba's outstretched arms of welcome, Baba's mouth grinning in a wide hello. Andrei walked forward to meet him. Their mutual delight was obvious, yet once they stood face to face, a formality came over them. They shook hands, smiled, but did not embrace. I sensed an established boundary that could not be crossed, like the starched custom of some other era.

The closer Andrei got, the more handsome he appeared. Broad forehead, defined cheekbones, angular jaw—strong, balanced, masculine. Just the sort of face that women are generally attracted to.

As the manager walked him around, making introductions, I noticed the first signs of an endearing awkwardness. He gave everyone he met his rapt attention, but said odd things like: "I am extremely happy to be here. And you? Are you satisfied?" He scribbled quickly in his notebook while the manager explained various office matters to him, but every now and then I would catch him nodding repeatedly like a catatonic child. He seemed oblivious to the people eyeing him.

Andrei was assigned to sort the "intact parcels." On his first day following his training, I watched as he systematically organized his desk, lining his pens to his left in order of size and colour and stacking his notebooks to the right so that they aligned exactly with the corner of the desktop. Then he methodically positioned his chair to ensure that the sun, which was streaming through the windows, no longer troubled him.

Though his desk was next to my own, we didn't have our first true conversation for several weeks. The first time I ventured a hello, Andrei said hello back so punctually that I was left speechless. Had I been snubbed? Or was he simply asserting his right to privacy in an open space without walls or office cubes? When the manager walked by to pick up our time sheets, the interruption was a relief. I began running through my head two or three sentences that I could use to engage him at the next opportunity: friendly but not overeagerly so.

My preparations proved to be unnecessary. A few days later Andrei initiated a conversation by asking me how long I had worked at the office. He was starting to note my existence and I could feel him studying me as if judging whether I could be trusted. He spoke English comfortably, though his speech was deliberate and strongly inflected, the words strung together with a Romanian rhythm. Even when he mixed up words, such as "undecorating" or "earwitness," it was clear what he meant. When he couldn't think of a word, he moved his hands in the air like whisks.

The third time we spoke, Andrei was sorting the plain brown packages from the ones that came gift-wrapped for birthdays and holidays. He was wearing a navy blue sweater, one of the few he seemed to own. His face was scrunched in concentration. I followed his hands, his gestures of gently raising each package, inspecting it, setting it down again and then writing on his clipboard. He stopped at a small yellow package. He tested its weight, squeezed its contents curiously. It was taped down at the lip and edged with animal stickers and flowery doodles.

"Look at this," he said. "A child's handwriting. It's addressed to her 'Daddy.'"

"What does it say there?" I pointed to a tiny square of writing in the bottom corner.

He held it closer and read, "'Fragile. Keep flat.' Or, more precisely, 'Frygil. Keep Fat.'"

We both laughed. Then I examined the package. "It's sad. The kid probably doesn't know the package was lost and her father may not know it was ever sent."

"Hmm," he said, then took off his new glasses and held them up to the light. "But life is full of bad connections. We all know it; we just trust in luck." He exhaled on the lenses and then wiped them with the arm of his coarsely knit sweater.

I looked at his face, at his pale lips and his boyishly smooth skin.

"Let me see what's inside," he said, slicing open the end with an exacto knife. Out slid a folded note, a packet of powdered cake mix and a box of candles. He picked up the paper and looked it over on both sides. After a moment he shook his head. "No luck." He made a note of the contents, closed the package back up with adhesive tape, then printed the word *Abandon* across the front.

Beside him was a stack of parcels with blurred writing. Black ink ran like spider legs across the face of the top parcel. The signature of a cloudburst.

The manager passed by our desks, scrutinizing, frowning. I glanced up and he nodded slightly. I got back to work. Andrei had moved on to the other bundles, devoting sleuth-like attention to those that still had a chance of being repatriated. Careful fingers worked at each sealed seam until the contents spilled out.

When the packages and bins contained money or other valuables, we laid them carefully on a side table. These items were later collected and delivered to Baba's workstation. It was Baba's job to attend to "major" valuables, but he had a love–hate relationship with his work. In the abstract, he accepted the delineation between items of "major" and "minor" value as a necessary part of postal organization, but anyone who spent a week in his company was bound to hear him soliloquize about the West's tendency to separate "matter" from "spirit." Under Islam it was important to show respect for the humbler things in life.

"Why differentiate? Why put money before sentiment? This pen is the means of poems. And even the silliest poem says more than that monstrosity!" he said, pointing disdainfully at a gold bracelet. "Why are people addicted to junk?"

Despite his philosophical reservations, which were always stated with good humour, Baba continued to preside over the subdivision of items deemed by Canada Post to be of "market worth." He was chosen because he was conscientious and fast. (In the early days of mail recovery this branch of the office tended to be run by retired clergy, whom it was felt could be trusted with items of value. Baba was our man-of-the-cloth equivalent.) He was a first-rate decipherer who had a genuine flair for working out the scrawled addresses on international mail. He also had expert penmanship—small, perfectly sloped script, which he had learned at boarding school in Beirut. If an envelope addressed to Benji Williams containing a hundred-dollar bill and a note that read *For your wee pocket. xxo Grandma* went astray, Baba could be trusted to record it. Turning to *W* in his ledger, Baba would find the number 12796 and, beside it, enter the name "Williams," the postmark date and the amount "$100" in careful block letters. In the column marked Addressee, he would enter "24 Dover Crescent, Oakville," and a note "No Known Party," followed by "Illegible Return Address." If the gift was claimed, the word "Returned" would be added to another column along with a date.

We still worked in an archaic world of longhand, carbon paper, rubber stamps and filing cabinets. Computers were slow to arrive at the mail office. Despite their renovation of other public institutions, their benefits for our work were still unclear. The job of sorting through mangled mail and defunct correspondence relied so much on the analog process of touch, on logic, or, failing that, on hit-and-miss.

Many of us secretly adapted our record books so the entries would tell us more at a glance. Baba added his own final column, a sliver-thin space in which he marked an *S* if he felt an item was particularly special and a *U* if he thought it was useless. I developed a star system, with four pencilled stars designating the objects I cared about the most, the ones I would spend the most time and effort attempting to repatriate. Some things resisted automation.

"Three minutes per package," Andrei said.

"Is that what they told you it took?" I asked.

"Yes. If you go by The Manual. The mail recovery book says that three minutes is the average time needed to trace a package back to its owner."

"Ah, of course. The Manual."

"Three minutes is just enough time to take in the essential things," he said.

"Meaning that there's no time to snoop."

"Exactly."

Even so, I felt a dash of shame when I came across anything that was unmistakably private. Riffling through a woman's diary, handling her most personal keepsakes, the sentimental poems she had written on scented paper, the pornographic pictures someone had taken in a bathroom stall. At such times it helped to work swiftly, with the composure and efficiency of a doctor carrying out a pelvic exam. Voyeurism was the tendency to linger.

I have to admit that Andrei was a consummate letter opener. By this I mean he was ethical in the extreme. He treated his access to other people's lives as a privilege not to be mistreated. If Andrei's lost mail contained secrets, so they remained.

Three minutes per package. Andrei was studying the contents of a small green tin. Snuggled in a nest of shredded newspaper was a bag of homemade cookies to be disposed of immediately, as were all perishable things. He placed a red pencil mark on the accompanying greeting card, a chocolate-brown stamp on the envelope, the Latin phrase *Post Obitum*—and the gift was dead.

The truth is that fewer than half of the thousands of packages that pass through the building reach their intended destination. The rest lie stacked on shelves and stuffed into storage bins: annals of doomed friendship, misdirected love, lost relations. The backroom is always crammed with canvas bags, their mouths cinched closed, their sides tattooed with the word *Undeliverable*. A thick cover of dust coats everything. Particles float in the light. Spiders twirl their threads and the husks of dead insects lie in corners.

An archive of misery. Or so I had always thought.

I can see now that only after Andrei's arrival did the daily dead mail offer new life. The piles of misfortune didn't dampen Andrei's morale; rather, they revealed his optimism, as if misadventures were part of him and all his life he'd been sorting them out. Wasn't it remarkable, he'd say, that anything ever reached its destination at all? Wasn't it wonderful that things sometimes turned out as you'd hoped?

Did some lost token of love ever touch him deeply? I never asked and he never said. Occasionally, I would notice him create a careful line drawing in his beloved notebook of an item on his desk—a bicycle pump, a model ship (the latter rendered in cutaway perspective)—but these drawings seemed less an expression of sentimentality and more a study in technical design: a reminder of the engineering student he had once been, and the inventor he hoped to one day become. I assume that for every pile he waded through, only a handful of objects stood out. The remainder would have been perfunctory messages sent on the occasion of a birthday or to someone travelling: John getting over a cold, Sylvie having a new baby, father's upcoming surgery, the weather, the food. Flat, formulaic words sent without much thought; words that feigned interest but escaped involvement, words that maintained a distance.

The morning he showed me the "Frygil, Keep Fat" package, Andrei offered to make us some tea. As he drifted off to the kitchen, I found myself staring blankly at my bin. All the objects from the morning delivery beckoned to me eagerly. Crocheted baby clothes, a satin scarf, a bottle of body lubricant, pencils with fuzzy pompoms . . . I sifted the satin through my fingers, enjoying the slippery smoothness. I tucked two fingers into a tiny cashmere mitten.

Andrei returned with two mugs and sat down. I turned my chair toward him. The steam curled slowly from the surface of the tea.

"I keep thinking about what you said about bad connections," I said. "Because really, when it comes down to it, I'm not what you'd call a virtuoso of personal interaction. It's like I'm lacking some sort of social gene. I'm either half-communicating or half the time missing the point."

Andrei massaged the bridge of his nose, didn't say anything. We sat in comfortable silence, drinking our tea. Finally, as if arranging space for a reply, Andrei pushed his mug a few centimetres away from him.

"Do you have a husband or a boyfriend?" he asked.

"Yes," I said, surprised by his directness, "Kind of. Yes. A boyfriend. His name is Paolo. He's from Argentina."

"Do you talk well together?"

"You mean are we open with each other?"

"Yes."

"Most of the time."

"So you trust him?"

"Yes."

"And he trusts you?"

"I think so."

"And generally you understand each other?"

"On good days."

"Well then, you should consider yourself fortunate. You have a good connection with someone. You can share your specificity."

"Specificity?"

"I don't know if I am saying it right," he said. "What I mean is the opposite of generality—you know, your surface. Your public face." He paused. "Most people need the comfort of generalities," he continued. "They want to say only the correct things. They prefer conventions. They hide their specificity."

I thought, at that moment, of my late grandfather. He was a smart man, but he couldn't bring himself to say anything that wasn't brilliant. His words and finally his silences had to be profound, so that he couldn't tell his children that he missed them, or his wife that he loved her.

"But some conventions are important, don't you think? They're reassuring," I argued.

"You're right. Some conventions are necessary. They are deeply felt."

"But you think most aren't."

"No. Most are filling."

"You mean filler."

"Yes, *filler*. We avoid being precise or specific because we are lazy, or scared, or indifferent. Every day we say to someone, 'How are you?' but we really don't want the details."

"Unless the details are exciting," I said. And I held up a burlesque-dancer salt shaker. "*Comme ça.*"

Andrei laughed. We sat there smiling at each other for a moment. As his mouth widened, I noticed a few missing molars, dark gaps at the back.

"Now, if you will excuse me," he said, stretching and rising from his chair, "I must go precisely and specifically to the loo."

I sifted through the bucket beside me. Picking up a small wooden music box, I lightly traced its border of seashells, thinking again of what he called the comfort of generalities. Of course, he was right. After all, intimacy would be diluted if expressed too readily. Even with Paolo, I often felt myself coasting on the surface, relying on physical instead of emotional closeness.

Was it self-preservation, dishonesty, lack of courage? I tried to imagine a life in which every conversation was a revolt against triteness. All that unfettered frustration, euphoria, nostalgia, sullenness and anger suddenly loose in the room.

Imagine the fatigue! It was a wonder, I thought, that anyone ever speaks from the heart. Most occasions call for a defiant shallowness. More impersonal, maybe, but more sensible, too.

Three

*W*hen I learned from Baba that Andrei was a refugee, I began to study him more intently.

"No one would think you're a refugee," I said.

"Well, I am. And what do you think a refugee should look like?"

I called to mind images of refugees—images formed from what I assumed must be their suffering. Columns of muted people travelling on foot, inching westward. And where had these images come from?

Honestly? The Concert for Bangladesh. George Harrison's charity event for homeless Bengali refugees, which I had first seen on television in the early 1970s. (I was embarrassed to admit to Andrei that my first impressions had come from a rock concert.) What I remember most clearly about the event was the song "My Sweet Lord" accompanying a fundraising appeal during a concert intermission, the euphoric, pot-stoked chorus playing as a flow of soundless people passed across the screen. Exhausted women balancing precious possessions on their heads, clutching pots, pans, bedding and babies—always their babies; desperate people whose salvaged belongings seemed at times incongruous, like the woman bearing a rice-sack to which she had tied a small painting of gold flowers. I remember a boy walking beside her. The sun above them was bright and constant, a hot, indifferent sun. I remember fighting the impulse to look away. I could see that the boy was about my age and for this reason he was harder to watch.

What happened to that boy and his family? Did they ever return home? Did they reach across North America and establish new villages—such as the Somalians with their New Mogadishus or the Vietnamese with their Little Saigons? Were they transformed into parking lot attendants or night watchmen or pizza delivery "boys"?

What made Andrei a refugee? Was it his bony chest? No, that was too obvious. His second-hand wardrobe? Perhaps, but that could also be attributed to general thriftiness. (I, for one, regularly shopped at Goodwill.) The reality was that there was no single outstanding characteristic—and why should there have been? Andrei frequently saved half his sandwich and kept the remaining Saran Wrap to use later, but to a different degree, I, too, was frugal. He appeared to own few personal belongings, but so did I. As to his deference to the manager, which seemed then the classic survivalism of the refugee, well now so much later I look more closely at myself, at my own often deferential demeanour. There were layers and layers to Andrei, I would discover, and refugee was but the latest, and thinnest.

"Anyway," Andrei was saying, "people don't generally like to be called 'refugees.' That's a file word. Like 'asylum-seeker.' Or 'displaced person.' People have their prejudices about refugees."

It was a clear message telling me how to be his friend, and so, in the coming months, I learned to listen as a diarist might, without presumption or pity. I was not to cast him among the earth's indigent—the limbo dwellers, the invisible people.

"Don't forget," he said, "Einstein was a refugee."

Despite Andrei's previous friendship with Baba, I quickly became his closest companion at work. He did most of the talking. Every now and then I asked a question, and as the weeks passed I could sense the foundation of our friendship strengthening with every revealed detail, every shared idea. I never thought to ask, *Why are you telling me?* It just seemed natural and necessary.

I recognized, early on, that Andrei was withdrawn—it's what he preferred. Only gradually did I uncover his specificities: the sketches of his eccentric inventions, his collection of newspaper clippings, his passion for chess. When he spoke about anything he loved (his mother, the river near his house in Romania, the sound of a steel-string guitar), his eyes lit up, and his very skin seemed to glow.

Early in May, two months after his arrival, he pushed his chair around his work table so that we sat back to back. I remember the wonderful feeling of sitting close to him, a softly humming body warmth. Such a warmth that I felt I must have wished for it—yet to what end I did not know.

And I realized that just as I had been drawn to Andrei, something was drawing Andrei to me, and it eased my image of myself: the bumpy texture of my skin, the solid unmoving mass of hair. With Paolo, it sometimes felt as if there was nothing more to know. With Andrei it felt as if I was at the beginning of knowing. He pushed me into a dizzying world of defectors and stowaways. He was like one of the mystery packages that arrived at the office come alive.

One afternoon while we were sharing a lunch break, he confessed to me that homesickness was interfering with his sleep.

"Can I be personal for a moment?" he asked.

"Of course. What is it?"

"It's a dream, you know, one of those night horrors. I'm worlds away from everyone, feeling very lost, trying to reach out to others and panicking that I'm forgotten, that I'm nothing, and the part of me that knows how much I have to be thankful for, well, it's sliding away. When I wake up—I hope you don't mind me telling you this—there's you and Baba. And my job, and my birds, and all the bits and pieces I remember about my country, and I'm so grateful!"

It was such an unexpected moment, so revealing of his emotions, and of my part in his new life, that I can no longer remember my exact response. I know I reassured him, but I can't recall the words I used. Still, I know I was deeply touched. You see, Andrei took several months to tell me the story of his life. It was a long story with many offshoots and detours, so that what I am recounting here is a reassembled summary. Have I remembered it correctly? Have I imagined scenes he never actually described to me? He sometimes told me several versions of the same event and perhaps I have been selective. What is clear, however, are the key moments that shaped his life.

ANDREI ARRIVED IN TORONTO in the summer of 1984. A room had been arranged for him at a settlement house in the west end of the city. He spent the mornings in a vocational placement program and in the afternoons made his way to the local library, where he read through recent newspapers and magazines. There were regulars at the library. A skinny woman with a faint moustache, and a clothing fetish for any shade of yellow, who surrounded herself with gardening books. An older white man in a sweatsuit who quietly read aloud from the Koran. Another man who was teaching himself German. He sat among these people and before long was greeted with familiarity by the library staff.

Every day between the hours of 1 and 6 p.m., when the library closed, he gathered facts about his adopted home and copied them onto a pocket-sized writing pad. He looked for what was current, the catchphrases, the names of politicians and celebrities, recent films (although he rarely found the time or money to go to the movies), the names of local parks and city landmarks. He wanted to collect as many household terms as possible, out of curiosity, and also out of eagerness to occupy himself. He read and read. When people spoke of something he didn't know, he listened attentively, leaping at unusual or unfamiliar bits of speech. He was cracking the social codes and behavioural patterns, the hierarchy of education and class.

He copied people's attire and habits, creating a safe character acceptable to his new world. He took to wearing a baseball cap, he dressed in blue jeans and a grey T-shirt with the words *Dalhousie Men's Diving* emblazoned across the front in a distinguished, collegiate typeface. Every morning he put aside his dimes and nickels for the library's photocopy machine, double-counting his change so that when he dropped the coins into the slot he could do so with the unthinking ease of a regular.

It took some time to get used to the eccentricities of his new home. Exiting a streetcar. Operating a pay phone. Reading a map. Finding an address. Such simple everyday things, which at first held the fear of failure, became a test of belonging. Each misstep left him feeling alien and unprotected.

When Andrei spoke with the other men at the settlement house, men who had travelled from all over the world fleeing wars and political oppression, they shared only details from the present, safe things, in scraps of English. They were not down-and-outs; they would be moving on. They were all just biding time until the day they could begin their real lives.

Every few months one left and another arrived.

The settlement house reflected their transience. There were pots and pans, clothes, milk crates, pillows, plates, towels, a TV set, mattresses, an electric stove, a fridge. But there were no pictures, no scented candles or ornaments, nothing personal that tied them to this place and time whose memories they would someday erase. By Andrei's fourth month, a sense of kinship had developed among the men, but they were a momentary family who could disperse without regret or record.

Of the residents, only Andrei and a South African spoke English prior to their arrival. The other men knew the words *revolution, interrogation, embassy, displaced person, exile, death squad,* but otherwise spoke like children, stringing together disjointed phrases—words that didn't have much to do with the thoughts they were having, or the half world they lived in. Urged on by an exuberant ESL teacher, they mouthed the language of parrots: *Hi, how are you? Nice day, isn't it? Would you care for a coffee?* Their accents slowed them down, but no more than if they had been taught to say, *Do you know what's happening in my country? Do you know what brought me here?*

As time passed and the expected days and weeks at the settlement house grew into months, the men increasingly began to share, if not their secrets, their daily routine. In the evenings, they did domestic chores, played cards on the bare floor surrounded by empty pizza boxes, smoked cigarettes or watched the international news on a springless couch, whispering, praying, cursing. There was footage of floods in Indonesia, famine in Ethiopia, drought in India and earthquakes in Peru. There were ads for cars, sugar cereal and floor cleaner. There was a story about the U.S. president's favourite jelly beans.

For Christmas, his first year in Canada, Andrei received from his roommates a bottle of wine, a digital watch and a clear plastic cube with Canadian coins embedded inside. In Andrei's mind, there was a distinct line that divided Romania from Canada. On the Canadian side of the line were the gifts he received from those first roommates in Toronto. On the Romanian side was a pair of shoes.

Four

 ndrei could never forget that on the morning he left his home for the last time, his favourite shoes were somewhere under his mother's bed. They were leather shoes the colour of dark grapes. He hadn't intended to leave them behind, but by the time he remembered them, his mother was asleep and he did not want to risk waking her. The previous evening he had left a letter for her with a woman named Ileana with instructions that she was not to deliver it until two days had passed. He knew that it would be impossible to depart with his mother's blessing. He rummaged through his closet and found an old pair of running shoes that he laced shut with a piece of packing string. At 4 a.m., he hurried from the house. In his right hand he held a plastic bag containing his belongings. His boyfriend, Nicolae, awaited him as planned in a car parked just off the town's main square.

During the preparations for his departure, Andrei had convinced himself that he was reducing his mother's burden by leaving. And although he was heartsick to part from his family, it was the only thing he could think to do. The state police would soon arrest him. Yet now, as he rushed toward the square, he was struck by another truth: he was a deserter. That sudden thought so stunned him that he halted in front of the pharmacy. He contemplated turning back. There was still time to change his mind, to go directly to Ileana and tear up the implicating letter.

Had he misjudged the severity of his situation—the threat of the Securitate, his own helplessness?

He stood there, cemented to the ground. The sky began to lighten, the first minutes of daybreak passed, and then, as abruptly as he had stopped, Andrei continued walking. Whatever motive had propelled him to this point had been right. Turning back was as precarious as going forward, and his heart and mind said *forward*. It was June 1984 and he was headed for the port of Cernavoda on the Danube–Black Sea Canal.

Andrei had grown up in a small bordertown in northern Transylvania that had at various times belonged to Hungary and Romania. Once known as a smuggling centre, the town had long since lost allure. Gone were the days of gambling houses and brothels. All that was left were poorly stocked stores: a government ration shop for flour and sugar, and vegetable stalls reduced to selling wormy apples and withered cabbages.

The food shortages were so severe that the government had announced a "scientific" diet for its citizens. Meat and excess starch and vegetables were unhealthy, declared the Health Minister. At the same time that truckloads of fresh crops were being transported to the capital for export, pamphlets began appearing that showed thin but happy families sitting down for dinner together. The pamphlets, which made a virtue out of eating less, were not warmly received. Within a week, they could be found littered around public spaces, defaced with drawings of corpulent politicians, overinflated balloon faces with Dracula-like fangs.

Thinking of food was excruciating; Andrei fantasized about bright red tomatoes, buttered bread, spiced meat, honey loaves with centres as soft as cotton. At night the craving was overpowering, and he would chew on his leather watchband, twisting the straps between his teeth to extract some imagined meal.

Andrei and his mother and brother fished from the river and grew their own food when they could. They relied on a small garden plot of hardy root crops, tucked discreetly behind the house. Sturdy beet leaves, feathery carrot tops, and pale-green onion stalks; a sweet earthy fragrance filled the air when the muddy harvest was pulled from the ground. Each morning Andrei would kneel to pat down the soil, delighting in its wet heaviness on his hands. Before she left for work at the dressmaking shop, his mother, Sarah, prepared an evening meal for the family, creating soups and stews from the meagre supplies. Pearls of barley sinking into vigorously boiling pots of liquid, adding a bit of thickness and bulk.

They had the mountains to thank, Andrei once said.

The Carpathians. Their snow-capped peaks were visible from the kitchen window. The mountains were their blessing, their shield. Foothills were strewn with tough bushes and wildflowers. Mechanized farming was impossible on this kind of land. In other parts of the country, bulldozers were razing villages to pave the way for agro-industrial complexes. Throughout the early 1980s, high-rise housing projects shot up everywhere, an endless horizon of concrete conformity. The dictator Ceausescu crushed homes and carted families off as if he were forklifting boxes in a warehouse. Anyone who asked questions or resisted found themselves summoned by the Securitate.

Unlike villages to the south, Andrei's village had been preserved for centuries. Some of the houses still had their original wooden mouldings and fixtures. Andrei's house had belonged to his mother's family since before the deportations in 1944. Nearly four decades later, it was still identified by locals as an *Evreica,* or "Jew," house on the basis of its design. Blue walls the colour of robins' eggs and pale yellow trim. Filigreed borders. Large arched windows. "The house that still stood" was what his mother called it.

Not that their house had always been so intact. Not that the villagers had watched out for it. Quite the reverse. Andrei's mother, Sarah, was Jewish. The only member of her family to survive the war.

Back in 1945, piles of overturned earth surrounding former Jewish homes and gardens were pitted with deep holes where neighbours had dug, searching for any valuables hidden by Jewish families in their final hours. Many deportees had committed their cherished possessions to the earth—wrapping jewellery, photos, silver, paintings, everything they hoped one day to rescue.

So when Andrei's mother returned alone at the end of the war at the age of fifteen, a survivor of Ravensbrück and a twelve-day march out of the camp, her family house was empty but filled with traces of uninvited company. The delicate film of dust that should have accrued in the family's absence had been disturbed. The sheer range of footprints and fingerprints suggested that the house had been searched exhaustively on several occasions: scratches and dents on the remaining vandalized furniture, dark yellow rectangles on the pale yellow walls indicating absent pictures, water stains weeping across the dining-room table. Where once there had been light fixtures, there were now only naked bulbs with broken insides, hanging from wires. Holes where windows used to be. Chairs repositioned. Bare bookshelves. Cabinets with sagging doors.

The remaining contents of drawers were strewn on the floor, items nobody wanted: a single glove, a dried inkpot, a box of clarinet reeds, a tub of skin lotion, a ball of twine, candle stubs. And yet to Sarah this valueless debris seemed as precious as heirlooms.

She spent the first day of her return in tears, moving from room to room. Toward early evening, she tried to tidy up. She returned the objects to their places, hanging the glove on a hook in the hallway, sliding the inkpot against the wall where her father's desk had been. She scraped wax drippings from the floor with her fingernails, and used her head scarf to wipe all the doorknobs and faucet heads. She scrubbed the door frame where a brass mezuzah had been pried away, reciting the *Sh'ma* as she touched her fingers to the bare wood.

Near midnight, she sealed up the windows as best she could and set up a bed and lantern in the kitchen near the wood stove. She ignored the scuttling sounds coming from the closet and rested her head on a folded towel. When she dimmed the lantern, the discoloured patches on the walls stood out like holes made by a giant fist. She filled them with her memory, creating ghost portraits of her parents and grandparents. She stared at each one of them until she could not imagine the walls without them.

Sarah's return to her village elicited total astonishment. She had vanished from the streets and shops of the town and now she had reappeared. She was a spectre, Lazarus returned from the dead, a phantom of the wind. The man at the dairy turned down his radio and stared when she walked in. His mouth gaped. He extended his hand as if reaching to touch, to prove she was solid, then stopped himself. A former schoolmate looked at her and then, without breaking her pace, crossed the street to avoid passing her. Many of them remembered the morning the town ghetto was emptied and the Jews were told to meet at the village school, where they were taken to the trains. Sarah's existence forced them to recall what they had seen and not . seen, how they had watched and how they had looked away. Her survival had the double effect of both allaying their guilt (she was alive) and intensifying it (she was alive in spite of their inaction).

Sarah knew that she was an unwanted reminder of shameful times, fated to become the conspicuous Jew, to be either pilloried or patronized, treated with too little or too much kindness. Yet she had to remain in the village, a survivor praying for the return of other survivors. The looks of curiosity, of pity, of disdain were the price one paid for waiting in a world that preferred to forget.

Waiting was Sarah's way of warding off a conclusion, of delaying the pain of final knowledge. A state of permanent suspension that might have driven others to madness kept Sarah from falling apart. The shock of the war never lessened, but as time passed, Sarah learned that it was possible to form a kinship with even the most shattering of absences. Her shoes resounded across the open floor as she went about keeping house.

A month after her return, Sarah removed an old door bolt from the basement and brought it upstairs, to protect herself in her new, old home.

How can I truthfully know the lives of people I have never met? I reassure myself I am as good a detective as any. After all, it has become a life work reconstructing other people's stories. I spend each day before my mountain of scraps, and imagine.

When Andrei first told me about his mother what I imagined was this: one girl among hundreds of thousands of silhouettes set against a vast plain of packed snow. I saw the crunch of feet, the march of death. The recesses of the mind are full of the grim images of history waiting to be summoned, and this image possessed me—the figure of a girl trudging along an icy path, slowly fading into the swirling snow.

"I'm remembering those newsreels we were shown in school about the liberation of the camps, but we were never told what happened to the Jews who survived," I said.

"Many people died from disease. But others spent years in other camps, waiting to be resettled, like my mother."

"Do you ever wish she had gone west rather than returning to Romania?"

Andrei was quiet before he answered. "I can't think that way. If she hadn't gone back, she wouldn't have met my father . . . my brother and I wouldn't exist . . . I wouldn't be sitting here now." Then he paused and smiled, pointed to the stack of work on his desk. "Just imagine the backlog."

And we laughed.

Once, when I asked Andrei to tell me more about his father, this is what he said:

"There's not much to tell."

We were walking to the bus stop together after work.

"When did your mother marry him?" I prodded.

"When she was eighteen. He was double her age and already a widower. I don't know if they were ever happy," he continued. "My father was away so much of the time, working as a miner in the mountains, I don't know . . ."

I nodded.

"He had one long holiday every year, around New Year's, which probably explains why both of us, my younger brother and me, were born in September."

As we walked, a smile spread across Andrei's face. "My favourite memory of my father is of lying with him on the couch, singing songs by the Mamas and the Papas that we had memorized, by phonetics, off an illegally copied album.

"We were lying close together, which is probably why I remember it. My father wasn't a very touchy kind of person. He didn't kiss or hug us. My mother was affectionate, but never my father—although he could be sweet with my mother. He had strong ideas about what it meant to be a man."

I saw a bus approaching in the distance.

"When did he die?" I asked.

"In 1968, when I was eleven. He had emphysema. There was nothing the doctors could do. He wasn't even sixty. For the last month of his life, he just lay on his bed, taking short breaths from an oxygen tube he held in his hand. Then one morning I woke up and he was curled up on his side, trying to get air. When he stopped breathing, the whole house turned quiet.

"After he died, I stayed in my room. I had a short-wave radio my father had built years before and I lay on the bed and listened to the music shows on Radio Free Europe. Phil Ochs. Bob Dylan. That sad sandpaper folk music. Every night I listened until the radio transmission stopped. One morning I woke up and found an extra blanket on the bed and my brother, Eli, sleeping close beside me.

"Seeing him there made me pull myself together. I remember thinking, *If Papa is dead, then it is up to me to protect everyone.*"

SHORTLY AFTER SHE BURIED her husband, Andrei's mother was presented with an opportunity to emigrate to Israel. News had spread that the dictator was selling Jews to Israel for hard currency, ten thousand dollars for each exit visa. Sarah declined: she refused to be treated as a commodity. Instead she went to work. She joined a local co-operative, and eventually became chief tailor of a small dressmaking and dry goods shop in the middle of town.

She sat at the sewing machine from morning until evening, making clothes, bedcovers and curtains; unfurling metres and metres of stiff buckram, a coarse blend of linen and cotton that could refurbish a chesterfield or "shield an army from bullets," as she put it. Though she worked with fabric of various colours, she herself never wore anything but black. Not just any black but the deep charcoal black of mourning. Even ten years after her husband's funeral, she wanted the villagers to know that his was not the only death she remembered.

Andrei helped his mother at the co-operative as often as he could. The rumbling of the roll-up metal doors was a signature sound—*we're open*—heard from blocks away. Sarah taught her sons to wind a bobbin, chalk the pattern marks onto fabric and use the foot-pedalled Singer (and, later on, the electric Singer) so that they could assist her when she was especially busy. The women of the town came to the shop for their dressmaking needs, and Sarah gained a reputation for her ability to make new outfits from old garments. She could cut down a sack and turn it into something stylish.

A few months after she started work, the co-operative ordered a second-hand mannequin from Bucharest. Delivered to much acclaim on the back of a truck that also carried blackboards for the local school, it had red hair, a large upturned nose, eyebrows arched like arrows and wide red lips. The bust was large and placed very low; the hips were marked by jutting pelvic bones. Wearing a fitted wool suit, demurely arranged in the store window, "Shirley," named after Shirley MacLaine, one of several American actors who had visited Romania during Andrei's childhood, became a symbol of Western glamour and sophistication.

On the day Andrei turned thirteen, his mother presented him with his father's old belt. The buckle was a hand-hammered brass square. The strap was enormous on Andrei's small frame, so she used an awl to punch extra holes in the brown leather, spacing the holes evenly until, on the eighth hole, it no longer slipped off his waist. The newly tailored belt became Andrei's pride and joy. He wore it everywhere, fitting it through his belt loops, tucking and winding the extra foot of leather so that it was artfully distributed around his middle. Even with the extra holes, it looked ungainly, a belt designed for another body, but Andrei refused his mother's offer to trim its length. And she never insisted, perhaps because secretly it gave her pleasure to see it left intact, a kind of continuance. The final, awkward embrace of the father.

Five

Does the sender have any obligation to the receiver? Andrei was not always reliable when it came to recounting the events of his departure from Romania. He had a tendency to bounce around in time, so that I was often left to piece his story together morsel by morsel. This was especially true in the early months, when our encounters were confined to breaks during the workday.

On one such occasion, Andrei was reminiscing about wading in the Tisza River as a child. It was a humid summer morning, and we had been sitting outside on a concrete planter having a coffee. A group of pigeons was waddling around us, pecking at bread crumbs Andrei had tossed a few seconds earlier. A car approached and the flock took flight in a sudden updraft of wings. I turned toward Andrei, saw the way the sunlight passed through his fair hair. As he spoke, the sweat gathered on his upper lip. I blushed and turned away when he noticed me staring at him. Passersby would have seen us as a somewhat odd couple: a slender, boyish man leaning toward a full-bodied woman. I often felt that no matter what adjective I applied to Andrei, the opposite could be said of me. Thin/Wide. Bony/Voluptuous (if I flattered myself). Light/Dark. Male/Female. Gay/Straight. Our differences piled up. His proletarian provincial childhood. My two-car suburban upbringing . . .

"You know," Andrei said, gently knocking my shoulder, "I think we make a wonderful pair."

"Do you?" I said, with feigned casualness.

"Yes. Like—" He paused. "Like Ginger and Fred . . . Like igloo and polar bear . . . Like peanuts and chocolate."

A smile glowed in his eyes.

I laughed. "You're crazy."

I could feel a hum of activity between the two poles, an electric exercise of imagination, an unwritten correspondence.

This platonic attraction of ours grew into a need, an urgency I had never before experienced. It was not a matter of Andrei being more attractive than Paolo. Paolo was handsome in exactly the brooding, tossed-together way I liked. Dressed in jeans, a plaid flannel shirt, work boots and glasses, he looked like a skinny, intellectual lumberjack. We had our rough patches, but no more than any other couple. In essence, we were well-suited. Right? That's what I began to wonder. The more I got to know Andrei, the more I found myself silently comparing. Paolo was my boyfriend, but it was Andrei who made me feel vital—important and alive.

Paolo had grown up in Argentina with rigid ideas about social etiquette. He was not the type to stop on the street, for example, and greet the corner-store owner and ask about his children's piano recital or his recent trip to Vietnam. Paolo was the product of the prolonged dictatorship that had set neighbour against neighbour. He avoided situations that might call on him to intervene. This was the crux of our difference (as I understood it then). A part of Paolo still lived in a country his family had left almost ten years before, a world of grated iron shutters, where people closed themselves off from one another and learned to ignore the comings and goings of strangers. In this world, it was entirely possible for someone in the same apartment building to disappear, his fate never to be questioned or mentioned.

Then again, perhaps Paolo's temperament had nothing whatsoever to do with his history. Perhaps his aversion to crowds, his bystander apathy tempered by his fierce loyalty would have all been present even if he had grown up among auto dealers in Windsor or dairy farmers in Vermont.

THE TISZA WAS ONE of the longest rivers in Europe. As it rambled along the edge of town, within walking distance of Andrei's home, its current slowed. A few months before Andrei was to leave his village with Nicolae, a terrible accident occurred in a neighbouring town when the dam surrounding a mining reservoir containing cyanide burst. The contaminated water seeped into an adjoining river, and eventually into the Tisza, which drained from the Carpathian Mountains into the Danube.

Andrei was twenty-seven at the time and cramming all night for his final exams at the regional university. At 3 a.m., seeing that it was a full moon, he decided to take a break from studying and go for a walk in the woods by the river. There was no one else around. Other than the occasional rustle of an animal, the hoot of an owl, the night was silent.

As he approached the river, he noticed an acrid smell in the cold air, a strange taste of bitter almonds on his tongue. He shone a flashlight on the water. Clusters of fish twisted on the surface, mouths open and gills heaving. A few metres away a carp bumped violently against a rock then began swimming in circles. He moved the beam slowly along the river's edge and saw that several larger fish had veered into lather by the bank, trying to escape the poison.

It seemed inconceivable that a great river like the Tisza should suddenly die. So the following day, when men wearing protective suits and thick rubber gloves came from Baia Mare to pull the dull-eyed fish from the river, the town went into deep mourning. People came to throw flowers into the current and silently cursed the dictator for the accident. No one expected the river to recover.

The mine spill deeply affected Andrei. That evening by the banks of the poisoned Tisza, a feeling of doom spread through him. It frightened him to watch the fish drift by. Their dying reminded him of everything he had lost before—his father, his grandparents—and he couldn't bear the thought of another death.

It was dawn by the time he returned home from the river. Careful not to wake anyone, he crept past Eli's room and quietly ducked into his mother's curtained bedroom. He stood several paces from her bed. As his eyes adjusted to the blackness, he studied her sleeping form. Her greying hair tied in a long pale braid and drawn across the pillow. Her sunken eyes, the loose skin around her neck, her chiselled chin.

He willed his mind to journey back to childhood, to recover a younger, more consoling image, something that would be less distressful to carry away with him.

He stood there for a moment, and then he left the room without looking back.

IN ANDREI'S STORIES I had pictured his mother as invincible. She was always making, arranging, mending, planting, polishing and carrying things. To hear Andrei speak of his mother in other terms was disquieting. And I was disturbed by all this talk of death. I remember it made me think of my own mother, now living close to the mail office at Sakura, a seniors' home for Japanese Canadians. My mother was sixty-nine and by all accounts less active than Andrei's.

My mother's was a body gradually subsiding. Hands in need of regular massage to relieve crippling arthritis. Soaring blood pressure in need of pills. It wasn't just her body. It was her mind. She was more forgetful every day. And because I had a tendency to mistake forgetfulness for fretfulness, I had to remind myself continually that she was not especially miserable. (I once received a gentle reprimand from another resident at Sakura, Gloria Kimura, who said: *When you are old, Naiko, it becomes almost impossible to persuade other people that you are still sharp, current or—hardest of all—happy!*)

I was determined that my mother shouldn't feel abandoned, particularly by me, so I visited her at every opportunity. My sister Kana wasn't immune to our mother's decline just because she was far away. I could tell from her letters and phone calls that she was upset by my reports, and sometimes incredulous. To protect herself she insisted that our mother was exaggerating her memory loss. Strangely, I think she felt cheated. I was managing to sustain a relationship with our mother, who even in her declining state was a more active parent than our father.

As Andrei spoke, I pictured my mother's dark head nested on the bed, covers bunched in her hands, a spare pillow cushioning her body.

"Did you think about your mother a lot?" I asked him.

"Of course. She was at the front of my mind."

"But something pushed you to leave anyway."

Andrei glanced up, then down again. We were having lunch by the loading docks. The picnic table was covered with takeout wrappers from the falafel shop down the street, dribbles of tahini across the surface, but Andrei seemed not to notice or care. His attention was fixed on his notebook and a drawing of a suspension bridge he had started as soon as we finished lunch. His long rake-like fingers gripped a thick mechanical pencil. I studied the graphite dust on his shirt cuffs, then peeled back the lid of my coffee cup and took a sip.

Andrei's hands were seldom idle. He was always sketching or picking at his fingernails or tearing off pieces of paper napkin and twisting them until they resembled tiny maggots.

"The hardest part was leaving my mother, but I don't feel that I abandoned her," he said, and rested the pencil in the gutter of his book.

"I'm sorry, Andrei. I didn't mean it to sound that way."

"I wasn't a runaway like you see in the movies. There was no thrill to it. I didn't *want* to leave; there just came a point where I had to. There was a rumour that our names were on a list of people suspected of anti-government activity."

ONE AFTERNOON, ANDREI HAD returned home from school to find his mother sitting at the dining-room table. She had placed her hands flat on the table surface with an intensity that suggested an effort to remember or to communicate. Her gaze was toward the living room, focused on one corner, though there was nothing there.

What she was staring at was the apparition of an old armoire, which once stood behind a dark velvet sofa. She was staring at it in the same way that she would sometimes gaze at an empty bookshelf, stacking it in her mind with leather-bound editions of Eminescu, Dostoyevsky and Shakespeare, dictionaries and the Talmud, the hundred different titles that had formed her father's collection. Andrei knew his mother would enter this trance-state occasionally, revisiting her childhood home, taking inventory of even the smallest objects: a crystal bowl full of lemon drops, a favourite fringed pillow, a silver wedding platter. In this restoration, the vacant areas were bright colourful spaces, not the hazy, white light of memory.

Andrei greeted her with a kiss and lifted her red cardigan back onto her shoulders. He gave her neck a quick and gentle rub. She smiled and an eyelash slipped off her cheek onto the table. He felt that, inside, she was flinching in his presence.

The next morning, the street was bustling with people engaged in early spring chores. A woman several doors away from Andrei was beating a knotted rug she had draped over a washing line. Every time she gave a hard whack with the cane pole, a cloud of brown dust exploded in the air. Neighbours on the other side were mending their fence with a ball of wire. Someone fixed a roof leak. Another person cracked a piece of wood in half with a hatchet. A child skipped on the pavement. Yet at the moment Andrei appeared on the front stoop of his house, everyone froze. The entire street seemed to refrain from breathing until he had passed from view.

There was never a direct accusation, but everyone gossiped, and the gossip that surrounded Andrei and Nicolae grew savage; neighbours and classmates were like pack dogs sniffing the prey. Perhaps Andrei and Nicolae were stepping out of class, or walking toward the forest, or sharing a quick embrace—suddenly the torchlight was on them. People said they were in league with the Magyars, the Jews, the foreigners, the orgiasts, the anarchists. They stared and whispered about obscene excesses and sexual perversions. At first, Andrei stared back, but the merciless faces troubled him. They glowed with smugness. His treachery not only reinforced their loyalty, but also purged them, made them feel holy. For if he was guilty, then they were pure.

Why did he risk so much?

He didn't know. He was swept away. Maybe it was his need for something more, his desire to live a life of his own choosing even if it meant paying a price. Maybe he just needed to believe in something. Or maybe it was simply the way Nicolae put his mouth to Andrei's ear and murmured, *Because I love you.*

The effect was narcotic. Suddenly he experienced a swell of sureness telling him that everything would be all right.

Nicolae and Andrei met always in secret, always at different times of the day and night. When it became difficult to meet, they confided their thoughts in letters slipped discreetly between the pages of textbooks and passed between classes. Intoxicated poems, burning declarations and carnal prose, scrawled on envelopes, opened matchboxes, napkins. The naughtiest had a cartoon sketch of two humping cats, and, below it, a heart inscribed with the flowing words *Te Ador.* They took the precaution of leaving their letters unsigned, but Andrei could not bring himself to part with them. Instead, he wrapped his stack carefully in an old tea towel and tucked it between his bed and night table.

One day he came home and found his mother smoothing out a small mound of earth in the garden by the kitchen. A small shovel lay at her feet. As soon as she spotted Andrei, her cheeks reddened and she reached with a shaking hand for a cluster of dandelions.

"So many weeds," she said, and feigned an exasperated sigh. The digging had left her short of breath.

Andrei watched while she finished.

"You work too hard, Mama," he said, and managed a smile of encouragement.

When he went inside to change his clothes, he found that the bundle of letters by his bedside was gone, the tea towel along with it.

He waited, but she never mentioned the letters. That evening, he spent longer in the kitchen, stacking the dishes away, wiping the counters. When it began to rain and the earth turned to mud, he thought of them, buried in haste, absorbing the moisture, ink sliding off the pages, everything melting into grey mush. But still she said nothing. Even when the storm winds were so strong he thought the roof might blow away, even then, not a word.

At the time, Andrei thought he was going to lose his mind. He remembered she talked about crocus blades she had seen slicing through the soil and whether or not the carrots needed to be replanted in the shade and the importance of composting the soil and turning it over . . . and the entire time his heart was pounding. He wondered whether things would have turned out differently if they had talked about the letters, but they never had the chance.

After Nicolae was interrogated he convinced Andrei that they had no choice but to leave. Andrei knew that if they stayed, things would get worse. For them. For their families. For his mother.

Andrei and Nicolae fled Romania at the end of the school year. Their point of departure: the port of Cernavoda, just east of Bucharest. The journey southeast to the port took an entire day and night.

During the long drive a silence grew between them. As they barrelled along the gravel roads, the engine's vibrations ran up their legs. They rolled the windows down against the thickening heat and caught glimpses of the Danube as it slipped through the pale green countryside. The tracery of forest. Clusters of oak and beech. Orchard-covered hills. Once they were out of the mountains, the trees thinned out abruptly. There were stumps burned to the colour of coal and broken fences. Vast areas with no grass or underbrush, just a blur of grey fields occasionally strewn with scraps of machinery—a rusting plough, mangled iron chains, an abandoned backhoe. Other cars rattled past them on the road, then a heavy transport vehicle throwing up black gusts of dust and diesel. They rolled up the windows. When it started to rain, Andrei focused on the road ahead of them through the flapping of the windshield wipers.

They had taken this route once before. A month earlier, they had travelled with a group of graduating students from the University of Baia Mare to Cernavoda for the inauguration of a new canal. Flags were hiked to the skies. Children belonging to Pioneer organizations with red kerchiefs knotted around their necks and hair glued down with glycerine tugged at balloons shaped like giant ships. The lavish ceremonies, which continued for several days and nights, began with a state presentation and ended with a fireworks display. Overblown speeches by local Party leaders were delivered beneath a giant portrait of the dictator—emperor-like and brandishing an enormous hand-carved sceptre. A choir of peasants in ceremonial costume stood off to the side, holding sheaves of wheat and mechanically singing traditional hymns.

Thousands of workers had toiled during the canal's thirty-five-year construction. Not one mention was made of them. No one divulged that the canal, which linked the Danube at Cernavoda with the Black Sea to the south of Constanta, a sixty-kilometre stretch, had been dubbed the "Canal of Death."

All through the speeches, Andrei shifted restlessly from one foot to the other, aware of the bored audience around him, the ocean of numb faces. At the end there was obligatory applause and the acrid stench of gunpowder. Silk streamers in red, yellow and blue lapped at the wind.

Once the canal was officially opened, the crowd scattered, then departed. Andrei and Nicolae headed for the pier, where they spent the next few days studying the ships. There were rickety fishing boats, Soviet tankers, Bulgarian coal freighters. They familiarized themselves with the funnels, masts, bridges and planks. "Naval architectural research," they explained to anyone who asked. By the time they were ready to go home, a week later, the dockmen and loaders acknowledged and greeted them when they passed. Even the stray dogs scrounging by the garbage heaps barked and nudged at them in recognition. It was time to move on.

The following month, after they had decided to flee, Andrei and Nicolae arrived at the pier just before sunset. The air was cooling, and with the garbage cleared, the friendly dogs were gone. They sat in the car watching the fishing boats growing darker on the water, watching the warm light reflected from their sides until night arrived and their silhouettes melted away. They waited until they were approached, as planned, by a man who conducted an underground business of smuggling refugees across the water. For a fee, he would carry them across the Black Sea to the Bosporus.

Soon after, they found themselves on the *Zenica*, a rundown Turkish freighter. The dark blue paint was chipped and cracked; rust was thickening on the hull; a red flag flapped in the breeze, stained and ragged at the edges. The man disappeared below deck. After a few minutes, he returned and gestured for them to follow. Andrei and Nicolae accompanied him down the ladder into the belly of the freighter. They were thirsty. They were scared. They had heard stories of stowaways betrayed by the very people they had paid.

When they reached the bottom, the man smiled and reached for Nicolae's wrist, silently removing his watch. He slipped it into his back pocket, then reached again for Nicolae's wrist. He circled it with his hand, touching his middle finger to his thumb, bounced it lightly, then dropped it like a twig.

"Are you strong swimmers?" the man asked. "I hope so. The shore will not be easy to reach."

"We'll make it," Andrei replied. Then added, "We've practised."

Before the man turned to leave, he gave them a blanket, a flashlight and a jug of water.

He climbed the ladder and lowered the wooden hatch.

The fisherman who found Andrei later on dry land noticed him from a distance, an ill-defined shape curled beside a rock.

Andrei had collapsed on the shore of a small Turkish village. The man who discovered him had come to fix his cast nets. When Andrei was revived, he was on the edge of delirium, sweltering in the midday sun. Only the breeze masked the scorching heat. His face and body were burnt on one side, almost raw at the shoulder blades and neck. His hair was still plastered to his face from the oily water.

The fisherman brought Andrei home, wrapped him in blankets and put him to bed, where he spent the next few days resting and waiting. Andrei was convinced it was just a matter of time before Nicolae would appear, staggering from exhaustion but grinning with relief.

Several days after he washed ashore in Turkey, Andrei had satisfied his hunger and thirst and felt strong enough to ask his hosts for permission to call his mother. The fisherman's teenage daughter led Andrei to a telephone in the dining room, brought him a wooden stool and politely excused herself as he began to dial the number of the dressmaking shop. He sat, cradling the phone against his ear, and focused on the ringing. He felt as nervous as if ringing the Securitate directly.

After four rings there was a *hum* and a hard *click*, followed by a sound like air rushing through a shaft. Then her voice, so clear he caught his breath.

"Hello?"

He exhaled and began to speak quickly. His eyes were already wet.

"Mama, it's Andrei. Please don't say anything. Just listen. I want you to know that I'm safe and not to worry. I love you." His words were followed by a forbidding echo.

He heard his mother sigh and then the sound of something heavy being set down on a solid surface. He pictured his mother's fabric shears, the plywood shop counters. He pictured the white walls speckled with starching spray, the window propped open with a stack of old textile catalogues.

"Please hug Eli for me."

He thought he could hear his mother's steady breathing and in the distance the call of children on the streets. Emotion swept over him. Romania was still there, people coping as they always had. The world hadn't shattered just because he left.

"Mama. I love and miss you so much, but we have to be careful. I have to hang up now. I want you to lock up, go for a walk right away. Right away. Walk where people can see you. Don't say anything, just do it. Now, Mama."

Then, above the buzz of static, he heard the jingle of a bell and the closing of a door.

The next time he phoned his mother, the call was intercepted. After several loud clicks, the line went dead. That was his last call. After that, his only contact with her was through his letters, which he knew were vetted, and through the letters she dropped into a blue mailbox every few months. On rare occasions, obliging tourists smuggled out missives filled with small talk and the most innocent details of her life. But for the most part, her envelopes arrived covered in censor markings and resealed with brown tape, their contents black-pencilled by the letter opener of the Central Post Office. But it made no difference. Sarah could have sent squiggles and ink blots. Her love was uncensorable.

Dear Andrei,

███████████████████████████

The walls are bright again. I thought you'd want to know. Eli has painted them with a fresh coat of canary yellow, which will take a day and a night to dry. He wanted to finish the whole room in time for my birthday, but he ran out of paint before he reached the ceiling. I could see he was frustrated, but he laughed as soon as he saw how surprised I was. The living room walls are still glistening as I write █

Six

My conversations with Andrei gradually became more intense. At times, words seemed to spurt from him. Sometimes he moved wildly off course, speaking in surges, sometimes remembering things partially, sometimes stopping abruptly as though overcome. If something excited him, he would gesture in the air until, embarrassed by his own exuberance, he would lock his hands between his knees as if to subdue them.

Yet, as I listened, I sensed that some part of his story remained unreachable, like a dark, cold stone that sat at the depths of a distant ocean floor. While everything else around it drifted and swayed, shifted and resettled, this core remained impervious.

In June, Andrei was sick for a week, and I tried not to think about him. But through the sprawling hours of the day, stories and scenes he had recounted came tumbling back. I thought of calling him, but that wasn't the kind of relationship we had. I didn't even know if he had a phone. Then I recalled Baba telling me once that Andrei lived downtown in an apartment in Parkdale. That weekend I called Paolo and convinced him to take a stroll with me through the west end to look at used furniture stores.

When we got off the streetcar, the streets were filled with the sound of summer construction, a bulldozer beeping in reverse, a pneumatic drill pounding up the pavement. Sturdy-legged women chitchatted past with armloads of groceries.

Paolo was in a cheerful mood, happy to face the world on his own intermittently engaged terms. He smiled at a baby in a stroller and played hide-and-seek with his face behind his hands but withdrew impatiently when the child's father addressed him. He stopped to pet an affectionate terrier while barely casting a glance at the owner.

We passed by apartment buildings, and now and then a door would open and someone would emerge. I imagined that, wherever he was, Andrei probably lived on the bottom floor—maybe it was a remark he once made about a fear of heights—so I casually searched the first-floor windows. I didn't tell Paolo what I was up to. I began to feel ridiculous. The prospect of running into Andrei suddenly seemed embarrassing. How would I account for my presence on his street?

Paolo and I must have spent two hours walking through Parkdale, weaving along every street east of Ronscesvalles. The sun was baking the tar on the roads and the flowers drooped in the heat. Paolo had taken off his cotton jacket and there was a dark sweat patch between his shoulder blades. My feet were throbbing, so when Paolo pointed to a small Vietnamese noodle shop, I quickly agreed to stop for lunch and aborted my secret search.

Until Andrei came along, it was just Paolo and me. For nearly four years, Paolo was the centre of my life outside of work.

We met at a record store in a downtown mall. I noticed his T-shirt first. It had a picture of Thelonius Monk in profile. I asked him where he got it. His fingers were deftly flicking through rows of vinyl but he stopped, kept one finger on a record jacket to mark his place, peered at his watch and replied, "One thirty-five." I laughed at the misunderstanding. His voice was strangely melodious.

Paolo's eyes were steady and smiling. They peered out from behind a pair of rectangular glasses. He was wearing a belt that missed two loops on his black jeans. We ended up talking until his lunch break was over and he had to return to work.

Before he walked away, he told me the name of the flower store in the mall where he was employed. I followed him a half hour later, enjoying the continual flow of the shopping concourse, its expanding and contracting sense of space, the brightly lit signs for shops called Desire and Mecca, the din and drift of closely packed people.

Bloom, at the north end of the mall, had elaborate gift baskets hanging at the front. One wall was lined with a refrigeration system, the other with flower boxes. Misted roses glistened in a glass vase. Paolo was cutting up bright yellow organza ribbon to tie around bouquets. Clippers, a watering can, loose stems of baby's breath were scattered on the counter. Tiny white flower heads were burred to his brown cardigan. His face opened when he saw me. He pushed his glasses back on his nose with a knuckle, reached into the refrigerator behind him and handed me a purple flower with a long, thin stalk. It smelled sweet and spicy.

"It's pretty. Thank you," I said as I rolled the stem between my middle finger and thumb. I wondered what it would be like to kiss his mouth. There was a fullness to his bottom lip that made me feel agreeably agitated.

"It's a bit overripe."

"Overripe?" (His lip? No, silly, not his lip.) I blushed.

"Withered, I mean. The petals should be crisp, not so limp."

"It still smells good." I smiled.

"I think so too." He smiled back.

All sorts of people came into the flower shop from day to day, excited brides-to-be, nervous first-daters, corporate banquet planners. Paolo created hand-tied bouquets of the silkiest Ecuadorian roses, flamboyant arrangements of lilies and towering displays of birds of paradise. The rhythm of retail life, the comfort of familiar tools and props, allowed him to engage people in social exchanges he would otherwise have avoided. Like the shy intellectual who comes alive on the dance floor, Paolo had an extroverted shop persona. The flowers were an expression of some inner exuberance.

It was from Paolo that I learned to tell the difference between freesia and lisianthus, bearded irises and orchids. It wasn't a simple or transparent relationship; there were times when the man sitting across from me was a stranger, one who revealed little about himself or Argentina, the country of his birth. Yet some force, some mutual want, held us tightly.

Paolo was twenty-nine when we met, four years my senior. I had assumed from his face that he was even older. Top and bottom relayed contrasting messages. His body was lank like a teenager's, but the skin around his dark brown eyes was creased and shadowed and his dishevelled hair was already flecked with grey.

On our third anniversary, Paolo suggested we move in together. We were sitting at the kitchen table. My cat, Miko, was curled up on Paolo's lap.

"It seems natural," he said. "Why should we both be living alone and be paying double rent when we don't have to?"

"I don't—" I started.

"We could share this apartment or find a new one, something with three bedrooms, maybe a small garden."

I felt my stomach tighten. "I like the way things are."

"I'd cook and clean," he said, ignoring me.

I know of people who adore the idea of having a live-in companion, couples who toss their laundry casually into the washing machine and delight in knowing that their clothes tumble dry together, couples who believe that cohabitation represents the pinnacle of love. As much as I love Paolo, as much as it reassures me to be in his company, I cannot imagine being part of such a couple. Ever since I was a child, I've needed space to myself. I've always enjoyed the melancholy world of single portions, solitary walks and undisturbed nights. I thought he shared this inclination. It was one of the qualities that made him attractive to me.

"I'm here half the time as it is. I just don't have my stuff here."

My silence was too long; it angered Paolo. "It's only stuff, for God's sake," he shouted. Miko, startled, jumped off his lap onto the floor.

"It's not the stuff," I said. Even though it *was* the stuff. Having defined myself for so long by my solitude, I greeted the prospect of Paolo moving in with a vague sense of loss, followed by a wave of fear. No matter how hard I tried, I was unable to achieve the offhand attitude some people have toward cohabiting. It did not please me in the least to imagine my personal effects being joined with Paolo's.

Though I always did a botch job trying to explain it to Paolo, I saw two major drawbacks to living together. The first was the likelihood of physical and mental disruption. There are certain assurances that come with living by yourself. No matter how many times you may come and go, you know that your furniture and belongings will remain a beacon of reliability. If you decide to place your sandals on top of the stereo speaker, for instance, you know they will stay there until you decide to move them. If you have to go to the washroom in the middle of the night, you know you won't do so at your own peril, tripping over someone else's misplaced gym bag or guitar case. When you live with someone, such guarantees of equilibrium go out the window. Suddenly the person may decide to put down a zigzag column of orange traffic pylons.

The second and more significant drawback is that if and when the relationship ends there is more to sift through and separate. In my experience, what gets blended eventually gets divided. Then you're left with bare hangers, blank shelves and jutting nails where framed pictures hung just the day before.

"Things are good," I said.

"Okay, okay, I'll drop it," he said, in a tone that indicated he intended to do no such thing.

He paused, then added, grinning, "I could section my things off from yours. Get some of that yellow police tape."

"Very funny." I punched him lightly on the arm. "Listen. I'll promise you Tuesday, Thursday and Friday nights from now until eternity."

"That's just it. Wouldn't it be nice to have a relationship that was a little less programmed?"

While Paolo had revealed himself to be a coupler, a nester, I took it for granted that Andrei was a loner, that he was predisposed to keeping his own company most of the time, and that we shared this tendency. I once tried to determine what he did when he was not at work or with me. (Did he have lovers in Canada? Would he tell me if he did?) When I asked what he did to amuse himself on his days off, he shrugged and said:

"I read. I exercise. But mostly, I practise."

"What do you practise?"

"I must learn to speak better, so I practise English. I am only a mediocre draughtsman, so I practise drawing. In the evenings sometimes I go to a café near my house and I practise chess because my playing is only so-so. It allows me to meet my fellow expatriates."

When he said this his eyes brightened. "There is an older Pole I know who is a grand master. He used to play with Khalifman in St. Petersburg, and one of my true desires is to beat him just once. Last time he won he teased me. He reached over the board and pulled my bangs to one side and said: 'Draw the curtains next time or I might think you're sleeping.'"

Andrei touched his newly cut hair as an epilogue to the story. Then something seemed to catch his attention and he traced a finger along the base of his skull. "I am turning into my father, how do you say it, spitting image? These dents at the back. I'm like a bowling ball!" Then he smiled in a way that seemed forced.

I struggled to convince Paolo that our current arrangement was the best way of ensuring our relationship would last. As a consolation, I made an extra set of keys and invited him to keep a few of his things at my place. Despite the offer, he didn't end up storing much—a toiletries bag, some extra clothes, a few CDs, a bottle of chimichurri sauce, some Maalox.

I made one other concession. I let him do my laundry when he needed to fill out a load. I know "let him" is an odd way of putting it, but everyone has chores they like to take care of by themselves and it took a while for me to get used to seeing Paolo stuffing my sheets and clothes into the washer, measuring soap and setting dials, waiting for the *whoosh* of the water into the machine.

My friendship with Andrei was something that Paolo took a long time to accept. In Paolo's mind, Andrei's arrival coincided with my rejection of his proposal that we live together. As he saw it, the closer I got to Andrei, the more my attention toward him seemed to fade. There was no doubt that it shaped his attitude toward Andrei.

On the rare occasions they saw each other, usually when Paolo came to meet me after work, Paolo acted distant, almost condescending toward Andrei. The tension in the room was palpable, but I refused to be on edge as I often was when I tried to hinge people together. I did not want to be a connector or a message carrier, something I had announced long ago to my parents. So I left it to them to sort out their differences, and over the summer their relationship seemed to improve. Paolo behaved more sociably toward Andrei and Andrei eventually returned the gesture by inviting us to join him at his apartment for a meal.

The dinner took place in October, right around Thanksgiving. We got off to a strained start, but by midnight we had settled in. The dirty plates were soaking in the sink. We were lounging on the floor around a glass-topped coffee table. The pie that Paolo and I had brought was warming in the oven. I was feeling happily wine-drunk. Paolo and Andrei were immersed in a discussion of the music they liked. Delta blues. Charlie Patton. Robert Johnson. A cassette played. Scratch and hiss. Sliding steel strings. Johnson's rasp rising into a flickering falsetto howl. I was so relieved that they had found something to talk about, I left them alone and floated around the apartment, tidying, nudging newspapers back into stacks, stopping at Andrei's desk to note a copy of *Time* magazine beside an open Oxford dictionary, peering at a familiar mother-and-child Klimt picture pinned to the wall beside a postcard of two men seated on a camel. The smell of baking apples sweetened the air. I offered to run to the all-night store and get some ice cream, and was gone for about fifteen minutes. We ate our dessert and Andrei opened a bottle of port he had been given by a Portuguese neighbour.

When we left that evening, Andrei gave us each a hug, and then kissed me on the cheek. For a second I thought he wanted to say something, but the second passed and he raised his hand and gave me a goodbye salute. Paolo and I walked slowly down the stairs, both lost in our own thoughts. As we wove our way down the street, the night was filled with the smell of raked leaves and wood smoke.

I have often wondered what happened after we left. Did Andrei begin washing up? Did he switch on his television or turn on the radio? Did he contentedly fix himself a cup of tea? Or did he have a troubled, sleepless night knowing that he would soon be leaving us all behind?

I asked Paolo one night following Andrei's disappearance what they had discussed while I was gone. We were lying in bed.

"There is something . . . I was wondering . . ." I started tentatively. "Do you remember the last time you spoke with Andrei? We were at his apartment. I slipped out to the store and when I returned the two of you were deep in a conversation. When I walked in you were saying something about jet lag or flying. Something about the first time you travelled by plane, and how it was so fast there was no time to withdraw from the place you had left and adjust to the place you had arrived in."

Through the bedroom window I could see clouds tracking slowly across the moon. I needed Paolo to share his thoughts, but I was cautious. I feared an argument.

In the darkness beside me, Paolo said, "He didn't say anything about leaving, if that's what you're asking."

His yawn told me there should be no further questioning. I took the cue—what good would pressing do? Andrei was gone. I had dissected every minute of our last moments in early December. I had tried to understand what had happened, but so far I could detect no motive or forewarning. Andrei had simply vanished.

I stayed up reading after Paolo fell asleep, not yet tired enough to close my eyes. When I did eventually sleep, the dream returned. This time, I was standing away from him. I could see the circular motion of the birds, hear the beating of wings. The movement was now smooth and regular. As the birds rose they appeared to melt into an orange sky. Once they had disappeared, Andrei lowered his head and saw me. Our eyes locked for a moment. When I awoke at 4 a.m., the warm colour of the dream stayed with me.

I got up for a glass of water, and when I returned to the bedroom, I slipped into bed as quietly as possible. Paolo's sleeping body was radiating warmth. His mouth was slightly open, and as I peered into his deeply dreaming face, I could feel my heart quicken. Sleep had laid him open. All the muscles of his face had relaxed, rearranging his features. His nose drooped closer to his mouth. The distance between his eye and his cheek had diminished. I observed a fresh vulnerability. As I shifted toward him, he stirred for a moment, then gave a soft grunt. I curled my body against his. The steady rhythm of his breath was reassuring. I closed my eyes.

Paolo, I knew, wanted to make me happy, but for that he needed more from me. It was in his blood to take care of things—plants, flowers—just as it was in mine, despite the nature of my job, to mess them up.

I felt a light touch on my arm, and I looked to see Paolo staring at me. He kissed my forehead.

I gently rubbed his chest. "Do you think we're good together?" I whispered.

"Most of the time," he whispered back.

"What makes us good?"

"Balance. I don't know. We're a nice combination, I suppose." His eyelids were heavy. He yawned. His tongue clucked for moisture.

"Like igloo and polar bear?" I said.

"Hmm?" he said faintly, drifting off again.

"Never mind," I said to his sleeping face.

As I lay beside him, the sound of a streetcar wafted through the window. In the fluttering of near sleep, the distant clanging became abstract, spinning and shifting in my mind until it was the groan of an anchor being hoisted above the water. The pull of it was hypnotic. The sound splintered again and the flotsam of a world I could never have known came streaming in.

Before Andrei arrived, I had enjoyed the hush in my mind. But he brought with him the racket of the Cernavoda port, the clamour of the canal opening, the *clink* of a jib hitting a mast, the lapping of water against the hull of a boat, the *creak* of a wooden storage crate. Each sound brought an image, each image expanded, gathering in the eaves of my brain and overflowing, spilling into everything else. At times, the sounds obsessed me, pulsing with urgency, like a far-off distress signal.

How could this be? I had never been inside the depths of a ship or at sea. Could another person's memories capture my mind, draw me unresistingly into someone else's past?

Seven

*B*aba kept a desk on the main floor but spent most of his time in the only separate room, a vault-like chamber, sorting valuables and precious items and depositing them in a row of security lockers. On slow days, I liked to take my break in there and watch him while he worked. I found it mesmerizing, the swiftness with which he arranged things into piles, the theatrical way he lowered his eyebrows and pushed out his lips when he encountered a clue, his Hercule Poirot manner when it was necessary to investigate further: a white-gloved hand slipped into the cool neck of a silver vase, a jeweller's eyeglass placed on a locket.

My job as a mail recovery worker involved restoring more ordinary things. Lesser goods. The sort of things that fell into the cracks of people's couches or cropped up at neighbourhood flea markets. Boy Scout badges, vacation photos, Magic Markers, teeth moulds.

A medical X-ray. A book of Sufi poetry. A Leonard Cohen audio cassette. Nothing was too small to matter to someone, somewhere.

Every day, inquiring letters arrived at my desk. Some had photos of the lost object enclosed; some attached a hastily sketched facsimile. Many letters contained exceptionally detailed accounts, proceeding on the assumption that an item was likely to be handled more carefully and/or returned more promptly if it was given a personal identity.

> *"Moo-moo" has been part of the family for generations. Over the years, he has travelled to Birmingham, Berlin, Montreal and the Hamptons. I sincerely hope he can be found and forwarded to my grandson at the enclosed address.*

Others were written in handwriting distorted by grief.

> *All we have left of our son Stewart is a toothbrush, a digital wristwatch and a few other personal effects, which the hospital gave us in a clear plastic bag when we went to sign the death forms. We were sending a few of these keepsakes on to his brother in Yellowknife . . .*

A few people chose to write their letters from the object's vantage point.

> *I am a silver heart-shaped locket. If you open my belly you will see a tiny picture of a man with wavy blond hair and a tan. That man sent me to the woman who he plans to marry but I must have got lost on the way. I am anxious to be united with her . . .*

Once in a while there was a cranky, blaming letter about bureaucratic incompetence. (These tended to be in uppercase and full of demonstrative punctuation.)

I AM UNFAILINGLY AMAZED AT YOUR GROSS INEPTITUDE.
TWICE THIS YEAR, I HAVE SENT A PACKAGE THAT HAS
NOT ARRIVED AT ITS INTENDED DESTINATION. ARE YOUR
POSTMEN PILFERING FROM THEIR CUSTOMERS?! THIS IS
A PUBLICLY FUNDED INSTITUTION: ARE YOU SLEEPING
ON THE JOB!?!!?!

I tried not to let the complaints get to me.

I liked the act of salvaging, and the feeling of goodness and purpose it gave me. Then again, maybe I was just nosy, a little too fascinated by other people's property.

In Andrei's absence, I felt increasingly indebted to my work. I found myself sorting cutlery with the exacting patience of a 1950s housewife. I folded clothing with a newfound tenderness, in the way an expecting mother folds a freshly laundered layette.

I plunged my arm zealously into the bucket and brought up one item after another. A canvas museum tote bag suggested an older woman; Hong Kong movie magazines suggested a teenage boy; a silver tie pin suggested a businessman; a pink Free Tibet T-shirt suggested a young, possibly style-conscious activist. Each item, no matter what it was, comforted me. I could lose myself in the lives piled up on my table.

I lost track of whole days, in fact—until an entire week had disappeared. The repetition of matching things up, sorting them into boxes, allowed my mind to soften and blur. I knew from practice the perils of too little concentration: overlooked clues, incorrectly attributed belongings. But I'd also learned it was a mistake to concentrate too much. Part of the mind always has to remain open.

The first thing that caught my eye the day after Andrei disappeared was a brown plastic rosary nested inside a white vinyl pouch. Taped to the back of the pouch was a small photo of a woman wearing a flimsy paisley dress that adhered to her hips, emphasizing her thinness. I brought the rosary to my lips, as I had seen Catholics do in prayer, and discreetly kissed several beads before placing it back down on the table, struck suddenly by the eroticism of the gesture. I hoped none of my co-workers had seen me.

By mid-morning, the rosary had been usurped by: a small tin of Scottish toffee, a set of newborn baby photos, a package of old *Penthouse* magazines, a plastic crocodile. I set each object on the steel table. At the centre was a cracked porcelain pillbox, oval shaped, loosely wrapped in brown craft paper, fragile in my hand. But the metal clasp flicked open with a pleasing *snap* to reveal a misty pond scene.

There was a time when the Undeliverable Mail Office was called the Dead Letter Office. The name was used from 1875, when the practice of opening undelivered letters was first authorized by the Canadian government, until 1954, when Canada Post opted for a less depressing name. Perhaps it was a sudden burst of optimism that encouraged them to change it. In 1954, for a brief interval—after two world wars and the Korean War and before the start of the Vietnam War—people were dying less prolifically. The world was almost at peace. Before that, the office must have felt like a tomb, a record of numerous sons and lovers forsaken to various battles. The staff then must have despaired at the futility of their jobs: so many of life's senders and receivers riven by death, never to be connected.

The facility is still sometimes referred to as "the postal morgue," "the letter cemetery," "the limbo of missent mail." As a child, I remember asking my mother to explain the idea of limbo to me. I had in my mind a picture of bodies melting in an oven-hot anteroom to hell, an image drawn from some Warner Brothers cartoon. She surprised me by saying that limbo was not a place of anguish or fury but a place of suspension.

"You mean people just float there in mid-air?" I asked.

To which my sister, who was always explaining things, responded, "Yeah. And they swing around, trying hard not to puke. That's their punishment for being bad people."

My mother, in her placid, comforting voice, responded, "No, Kana. Not that kind of suspension. I meant waiting. Imagine a very long hallway . . ."

When I pass through the heavy metal doors of the Undeliverable Mail Office it's as if I am suspended in time.

"Are you ready for lunch?" Baba asked a few days after Andrei disappeared. "It's ten past twelve."

"Not quite. You go ahead. I think I'll stay and finish this last bin."

He nodded and left, and I was alone.

As I had drifted through my work, occasionally taking breaks with Baba and going off with him for lunch, I had been waiting for a moment like this. The office was empty.

I stood up and walked toward Andrei's work area, which the manager, after some coaxing on Baba's part and mine, had agreed to leave untouched for a few more days. Andrei's blue sweater hung over the back of the chair. Magazines fanned across his shelf.

I sat down at his vacant desk, pulled out the drawer and swept around with my hand. I discovered an old roll of mints and some paperclips. I pushed my fingers up into all the corners, but the picture I was searching for was gone.

If I made an effort I could call an impression of it to mind. I could see a figure in a woollen hat and a dark pea jacket sitting on the steps of a building, a cheerful face, thick brown hair drifting across his forehead.

"So who's behind the camera?" I once asked Andrei. "Who's put that big grin on your face?"

When I looked across the table at him, he was staring down, blushing. He glanced up again and his face seemed soft and sad—like that of a different Andrei.

Another picture existed. A picture of Nicolae sitting on the same steps. But that was gone, too. I remembered remarking that Nicolae looked too timid to be a revolutionary firebrand, but according to Andrei he was active for a brief period in an underground student movement. His activist career ended abruptly when he was detained for hand-copying a quote from Solzhenitsyn's Nobel lecture: "The simple step of a simple courageous man is not to partake in falsehood, not to support false actions! One word of truth shall outweigh the whole world!" Nicolae had written and distributed a hundred copies of the slogan, almost all of which had landed on the desk of a Securitate officer. The officer had said, setting the handwritten leaflet beside Nicolae's matching handwritten statement, that Nicolae was fortunate it was a first offence. Even so, his father, a longtime Party member and a distinguished professor of chemistry, had to bribe the police for his son's release.

I ran my hand along the shelf, touching each object. A silver ball, about palm-size, made of the foil that came in cigarette packages. A small plant that Baba had watered recently, and beside it, Andrei's notebook of inventions. I flipped through the pages, filled with sketches and roughly hatched plans that he had never brought himself to patent. I followed the contours of curves and the collision of lines, appreciating the satisfying crispness of graph paper filled with 2B pencil. Each idea was rendered meticulously:

- A self-cleaning device for window blinds.
- A chess timer with coffee-warming attachment.
- A prosthetic limb with a hidden compartment for storing house keys and money.
- A hand-operated brake for Rollerblades. (He showed me the sketch during one of our first conversations. "I will revolutionize this activity, channel the force in motion," said Andrei, with a seriousness that placed him somewhere between physicist laureate and Obi Wan Kenobi.)

Everything that was left of Andrei rested on his shelf. And I stood there, crestfallen, because all of a sudden I realized that I had no pictures of him.

But there *was* a photo. Not the one I was searching for, but a photo nonetheless. I found it a few minutes later, tucked into a pocket at the back of his notebook. A picture of Andrei and his settlement class taken during the first year he lived in Canada—a studio portrait set against a sunset orange curtain. Two dozen people stared out from the photo. Andrei was in the front row, dressed in blue jeans and a black long-sleeved shirt that made his torso look even lankier than it was. He was seated at a three-quarter angle to the camera, his hands folded in his lap in a touching, overly posed way. His face was newly shaven, his hair combed, his eyes . . . Was that a piece of paper in his shirt pocket?

I shuddered slightly, frightened now at this attachment to someone who had inexplicably vanished. All I wanted was to have things return to what they were, to live my life in a familiar world. I needed Andrei at his desk: a solid, warm, unfailing presence.

I couldn't accept the ambiguity that surrounded Andrei's absence or trust Baba's assurance that it was only a matter of time. Instead, I felt adrift, somewhere between sinking and surfacing.

Eight

*I*n my experience, if a person does not take note of an item's disappearance within a few weeks, they are unlikely ever to do so. Some
things simply go unmissed.

In the limbo of Canada Post, items that went unclaimed after seven
months were either auctioned off by Head Office or destroyed. An
overhaul of non-valuables happened twice a year. We called them
"days of reckoning" and, with the exception of statutory holidays
and staff birthdays, they were the days most anticipated by all of us.
Dumpsters full of odds and ends were emptied. A great crunching
ensued, a spinning of blades, a sizzle of cardboard, until everything
was reduced to fibre and dust. The sound of hydraulically powered
disintegration echoed in the warehouse, weaving like an avant-garde
composition through the hum of daily work.

A day of reckoning was an opportunity to get out of your seat. I spent most of the afternoon by an industrial shredding machine. Cardboard frames, sheets of loose paper, receipts, composition notebooks, photographs were reduced to ribbons and confetti. The order I had imposed on my collection was coming apart. Chaos was being reinstated. Yet as I stood there feeding handfuls into the machine, I found myself contemplating what it would be like to divest oneself of everything one owned.

I cheered myself by considering the long-term benefits of my work: I was dispensing with the world's rummage so that future generations would not suffocate beneath the accumulated surplus. (Even museums de-acquisition their holdings from time to time. Without regular purges, the dead weight of everything in the mail recovery office would surely cause whole cities and countries to sink into the sea.) And yet—what was trash? So often I'd worry that an item casually chucked might be the protective charm of someone's future.

Could someone's entire life be derailed by an undelivered object?

I imagined mailboxes across the country filled with nothing but snow, household letter slots opening only to a shiver of wind.

The morning immediately following a day of reckoning always felt quiet in contrast. People kept to themselves. When I arrived at the office, Doreen was hunched over a mound of files, faxes and memos. Her coffee and Chelsea bun were untouched. She was executing her work with the gusto of someone involved in a vital project, not her usual attitude of secretarial indifference.

I said hello and she said hi in return. I hoped she might have some new information about Andrei to pass on, but she didn't say anything. I felt silly just standing there, so I asked her if her skin was still bothering her. The last time we had spoken she had been complaining about her eczema, which she said should be improving because she was taking new vitamin supplements.

She touched her pen to her neck and replied, "Yes. But not as much."

Beside her desk was a new poster and written in yellow were the words HOW TO DETECT SUSPICIOUS ITEMS. There was a picture of a dishevelled package and a list of things to look out for when sorting mail. I studied it for a moment, but the words began to blend together in a series of alarming haiku:

LIVE DANGEROUS LEAKS
SHARP LOPSIDED STRANGE ODOUR
NO RETURN ADDRESS

PROTRUDING WIRES
EXCESSIVE WRAPPING PAPER
OIL STAINS RIGID BULK

It occurred to me as I walked across the floor toward my desk that I was the only one who still seemed to notice or care that Andrei was missing. An insular silence had crept over the hive. Ten days had passed since I last saw him—or was it eleven?—I was losing track of time. I had also not kept on top of my work. There were many things to sort through if I was to catch up.

By 9 a.m., I had chosen three objects, more for diversity than priority. One was small and round, an American Legion pin; another, hard and heavy, a box containing two Qigong balls; the third, pleasing and soft, a pair of leather gloves.

Over on the side, several plastic jars of medicine had burst through an envelope. Easy to trace. A name of a doctor and a number to call. A set of dentures sat like a museum piece in a box of light cast from the skylight.

By mid-morning, I was transfixed by a Polaroid photograph. A red sunset sky. Trails of violet cloud. Two backpackers walking down a sloped road. It was a fairly standard travel photograph but the surface was strangely beaded. The emulsion had partially peeled away, lifting away random details. The longer I peered into its tiny window, the more I felt as though I had entered a bubbling lava world where everything was liquid and alive.

reason to recreate herself

Did the work ever take my mind off Andrei? Yes and no. Something new to identify could so totally preoccupy me, like the photograph that morning, that my mind emptied. But most days Andrei's absence was a presence I felt from the moment I entered the building until the time I left.

That day during my lunch break, I dialled Andrei's number five times and listened to it ring. The answering machine was either full or broken. I asked the manager to double-check Andrei's personnel file, but there was no emergency contact information. There was nothing written under "Next of Kin."

"Maybe it should be more precise?" the manager said, pointing at the blank spot beside "In case of emergency, call."

"Precise?"

"You know, for different sorts of emergencies . . . in case of electrocution, call . . . in case of shooting, or heart attack or alien abduction, call . . ."

I stared at him. He pinched the knot in his necktie and gave a shrug.

"Sorry," he said. "Dumb joke."

How ironic that the combined tracking skills of all the employees at the office led us no closer to finding Andrei. (And indeed such were the skills at the UMO for locating people that there were occasions when we were recruited to help trace a loved one. For example, one man who had been out of touch with his sister for nine years mailed a letter vaguely labelled, *To: Miss Emily Harwood, Registered Nurse, Regina, Canada*. We eventually discovered Miss Harwood's whereabouts. She had traded in her nurse's uniform for a nun's habit and was now living with the Sisters of Charity in Saskatoon. Within a few weeks, Mr. Harwood wrote to express his thanks and to tell us that he was now corresponding with his sister on a regular basis.) We could sometimes solve the nation's postal puzzles, but when it came to finding Andrei, our ingenuity and analytical talents seemed to get us nowhere.

I made the decision to visit his apartment. If he was not there, I would tape a message to his door. The landlord had told me that he could not give me permission to enter the room until Andrei's rent expired. That left nineteen days until the end of the month.

Nine

*A*ndrei lived in a top-floor apartment of a six-storey building, overlooking the street. It was a modest one-bedroom with a bathroom and kitchenette. The main room came furnished with a fold-out couch in brown corduroy, two director chairs made of faded red canvas, a glass-topped coffee table and a heart-shaped ottoman. Every available surface was thick with yellowing newspapers and clippings, some in Romanian, others in English. The upholstery was dull and worn but the shapes felt modern—a feature he appreciated, coming from a world of patina and weathered wood. The walls were a freshly painted mint blue. The ceilings were high. It was a home relatively unsoiled by history.

In his second year in the building, Andrei had built a small wooden loft on the roof to house a family of pet pigeons. Like the birds he cared for, Andrei moved about his nest with immense nervous energy, always garnishing and gathering, one minute adorning his walls with landscape photographs he cut out of travel magazines, the next minute filling his cupboards with used plastic and paper bags, which he expertly bundled and folded. Nothing was thrown out.

I visited his apartment only twice during the course of our friendship. On the first occasion, I had been invited over for tea. It was a Saturday afternoon in July (exactly one month after I had dragged Paolo through Parkdale in a vain effort to locate Andrei). I remember that it was a particularly muggy day, with the kind of suffocating humidity that usually precedes a summer storm. The air on the top floor was almost unbearable. I had brought strawberry tarts that had turned soggy around the edges, the custard on the verge of liquefying. Andrei welcomed me, gallantly placed the tarts on a small table and made his way across the uneven floor to the kitchen nook to fetch two plates. When he returned he was also carrying an electric fan. We placed the fan on the floor, then opened the window and door to create a cross breeze.

A pigeon swooped onto the wide ledge, a broken coo rising from its throat as it landed. Another followed. Then another. The birds were prim and polite, displaying avian precision in the way they spaced themselves on the perch.

Andrei picked up one of the birds and held it for me to touch, his hands cupped around its breast. The sensation was damp and cool. Then he put it back down and headed for the kitchen, returning moments later with a small bowl of water and a handful of raw popcorn, which he delicately dispersed on the sill, carefully avoiding a splatter of droppings. The pigeons pecked at the kernels, the sunlight transforming their slate-grey feathers into a silvery blue.

Despite the fan, sweat trickled down my chest, my clothes felt clammy. I could feel that my face was shiny.

"They prefer the kitchen ledge because it's wider, but they'll come wherever there's food," he said.

"They're yours?" I asked, nudging my hair behind my ear.

"No, no. They're not mine. I feed them occasionally and that's why they return."

Out of the open window, I noticed a large sign for a food mart in the distance, a bright band of orange with bold blue letters spanning an entire block. As we nibbled our tarts, Andrei followed my gaze and began to speak.

Andrei first entered a North American grocery store three weeks after he arrived in Toronto. He was still staying in the settlement house, wearing mismatched clothes and his baseball cap, dreaming of a job and an apartment of his own. He moved timidly about the city, quietly studying the transactions of people around him. Before long, he knew how to ride the streetcar, how to operate the coin laundry, where to buy coffee and cheese in Kensington Market. Just from observing and copying others, he was slowly gaining confidence and adapting to his new home.

But entering a grocery store as large as a sports stadium was an entirely different matter. Andrei walked in on a whim, and found himself happily lost in a maze of aisles offering a variety of products beyond anything he could have imagined. Shrink-wrapped hams crowned with pineapple rings. Frozen meat pies with puffy gravy packets. Thigh-sized tubs of coffee-flavoured yogurt. Sausage rolls the size of a man's fist.

He stopped in a section devoted to pet food. There were small tins with special pull tabs, unidentifiable cow and sheep parts gussied up to sound like a gourmet French feast. His stomach tightened at the sight. A swell of nausea overcame him as he saw orange-coloured frozen pizza samples, pepperoni sticks dotted with fat. In sight of the exit, his mind numb, he hurried past mounds of oversize produce, deaf now to the *ping-ping* of cash registers and overhead speakers announcing the day's specials. He stumbled through the automatic doors, feeling the cold from inside mixing with the heat outside. The air shimmered.

He inhaled deeply and walked to the edge of the pavement, his back to a row of open car trunks. A woman dressed in a bright pink halter whipped grocery bags into her Jeep. Two girls picked through a book of stickers while the mother of one of the girls hunted for her car keys. A young clerk helped a well-dressed older man carry a crate of soft drinks to his hatchback. Andrei felt torn, part of him repelled by all the indulgence, part of him wanting to fit in, envious of the self-possessed shoppers rushing home to their families. Such purposeful people—had they ever felt at odds with the world? Had their own actions ever horrified them?

As Andrei stood and watched, he felt more and more inconsequential. He didn't belong. Strangely, what struck him most was the awareness that there was no one watching *him*. Back home, he had experienced an intimate nearness to others, with all the accompanying strife and harmony. Here, it was as if he didn't exist.

Yet in the same instant Andrei knew he was everything he hadn't been before. He was free to sleep with men and not marry, keep a pet or two, buy a colour television, practise religion, listen to Bach or AC/DC—any of which, back in Romania, would have marked him as a likely enemy of the state. In his newly adopted home, he could count on a certain degree of tolerance. Provided he was discreet, provided he did not overstep anyone's idea of decorum and good taste, his personal preferences would remain his own affair.

It was his dream. His big North American dream. The freedom to do what he pleased. Opportunities everywhere. So why did he feel so miserable?

The fight had gone out of him, he realized, because there was no longer a monolithic force to fight against. He felt oddly diminished. He was a man standing on the periphery of human activity. He could be waiting for a friend. A child. A spouse. He could be Albanian. Or Italian.

As he contemplated his situation, a young man swept past, accidentally brushing against him. Andrei's heart raced at the sight of the man's wavy dark hair, the sleek neck rising from a white T-shirt. A familiar smell. Andrei tried to concentrate on a billboard at the farthest edge of the parking lot, but a memory had been roused. Unsure, he remained still, but there was a stirring, and the blood filled him, a bolt of longing shot directly to his groin. He crouched, embarrassed by this sudden flicker of excitement.

When the arousal faded it was replaced by a dull ache in his chest. He blinked back tears. All the tension that had been building inside of him needed to be released. How could he be heard? Throw himself on the ground? Pound the concrete? Blurt out some profanity that would trumpet his presence, like a brick shattering a pane of glass? But when the moment passed, he was still standing, appearing as nonchalant as everyone else who walked through the In and Out doors of the grocery store.

A sweet yeasty aroma drifted from a nearby bakery. A dozen bagels for three dollars. Poppyseed or sesame. Andrei couldn't remember the last time his cheeks had been stuffed with food. Meringue that melted decadently on the tongue. Diabolically rich eclairs. He made a mental note to buy a toaster the minute he could afford one. So many choices. Shirt pressed or crumpled? Shoes re-soled or replaced? Hair freshly cut, with or without a shave? Choices that would have been momentous back home were minor here.

Andrei walked by a family-style restaurant and through the window saw a couple dining on giant steaks. He saw the woman pare away the gristle with a sharp knife before taking a bite.

Nibbling diamonds and chewing hundred-dollar bills was the way he thought of it.

Andrei wrote his mother one letter after he had settled in Toronto. He tried postcards, but within a year he stopped sending those. By that time, he had heard a story about a Romanian family who were forced out of their home for having a defector son. The Securitate chose the middle of the night to evict them, boarding up every window and door of their house, then plastering the exterior walls with every letter and postcard the son had ever sent home. Years of intercepted correspondence neatly pasted up like wallpaper. Why the Securitate had waited so long wasn't explained. The story sickened Andrei, and after that, he opted for the painful but less incriminating course of silence.

"But you wrote to tell her that you had arrived in Canada safely."

"Yes. And out of homesickness."

A squeaky ceiling fan was whirling directly above me. My face now felt dry. A warm breeze passed through the window.

Andrei was standing by the sink preparing iced tea. When the kettle reached a boil, he poured the gurgling water into a teapot. I watched him empty a tray of ice cubes into two wide glasses and thought about homesickness. I was trying to fathom what it would be like to leave everything and everyone I knew behind. How, after thirty years, could someone suddenly pack a bag and walk away? There had to be some single moment of decision.

"Were there many people—?"

"At the grocery store?" The ice cubes popped and crackled as he poured the warm tea over them.

"No. In your country. Were there many trying to leave when you did?"

"Yes. Then, before, after. There were always stories, from as early as I can remember—people hiding in the seats of cars, in wine barrels; people escaping by sea, through underground tunnels, even by hot-air balloon."

"But what happened to the ones who didn't succeed? Did they end up in jail?"

"Some did. But soon there weren't enough jail cells for all those trying to run. And to improve his image with the West, the dictator released all but the most dangerous opponents. Anyway, it didn't matter. We'd become our own jailers. We were so used to being watched, we began watching ourselves."

IN NICOLAE AND ANDREI'S class there was a student by the name of Ion who had succumbed wholeheartedly to the influence of the dictator and expressed his devotion by betraying others. Still in his early twenties, Ion already looked like the comedic image of a rising bureaucrat, in his imported clothes, always reeking of cologne.

He was the one who had reported Nicolae for handing out *samizdat* leaflets a year earlier. So when Nicolae was summoned again in February, they assumed that Ion was the one responsible. Four months before Andrei and Nicolae's defection, three men in heavy coats approached Nicolae as he walked toward the university engineering building. A routine check, they said, and escorted him on foot to a small apartment near St. Stephen's Tower, one of several rooms the Securitate leased around Baia Mare.

Nicolae was directed toward a desk in the far corner and told to keep his coat on and remain standing. The room was horribly over-heated. But he tried to appear calm, waiting for his eyes to adjust to the room's dimness. Minutes passed and finally an officer emerged from the kitchen holding a plate of dumplings. The officer sat down at the desk, removed a pair of cufflinks, rolled up his shirt sleeves and began eating the food with his fingers.

He ate with his eyes fixed on Nicolae. Apricot syrup dribbled onto the wood surface. The officer's moustache became sloppy and wet. The room seemed to grow warmer. Why did the officer insist on eating so slowly? Nicolae wondered. At last, the officer wiped his fingers on a napkin, reached for his notebook and began to fan himself, revealing the silver roots of his dyed hair.

The interrogation was quick. A round of questions, seemingly ran-dom, but precise. Nicolae was kept standing, and his mind took a zig-zag course as he tried to follow and then anticipate the abrupt changes of subject. The officer's tone was direct, his face inviting and amiable. Nicolae knew that they were trying to disarm him; replacing shouts and threats, his interrogator's informality and false camaraderie was disconcerting in its own way.

" . . . no more Solzhenitsyn?"

" . . . copy of Saul Bellow?"

" . . . brother-in-law, a backroom abortionist?"

" . . . practise chemistry like your esteemed father?"

" . . . anti-state activities?"

" . . . contacts in the West?"

To seem co-operative, Nicolae would nod or shake his head. When it was unavoidable, he gave brief answers.

" . . . a fiancée?"

"And children?"

" . . . your duty to replenish the population?"

Next, he was given a blank piece of paper and commanded to write down the name of every "dissident" he knew. Nicolae picked up the pen, pretended to think for a moment, then handed back the pen, shaking his head. The officer returned to his seat and stirred his coffee, clinking the spoon against the cup.

The immunity Nicolae had experienced for being the son of a long-standing Party member was eroding.

Two weeks later he was summoned again. This time, he was seated in front of a blank paper and ordered to write down the name of every homosexual he knew. He remembered the interrogator's thick, diamond-centred wedding ring, as a heavy hand clapped his shoulder. Nicolae considered his options and picked up the pen. He wrote two names: *Dinu* and *Pavel*. And then he lowered his pen, his hand shaking. Dinu and Pavel were already notorious. Old men from the outskirts of Baia Mare, the thought of whom stirred up complicated feelings in Nicolae. They encapsulated all his fears of becoming vagrant and disparaged, yet they represented all his dreams of certainty; the self-acceptance he coveted, they wore as a shield.

" . . . their addresses?"

"No."

"Where did you encounter them?"

"Only once. At the park," he answered.

The officer picked up a piece of bread and moved it to his mouth. He stood up and began pacing behind Nicolae.

"By the university," Nicolae added.

"What were you doing?"

"Studying for my exams."

"And Dinu and Pavel?"

"They approached me separately."

"You knew they were homosexual?" The officer stopped and stood behind Nicolae, waiting for a response.

"I was propositioned," Nicolae replied.

The officer appeared pleased, patted Nicolae's shoulder and offered him a pen. "Sign the paper. Then you may go home."

"Thank you." Nicolae felt that his throat was coated with dirt.

He was summoned several more times by the officer, a chameleon of a man whose physical presence seemed to change—at times ominous, looming above Nicolae like a bully, at other times, big and warm, like a comforting friend. Nicolae was asked to submit further names. Enemies of peace and Communism. Anti-government conspirators. Each name was shuffled away. There was the ritual pretense at kindness, small gifts of food, a package of coffee, which he couldn't easily decline but which made him nervous.

More tricky were the intermittent jokes. As the hours crawled along, every now and then the officer would fire off a new one. The humour was often irreverent.

"Why do the Securitate travel about in threes?" the officer asked.

Nicolae shook his head.

"So there's one to read, one to write and one to keep an eye on the two intellectuals."

Between jokes, the officer would toss out names to gauge Nicolae's response; some he didn't know at all, some he knew slightly and some intimately. Nicolae practised his reactions at home between interrogations. He did not flinch or allow his face to crumple. He learned to keep his expression relaxed but closed.

And then suddenly a new name popped up. A name that shattered his defences. After uttering it, the officer tilted his head ever so slightly to the side. He picked up a lemon cookie from the table and began to chew. Nicolae nodded and then looked away. "I must use the bathroom," he said. He could feel eyes on his back as he walked across the room.

Nicolae's father, a professor emeritus who presided over his class-rooms and his house with authority and who had once advised the dictator's wife, Elena, on affairs of "science," was powerless to stop the Securitate from harassing his son. When Nicolae returned home from the final session, his parents met him in the front room. He embraced his mother, then took one look at his father's face, seeing an embedded sadness his father could not hide, and knew that they would not speak of anything that had passed.

In the days and weeks that followed, he tried to resume life as usual, but all his routines and certainties had been upended.

It wasn't Ion after all, Andrei later discovered. The informant was a neighbour who had known Nicolae since he was a child.

It made sense. It could have been anyone.

Nicolae had been taught from an early age to believe in the prom-ise of a utopian socialism, as a kind of twinkling light on the dis-tant horizon. When he was eight, his father had introduced him to a reading syllabus beginning with the easy bits of *The Communist Manifesto*. By age eleven, he was reading the revolutionary writings of Che Guevara, Walter Rodney, Ho Chi Minh and Amilcar Cabral. He took his father's assignments seriously and followed world events as closely as possible.

In September 1969, when Ho Chi Minh died, the state newspaper, *Scînteia*, ran a photo of him on the front page. Using a thin blue marker, Nicolae created a pointillist impression of Ho's delicate bearded face, wisps of thin hair on his chin, which he mounted on cardboard and hung on his bedroom wall.

He dearly wanted to please his father, and in return be treated as a thinking young adult. But the more he read, and the more he compared what he read to the hardship and corruption he witnessed around him, the greater was his suspicion that something was not right. Of all the revolutions that had occurred in the Socialist World, Romania's, he concluded, was a travesty. The missives that Marx, Lenin and Trotsky had posted many years before had clearly been lost in transit.

Nicolae maintained his faith for as long as he could. But his repeated visits to the Securitate became layers of depression, harder and harder to shake off. One night, unable to sleep, he hit rock bottom. He felt an emotion more harrowing than any he had ever experienced, a feeling that was intensified by the voice of a state radio announcer discussing the dictator's visit to Buckingham Palace. The radio was in his father's study. At half-past twelve, Nicolae contemplated killing himself.

It was at that point that Nicolae realized he had nothing left to lose. A clarity came to his thoughts. A door opened. The idea of escape.

Andrei dismissed Nicolae the first time he approached him with his plans. But not long after, the circumstances of his own life changed considerably. The Securitate began visiting Andrei's house and his mother's dressmaking co-operative, questioning her while he was away at school. His mother tried to calm him. It's just harassment, she insisted. But clearly she was upset, more so than Andrei had ever seen her. She paced the kitchen restlessly at night. Andrei noticed her body startle when the wind rattled the shutters or a visitor knocked on the door. He too alternated between panic and resolve, and he vowed to himself that he would protect her—even if it meant leaving Romania.

In the plastic bag that Andrei packed in haste while his mother was sleeping, there were two changes of underwear, an extra shirt, marine goggles that would replace his eyeglasses, some matches, food and water for two, and a slender waterproof packet containing a few photos and personal effects. He wore a bathing suit under his clothes. In contrast, Nicolae carried virtually nothing—a snorkelling mask and, pinned to his bathing suit, a tiny enamel portrait of Che Guevara given to him by his father.

Nicolae had spent weeks secretly dispensing his belongings. He did this partly out of concern for his family, for he truly believed it would be easier on everyone if there was nothing left to tidy up, but also because it provided him with an almost therapeutic sense of ceremony. To begin another life, Nicolae believed, the past life had to be given away.

On board the *Zenica*, however, Nicolae's confidence quickly dissolved. The faint smell of laundry soap on his shirt filled him with longing. He was rid of possessions but not emotions: the unsaid goodbyes weighed heavily. He reached for Andrei, who moved closer and rested Nicolae's head against his shoulder, softly counting down from one hundred as the Turkish freighter lifted anchor. When he reached fifty-seven, they heard the nasal sound of a ship's horn.

The wooden crate in which they hid was hardly large enough for them both. After an hour, their flashlight began to flicker and fade. Andrei turned it off and immediately a damp blackness closed in. He shook the flashlight and turned it back on. The boat was tipping and sliding on the waves, water hitting the deck above them. He tried humming to subdue their fear, but quickly stopped, reaching instead for the jug of water they had been given earlier by the man who hid them. Nicolae's eyes stayed on him as he lifted the jug, took a long gulp, then offered it.

"We're going to be all right," Andrei whispered, and Nicolae nodded.

The flashlight faded out one last time and then they were in darkness. Nicolae, who was pressed up against the side of the crate, felt the retching onset of seasickness. His stomach tossed each time the hull hit the water. He sagged into himself, his arms wrapped tightly around his legs, until he passed into sleep. Though they had been told to stay hidden away, Andrei felt his way up the ladder and wedged a small piece of scrap wood in the hatch to allow for fresh air.

At half past one, a puff of light and sulphur scratched the air. Andrei checked his watch, then extinguished the match. He reached for Nicolae's hand, distressed at its clamminess, and gave it a gentle tug. Their plan was to enter the water at the mouth of the Bosporus. It was three hours before sunrise. Andrei groped carefully up the ladder and lifted the lid. On deck, he released a long sigh, relieved to be able to stretch his legs. He took pleasure in the moon, watching its reflection carve the black water in two, the sea now so quiet.

Then Nicolae arrived at his side, pale from fatigue and nausea, whispering, "Let's hurry. I'm more than ready to throw myself overboard."

Together they spread an insulating layer of petroleum jelly over their skin, along their arms, onto the backs of their legs, slipping against each other for a slick and final embrace. It was agreed that if they got separated, they would reunite on the shore.

Nicolae lowered himself by a rope and entered first. Andrei tripped on a winch, lost a few seconds righting himself, and entered a minute or so later. The freighter travelled slowly along its course, leaving a soft wake across the surface. It was still too early for the passenger ferry boats to begin brightening the water with their lights. The blue-black water and sky merged.

Andrei felt a strong wind quickening the current where the Black Sea filled the mouth of the Bosporus. The water was choppy and he dipped under for longer stretches of time, sinking and spluttering, fighting to the surface as water swelled over him, coming up with a gasp and then sinking again. The pressure was almost more than he could bear. The force of the sea was crushing, and his lungs were heavy and sore. When the water calmed down, he rolled onto his back and floated for a few minutes to regain his strength. His chest was heaving. The Black Sea was behind him.

Through a surface skimmed with iridescence, swirls of pink and blue petrol, he swam out of one world and into another. On the Bosporus, he was surrounded by tankers anchored in the night, a spew of industrial waste. His mouth clamped shut. Three hours after they had entered the water, he experienced the first grey light of morning. Ahead he saw a dark, shifting stripe of land.

When his feet finally touched solid ground, he looked up and noticed the sky spinning above him. For a moment, his eyes pulsed with spots of darkness, then his body gave way, like ink spilled on the shore. He crawled toward, then collapsed against a large rock. For hours, he slipped in and out of awareness.

He dreamt he saw Nicolae's head bobbing above the water's surface. He called out, but there was only his voice and its echo, receding upward to the sky, then caught, gone on the wind.

> Andrei Dinescu, age 27, from Northern Romania, was
> found alive on a shore near Yenikoy by local fisherman
> Metin Saygin. He is in stable condition after many hours
> in the water.

Metin Saygin, the man who discovered Andrei, was interviewed by the local paper. Wasn't he afraid the man he rescued might be dangerous?

"No. I trusted my first impression completely," Andrei's rescuer replied.

And what impression was that?

"It's very simple. I saw someone's son."

Metin saw in Andrei a child who was near death. He took a flask of water and held it to Andrei's lips. When Andrei failed to respond, he dipped his fingers in the clear liquid and swabbed his parched lips until the child suckled in appreciation. He wiped his shirt across Andrei's forehead to draw off the sweat.

DESPITE THE PASSAGE OF several years, Metin had remained undiminished in Andrei's mind. So much so that the moment he finished describing his rescuer to me, he began to cry. We had moved from the living room to Andrei's small kitchen table. The electric fan, set at medium, was now perched on a stack of newspapers. Its vibrating tone blended with drifts of city noise. Strands of hair fluttered across Andrei's forehead as he wiped his eyes. There was a vase of daisies in front of us with a penny sitting at the bottom of the stale water. Bubbles clung to the stems. I pushed it aside and reached for his arm.

We stayed sitting in adjacent chairs. I remember being struck by Andrei's nearness, the closeness of his warm body smelling of soap and sweat. I remember looking at him and having a funny feeling in my chest.

He moved his chair closer, put his palm on my shoulder, tilted his face close to mine and kissed me. It started with a delicate touching of lips, then his mouth opened on mine and the kiss became loose, moist. I didn't stop him—suspended by surprise. He kissed me tentatively, and then more urgently. It was pleasant and then exciting and then . . . strange. When it was over (maybe a minute had passed, maybe two), he looked at me and shifted in his seat.

"That's my first kiss in a long time," he said, and began to blush.

I nodded and smiled, equally embarrassed, knowing what he was going to say.

He continued, "I have to tell you that—" He paused and looked into the vase.

"It's okay. I know."

"That I—I care very much about you, but—"

"It's okay, Andrei. I care about you, too," I said, trying not to feel rejected.

He looked away. "Forgive me?"

"Yes," I said, feeling guilty now as I thought of Paolo. "I forgive you."

When it was time for me to leave, we stood in the hall and hugged each other for a long time. Then we said goodbye.

We never discussed that kiss again. After a few days of awkwardness we slipped back into the roles we had established. Though it was unspoken, we both seemed to agree that friendship was the best thing for us, the easiest intimacy. I took the kiss to be merely a symptom of his increasing loneliness.

When I returned home that evening, still flustered by the afternoon's events, the entrance to my apartment was festooned with streamers. A scratchy fibre door mat—HOME SWEET HOME—had been placed across the threshold. On it was a letter from Paolo with an amusing poem he had composed about a dog named Hindrance that insists on squatting at a woman's doorstep until she adopts him. Paolo ended the letter by saying that he knew I was following my instincts, but soon he hoped my instincts would convince me to invite the dog in. "We can all learn new tricks," as he put it.

Inside the apartment, the answering machine light was blinking. I pressed Play and after a pause I was listening to a canine rendition of the song "Our House" by Crosby, Stills and Nash, Paolo's familiar voice performing a sequence of off-key bellows and howls. The whole production was so ridiculous and elaborate, it made me laugh out loud. A fitting end to a bizarre day, I thought.

But a part of me knew that Paolo wasn't joking. He was upping the ante.

We do not remember days, we remember moments.

From *The Burning Brand: Diaries 1935–1950*
by Cesare Pavese

Part Two

MY MOTHER'S THINGS

27 hotel toothbrushes (from my sister, Kana)

35 bars of hotel soap (also from Kana)

51 egg cartons (empty)

117 matchboxes (full)

163 ballpoint pens (new and used) divided into bundles of 20
and tied with elastic bands

11 rolls of digestive biscuits (unopened)

22 brown sugar packets

7 tins of cocktail nuts (6 unopened, 1 opened and partially eaten)

15 cans of chicken broth (unopened)

Ten

In early October, I invited Andrei to accompany me to visit my mother at Sakura. For some reason, I decided not to tell Paolo. It was a cool day and when we arrived most of the residents were inside busily preparing for the annual fundraising bazaar. In the dining area, several women dusted homemade *manju* cakes with rice flour, while others prepared marinated sacks of bean curd for *inarizushi*. The sweet tang of rice vinegar and cooking sake drifted through the air. Mary Yamada offered us some *mugicha*, roasted barley tea, which Andrei drank gratefully. I cupped my hands around a recycled office mug and brought the earthy liquid to my lips. It warmed my throat.

As we finished our tea, Andrei's eyes began to inspect everything— the upright piano and craft table in the common room, and the scenic posters of Kamakura and Mount Fuji that lined the halls. Near the entrance was a round brass medallion engraved with small-petalled flowers and the words: SAKURA. A BLOSSOM OF LIFE. I left Andrei alone in order to call up to my mother's room, and when I returned, he had wandered away. For a moment I thought he had left, but I found him standing in Roy Nakano's room, carefully examining a garden of miniature trees on the windowsill, as if he were acquainting himself with each individual leaf. Ceramic trays of pine, azalea and bamboo were arranged on top of stacks of *Popular Mechanics*: each curiously curved tree positioned off-centre on a small hill of earth. Bonsai. The art of cultivated deformity. Roy had packed soft green moss around the base of each creation.

When Andrei noticed that I had entered the room, he walked over to the shelves and pointed to an old photo of Roy, taken in an internment camp.

"Is this man a professional gardener?"

I shook my head. "No. I think it's just something he picked up during the war, in the camps." I said "in the camps" as flatly as I might have said "at school" or "at the cottage." "It's twisted, isn't it? So-called dangerous enemy aliens tending their flowers."

"Ah, yes. The manure-loving pacifist as treason suspect. I know very well about the state and its villains."

"If it wasn't so tragic, it would almost be funny. Just think of all the crimes against national security committed with a trowel and spade," I said.

He grinned. "Well, it's incredible what he's done," he said, pointing at the collection of bonsai. "I've never seen anything like it."

We left Roy's room and walked toward the common room, where my mother sat waiting with her hands clasped around a small pleated-leather handbag. Her black, shoulder-length hair was loosely arranged. I said hello and introduced Andrei. She smiled and pulled her shawl close to her, twisting the ends at her chest. I gave her the oranges I had brought. She placed them on the table and then massaged her knees.

Shiro, the white kitchen cat, tiptoed by with a bandaged stump where its tail had been severed.

When my mother finally spoke, her voice sounded cracked from underuse. "See the cat?" She pointed. "Gloria thinks that someone in the building chopped its tail off deliberately."

"That's terrible. Why would anyone do something like that?" I said.

Her voice, now that her throat was cleared, suddenly became warm and buttery. "To make it look like a Japanese bobtail."

I leaned forward and reached for the purse she had just placed on the table. It contained a fresh package of tissue, nail scissors and loose change that jangled like spurs when she walked.

"Gloria has a morbid imagination," I said, examining the purse.

My mother stared at my hands.

"It's almost broken," I said, gently tugging at the leather purse strap. The stitching was unravelling.

"Please give that back." She reached for the purse and turned to Andrei. "Will you put your mother in a nursing home when she becomes old and inconvenient?" A playful smile crept across her face.

"Jesus, Mum."

"Perhaps," he said, also smiling, "but if I did, I would be like Naiko and visit often."

There was a pause as my mother contemplated his answer. I raised my eyes to look at Andrei, who seemed to be enjoying her directness.

"Are you married?" she continued.

"No," he replied.

My mother studied Andrei in silence and then began to nod. "Yes. It's probably better that way."

I turned tensely to my mother.

Andrei laughed. "You must be the first mother I've met who doesn't believe in marriage."

"*Pfft*," she said, and relaxed a little. "I say *pfft* to marriage." Then she leaned over and whispered, "But last night I had two offers."

Andrei and I both laughed in surprise. She giggled.

When we were ready to leave, Andrei walked over to my mother's chair and offered his hand as she stood up. Their spontaneity and the casual way he touched her made me envious. Here was a man with an abundance of history, but none whatsoever with my mother. She was possibly the only maternal figure he had encountered since arriving in Canada and he was blissfully free to enjoy her company.

He hugged her. "Bye-bye, Mrs. Ayumi."

Although it felt awkward, I hugged her, too.

When I stepped back, I noticed that the blue cardigan she wore under her shawl was buttoned incorrectly, but I stopped myself from saying anything.

"Thank you for coming, Mr.—" She smiled and tilted her head for a moment, but the name didn't come to her.

"Andrei," he said gently.

"Mr. Andrei. It was a pleasure to meet you."

Her face was glowing and her eyes had a bright, almost lucid look.

Aging is a form of estrangement. We feel psychically matched to our image until our skin begins to soften and sag, and then one day we look in the mirror, dismayed to see an intruder with jowls and creases. When I was little, my father told me that the bags under his eyes were pockets stuffed with all the visions and images that had slipped away.

My mother's apartment at Sakura consisted of a small bedroom, a sitting area, a bathroom and an intercom connected to the caretaker's station. I found it pleasant but cramped, preferring to meet my mother in the common room, where there was more space to socialize. The walls were painted a cheerful sunflower yellow. Shafts of light streamed through the windows and, in the early afternoons, a large-format television played American soaps or *doramas* videotaped from Japanese TV. On the days she remembered to do it, my mother joined the other residents who congregated on the couches between two and four o'clock, eyes glued to the television, avidly enjoying its young models, its undiluted bursts of passion.

There were many Saturday afternoons that I sat with them on the couch, eating *osembe* and peanuts, enjoying the confinement that aging permitted, the ever-decreasing perimeter of choice and movement. It startled and amused me to realize that I was a young woman with the precise, repetitious habits of an old woman.

Before my mother came to Sakura, a social worker arranged to do a cognitive evaluation. He showed me the list of questions but told me he would have to be alone with my mother, presumably so I wouldn't give her any signs or clues. To test her long-term memory he asked: "Who is the prime minister of Canada? When was the Second World War? When were you married?" To test her short-term memory, he named three objects—motorcycle, earmuffs, pineapple—and asked her to repeat the names immediately and again five minutes later. To test her judgment, he asked, "What would you do if you were walking down the street and saw a wallet on the sidewalk?"

My mother did all right on some of the questions, but not well enough overall to warrant an unconditional pass. In her ability to remember and master new things, for example, she was assessed as "considerably impaired." By the end of the visit, the social worker had determined that my mother was exhibiting signs of confusion and mental decline that could no longer be attributed to forgetfulness or mere distraction. When he suggested that she was an ideal candidate for assisted-living, somehow making this sound like a lavish compliment, I numbly accepted his opinion and moved her to Sakura—prompting a series of arguments with my absentee but nonetheless disapproving sister. That was twenty-two months ago.

Kana said, "It'll just make it worse. There are studies that show—"

"She needs help. And you're not around to help her 'get better again.'"

"The studies say institutionalized care can lead to a downward spiral . . . rapid deterioration . . . intellectual decline. She's just overtired. What she needs is a good, long holiday."

Kana was annoyed because she thought our mother was acting older than she was. She didn't like admissions of weakness or defeat. She believed in self-diagnosis, self-help, the idea that everyone—with hard work and an occasional spa treatment—was perfectible.

My mother was now entering Alzheimer's middle state and I began to picture her mind as a Jackson Pollock painting: repetitive, overlapping loops, bundling and broken lines, all searching vigorously for a beginning.

Anyone who knew my mother well could see that her mind had become tangled.

My mother was once a scrupulous organizer. When we were little, she held on to all the photographs we ever took, every letter and birthday card she had ever received. She slipped everything into clear plastic sleeves and made raised print labels with her Avery label gun. My sister and I took my mother's stashes for granted. We thought she was uptight when really she was just a firm believer in posterity. She was showing us that keeping a record of life gave it meaning.

Then, around the time of my twenty-first birthday, after Kana had left for Europe to work for a British newspaper, my mother suffered a mild concussion after slipping on a patch of black ice at a subway entrance. She quickly recovered, but soon after began acting oddly. My sister came back and discovered while doing laundry that my mother's pant pockets were filled with small scraps of paper. Smoothed out on the kitchen table, they formed an inventory of our mother's mind: things she needed from the drugstore, bills that needed paying, names and numbers of close friends, family birthdays, places she had visited or hoped to visit, the dates and times of television shows she planned to watch, the bloom time of various flowers in our garden.

> multi-vitamins, dental floss, hydro, phone, Anita 922–6190,
> Ellen 304–1211, March 22nd (Jody's Birthday), Ronchamp
> (Notre Dame-du-Haut), Kyoto (Ryoanji), Paris (Ste.
> Chapelle) . . .

By the time I reached my mid-twenties, my mother was regularly losing things like her watch and datebook and acting genuinely bewildered when they appeared in places she professed never to have left them. Her secret lists multiplied with these slips of short-term memory. The contents of her dresser became a source of preoccupation and constant rediscovery. When something caught her eye it was adopted—like an Expo 67 pin she attached to her tennis visor, or a cosmetics case she carried around with her everywhere for weeks, a pincer grip sliding the zipper back and forth, her other bumpy hand kneading the fabric like pastry dough.

"I never want to be like her."

Kana made the observation one afternoon a few years back as we sat at the kitchen table, casually observing Ayumi in the other room. It was the harshest thing she had ever said about our mother and I was taken aback by the coolness in her voice.

"It's so depressing." She frowned. "All that fussing and tinkering. All her fucking paraphernalia."

It was a Sunday. Kana was wearing a shoulder-baring alpaca sweater and dark fitted jeans. Her hair was piled in a knot on top of her head. She looked casual and glamorous at the same time. Sometimes she was so beautiful it stupefied me.

Our mother was matching teacups and saucers, carefully dusting each set as she removed it from the glass cabinet and placed it on the dining table. She was concentrating in such a way that I knew everything else was blurring into the background. It was clear that she would be lost for hours.

Kana continued. "I pity her. Imagine having to rely on possessions to tell yourself who you are. Why do women do that? It's a woman thing, isn't it?"

I nodded but I felt secretly unsure. My mother had always been a collector. I remember shelves from my childhood lined with thickly glazed bowls and translucent egg cups she had gathered over the years. Painted china cats arranged in order of size. Plates that were never used because they were too beautiful. It was never just "loot." Her collection rivalled the stock of most antique stores. But more recently her formidable stash had come to include detergent samples, elastic bands, old issues of *TV Guide* and blister packs of pills.

I wondered if a man in her position would behave the same way. Was it women's particular dementia—or salvation—to obsessively tend to the order of the material world?

Shortly before my mother moved to Sakura, I went to visit her at home one evening and found her sitting at the top of the stairs with red, tear-filled eyes. She was holding a can of lemon furniture polish in her hands. When she noticed me standing by the banister she stood up and tried her best to fake a cough. I remember she even placed a hand against her forehead as if feeling for a temperature. The onset of the flu, she said. When she passed me, she patted my shoulder in a way that was completely foreign to me.

That same evening I discovered that she had killed her house plants, not by neglect but rather by drowning them with overvigilance, watering them over and over again.

The first few nights at Sakura, my mother told me, she lay awake, listening by habit for the CN trains that used to pass along the tracks near her house. She heard instead someone walking up and down the hall, a patter of footsteps receding then approaching, receding then approaching. Eventually the sound soothed her to sleep.

I stopped by on my way to work the next morning to see how she was settling in. The nurse came by with her medication shortly after I arrived.

"*Ohaiyo*, Ayumi-san, I've brought you your magic pills," she said, and laughed warmly.

"They're so tiny." My mother stared into a small paper cup at two round, buff-coloured pills.

"*Dozo*, three more," the nurse said gently, passing another cup with two vitamin E soft gels and a single ibuprofen tablet.

My mother stared into the second cup while I stared at the nurse's fingernails, each one rounded and perfect. My mother rose to get some water from the bathroom. When she returned, I noticed that the tap was still running and went to turn it off.

There was nothing that could stop the wires from crossing in my mother's head. Drawers full of mixed-up belongings: winter gloves packed in with pyjamas, undergarments in the vitamin drawer. She continued to misplace her possessions and it continued to upset her— "But it was here just a second ago . . ." It affected me deeply, until one day I had another meeting with the social worker.

We were sitting in his small windowless office. He had eyes that crinkled at the corners behind round glasses, tufts of greying hair by his temples and a horrid habit of picking at the wax in his ears as he spoke. But he was kind—effortlessly kind. The important thing, he emphasized, was that my mother still cared. She hadn't given up. She still remembered to put away her clothes every evening, folding then refolding the sleeves, arranging her shoes under the bed. Most important, he continued, she still remembered what belonged to her. (Underwire bras, Clinique moisturizer, digital travel clock . . .)

Whereas people with advanced Alzheimer's forgot what was theirs until they had nothing of their own—their lives a mishmash of unfolded clothes, unrecognized children, mouldy refrigerators—my mother's world was yet governed by orderliness.

"Naiko," said the social worker, "you must keep in mind that the older we get, the more we have to remember. There's not an aging person around that hasn't at some point feared having the circuits of their brain blown out by dementia. If you're thirty and you lose a second set of keys, it's a joke: you're in love, daydreaming. If you're sixty, it's a crisis. Everyone around you reaches for the panic button. Generally families can do more to help by remaining calm."

I realized that the moment my mother showed indifference when everything she once owned was gone from her memory, I would know that the end was coming. The more sick she became, the less she would carry in her purse.

"Andrei, what am I going to do? She's lost her wallet again."

"There are worse things to lose," he said.

"Of course there are, but . . ."

"We lose things all the time."

He was carefully extracting a rolled-up diploma from a slender cardboard tube. He examined the silver seal and continued, "Most people can't remember what happened last week, let alone a few months ago. Tell me. Do you remember what you ate for breakfast yesterday, or the face of the person who sat beside you on the bus to work?"

"No—but . . ."

"How about your first kiss? Do you remember that?"

"Yes, of course. But, Andrei, I don't see how this relates to my mother losing her wallet."

Andrei had a theory that the ability to adapt to losing things was one of the reasons very old people had such peaceful faces. They accepted it as part of aging, he said. But I could see nothing positive about my mother's illness. There was no tranquility. The ease with which she used to open a door, talk on the phone, pick up a pen, search through her purse—all gone.

"She has been losing things for eight years. You might think it's perfectly normal, but I still can't get used to it." I knew there was an edge to my voice.

Andrei nodded slowly, his guard dropped, and he said quietly: "I'm sorry. It's just that . . ." He shrugged. "I think we worry a lot about our mothers. And maybe it doesn't help . . . any of us."

I changed the subject. "You know, she's started taking watercolour classes. She's actually very good. She knows how to capture trees, flowers, water, all that landscape stuff."

"That's wonderful. To have a grasp of nature."

Andrei had experienced his own battles against forgetting, which made his seemingly casual attitude to my mother all the more puzzling.

A few weeks after he started working at the Undeliverable Mail Office, he developed a sudden spell of insomnia. He came to the office dishevelled and exhausted. His face suddenly seemed to be composed of sharp planes and dramatic shadows. His eyes became dark and grief-filled. As he later explained it: "One morning I woke up from a bad sleep and I couldn't remember any of the shop names or streets signs of my childhood. I tried to remember the name of my favourite grade-school teacher but that was gone too. Was it Mr. Giurescu? Georgescu? I tried to picture the animal that appeared on our school badge. That little slice of moon, the tree. Was the tree an elm? Was the animal an owl? For nights I lay awake, fearing sleep, fearing that my dreams would swallow up other things."

He called it his "memory flu." In bed, he stared for hours at the stuccoed ceiling, making connect-the-dot shapes in his mind. Tree. Hammer. Cloud. By daybreak, with the sky lightening, he found himself drifting in a state of half sleep, rehearsing the Romanian words for willow, carpenter, thunderstorm. A kind of pre-emptive rescue mission. Was it his way of not forgetting the world of Nicolae?

Images of the Carpathians sat on one shelf of his mind, the words to "Awaken, Thee, Romanian!" sat on another, waiting to be retrieved whenever someone mentioned Romanian mountains or anthems.

But no one did.

Toward the end of the second week, Andrei was on the verge of collapse. He would awaken to the morning sun piercing the bedroom window, then, sleep-deprived, drowse during the day. He dropped and spilled things at work. He developed a pulsing tic in his right eye. His pride took a plunge along with his blood sugar. Eroding his sanity, heightening his sense of fragility, was the feeling he was utterly alone. That's when he reached out to me.

The Undeliverable Mail Office is where all the lonely hearts end up. It was destiny, I believe, that he started working here when he did. Maybe I had a sympathetic face, high eyebrows that made me look perpetually interested. Maybe he had a nose for a good listener.

Together, we resurrected his past, and eventually Andrei began to sleep again. He laid claim to his memories as doggedly as he recovered misdirected mail.

For my part, I was grateful to be able to help him. Most of my mother's memories were already unreachable.

The other night I was lying in bed wondering about the mischievous nature of recollection. Why our minds stop at some things and skip over others. It started with a stray childhood image of me standing at the end of a tall diving board in a red bathing suit, the board sloping slightly under my weight, my hands folded between my legs, hot pee trickling through my fingers. Why did that forgotten image flash into my head when it did? Where had it been kept all that time?

One cannot predict what portions of the past will be carried into the future. I work in a place where there are no guarantees of delivery. Letters or parcels sent to easy destinations arrive damaged or in tatters, while other mail, perhaps subjected to wars or hurricanes, arrives in near-perfect condition.

A few days ago something special happened at the Undeliverable Mail Office. A birthday card turned up that had been sent from Brighton, England, in 1896. It had arrived in Canada, in an official postmaster's envelope, having spent nearly a century lost in the

British Royal Mail. A long-ago, offhand greeting had become a symbol of imperishability. I looked at the handwritten script, the curlicue accents, the quaint image on the card of a Victorian child holding a butterfly net and playing in a summery meadow.

Maybe in the torrent of the new, old memories get swept away to some corner of the mind that is custodian of the future, until years later they mysteriously reappear, pristine in their innocence.

Eleven

There are seventeen days until Andrei's rent expires. And Christmas is coming.

Kana has called to tell me that she won't be coming home for a while. The general strike in Prague has led to the resignation of the president and a demand for democratic elections. They are calling it the Velvet Revolution and it is being led by Václav Havel, a dissident playwright who was still in jail only three months ago. They adoringly refer to him as the Lennon-loving—as opposed to Lenin-loving—champion of Prague.

At the end of November I had received an excited letter from her.

Dear Nai-chan,

The past week's events have been incredible. Students have taken over the streets calling for democratic reform.

*Families march through the city and jangle their keys—a
symbol that means it is time for a change in leadership. The
other night there was a standoff near Wenceslas Square in
which the students offered flowers to the riot police. The
police began beating the young demonstrators with night
sticks, bringing out dogs and water hoses. It has angered
everyone I speak with. They are expecting an even bigger
demonstration next week at Letna Park. There are even
rumours of a general strike.*

*I just spoke with Mummy on the telephone. It was very
discouraging. She seems to be getting worse—more absent-
minded every time I call. Have you noticed? She keeps
repeating the same stories. Tonight she told me (twice!)
that you have been bringing someone other than Paolo to
see her. She didn't mention his name but she says he speaks
English well, but with a heavy accent. What's going on?
Is she making all this up? If things settle down here I am
determined to come home for Christmas, but I'll call as soon
as my plans are confirmed. Let's talk then.*

XOXO
K-chan

*p.s. Is everything okay between you and Paolo?! Have you
come to any decision about living together?*

This evening when I arrived at Sakura after speaking with Kana on
the phone, there was a handwritten sign taped to the main door:
Because of a small fire all residents had been temporarily relocated to
Grace Church. The sprinkler system had been set off in the morning.

Water had spouted out in circles, drenching the corridors and the bedrooms of several residents. Fumes of melted plastic permeated the air. There was so much smoke that the white tiles of the main-floor washroom had turned grey. Shortly before I arrived, the residents had been escorted to the simple red-brick United Church building one street over. A firefighter pointed me in the direction of its squat, cross-topped steeple and I walked there against a lashing early winter wind. Grace Church, a strange building that butted up against a real estate office on one side and a video store on the other, boasted a giant stained-glass window of the Resurrection. It would have been no surprise to find a singing choir or a minister reading a sermon, but when I opened the door and peered inside, there was only a balding middle-aged man holding two fold-up chairs. He gestured for me to follow him.

Inside the church, the evacuated residents were resting in a large basement room. There was a peaceful after-supper feel to the place. Roasted chicken legs, dinner rolls and the remains of a shredded-carrot-and-raisin salad sat on a rectangular banquet table next to a stack of unused paper plates. An aroma of greasy meat lurked in the air. Roy Nakano sat on a chair eating a piece of Black Forest cake, a tissue stuffed up one of his nostrils. The darkening spots from an earlier nosebleed matched the dark red cake filling. I stopped to say hello.

The woman to his right, Grace Shimura, was wearing a red cowboy bandana as a head scarf. She had a wonderful, happy face, and seemed, along with a few of the others, genuinely thrilled by the day's events.

"You poor thing, you look absolutely frozen," she said.

I pulled the collar of my jacket closed and nodded. "The wind just picked up. I didn't realize it would be so cold when I left for work this morning."

She smiled. The bandana gave her a scatty appearance. By way of apology she adjusted it.

"I know this is a peculiar thing, but Roy, now, he tells me when he doesn't like the way I fix my hair. And today, with all the commotion, I didn't have a chance to pretty myself."

Grace rested her hand on Roy's leg, patted it lightly. Roy scraped the icing on his plate and piped in: "They're still trying to figure out what started the sprinklers. The goddamn system went haywire. I had to throw plastic bags over my trees so they wouldn't get flooded. What a mess!"

His gaunt face puffed up in excitement, an emphatic plastic fork poked the air.

Across from Grace, a woman bleated, "*Hidoi yo* . . . it's just terrible . . ."

My mother was sitting in a corner holding an orange drink box, drawing short sips through the straw, a lonesome plastic chair beside her. She was wearing most of her costume jewellery, strings of coloured glass beads and silver pendants around her neck. Her hair was held in a bun by handfuls of black bobby pins. She looked more uncertain than usual, and even after I arrived she kept nervously watching the door. When I sat down, she leaned close and took my hand, holding it tightly.

She whispered, "They can't find Gloria."

She let go of my hand and twisted a garnet ring around her baby finger.

I sat silently with my mother for an hour, and watched Roy Ishii (another Roy) pacing back and forth with a down jacket around his shoulders. Whenever he passed a window, he would stop for a moment to peer up at the sky. A layer of curdled cloud spread as far as the eye could see.

I liked Roy. He was probably the most solid, unwavering person I had ever met. When he was a kid in Vancouver, he decided he wanted to be a weatherman. He dreamt of being a master of the elements. While forecasting the weather didn't mean you could transform it, and while there would always be days that you'd get it wrong, he said that learning how to interpret the skies and gauge the winds gave him a feeling of confidence he had never had before.

During the forced evacuation in the Second World War, when the Ishii family was relocated to Tashme, a former cattle ranch in the British Columbia interior, Roy's weather predictions were treated as a welcome diversion. He taught the other children to read the clouds—widely scattered puffs, low twists and tatters, wisps with rust-coloured haloes—identifying each by name and thickness. A harmless hobby, everyone assumed, until October 1944, when Roy wrote a letter to an uncle in New Denver, describing as an aside the low-level nimbostratus obscuring the sky above Tashme. This edgeless dark mass would sit for days above their heads, producing a steady dump of snow.

The letter was returned opened but undelivered: a first warning. It turned out that if you were Japanese Canadian, amateur weather forecasting was considered an offence. The post office was under government orders to scrutinize any letter being sent by or to any Japanese Canadian. Information concerning such things as meteorology or road conditions was blacked out as intelligence helpful to the enemy. The weather was no longer a staple of conversation—it was treachery.

Despite a few inauspicious years, Roy continued to nurture his interest in weather after the war ended. And when he moved into Sakura, decades later, his worldly goods reflected a lifelong preoccupation. Posters from NASA's image spacecraft covered his walls, offering a ghostly vision of Earth—a blue-and-white orb glowing in the blackness of outer space surrounded only by a thin membrane of air, which Roy referred to as Our Fragile Envelope. During a visit one afternoon, he showed me a storms-and-fronts index that went back to 1955. He surprised me by asking my birthdate. I told him it was April 14, 1960.

He grinned. "Overcast. Showers in the afternoon," he said.

And when we looked it up, he was right. (He confessed later that my birthday coincided with Maurice "Rocket" Richard's last game in the NHL, when the Montreal Canadiens swept the Toronto Maple Leafs 4–0 for the Stanley Cup. Roy remembered walking to Maple Leaf Gardens in a rain slicker.)

Now, I watched him sauntering through light shafts in the church basement, wearing his down jacket as a cape. He raked his fingers through his thinning hair, unruffled by the day's events.

Noting my presence, he smiled and nodded. "Looks like she's going to storm."

Cumulonimbus clouds, a cold front moving gradually across the early night sky.

"Your mom. She sounds kind of tense." Paolo's hand was over the mouthpiece.

He held the phone down toward the couch where I lay that same night, overcome with exhaustion. It was just past ten o'clock. My mother and the other residents of Sakura were staying at a local inn until their rooms were restored.

"Naiko?" She had to be calling from the hotel front desk.

"Mom, is everything okay?"

"I'm not sure. It's Gloria. She's still missing."

Gloria Kimura lived on the same floor as my mother. I knew her as a fidgety woman who collected dolls and combed her grey bangs compulsively.

"Get them to phone her family. Where else would she go?"

As I said this, I imagined Gloria wandering alone through the cold streets.

"They're calling now. Oh dear, it has been such a crazy day. Only . . ."

"Only what?"

Silence.

"Mom?"

"This is awful, but I think she was the one who started the fire."

As soon as she said it, I knew she was right.

On a recent visit, I had stopped by Gloria's room to find her talking on the phone. I waved to her quickly from the doorway, but as soon as she saw me she tilted the phone onto her shoulder and gestured for me to join her, moving her free hand vigorously as if fanning herself. I stepped into her room, removed a stack of magazines from the only chair and heard the agitation in her voice as she spoke to her sister, who lives in Port Hope. The window was opened and the room was chilly, and as I flipped through an old copy of *Vanity Fair*, goosebumps spread across my skin. I noticed the sound of wind whistling through a tree just outside the open window. A few more minutes of heated conversation passed. Then, just as Gloria was saying goodbye to her sister, I was startled by a loud and sudden *bang*, something smashing against the rain gutter below. My head jerked back just as Gloria's arm returned to her side. My heart jumped against my chest. I kept my eyes on her face, but she was staring at the window ledge, where a wooden *Kokeshi* doll had stood only seconds earlier. Her expression and the tension in her hand told me that the doll's fall wasn't an accident.

"My God, Gloria," I said, one hand still on my chest. "What happened?"

She looked up. "It slipped," she said quietly.

I walked over to the window and looked below. "Someone could have been down there. You could have really hurt someone."

She didn't answer. Drooping with tiredness, she slumped onto the bed so suddenly it startled me. It took me a moment to take in her difficulty and to help her lie down.

"Bless your heart." She blinked and changed the subject. "You like *yokan?*" She aimed an arm in the direction of her mini-fridge. "Take some with you. I shouldn't eat it. Diabetes. Go on, take it all."

"Gloria, please rest." I began to pull up the folded quilt at the foot of her bed, but her hand blocked me.

"Please, no. The quilt's not quite finished yet." She sighed. "But almost."

And with that she rolled over and closed her eyes.

I ran my fingers over the fabric, then carefully folded it up and put it back at the foot of the bed before leaving the room.

The quilt had taken on epic dimensions since finding its way to Gloria the previous winter. Though she told slightly different versions of the story, the basics stayed the same:

In the spring of 1987, an elderly widow by the name of Mrs. Millie Kingston collided with a cyclist while taking a morning walk and died hours later of a cerebral hemorrhage. When her children were disposing of her things, they found folded away among the more obvious valuables a quilt embroidered with the words *For our dear friends, John and Margaret Kimura, Ucluelet 1944.* The quilt, which was now sun-faded and unstitched in sections, had been purchased at a small antiques market near Cobourg, Ontario.

How it ended up there is open to speculation. When Japanese

Canadians were rounded up and sent to internment camps, the remnants of their lives cropped up in various locations. Among the myriad disruptions of daily life faced by a people suddenly branded "enemy aliens" was uncertain mail delivery. Piles of undeliverable packages sat in Canadian post offices waiting to be rerouted. Most of these packages had been returned or retrieved from houses where families were not present to receive them, and were marked with the impassive administrative memo FORWARDING ADDRESS REQUIRED. Some found their proper destination, but many were left unclaimed.

The names on letter boxes throughout the coastal towns of British Columbia spoke of Japanese Canadians who hoped one day to return to their homes. The name TANAKA painted on a box imparted the impression that Kenta and Hatsuko Tanaka had not been evacuated by the RCMP, that if one opened the door to 526 Cordova Street, they might be right inside, preoccupied with mending the water damage to their bedroom ceiling following the heavy spring rains or busy unpacking a recent shipment of Japanese silk to display in their modest but successful import shop. A block away on Powell Street, a letter box bearing the name MAIKAWA awaited mail addressed to the owners of the community's only department store. One after another, the names on the letter boxes were replaced, but for a time it was possible to stroll through the streets of Vancouver's Japantown and believe that the community had simply stepped out for a moment, that everyone would shortly return.

The quilt was one of many postal orphans. After the war it was put up for auction, and it eventually found its way to Cobourg, where it was purchased by Millie Kingston, a retired primary-school principal. Decades of travel and use took their toll, so that by the time Millie died, the quilt was tattered and ready for the trashbin; only the intervention of Millie's perceptive daughter, Jenny Kingston, prevented such an end. Jenny, with intuition reinforced through a decade of work as a city archivist, recognized the quilt's sentimental and historical value and immediately packed it off to *The Kimuras of Ucluelet c/o Canada Post*.

From friendship token to stray artifact to craft souvenir to raggedy castaway to personal effect of the deceased to repatriated relic to cherished heirloom. The transmutation of matter.

The quilt arrived at the Undeliverable Mail Office toward the end of 1988. As I recall, I was poring over an elastic-bound set of Enid Blyton books, looking for a card or a dedication, remembering my childhood, when I was called over by one of the storage-room sorters. His name was Finn, short for Finnegan—though Andrei used to tease him by calling him "Fin, the End," because it was his job to declare the worth of items that were left unclaimed after six months. He was the gravekeeper; the storage room, his necropolis. For days at a time, its phantoms were his only company. Covered in dust, in actual danger of being crushed, Finn burrowed his way through bulging walls of packages and documents, his great mop of reddish brown hair floating through this contemporary catacomb along an increasingly narrow trench. Valuables were sent to auction. Non-valuables were destroyed. It was like sorting wheat from chaff: tedious but straightforward. Only on occasion did he call on anyone else for input. And when he did he spoke concisely.

"I've found something."

On a table lay the badly preserved quilt, star-shaped patches of red floral fabric hanging in flaps against an uneven blue background. Along one edge in pale pink thread was the embroidered inscription. He underlined the names John and Margaret Kimura with his index finger.

●

Did I know of them? Well. No. Not them. But I could make a few calls.

It turned out that the quilt, which had been on its way to the incinerator, had been made for Gloria's aunt and uncle, who, when given the choice of going to an internment camp or "repatriating" to Japan, a country as foreign to them as Norway, had chosen the latter. The quilt had been in the hands of strangers for four decades. After a bit of inquiring, it was given to Gloria as John and Margaret's closest traceable relative.

It was a "reunion" I regarded as a landmark in my mail recovery career. Gloria was an odd but good-hearted woman who tended to place everyone else's needs before her own. I'd long admired her cheerful disposition, the genuine, sometimes heroic smile that spared whoever she was with any sense of the distress she might be feeling at that moment. It gratified me to be able to give her something.

For Gloria, the quilt became a source of pride and purpose—like Penelope's robe, a perpetual doing. She worked on it every day, mending the broken stitches, repairing the stars. In retrospect, the labour probably staved off a depression that would have consumed her sooner. It was impossible to imagine Gloria without the quilt.

And when it was completed, a few days after I visited her, she got out of bed and wrapped herself in it, and then a woman whose days and nights had no centre walked down the hall and set fire to a waste-paper bin in the women's washroom.

Twelve

The morning after the sprinklers went off at Sakura, I woke up early with razors in the back of my throat. I went to the kitchen to fetch a glass of orange juice but it hurt too much to swallow. My ears were clogged and when I spoke my voice sounded faraway. I padded off to the bathroom and inspected my tonsils, gargled and padded back to bed, groaning as I lay down. A shaft of light passed through the window. It had snowed lightly during the night.

"It's probably the flu," said Paolo when I called him. "Stay in bed."

After I telephoned the UMO, I slept and slept, waking occasionally to take teaspoons of liquid, including chicken broth that Paolo brought over later in a big pot. After the virus travelled from my throat to my chest, a cough racked my entire body. During the three days it took me to recover, I hardly thought of Gloria or Andrei or my mother at all. I rested and watched television with filmy eyes, buried in a beige duvet that I had had since I was seven years old and surrounded by ribbons of toilet tissue to blow my nose. Paolo nursed me between his shifts at the flower shop, but for the most part I was alone, blinds drawn against the daylight, lozenge wrappers hidden in the damp folds of my overslept bed.

Day mixed with night, snacks replaced meals. A feeling of slackness gradually overcame me, as if my body had been filleted of its bones and was now melting into the mattress. The television was on but I looked through it. After some patting around, I found the converter and turned it off. There was a bulk at my feet where I had left the morning newspaper. I reached down and pulled it toward me, unfolded it on the bed as best I could, barely able to take in the day's reporting.

USA THREATENS TO INVADE PANAMA. OPERATION JUST CAUSE

90 HOMELESS EARTHQUAKE VICTIMS IN SAN FRANCISCO SLEEPING IN AN AUTOMOBILE SHOWROOM

ELEVEN PEOPLE KILLED IN A CAR PILE-UP ON THE 401

MASS PROTESTS IN TIMISOARA, ROMANIA, TURN VIOLENT

I refolded the paper and my mind started to roam, picking up thoughts then discarding them. The telephone rang. After four rings, I managed to reach it. My mother was calling with news that Gloria had been tracked down through her sister in Port Hope. Her breathing quickened with excitement as she spoke. Apparently, Gloria's sister had received a call earlier that morning from a nurse at a Toronto hospital. Some good Samaritan out walking his dog had witnessed Gloria fall on a pathway overlooking the Scarborough Bluffs and had brought her to emergency the night before with a hip fracture. They had set the fracture, but she would be in hospital for several more days. As she told me this, I could hear the note of disappointment in my mother's voice, the pout of a child who couldn't wait. I swallowed in an effort to unblock my stuffed ears and mustered a few words of encouragement. Something about time passing quickly enough, no need to be impatient.

After I replaced the receiver, I flopped back against the pillows with a mixed sense of relief (that the mystery of Gloria's whereabouts had been cleared up) and irritation (that my mother hadn't asked a single question about me, not a word about how I was feeling). My spine hurt. Sitting upright, I sipped my tea and shifted against the headboard, feeling sulky. The small of my back needed a good stretch. I flexed my feet, crossed my legs, tucked them under, straightened them, unable to get comfortable. At what point had she stopped asking?

Was it possible for a mother to forget to be a mother?

Don't, I thought.

But it was too late.

When they come, childhood memories are much like a wind in the trees, everything stirring at once.

ONE SPRING, WHEN I was ten and Kana was thirteen, my father and mother made the announcement that they were separating, a mutual and amicable decision.

"We've grown apart," they said.

To which we responded: "Can't you work it out? Can't you grow back together?"

But they insisted: "Don't make this harder. Someday you'll understand. And we'll still be friends, still be here for you."

We pleaded and bargained but it didn't get us anywhere. There were no miracles. We felt cheated. The way they had padded their announcement with niceties had broken our hearts.

It was almost summer but the world was grey, the shadows in our house multiplied. I became a faucet of sorrow, flooding the house with my tears. Kana cried in private, often in the shower under camouflage of cascading water, but her eyes bulged publicly with grief.

Everything happened so quickly. Within a few days, my father had rented an apartment near the college where he taught applied geography, and on my mother's insistence they began dividing the contents of the house bit by bit. Books, records, scissors, linen, unmatched chairs, mugs, photos, even condiments. I walked around the depleted house in a state of shock, while Kana spent hours in her room working on a jigsaw puzzle of Antarctica she could never complete.

When the first heartbreak passed, we imagined we were luckier than many kids in similar situations. We practised handstands and back walkovers in a space once occupied by two worn leather armchairs, and imagined our father's empty study as a time-travel machine, a device that could transform stillness into velocity, the present into the past.

Of course, in the end, the separation wasn't as tidy as they had led us to believe it would be. Old grudges began to reveal themselves. My parents became more aloof with each other, and stopped talking like old friends when they were on the telephone. Shared meals became less common. As the drifting apart gained momentum, we felt it acutely: the loss of their once combined energy and ideas. My father, an introvert by nature, sank further into his books, and into a monastic solitude that became harder and harder to interrupt.

But the most significant change was in my mother.

Through the initial stages of their separation, my mother fluctuated between matter-of-factness and giddiness. Strangely, her approach to keeping her composure was to keep moving. A figure of perpetual motion, she restained furniture, discovered the art of stencilling borders and reorganized the house from top to bottom.

Then one day, out of nowhere, following a conversation with my father during which he told her he had made the decision to spend half his sabbatical in England the following year, she came to an abrupt halt. When she got off the phone, the look on her face was that of someone who had lost her way. For a few minutes she moved about the room, repositioning chairs, picking things up and putting them down someplace else. She swept the vitamin bottles to the back of the kitchen counter, then sat on a stool. It seemed she didn't know what to do next.

As I finished eating the *onigiri* she had prepared for lunch, she stumbled past us to her bedroom, quietly but firmly closing the door. I followed her, with bits of rice sticking to my fingers, and rapped lightly on her door with the heel of my hand. There was no response. I licked the rice off my fingers, placed my hand on the knob and put my ear to the wood. Inside I could hear the rustle of bedsheets growing more insistent, like a mole was burrowing. I tried again. Still no response.

From early September to late November, she barely left her bedroom, sleeping through the day while Kana and I were away at school.

One childhood fear, still with me, comes from the mystery of my mother's collapse, the lack of any advance signal. At times, I have wondered, as children do, what genetic surprise awaits me. How would I know? What was her snapping point? What did it feel like to crack? A sudden pop, a jagged rupture, a slow seep?

My father ended up moving to England. A few years ago, when he came through town for a geography conference, I asked him, during a rare heart-to-heart, what he might have said to her during that ill-fated phone conversation.

He replied, "I can't think of anything in particular. I merely told her to take care of herself."

Perhaps he said it in such a way that she felt the entire wall of her ego cave in. Or maybe he didn't say it any particular way at all; maybe at that moment he was genuinely full of sympathy and concern. The words shattered her nonetheless. They were divorcing words.

Well then, my dear, he might have said as he held her over a canyon, legs dangling in mid-air, *take care of yourself.*

The truth is that my father has always been a bit curt. The thing he most dreaded being was tedious. It was a quality he despised in others. He believed that most people talked far too much, that fewer words denoted thought. But to my mind he simply feared the emotion of words. He should have had the courage to say more. The week before he went off to England, where he planned to investigate some breakthrough in electronic cartography, he took me out for ice cream. His parting speech lasted a confusing thirty seconds.

"I know it's hard but during this difficult interval, it might be beneficial to concentrate on your studies. Try to be generous with your mother and sister. Before you know it, everything will come back together. Dissolution and renewal are a part of life. What makes us human are our failings and flaws."

When I finally figured out what he was saying, I felt hoodwinked. He didn't really believe that dissolution was a part of life. Or if he believed it, he certainly didn't like it. As for our failings and flaws—my father loathed imperfection. He couldn't stand the asymmetry of his face, for example, the way his nose curved to the left, how one eyebrow was noticeably higher than the other. He abhorred the freckles covering his body. He judged himself relentlessly. He shuddered at people's image of him as a pure-blooded Scot, not out of ethnic dislike but because he despised clannishness—especially its rituals of kilts and pipes.

What he did like were straight lines and straight A's. He had a fondness for triangles. The equilateral was his favourite (three equal sides), next he liked the isosceles (two equal sides) and last of all the scalene (no equal sides). As a geographer, he looked for near-perfect formations: mountain chains, waterfalls, coral reefs. Best of all were near-perfect triangular formations: deltas, ice caps, the province of Madrid. He wasn't without a sense of humour. He liked making geography jokes such as, "No man is an isthmus." (An isthmus, I later learned, is a narrow piece of land connecting two larger bodies of land. When my parents separated, I became an isthmus.)

My father looked at his wife and saw someone too opposite. He was a minimalist. She was a maximalist. He was regular in everything, from his choice in coffee to his bowel movements. She was irregular—tea one morning, hot chocolate the next. He was a pessimist. She was an optimist. He liked the refined pleasure of listening to opera alone in his office. She preferred to pile up with us on the couch and watch television. Deep down I think he wanted to do the right thing for his family, but in the end he suffered from a failure of hope.

Yet at one time hadn't he thought she was the very incarnation of perfection?

In my memories of my mother's period of collapse, she is always lying under her comforter, the same floral *mofu* she'd had for years, originally shipped from Japan in an enormous piped-plastic package with a matching towel set that, once faded, was used as bedding for the cat's basket. A dark slab of television rises tomb-like at the foot of the bed.

Bouquets of elastic-bound junk mail are scattered across the floor. The warm autumn sun, then the white winter sun, slants through a gap in the curtains, casting a coffin of light on the bed. It is surely the dictionary definition of *wretchedness*. Her hands are folded on her chest. She looks like the dearly departed. And this is when I start to mourn her.

No matter how much she slept, there were dark stains under her eyes. Not a normal tiredness but undiminishing exhaustion. As the weeks passed, Kana and I did our best to hold the house together. Kana was the mother now. She did the laundry and laid out our pyjamas in the evening, our clothes in the morning. For dinner, she beat four eggs, added some slices of pepperoni, diced tomato, a large toss of salt and pepper, put some butter in a pan and prepared her one specialty: pizza scramble. On other nights, our meals came from boxes and cans. The papery corpses of dead bugs gathered on the kitchen floor by the fridge. I used plastic cutlery and pretended we were on a long camping trip.

When I tired of eating Kana's scramble, I thought briefly of asking the lady next door to help out on meals, but then she might have called Children's Aid—and such intrusion wasn't worth the risk. Looking back, we held up pretty well considering the strangeness of a mother who kept nocturnal hours and even then rarely left her bed.

At least I could count on knowing where she was. I experienced a rush of pleasure whenever I entered her bedroom after school. I knew that she'd be just waking up, that her body would emanate warmth. One day, while Kana stayed late at school for gymnastics practice, I joined my mother in her pillow fortress, crouching in the soft king-size bed, inhaling her faint sweat smell and glancing at her profile as we watched television together. By now, my mother had spent three weeks in bed, and I had a sudden irrational desire to be shut up with her, the security of her and me in an otherwise hazardous world.

Our stomachs were growling for food, but I paid no attention until I was starving and then ran downstairs to prepare a selection of snacks. I remember enjoying the hickory salt left on my fingertips from the potato chips and the thick texture of Nutella pressed off a spoon with my tongue. We passed hours into the evening, lying side by side. At one point, I went downstairs and prepared a tray with chocolate milk, a sludge of brown syrup at the bottom of each glass, a tin of Del Monte mixed fruit for my mother and a bag of trail mix for myself. When I entered the bedroom the cats were scratching up the woven silk wallpaper, shredding the brown fibre with their unclipped claws. There was a nest growing on the carpet.

My mother rested the glass of chocolate milk on her collarbone, taking baby sips as she watched a rerun of *The Mary Tyler Moore Show*. Mary had just knocked on Mr. Grant's office door. Suddenly there was a dull *thud*—in the room this time, not on the television. The unopened fruit salad tin had rolled along the downy slope of my mother's blanketed legs and onto the floor. I waited but my mother didn't stir. I let a minute or so pass, but it bothered me knowing that the tin was on the floor, so I went to her side, picked it up and placed it on the bedside table.

Perhaps at the time I wasn't entirely normal myself. What I felt inside me during those first few weeks seemed more like a strange curiosity than fear—not unlike the way I felt when my father drank too much at Christmas one year and I watched him waltz into a glass door.

My mother's face looked as if she had just competed in a marathon, conquering a task so strenuous that she had now earned as long a rest as she desired. Under the covers, she wore an old T-shirt and grey sweatpants. Though she didn't wear makeup, the room always smelled sweetly of honey skin lotion. A thousand pills of wool formed on a baby-blue cardigan she draped over her shoulders. Even her clothes were returning to an atavistic state.

Weeks passed, and Kana and I stopped waiting for our casserole-making, euchre-playing mother to return. I convinced myself that all mothers, even the good ones, maybe particularly the good ones, needed to take time for themselves.

The arrangement was that we would see our father once a week, but more and more frequently he would cancel or postpone at the last minute. I could always see the hurt on Kana's face before she could hide it. Our father had stopped being reliable. The more we needed him, the more distant he became.

My father always had a knack for fixing things. He spent much of my childhood sitting at a work table in the garage surrounded by warped bicycle wheels, lopsided picture frames and uneven table legs. The state of the concrete floor, strewn with nails and splintery scraps of wood, made entering off limits, but I counted on him to be there, and often stood at the doorway watching him. As winter approached, my mother would wander over and try to convince him to bring his work-shop into the house so he wouldn't have to be alone and in the cold. But he insisted he liked it out there by himself. He said it was his "bit of crust," a geographer's way of referring to his portion of the earth.

One afternoon after he left, I ventured into the garage. I was desperate to be in the spaces he had occupied. The garage was dim, but as soon as I entered I saw something wedged in the bench vise: one of my mother's shoes. My father had mended the wooden heel and left it there for the glue to dry. I walked over, unscrewed the vise carefully, and placed the shoe on the wooden table among his clamps and filing tools. It was the last thing he fixed before he left his marriage.

I tried to kept busy. In the morning we had school. I ate arrowroot cookies and orange juice for breakfast. In a burst of maternal feeling, Kana suggested I explore other food options, but I didn't like cereal and I was tired of eggs. So I continued eating cookies, added La Vache Qui Rit cheese triangles to my diet and sometimes substituted milk for juice. I begged off scrambled eggs forever, explaining, in a note I left for Kana on the fridge, that I had a "klorestral problem."

It was near the end of the first month that the novelty wore off. I hit a wall. Whatever my mother was thinking and feeling on the inside just wasn't getting through to us on the outside. No longer did she seem serene. She was comatose. Yet according to our family doctor—who paid a house visit after Kana called and pleaded with him to come—there was nothing physically wrong with her. He took her temperature and pulse, ran a few other tests and concluded that she was suffering from shot nerves, a "woman's problem," something we'd understand one day when we were grown up. Kana was ready to kill him when he said that, but I just thanked him and showed him out, feeling secretly guilty that I had wished our mother had a bona fide illness, something that involved wounds or lumps or spots. (Could the doctor show me an X-ray of her shot nerves? Would it look something like Swiss cheese?) I wanted splints and gauze and ointment. Maybe my mother was permanently deranged and the doctor was trying to protect us from the truth.

Oddly, I now found myself turning to television in a search for social explanations for my mother's unresponsive behaviour. At first, this convergence of fact and fiction was a lark. After watching an episode of *Gilligan's Island*, I told Miss Lowry, my grade four teacher, that my mother couldn't attend a parent–teacher night because she had a tarantula bite. (It was 1970 and, for some reason, television was glutted with stories about deadly spiders, piranhas and sharks.) Then a week later, after watching an episode of *General Hospital*, I told Miss Lowry that my mother had contracted septicemia.

"Won't you stay and talk with me? Please do," Miss Lowry said one afternoon in October, leaning forward in her swivel chair. "I know this has been a very difficult time for you."

I cut out of the conversation. My eyes flicked over the room.

" . . . divorce . . . immigrant mother . . ."

I stared at the orange-and-brown-striped curtains, then at a cluster of paper jack-o'-lanterns taped to the window.

" . . . at lunch or after school . . . someone to talk to now and then . . . So how does that sound?"

"Thank you, Miss Lowry. But I think I'm fine."

I knew she was genuinely concerned that I had lost a grip on reality. I tried to explain that it was just a game, but she simply stared at me, nodding.

Despite Miss Lowry's intervention, I kept telling stories.

Just before Thanksgiving, my father stopped by unexpectedly. My mother was still in bed. I was on the wood floor beside her, crawling forward on my belly the way commandos do in war movies, playing with the cats, trying my best to ignore the fact that my mother had been watching a mute game of *Family Feud* for over an hour. It was late afternoon. The doorbell rang and Kana let my father in. My mother remained upstairs.

"For you," he said when he arrived, and handed us an odd-shaped package.

I balanced it while Kana peeked through the foil wrapper and sighed. "Great," she muttered. "A plant." (For my sister that was the clincher. Our father had brought us something else to care for—the surest sign that he had no clue.)

"Pretty." I smiled.

"I thought your mother might like it," he said sheepishly. "She always liked mums . . . mums for Mum. Perhaps it'll brighten things up a bit."

Kana and I had grown accustomed to ordering in. We had collected takeout menus for every pizza and barbecue joint in the area. As supper hour rolled around, Kana made a dramatic performance of arranging our menus in a fan on the dining room table. Her eyes were flickering with defiance.

"There's a two-for-one deal at Pizza Palace," she said.

"It's chicken-and-rib night at Roasters," I said.

"Good idea," Kana said, pointing her finger at me.

"They have good sauce," I explained to our father.

"Or, if you'd prefer"—she turned to him—"I'd be happy to whip up a peanut butter and mayonnaise sandwich."

He smiled. "How Julia Child of you." There was an awkward silence, then he said, "Actually, I had a late lunch. You two go ahead. I'm not hungry."

"I could make spaghetti," I offered.

Kana shot me a killing look.

"I'm fine, Naiko," my father said, his voice thin and tired. He stood up and started moving toward the living room. He looked pale. On his face there were wrinkles I had never seen before. I ran ahead of him and scooped a pile of dirty clothes from the couch so he could sit down. I was afraid he would dash off and leave us alone again.

He spent the remainder of the visit trying to get Kana to look him in the eye. She behaved as though his presence meant nothing at all to her, but I knew better. Whenever he turned away, I saw her watching him. I wanted to catch his eye, roll mine knowingly at Kana's behaviour, but he kept passing over me. Ping, ping, ping, our eyes ricocheted around the room.

Kana was sullen. I rubbed my socked feet on the carpet and touched the cat to watch the sparks fly. I felt my heart zip itself up.

Thank you. Yes. Yes. Great. Not at all. Not at all. I'm really glad you came . . .

The only emotion I seemed capable of expressing that afternoon was accommodation.

Perhaps the exaggerated way we discussed takeout options tripped a guilt wire in my father. The next week he packed us in a rented car and we headed for the Caledon Hills for Thanksgiving dinner in the country. This time he insisted that our mother join us.

Suddenly we were one family among many on Highway 401, cars braiding their way across the three lanes. I remember watching other people pass in their hatchbacks and station wagons, replicas of us—father, mother, two kids—other odd-acting clusters, and wondering, *Were they better or worse?*

I was wearing a pair of Mary Janes that I had polished with cooking oil and a blue-and-white sleeveless dress my mother had sewn for me years before from a McCall's pattern. The dress was now a size too small and much too summery, but I wore it all the same, layering it on top of pants and a turtleneck. I played with the long trailing ribbons attached to the bodice, dangling the ends in front of my mother's face during the car ride. Perhaps I wanted to remind her that she did once make things. But she was lost in her own world, concentrating perhaps on the soft drone of tires on the highway.

My father broke the silence by asking if we had ever tried venison. I asked what it tasted like and he said: "Gamy. Like strong liver." Kana made a moan of disgust. "Now, now," he continued, "it can be quite excellent with a dash of clam marinade and a spoonful of pork gelatin."

Kana and I were clutching our stomachs and writhing in mock pain. Our mother, sitting in the front seat, wasn't blinking.

Our father dropped us off in front of the inn while he went to park the car. We entered the restaurant foyer. My mother was dressed in a special-occasion outfit, selected by Kana. It consisted of a yellow silk blouse and a long skirt with a black-and-red diamond pattern. Kana was wearing a brown duffle coat over her favourite velour jumpsuit. We must have looked like a family of hippies on our way to a jamboree. The fact that we arrived without a reservation did not endear us to the maître d', who seemed, in the particular long-necked manner of maître d's, to challenge our right to be there.

The room smelled of buttered yams and roasted turkey. There were hunting pictures on the walls. The other diners looked very dignified, satisfied: life going as planned, members of a circle. Our presence seemed to make them uneasy, hostile in a genteel, don't-display-it sort of way. Even if we had dressed in black gowns, the other diners would have seen what a calamity we all really were. But as soon as my father arrived some unspoken agreement was made, some secret aristocratic handshake exchanged, and we were seated in that tiny, crowded room. Soon, the waitress was bringing us our menus, and no one seemed to entertain any grudges, at least not openly. I picked up a fork, held it under the tablecloth and began scarring the soft surface of the wood table.

My mother, years later, denied the dinner had ever taken place. She said, "You must have dreamt it," then she fell silent. But I have enough memories for the both of us.

I remember the oval table, the amber light and the wine-red velvet upholstery. I remember watching the diners around us—the men with their white cuffs, the women with their tasteful bracelets (my mother with her heavy silver bangles, courtesy of Kana). I remember that Kana insisted on wearing her coat throughout the meal despite the wood fire roaring a few metres away. I remember my mother putting down her soup spoon to ruffle and rearrange the flowers in front of her, my father bending down to pick up the serviette that had fallen from his lap. The server kept refilling his water glass and my father kept drinking it in long gulps, as if he needed to flush something inside himself.

I remember the white candles, bowls of liquid wax melting around the wick. I tipped drops onto the linen tablecloth. No one scolded me. Deft hands came and removed the filigreed soup bowls; the server's steps were light, so as not to scuff the polished floor. The quails on my plate were too small to eat. The steaming pool of meat juice that seeped off them made my stomach churn. I stared ahead at a painting of a dead fox draped over a man's shoulder. I remember thinking that my family was like a dead fox that I would carry around for a long time.

I wanted to scream: WHY CAN'T YOU LOVE EACH OTHER? ISN'T LOVE SUPPOSED TO LAST FOREVER? WHAT DID I DO?

I wanted to say so much, but I didn't. I never do.

My father left again, and finally, one afternoon in late November, my mother got out of bed. I came home from school and my mother was walking around the house in white jeans and a floppy peasant shirt, calmly watering plants. I wasn't prepared to see her upright and without the sweatpants. The whole thing took some adjusting to.

"I like your shirt, Mama. You look pretty."

"Thank you, Nai-chan." She touched her hair.

I smelled a faint whiff of starch, rice steaming in the kitchen. After so many weeks, the scent filled the house with promise.

My mother quickly set about restoring order. She sent me on an errand to buy scouring pads, bleach and a bottle of detergent. When I returned she was heaving a wooden hutch away from the wall. Beneath it, in a dust mound containing hair, bread crumbs and shrivelled grapes, was a desiccated mouse. Without a moment's hesitation, she pulled a rubber glove from under the sink slipped it over her hand.

It was soon clear that my mother's hibernation had worked wonders. She had never looked or acted younger. Toward spring, she called up an old friend and got a job working at his art supply shop. She liked touching all the fancy paper and grouping the paints together by colour. It turned out she had a knack for dealing with the customers, and before we knew it she was dating—nothing lasting or serious, but the attention boosted her confidence. One guy came by every Friday night for several months. He was a painter with long silvery hair and eyes that were too close to his nose, so they always looked crossed. He wore a brown sweatshirt with a mandala silk-screened on the front. When I told my mother that his face reminded me of a ferret's, she just laughed. She was now as permanently happy as she had once been tired. Everything around her was showered with affection.

Even her body language began to change. As our father became more clean-cut in appearance and more reserved in his mannerisms, our mother became less inhibited. I saw it in the way she interacted with people on the street and at the store. She pressed up close in a way that made me squirm in embarrassment. She was constantly pinching her cheeks to make them rosier and throwing her jeans in the dryer so the fabric tightened and hugged her bottom in an alluring way.

Kana said our mother was experiencing a sexual rebirth.

I came home from school one day and found Kana in our mother's bathroom. She was sitting on the counter in front of the mirror, her mouth puckered, dabbing on Nivea face cream before slowly smoothing it into her cheeks with her fingertips. She made small circles, moving up from her jaw, just the way our mother did.

When she saw me staring at her, she stopped and said, "The Ferret slept over again last night."

I picked up a tube of lipstick, rolled it up, gave it a sniff. "Why is she acting this way?" I said.

"Don't be a knob. People have sex. Grandpa and Grandma had sex. Mom and Dad had sex." She washed her hands. "How do you think we got here?"

"Oh God. Kana," I groaned. "But how do you know Mom and he—?"

"Come with me," she said. Then, to prove her point, she pulled my hand, towed me into the bedroom and opened the sliding door to our mother's closet.

"Exhibit A," she declared triumphantly.

In front of me were fancy blouses and slinky dresses I had not seen our mother wear in years. The hangers poked out at angles, indicating how recently and how hurriedly she had tried the clothes on. On the floor were stilettos, sling-back pumps and sequined shoes that we used to slip onto our small feet when we played dress-up. I turned around and noticed several puddles of black silk on the bed.

"She's doing her own thing," Kana said.

"She's totally lost her mind."

Kana flipped her hair. "People change."

"Not mothers. Not like this," I said in horror.

She stood back and studied herself in the full-length mirror, and said, "As long as it makes her happy . . ." She poked her chest out and ran her hands across the two lumps there.

I didn't say anything.

She glanced at me and smiled. "You'll see," she said. "'It's a woman's problem,'" she added in a low voice, imitating the doctor who had paid us the house visit. Then, in her normal voice, she repeated, "One day—when you're older—you'll see."

PAOLO ONCE ASKED ME if I thought that period of my life had left a mark on me. "No," I said. But he pointed to the way films and television shows

stick in my mind, affecting my moods. A good film can fill me with optimism or a sense of inadequacy. He says that unlike most people who
see movies as art or entertainment, I seem to turn to them as personal
allegories. Paolo is convinced, for instance, that I graft his head onto the
bodies of unreliable men.

On the night before I returned to work after being sick, he came
over with a film called *Another Woman*. Because it was right beside
Woody Allen's *Sleeper* on the video store shelf, he assumed it was a
comedy, something light and cheerful, and failed to notice the orange
genre sticker on the cover that said Drama. Within a few minutes it
became clear that we were in for a depressing two hours. Paolo made
a noble effort to step in and save the evening, but I resisted.

"Oh. Boring movie," he said quickly. "Let's find something on TV
instead." He reached for the converter.

"No." I held his arm.

So we watched Gena Rowlands reckon with a missed turn in her
life—the fear that prevented her from ever succumbing to her pas-
sions, her crumbling relationship with her husband (Ian Holm)—and
I felt a salty sting rise up my nostrils. Before I knew it the tears were
plopping onto my lap. Paolo looked over at me, concerned, not sure
whether to hang back or move closer. His torso had a strange twist to
it, caught between flight and approach. He held out his hand, which
I ignored as I searched in my pocket for a tissue.

"These aren't autobiographical tears."

"No. Of course not."

"Paolo, I can hardly imagine putting your head on the body of Ian
Holm or Gene Hackman!"

"Then look at me."

"I am."

It was impossible not to feel foolish. I blew into the tissue and then stuffed it back into my pocket. There was a loose thread on my pants I felt a sudden urge to tug. Paolo noted my attempts to look absorbed and laughed.

"Come here. Let's just forget it." He reached toward me.

I stood up. "I should probably go to bed. I have to be up early."

Paolo grabbed my hips from behind and pulled me back down. He kissed my neck, my shoulder and then my neck again. I felt my breathing change. This time, I didn't move away.

Thirteen

A few days' rest had distracted my mind. But when I returned to work after my flu, there was a lot of catching up to do. Two overflowing bins awaited me. The nation's hastily and carelessly wrapped Christmas presents had sprung open. I could see the bins from a distance and their contents looked like multicoloured candy. An explosion of plastic toys was combined with the usual bric-a-brac.

I could feel people's eyes on me as I passed. I heard, or imagined, Doreen whisper something to the manager. Something was odd, and deciding that it must be my appearance, I sent my fingers instinctively combing for leftover breakfast bits, unruly hair. I was still patting around my head when I reached my work area, at which point I suddenly understood what all the staring had been about.

Andrei's desk had been packed up. The pile of packages had been taken away. His workstation was now completely anonymous, the last trace of Andrei erased.

My head pounded and I sank into my seat. In the distance, I could hear the racket of Marvin arriving with the morning delivery. I felt a rush of grief and I picked up the phone to call Paolo, but he hadn't arrived at work yet. So I put the receiver back and looked around me, feeling how the world floated, nothing anchored. Everywhere there were careening wheels clattering across concrete floor, big yellow buckets full of things lost. My people were unmoored, close friends carried away: Andrei, then Gloria.

The people working around me were behaving as though Andrei had never existed. I felt a pit opening in my stomach. They had bagged him up. Baba was standing near the middle of the room, his back to me, discussing something with Maria, who was visiting from another department. It was a lively conversation, and on several occasions they burst into laughter.

It was Baba who eventually came to my desk to tell me that they had hired someone to replace Andrei. He would be starting in two days, to help with the Christmas surplus. I noticed a touch of embarrassment in his voice, but I could also see that something had happened to Baba while I was away. He seemed practically euphoric.

"Thank goodness you're back," he said. "I've been waiting to give you my good news. Françoise and I found out we're having twins. A girl and a boy."

"Twins! Baba, that's crazy. Congratulations!"

"I don't know how we'll afford it, but Françoise is thrilled."

At that moment, Baba revealed a side of himself I had never seen before: he stepped forward and hugged me. I laughed at this impulsive display of affection and we chatted for a bit about Françoise. When we finished, I turned to face Andrei's desk.

"Baba, we have to stop them."

Baba placed his fingers over his mouth, raked them toward his chin.

"No. Don't tell me," I said.

He didn't say anything. My face fell.

"Naiko," he said quietly.

I shook my head. "They've convinced you, too."

Baba stared down at my desk. "It's too late. The manager made up his mind. Really, he waited as long as he could. You saw how much work had piled up."

"But what if Andrei comes back? He's bound to turn up, just like you said happened last time." I tried to quell the panic I felt creeping into my voice.

"It's not the same as last time. He's been gone too long."

"So you've given up on him," I said, more as a statement to myself than an accusation. But his face froze.

"No. Not me. They have." He said it bluntly, pointing toward the manager's office, then continued, "Naiko, you know what I think? I think you should be angry instead of worried. Remember, he deserted us. Not the other way around."

He excused himself and retreated to the valuables room.

I felt ashamed at having upset Baba when he had been so excited; now I watched him walk away, as if he had turned his back on me. Maybe he was right. Maybe I was wasting my time.

I took a deep breath and tackled the workload, my hands resuming their familiar tasks. Counting came first. Wallets, picture frames, fountain pens, tape cassettes, passports, handkerchiefs and cufflinks. My calming stacks, my benevolent rows. I counted to keep order, to keep from crying. By mid-afternoon, I was surprised at how much time had passed and I wolfed down a sandwich. For the rest of the day, the others gave me a wide berth, perhaps believing that anything they said or did would set me off. Aside from Baba, no one talked to me about what had transpired. Was it human nature, or just the nature of government employees, to live in constant complacency? I wondered bitterly.

The next morning I went straight to Baba's desk and apologized to him for my behaviour the day before. He was gracious, but it was plain to see that things had changed between us. There was a certain reserve that had never been there before. Nonetheless, I contented myself with the fact that I had made an effort, and vowed to keep quiet about Andrei in the future.

It was still before 9 a.m. when I sat down, so I took a few minutes to glance at my newspaper. As I was reading, a moth flitted by and landed on my sorting tray. I tapped my finger beside it and it fluttered away, along a crooked path, before landing on the shelf beside me.

At exactly 9 a.m., I folded away the newspaper, popped a vitamin in my mouth and began looking through customer claims letters. I was halfway through my first pile when I heard a gasp from above and the exclamation "God Almighty." When I looked up, Marvin was gaping over the pile, craning dramatically as if it took great effort to find me. *Oh no*, he said. *They. Squashed You.* His stomach sagged over the bucket he had wheeled across the room. His shirt looked old and faded and said: "Draft beer, not boys."

The contents of his bucket, my morning delivery, merely added to my steeple of work, objects piled so high that an avalanche could have been triggered by a gust of air. I was literally days behind, but for some reason it no longer mattered. I felt strangely calm. Why keep rushing to catch up? Come morning there would always be a new pile.

A sunbeam hit my desk and the warmth pleased me, made me stretch, catlike. I watched Marvin as he continued to make his rounds. My fingers bumped against something soft. I slipped a pair of cufflinks from a black velvet pillow, turning one from side to side to watch the light bounce off a circle of tiny blue stones. The absurdity of concentrating on anything so tiny, given the mountain of material at hand, was perversely appealing.

Periodically, my mind buzzed with a thought: what if Andrei had left me a message somewhere? Where would he have put it? (I pictured myself entering his apartment and discovering an unshaven Andrei rocking back and forth on the floor, pen in hand, suitcase beside him.) Suppose I found a body? (This last image blasted away any fear I had of finding his room bare.)

Then the thoughts would pass and my eyes would fix on something else. A lacquer box with a hand-painted portrait of John F. Kennedy, inscribed in Vietnamese. A tribute or a hex? I brought out the magnifying glass, copied the script onto a scrap of paper and made a mental note to ask Nhi at the library. Next, a pair of men's briefs flattened in a glass frame. . . In this manner the morning passed. Poke as I might at the pile of objects, it did not seem to diminish.

Had my curiosity deserted me?

Thankfully not. There was an old wristwatch. A curved rectangle with a dirty yellow leather band. Popeye and Swee' Pea on the discoloured watch face. The winding pinion had stiffened from age, so that the time was always 4:25. The watch wasn't well preserved and it didn't look especially valuable. Why was a watch that no longer functioned being presented as a gift (tied to an unsigned card addressed to "Darling Adrian")? I lifted my magnifying glass to the back to look for an inscription.

Silverplated. 1957.

Could an object acquire life, a "soul" of some kind? Might this leather band recall the wrist it once touched, remember the sweat, the grime, perhaps even the passing of that person?

Baba had turned on the radio in the kitchen. A woman said something about Tchaikovsky and played the "Dance of the Reed Pipes" from *The Nutcracker Suite*. I watched him pour a coffee and open two packets of sugar.

What is the measure of love? Persistence in the face of brokenness? Devotion in the face of rejection?

In Japan, there is a tradition of honouring broken things, things that people have used for many years, in particular belongings that they have worn close to their bodies. It is a pleasing thought that something spiritual might rub off on objects that age with us. When the time comes for damaged possessions to be discarded, they are collected together and Shinto or Buddhist prayers—prayers of thanks—are said over them. *Harikuyo*, the Festival of Broken Needles, held annually on the eighth of February at shrines and temples across Japan, is typical of the practice. The festival allows seamstresses and tailors to express gratitude to the tools of the sewing trade they have used and worn out during the previous year.

Inasmuch as they are still practised, these Mass-like rituals teach people to pay attention to things that are near to them, to respect the disregarded or abandoned. A cracked rice bowl that has provided a year of nourishment. A damaged pair of straw sandals that have offered many miles of comfort. A decorative comb with snapped teeth that has adorned the hair of generations of women. Life's hierarchy of importance is turned on its head.

And here perhaps lies the true measure of devotion. Dedication to that which is beyond usefulness.

ON THE DAY OF my mother's cognitive evaluation test, two months before she moved to Sakura, the social worker asked if he could talk with me privately. As my mother napped, we sat at the table drinking tea. He had a clipboard in front of him and was writing something down. He said he needed my help in completing my mother's assessment.

What, in my opinion, he asked, was the strongest indication of her mental deterioration? He avoided my eyes and gazed at my hairline as he spoke, an affectation that I found disconcerting.

I shouldn't have answered; it made me an accomplice.

"She collects stuff," I told him.

"What kinds of stuff?" he asked.

"Thrift items mostly. She stores it all away," I replied.

"But many people collect things as a hobby. Stamps, coins—there is nothing unusual in itself about collecting things."

I shook my head. "It's the things she chooses to collect. Dried-up pens. Egg cartons. Twist ties and old coupons. Expired warranties. She collects things for my sister and me, too. She keeps old shoeboxes and stuffs them with items she thinks we might find interesting or useful. Rubber bands, disposable chopsticks, pens and more pens . . . I can't tell you how many pens."

I offered this information because I thought it was the surest sign that my mother had a degenerative brain disease, but as I spoke I began to wonder if I had missed something. Maybe my mother's magpie behaviour was a normal reaction to a world that had grown more cluttered and disposable. A hundred years ago, most people wouldn't have used sixty pens in a lifetime. Now we use that many in a few years. Perhaps after all my mother wasn't so crazy—merely subconsciously intent on salvaging our throwaway world.

What distinguishes collecting as a hobby, from collecting as an illness? The value of the objects themselves? Accumulation techniques? Conscious selection versus absent-minded accrual? Relevance versus irrelevance? Wealth versus poverty?

The boundary suddenly seemed razor-thin.

I have only faint memories of my mother as a younger woman. I remember the scent of the shampoo she used, the texture of her favourite sweater, the shade of her preferred lipstick. I remember my head reaching the slight slope of her tummy. I remember the callused part between her thumb and forefinger that I used to rub for comfort, until she delicately extricated her hand to go to the bathroom or make supper. I remember the cards we sent at New Year's, and others we received, but those cards are probably among the few things my mother discarded—too much a reminder of the abandoned ceremonies of family.

But mostly what I remember is the way she let her life shrivel after my father left.

Year one, the Watching: mostly television, though occasionally the tree by her window, and birds that landed on the tree. The year of her depression.

Year two, the Cleaning: and the discovery of the "art of homemaking" with its pressed sheets, spotless mirrors and strong solvents—a time of scouring, and defiant cleanliness. The year of her "recovery."

Years three to five, the Wrapping: of packages often using only one piece of tape, of couches in fabric, of television converters in Saran Wrap. A foreshadowing of her own unravelling?

Years five to eight, the Collecting: or should I say "the clinging to and clutching of" various bits and pieces. A declaration that the world could be arranged just as she liked if she owned it?

I know from experience the affection people have for second-hand objects: almost a kind of kinship with previous possessors. There are Dumpster divers and auction goers and everyday bargain hunters who spend most weekends buying up other people's castoffs at flea markets, thrift shops and yard sales. There are antiques fetishists who love the feel of worn velvet, the look of an embroidered sampler, the smell of old books. There are people who don't mind, who even enjoy, sinking into a deep and dusty armchair or wearing vintage dresses with loose hems. (There are even people who wilfully expose unused objects to the rain and elements so they will warp, fade, tarnish, and so become, in the words of decorators, "distressed.") I suppose I am one of these people, mulling over old objects and heirlooms, digging for history as others would for oil or gold. I admit that I have knowingly transported mites, dust and other asthma-triggers into my home for the thrill of possessing a newly rummaged treasure.

Yet, in the days following Andrei's disappearance, I found my tastes changing. The older an object the more thought it required, and now my thoughts were scattered. I couldn't cope with the shabbiness of it all. A rain slicker that had stiffened, a T-shirt with a baggy neck, a hairband that had lost its elasticity, a deflated ball squishing in my hand—such objects produced feelings of queasiness. I had a sudden wish for newer things, pristine gadgets and gifts, the smell of fresh rubber or vinyl—a whiff of a clean, lustrous future.

I found myself reassessing people who gravitated toward the synthetic world, who surrounded themselves with plastic flowers, fake leather, glossy ornaments and other objects that mimic happiness, that retain no memory. I had been in the habit of thinking that such people were shallow. But perhaps I had been wrong all along. Perhaps it was possible to prefer the synthetic world, as the very young and the very old often did, for simple and sensible reasons. Plastic dolls lasted. Plastic flowers would never decay.

Fourteen

$\mathcal{A}$ brackish vinegar smell hung in the air. A small jar of Swedish herring had fallen out of a package and shattered on the floor. The new person was seated at Andrei's desk. A skinny man with bushy sideburns and an extraordinarily long, almost simian space above his upper lip. Even when he was smiling, which was often the case, his mouth appeared to be too far away from his nose. He was introduced to me as Warren. I greeted him politely and then turned around, somewhat ashamed that I could not stop myself from silently judging him (the horrible brown-and-green-speckled sweater he wore, his ingratiating grin, the odour of fermentation surrounding us).

To avoid further chitchat, and the risk of saying something I'd regret later, I opened my newspaper and half-heartedly skimmed the head-lines. It was the twentieth of December. Five days before Christmas.

BEST OF THE BAD (ACTOR LEE VAN CLEEF DEAD AT 64)

OIL SPILL WREAKS HAVOC ON MOROCCAN COAST

BALLOT FEVER IN CZECHOSLOVAKIA

RIOTS ROCK ROMANIA (CEAUSESCU SAYS, "REFORM WILL COME TO
ROMANIA WHEN PEARS GROW ON POPLARS")

After Marvin arrived with the morning delivery, I slipped into an effortless rhythm. Every now and then I noticed Warren at the periphery of my vision. At one point I leaned back to stretch my neck and shoulders, and he looked up, mouth widening into a broad smile, his friendliness catching me off guard. I gave a quick smile and lowered my head. Was there any point in trying to understand what had happened to Andrei? A dozen different thoughts swirled in my head. How many days left until his rent expired? Twelve? Would I find anything in his apartment? And what about Gloria? Was she back at Sakura? And Kana? Was she ever coming home?

Another letter from Kana had arrived the day before. It was written on the back of a small Czech menu. In a quick scrawl that in its rollicking unconcern for legibility bore no resemblance to my own tidy penmanship, she wrote:

Dear Nai-chan,

Your present was delivered this morning. So thoughtful! My first granny cardigan! But seriously—it's just what I needed. It has been freezing here! I've taken to walking around the apartment with my overcoat on. So much is happening every day. Everyone is convinced that Havel will be elected president on December 29. The Independent has asked me for a feature story and post-election interview. The feature

will be called "The Power of the Powerless," based on an
essay Havel wrote just over ten years ago. I wish I could
have been home for the holidays, but this is a big one.

Love, Kana

p.s. See reverse. I've been living on item #6 (pork back,
cabbage and bread dumplings). Sounds revolting but it's
incredible, sublime food. I promise to take you one day!

The unstoppable Kana. Her letter brought forth a glint of resentment, the taste of some ancient bitterness that made me feel petty
and ashamed. (She didn't even mention our mother.) While I prepared
supper, I tried to picture her life in Prague. I knew she was probably
smoking too much, living out of her suitcase. Yet I also knew she was
doing all this happily. She had become a nomad, long ago liberating
herself from the commitments and consolations of family life.

When Kana decided to live somewhere else in the world, returning
from time to time to visit, it became my destiny to keep watch and to
tell her what she wanted to hear. I swallowed my resentment.

Dear Kana,

I wish I had some exciting news to share, but life here is as
boring and eventless as ever. If anything my days seem to
get more monotonous! I don't even have a new outfit or a
horrible snowstorm to report . . .

Then again, would I have wanted it any different? The morning
cup of coffee. The short bus ride to work. The mail that awaited me

when I got home. The pre-decided meals I shared with Paolo—pasta on Tuesdays, Szechuan on Thursdays and curry on Sundays. The scheduled amusements—rented videos, jazz night at the Rex, dancing at El Centro, a bottle of wine, an occasional pinch of marijuana. I had centred my life on simple rituals. It was irrational to turn on Kana because she had built a life on not knowing where she would be tomorrow, to begrudge her a happiness built on passing moments of passion and appetite.

It's probably true that Kana shuddered at the thought of winding up like me—domestic, unworldly, without enterprise (for in her eyes, to be a homebody at the end of the century was to be a true global pariah). It was also probably true, though harder to admit, that I lived in dread of ending up like her—drifting all over the place, prey to any sudden gust of wind.

When I returned home from work that evening Paolo was in the kitchen pouring a glass of juice. He was still wearing his pyjamas. He nodded at me and I greeted him in return. We had a brief exchange about the leaking sink faucet, after which he sat down and began pensively drumming on the kitchen table. I picked up the day's mail and made my way to the living room. I had intended to flop out on the couch, but the room I entered was in disarray. The curtains were still drawn and a twisted bundle of sheets and blankets was piled in the middle of the couch. Miko, my cat, was nestled on top. A few dirty plates and cups—my plates and cups, but not my dirt—lay on the coffee table. It was not a catastrophic mess, by any means, but every object had become eloquent. The room wanted to say something. On Paolo's behalf, it ventriloquized: *I'm tired of trying.*

I heard water running in the kitchen sink. It stopped for a moment, then started again.

Ever since Andrei had disappeared, Paolo had done his best to keep the apartment vibrant on the days he came to visit. Flowers appeared regularly on tables. Windows were cleaned and bared to the sun. Elaborate pastas and delicious pilafs materialized at dinner on Friday nights. The robust sounds of Charlie Parker and Jimmy Cliff played on the stereo. His efforts to distract and entertain me, to prove that he was still present and committed to carrying on with our patterns and cycles, helped keep me together. He was so good at making things relaxed that I hadn't noticed the distance deepening between us.

But that evening, everything threatened to break in two. It happened just as we were finishing a late dinner. I had been subdued throughout the meal, pushing my pasta around with my fork, pouring a glass of wine, tearing off portions of baguette. I was so lost in my own thoughts that I didn't notice that Paolo was seething beside me. When he eventually spoke, I started at the tone of his voice.

"We need to talk," he said. "I'm worried. You're beginning to show signs of obsessive behaviour."

Obsessive? I felt the bread stick in my throat. The word was a dagger, a cruel shorthand for my mother. Paolo used it knowingly. (He felt the need to be callous, to crack the shell of my "self-pity," as he later put it.)

"Face it, Naiko. He's gone. It's time to give up. That may seem cold-hearted, but it's not healthy to keep going on this way."

Paolo's theory was that his years in Argentina, while fraught with painful memories, had made him more discerning. He had learned how to tell whom to trust and whom not to. My theory was that it had made him an expert at kind indifference. Perhaps it was unfair of me, but I felt that years of living in a climate of non-response had left him detached from certain emotions. For evidence I thought back to a conversation early on in our relationship, when Paolo had confessed to me that he was unable to console his mother when her brother died. It was just the two of them at home when the phone call from Argentina came.

"I loved my uncle. Yet when I heard the news I had no reaction," he had said. Even when his mother's tears began to scatter, words did not come. He just stood there, mesmerized by the sight of her crying. "It was her eyes, so shiny with tears—how beautiful she looked. But I couldn't tell her that; it would have seemed insensitive," he said.

It was his lasting shame that he was able to appreciate his mother's beauty but not her sadness.

It isn't the child who comforts the parents, I tried to reassure him. But what I was left with was the image of a young man—he was eighteen, after all—observing his crying mother without embracing her.

I wasn't always mindful of Paolo's feelings. And neither was he of mine. There were times that I declared he was cold and insensitive. There were times that he accused me of being naive. We both had it in us to be harsh and uncompromising. But that evening in the kitchen when he challenged my "obsession" with Andrei was the first time I realized how easily our relationship could collapse.

"Are you in love with him?"

"No. I told you, Andrei's gay."

"Then what is it? What's there? Explain. Why can't you let go?"

"I can't just turn my back on someone I care about."

"Well, he could," Paolo said coldly.

I glared at him.

"Why don't you just accept it. Call it what it is," Paolo continued.

"Meaning what?"

"Meaning desertion. It's simple. Rushing off like that. Without a note or explanation. In the army he'd be court-martialled."

"Stop it."

"He ran away. Making excuses for him isn't helping. It isn't loyalty anymore, it's craziness."

I felt stunned by Paolo's belligerence. I stared at my hands and breathed in, breathed out. Panic welled up in me.

"Why do you have to be so intense about everything?" Paolo rubbed his temples and sighed. "Can't you be like everyone else?"

"Who?"

"Other people. The ones who stick to their own business." He paused. "It's strange. It's almost as though you take pleasure from it." He had stacked the dinner plates and was now leaning back in his chair, eyeing me coldly.

"What are you accusing me of now?" I asked.

"I have no idea," he said. "I don't have a clue what's on your mind anymore. Something changed when Andrei—"

"Nothing changed."

"Fuck, Naiko. This is impossible." He stood, paced for a moment and then stopped, placing his hand on the counter. "You know what? I'm tired of it."

I stiffened. "Tired of it? Or tired of me?"

"It. You. Both. Everything."

"Well then, I'm very sorry," I said.

"I'm trying to be straightforward with you. You know, trying to communicate. Clearly it's not working."

"No, clearly it's not," I said, and left the room.

Paolo and I rarely fought. What usually happened when there was a disagreement was that we temporarily became aloof. For a joyless day or two we were inaccessible to each other. If the argument occurred while he was at my place, we walked around the apartment like strangers passing on the street, bodies proceeding quickly and politely, eyes averted. It was soul crushing. But this was the way we did battle.

But that night was different, more troubling. I felt him starting to slip away from me.

I retreated to my bedroom and sat down at the edge of the bed. On a shelf set into the wall my books stood in neat rows, oversized reference books on the bottom, alphabetized fiction on the top. Most days, this vision of painstaking organization reassured me. I treasured my library, knowing that it would never be ripped apart. Yet who but me cared? And why did I care? It was all suddenly unnecessary. What did it matter how the books were arranged, or if Paolo's books were added to mine? I had to resolve the situation or he was going to leave me. One night, maybe even this one, he would give up, pack his duffle bag and walk out the door.

My door. Our door.

I'll lose him, too.

I felt dizzy. I closed my eyes, and when I reopened them the books had a funny look to them, as it they were see-sawing in mid-air.

It was too late to catch the subway, so Paolo stayed that night, but we ended up sleeping separately. At 2 a.m., I woke up and went to the kitchen for a glass of water. The table light was on in the living room and Paolo was sitting in a chair with a magazine. He didn't change his position, didn't even glance up, so I returned to the bedroom. About an hour later I heard him quietly open the door. I wanted him to lie down and hold me, but I was too proud and frightened to say anything. I pretended I was sleeping. But I felt the tears rising, a lump in my chest. He stood there for an unbearable minute and then I heard the faint *click* of the door closing behind him.

Fifteen

I went to Paolo before dawn. I crossed the dark apartment and lay beside him on the couch, then under him. There were no words. My tongue was tied in my mouth, but my body told Paolo to stay. I needed his existence in my life. His steady, unvanishing presence. We moved to the floor, entwined with each other, his familiar hand slipping between my legs, then inside me. The pressure of him toppled any remaining tension between us. I came with my mouth against his. The sky was still dark. He rested his head against my shoulder and we both slept.

The clock radio came on in the bedroom a few hours later. We listened to the announcer reporting the traffic news. I snuggled into Paolo before getting up.

"Why do you think it's so hard for me to let go?" I asked.

"It's your sympathetic nature," he replied, placing his palm on my chest. "Add to that the fact that you're irrational, stubborn, overly concerned with other people, and . . ."

"I have no life," I murmured.

"Hey," he said. "*We* have a life."

"Yes, we do," I said, reaching for his arm.

"You said we could move in together at the end of the year."

"I did?" I touched a mole on his wrist.

"I miss you. You haven't been very . . . here, lately."

"Oh, Paolo." I kissed his neck.

The automatic coffee maker burbled in the kitchen.

"Can I ask you something?" He traced his finger lightly along my arm.

"Of course."

"Promise you won't get angry or take it the wrong way?"

"Maybe," I said, and smiled.

He eyed me for a moment, then asked, "Was Andrei in some kind of trouble? Something with the police . . . immigration? Maybe a money situation?"

"No."

"Was there anything that might have upset him enough to run away?"

I stared at the wall, weighed the question.

"No. Not that I know of," I said, and sat up. I craned to look at the clock. "It's getting late." I kissed his cheek. "I better jump in the shower."

After showering I hurried to work. Snow was falling lightly. By the time I arrived, Marvin had already delivered my sorting bin. I sensed a few people watching me, but I ignored them.

Once Andrei's desk had been cleaned up, people's attitude toward me had changed. I was their last reminder of him, and they didn't want to be reminded anymore, so they avoided me. When I said his name out loud, even to Baba, I felt shushed.

At the top of my pile sat a small wreath of shellacked roses, a candy-striped necktie, a box of tree ornaments—seasonally confused bunny rabbits with Santa hats. I stared at a set of "Last Supper" Russian nesting dolls that I had lined up on my desk: John, the tiny apostle. I dipped my hand back into the bin, lightly sifting the torn wrapping paper, stray greeting cards, sales slips, bright yellow fleece socks, an inflatable beer bucket. Why the objects should have seemed so off that particular day, I don't know; I just couldn't imagine any of them being to anyone's taste. I picked up a small Pierrot doll, fidgeting flecks of silver glitter off its ceramic head.

There were only four days until Christmas and we were working late into the evening in an attempt to rescue last-minute presents. The kitchen was a banquet of treats that the manager's wife had prepared. At the edge of my desk was a plate with a half-finished sandwich left over from lunch. Handel's *Messiah* played on the radio, filling the room with an air of harmony and good cheer—amplified by waves of colour and sparkling tinsel, popcorn and cranberry chains, ladles of eggnog. I watched the manager's wife walk by in an elf's hat holding a bowl of sugar-dusted shortbread cookies. I contemplated joining in, but decided against it, feeling ultimately that it was beyond my ability.

At 6 p.m., when it was time for dinner, people began making their way to the kitchen. I was examining an engraved drinking mug when Warren walked over.

"Aren't you going to eat with the others?" he asked, preparing to join them himself.

"I can't," I said, and paused. "Too much catching up to do."

He looked at me and smiled. I smiled back at him with a shrug. We both knew my answer sounded like an evasion. I returned to my work, but I watched him more closely as he started toward the kitchen, seeing him differently right then, seeing him as Warren. It wasn't his fault he was occupying Andrei's space. He wasn't responsible for the circumstances that had led him here.

When he returned, he was carrying a small plate of food. He presented it to me, assuming the exaggerated posture of a waiter, body tilted slightly at the waist, one hand behind his back. I laughed. His friendliness was a relief—it made me feel normal.

Warren brought me back to the quotidian world I had abandoned. I believe this. His small gesture of kindness prodded me out of my slump. There is a limit to the amount of isolation and misery one can stand, and I had reached it.

I finished eating, then picked up the phone to call Paolo. When the machine clicked on I left a message asking him to come by my place that night. Baba was in the kitchen helping to pack up the leftover food. I could see him from my desk picking broken crackers and sprigs of parsley off the cheese tray. The manager's wife was wiping down the counter. Warren returned with coffee and a plate of honey-drenched sweets Baba had brought from a Lebanese bakery.

"Cheers, Naiko," Warren said, lifting his cup to mine.

Robert the janitor steered his wheeled mop bucket past our workstation.

I was sitting at the kitchen table when Paolo opened the door to my apartment later that evening. He unbuttoned his coat and slipped out of his boots.

"Look, I've been thinking," I said.

His face dimmed. "You want me to go," he said tonelessly.

"Go? Oh God no, Paolo," I said. The uncertainty on his face told me how fragile we were. "I was just thinking. I've never really told you about Andrei."

Paolo put his coat on the chair.

"I've kept quiet about it for so long, like it was some kind of trust I couldn't break. I don't feel that now."

One of the first things I told Paolo about were the letters.

MANY MONTHS BEFORE, TOWARD the beginning of June, Andrei had walked into work with a determined look on his face. He said he had made up his mind. He wanted to send letters to various people inquiring about Nicolae, to uncover what had happened to him.

Dear Consul General of Turkey,

I am writing to inquire about the whereabouts of my friend Nicolae Halmos, a citizen of Romania, who was last seen swimming off the coast of Turkey in June of 1984 . . .

We drafted the letters together and during our lunch hour typed them up on heavy bond paper. Andrei signed them at the bottom, making sure that each letter remained smooth and uncreased. He used the stamp machine at work, but insisted on posting the envelopes from a box near his home.

Dear Metin,

It has been several years since we last communicated. I hope your family has kept well . . .

We wrote eleven letters in total and then waited for a response. I expected letters to start arriving within a few weeks, but not one arrived. Then more weeks passed and still there was not a single reply. I began to wonder if our letters were even reaching anyone. Were the addresses inaccurate or outdated? Had the letters been blocked or detained somewhere?

Andrei remained unfazed. "There are thousands and thousands of Nicolaes in Romania, most of them named before the dictator came to power," he said by way of explanation. "Parents used to like the name because Nicolae is the patron saint of children."

"What an unfortunate coincidence," I said.

Andrei smiled, then continued, "I doubt there are many babies being named Nicolae anymore. Unless they're children in the state-run orphanages."

He paused, seeming to remember something. "There was a strange story in one of the underground papers about an orphanage director going to prison for naming all the boys in his care Nicolae. He must have been a bit crazy. Imagine a hundred malnourished Nicolaes running around. The director said he was tired of hearing the orphans referred to as 'nobody's children.' They are Ceausescu's children, he said. Ceausescu was the one responsible for creating a population of unwanted babies when he outlawed birth control and abortion so he could fill Romania's factories. 'So let's name them after their Tata!' the director announced. I don't know if he expected to get away with it. The minute Ceausescu heard of it he had the director locked up for treachery."

"Those poor kids," I said. "How did Nicolae feel about his name?"

"He really only thought about it when it came to leaving. On the way to the port, he said, 'Maybe I should change my name. I don't want people in the West to think I was named after *him*.'"

"What did he want to change it to?" I asked.

"Something light," Andrei replied. "Dan. Brian. George. It's hard to make up a name for yourself. Anyway, we experimented with the name Bruce. You know, Bruce Springsteen."

We both laughed.

Around the time of the letters, Andrei began collecting articles from various newspapers and magazines. Stacks of writing about and photographs of unidentified people who had been discovered in different parts of the world, either living or dead. He started spending his weekends at the city reference library, hunting through the international papers. He was not interested in the widely publicized cases, only in the cases tracking the lesser known.

> Unidentified man discovered in a state of unconsciousness on the Island of Rhodes. [?] ~~Middle-aged, grey hair,~~ dressed in black slacks, a green shirt and black jacket. Two Romanian coins were found in the pockets.
> (The Athens News Agency, 7 June 1989)

Two things struck me when I looked at the clippings. The first was the way Andrei had marked up each text, highlighting and striking through words, inserting question marks in places. The second was a feeling of overload, a sense that the world was crammed with people like Nicolae: missing persons, fugitives, runaways, abductees. Loose ends, all awaiting some finality.

> The body of a dead man was found 6 miles off the coast of Livorno. [??] The body is that of a tall, slightly built man whose features are typically Northern European. ~~Light~~ brown hair. Brown eyes. ~~A dimple on the chin.~~ Postmortem exams, performed at Pisa University, have not found any signs of violence or poisoning, so drowning was the probable cause of

death. A few items may help identify the body. 1) a worn rubber-soled brown shoe, ~~size 47~~, with a red logo. 2) a Casio digital wristwatch with a grey strap. The manufacturing number 47235 printed on the back could help trace the point of purchase. [??] 3) ~~a wedding band, 24 ct., size 27. The ring was made in Italy.~~ (From The Corsica Weekly, 12 June 1989)

Andrei kept a cardboard filing box filled with his clippings. Dates were carefully pencilled in at the top right corner. And everything was sorted according to geographic region. Even missing persons who didn't fit his search had a home in Andrei's box.

Soon, I was contributing to his collection. It started one morning when I found myself grazing through the newspaper, scissors in hand. Eventually, it became second nature. Sitting on the bus, waiting at the doctor's office: wherever there was a discarded newspaper, I busied myself. Lost and found people, I came to discover, comprised a sub-genre of journalism, tucked between the local crime stories and the obituary section.

I was drawn to stories of the transient: the bearded drifter who was discovered living in a high-school locker room. And stories of the unhinged: the man who woke up in a Toronto hospital bed with a fractured skull and no idea who he was. He was diagnosed with something called post-concussion global amnesia, or total memory blackout. His picture was sent to various police precincts across the country. Fingerprints, mug shots led nowhere. When months later the detectives finally gave up, the man in question asked to be given a new identity, but his request was denied.

The stories of people who were afflicted with amnesia presented one of the kinder scenarios. I had heard of people recovering their "blanked-out" memories over time—in some cases as suddenly and

inexplicably as they had lost them. Was it possible that Nicolae had
suffered a blow to the head? And if so, was it also possible that he was
now wandering around in some corner of the world, on the brink of
regaining his identity?

I avoided the stories of the dead.

Whenever I came across a photograph to add to Andrei's collection,
I felt a mixture of excitement and depression. Even living people in
newspaper photos somehow seem ill-fated, ethereal, as if composed
of grains of black sand about to blow away.

For a few weeks, it seemed that stories of human-smuggling opera-
tions were everywhere in the newspapers. My fingers were black with
newspaper ink.

In early July, twenty-five Chinese migrants from the province
of Fujian were discovered inside two shipping containers aboard a
Seattle-bound freighter.

The following week another cargo vessel carrying Albanian stowaways hit rocks off Turkey's Mediterranean coast, killing at least
eighteen people and leaving the rest to survive the treacherous sea.

Then a week later, twenty-four people drowned when another
Turkish vessel carrying thirty-one migrants from Southern Romania
capsized in the frigid, stormy waters of the Aegean Sea en route to
Greece.

Such items for most readers were just page-fillers, mere miscel-
lany, horrible but far away. Andrei, on the other hand, took it all very
personally.

Nonetheless he persevered. Throughout the middle of summer, he
continued his parallel projects, his letter-writing and his scissoring
of newspaper articles, with a kind of manic dedication. And while
it didn't occur to me right away, it soon became apparent that these
seemingly disparate activities were, in fact, intrinsically connected. If

Andrei's letters comprised a question to the world, then the clippings were the world's detached reply. Or so he would have me believe.

He seemed absolutely certain that our tenacity would be rewarded. That's why I was baffled when out of the blue he stopped. It was the second week of August. Suddenly there were no more newspaper cuttings lying on his desk. The filing box he had kept on his work shelf disappeared. He started sketching again in his spare time. Elaborate, technical illustrations that kept him occupied for hours.

When one day I suggested we draft a new batch of letters, he declined. What was the point, nobody's responding, he said, surprising me with his resignation. All efforts to motivate him just brought a shrug. As far as I knew, he never wrote another letter.

For several days, I hardly saw Andrei except at his desk. I knew something was wrong. He turned his face away whenever I tried to catch his eye. At lunch he would rush off by himself. I would call after him, and he would give a quick wave and keep walking. He seemed anxious to keep moving. I would catch up with him. "Where are you going? Can I come too?" A forced smile, a shake of his head, he was late for something or other. Sometimes he would be delayed getting back to work. He lost interest in the packages that arrived at his desk.

Even his gaze, once always watchful, now had a thousand-yard stare. Something had overpowered him. I didn't realize it at the time, but this was the beginning of a gradual letting go.

And what was it that he relinquished? Perhaps Nicolae. Or Romania. Perhaps his ties to the past. Perhaps something as simple as hope.

So much remains unclear when I look back on that time, but Andrei's pain was unmistakable. Photos of young men were the hardest on him—those who looked like Nicolae, even those who didn't.

Dead letters! Does it not sound like dead men?

From "Bartleby the Scrivener"
by Herman Melville

Part Three

Sixteen

Somewhere deep inside, I knew that the key to Andrei's disappearance was to determine what had happened to Nicolae. One missing person would guide me to the other.

Throughout my early conversations with Andrei, Nicolae had remained elusive—a blurry figure in a corner of my mind. I could put a face to him from Andrei's photos, but I lacked the fine character details to bring him to life. Much of this vagueness, I knew, was my responsibility. Wishing not to be intrusive or indelicate, I was at first hesitant to ask too much about their relationship. (Would I have been so circumspect had Nicolae been Nicola? I cannot say for certain, though I hazard to think yes.)

It had been the pattern with Andrei that I would wait for him to volunteer information, which he began to do more earnestly in early October, two months before he disappeared. It seemed to happen all of a sudden. For some time after we had aborted our letter-writing and newspaper-clipping campaign, Nicolae's name had been off limits. Then one afternoon, while we were sitting outside the mail office enjoying a warm spell, Andrei began to speak of him again. We had just come back from walking in a nearby ravine and I was using a branch to pick at dirt that had caked into the ridged soles of my shoes.

"I still compose letters to him every night in my head," he said.

He was looking straight ahead, directing his comments at the row of parked cars, the trees in their concrete planters. I put the stick down to show I was paying attention, but Andrei took no notice. I might not have been there: he was talking beyond any audience, to wherever he stared.

"The other day I ran into someone I met when I first came to Canada. He's a bank teller now. We ended up going for a coffee and before long he was showing me pictures from his wallet. There was a snapshot of his wife on their wedding day, one of his house and one of his two young girls feeding geese by the lake.

"It was as though he was trying to sell me something—you know, the 'good life' we're all supposed to be wanting. I felt relief when he finally closed his wallet and asked me what I had been up to in the five years since we had last seen each other."

"What did you tell him?"

"I told him that I had a good job. I remembered that he was a chess player himself and told him about my chess matches. It was all very friendly, which is why I was shocked when, just as we were leaving, he held my shoulder, looked me in the eyes and said: 'My friend, you must get on with your life. We must find you a wife.'"

"How horrible and presumptuous."

"That's just it. He wasn't being horrible. He was a nice man. But I realized that it didn't matter if I had won the lottery or been promoted to manager of his bank. Without a family, I was nothing."

"Did you consider telling him about Nicolae?"

He turned to me in surprise, perhaps puzzled by the mention of Nicolae in the context of family. He shook his head.

I waited for him to continue, but he didn't. He began fishing around in his pockets, looking for his lighter. I could tell from the changing expression on his face that he was becoming lost in his own thoughts again. I picked up the branch, this time whisking it along the tops of my shoes. I watched his hand curl, uncurl, then curl again, as if clasping something.

In his mind, perhaps he was walking with Nicolae along the banks of a river. Perhaps he was remembering how they used to slip off their clothes and jump in the water, swimming side by side, diving into the cold patches where the riverbed dropped away. Perhaps he was thinking about the way Nicolae's face used to break through the water, a whip of hair, a bobbing head, circles widening across the surface.

But it is more likely he was thinking about the splash: that final fateful moment when Nicolae entered the water of the Bosporus. Was Nicolae far enough away from the freighter? Did he shout? Andrei couldn't remember. The moment when so much happened eluded him; it had been left behind.

"Are you okay?" I asked.

"Yes, why?"

I placed my hand on his arm. "You're shaking."

Andrei lit his cigarette with a trembling hand and inhaled deeply. He exhaled. He breathed in again deeply, this time without the cigarette. I saw from the look on his face that he was back again, back in the sunlight.

Andrei pointed at an approaching truck. "Marvin." The truck passed, two honks and a wave. We both waved back and watched a cloud of dust rise in the air.

The particular moment Andrei couldn't remember was always a forbidding blankness; struggling with it would leave him anxious and confused. Every few days he woke up in a panic, his body covered in sweat. Every evening, he told himself stories about Nicolae to dispel these nightmares. The stories he invented spoke of happier circumstances. In one story, Nicolae was in Lisbon eating grilled sardines by the sea. In another, he was walking through the market in Biarritz, buying fresh tomatoes and spiced sausage. In Andrei's stories, Nicolae was always comfortable and well-fed. He wasn't languishing in some cockroach-infested room with only a hot plate for cooking and crates for furniture. He was okay. Far away, but okay.

These stories soothed his conscience. Only occasionally did he allow himself to wonder what it meant for Nicolae, assuming he had survived, to move on without him.

Had Nicolae even tried to find him?

But there were bleaker thoughts to which Andrei alluded: that Nicolae all along may have had his own plan of escape—escape from him included; or, most unbearable, that Nicolae may have held him to account for that moment of parting in the black of the Bosporus.

Outside the mail office, Andrei dropped his half-finished cigarette to the ground. I shuffled over in my seat and mashed it with my shoe. I wanted to jump into the silence and ask him if he would consider joining Paolo and me for Thanksgiving dinner the following weekend, but before I could put the words together, he spun around to face me.

"You know, all this time, you hardly ask any questions about Nicolae. Is it because . . ." But he stopped himself. "Why is that?"

I stared down at my feet. The question caught me off guard. I couldn't tell if he was accusing me of something, or simply inquiring.

"I . . ."

"Don't be shy," he urged.

I thought for a moment, then said, "Okay, then. How did you meet?"

Andrei raised an eyebrow, then smiled. "That's it?"

I shrugged.

"All right. Let's see. How we met. Well, we were classmates in our first year of university. Both of us were eighteen years old. We sat close to each other in mathematics class.

"It was mid-session exams. The classroom noisy with moving paper and chair legs scratching the floor. Nicolae was sitting by the window, leaning on his wooden desk. He was using a ruler to draw a gridding—grid?—a grid on his paper to complete the last question. Around us, everyone was concentrating.

"Only I was moving in my seat. I had forgotten my sharpener, and my flat pencil would not let me finish the final question. The more I tried to fix my . . . my grid the more messy it became, until I was looking at a terrible grey mark in the middle of the page. I must have sighed loudly, because a moment later there was a tiny sound on my desk. Nicolae had given me a new pencil. I held it up. The tip was a perfect point. I looked over to thank him but his nose was already back on his page.

"When the exam was finished I waited at my desk until everyone had collected their things and the room had become empty. Finally, Nicolae came over, and before I knew it we were touching. It was quick—I think his hand pressed my arm—but I could feel a shivering on my skin.

"'Keep it,' Nicolae said, pointing to the pencil I was holding. I saw that the end of his thumb was missing. The other fingers were long and skinny.

"'You don't mind?' I said. When he looked at me I felt warm. My cheeks were hot. His attention was pleasing to me.

"'No.' He was smiling, 'My father is a professor. He gets them from the university.'

"Just then a teacher put his head into the classroom. Nicolae turned and looked away, but I didn't.

"'I better run,' he whispered, looking back at me and smiling. He closed the buckle of his bag.

"After he left, I could still feel his breath right here on the side of my neck, his hand on my arm."

The hollow beneath Nicolae's shoulders where his shirt hung loosely, his trimmed fingernails, his missing thumb tip, his small front teeth, the light freckles on his arms: such intimate knowledge of body parts fleshed and warmed Andrei's memory of Nicolae. Now I was the holder of these small parts. As the sole keeper of Andrei's story, I had to determine its fate. But could I be trusted?

Andrei once said that every memory is a possible betrayal. Our memories are communal and so revealing them without the permission of those with whom they were created is a kind of violation.

Ultimately, it was my own desire for peace of mind that kept me recounting Andrei's story to Paolo, confiding in Paolo the way Andrei had confided me. In the end, I told him virtually everything. He listened closely, nodding at different points, stopping me every now and then to ask a question. This act of sharing generated a new intimacy between us, and any resentment he harboured toward Andrei seemed to dissolve. (I should mention that Paolo continued to demonstrate a characteristic mind for detail in the questions he asked. For example: Were the letters we wrote inquiring about Nicolae sent by registered mail? Was Andrei a good student? By which I think he meant: was he smart enough not to draw attention to himself?)

Something quite unexpected happened as I spoke. A feeling of calm resolve spread through me, a quiet hope that in recounting Andrei's story, I was somehow keeping him alive.

Seventeen

*A*ndrei carried the pencil Nicolae gave him everywhere he went. He rolled it in his coat pocket while waiting for the bus, always careful not to snap the point. He played with it during class, twirling it around his thumb, lacing it through his fingers, mindlessly doodling just to feel the scratch of the tip against the paper. He tucked it behind his ear while he ate. And he placed it beside his pillow when he went to sleep.

The pencil was the first sign of Andrei's lovesickness. The second indication was the sighing. He sighed prolifically, an entire dialect of sighs, as though life had many different ways of pressing the air out of him. A soft contented sigh when he was in Nicolae's presence. A mournful sonorous sigh in his absence. A grumbling sigh when Nicolae had to rush home. A grateful sigh of relief when he entered the room. Andrei had developed an uncommon, non-verbal eloquence.

He could summon the complete range of human emotion. But there was still one sigh that Andrei had not yet uttered, a sigh that had not yet found its proper occasion.

The occasion came in early October. Nicolae surprised Andrei one day by asking if he would join him after class. The invitation was written on the back of an exercise book and passed to him during the professor's morning lecture. Their professor had given them a hydraulic engineering assignment that involved designing a small dam for the Tisza. Nicolae's note read: *The river, this afternoon?* Andrei stared at it and felt his pulse jump. He picked up his pencil—*the* pencil—ready to reply in small neat lettering (*Yes!*), but thinking better of it, put the pencil down and gave a furtive nod.

By mid-afternoon, they had found an undisturbed area by the river. They set down their bags and tinkered with their drawings for three-quarters of an hour. Conversation was halting. Nicolae did most of the talking. Whenever Andrei tried to contribute he found himself speaking in monosyllables. For months he had fantasized about being alone with Nicolae, but now he felt almost numb with shyness, grateful when Nicolae launched into a monologue about "uncivil engineering." He listened as Nicolae described a recent trip to the capital: how horrible it was to walk through the potholed streets of Bucharest. Behind the shiny white exterior of Victory of Socialism Boulevard everything was grey, grey, grey. Thousands of people jammed into pitiful apartment blocks with horrible, uniform facades. Grimy, precast concrete for miles. It was monstrous! Inhuman! Evil!

Nicolae's words stabbed the air. They were hard, bitter words having nothing to do with the occasion—the occasion of their courtship as Andrei perceived it. Yet the truth was that Nicolae's words didn't matter to Andrei in the least. What mattered was his proximity. Sitting beside Nicolae gave Andrei a fluttering sensation in his stomach.

A feeling of unadulterated joy. His eyes, his mouth, his neck, his hands! The anticipation of touching Nicolae was enough to make him giddy.

He fought the urge to lick him. Right then. Run his tongue along the edge of Nicolae's ear.

Andrei realized he was being too forward, his eyes too eager, when Nicolae began to blush and look away. As a diversion, Nicolae massaged his chest pocket and pulled out a crumpled package of cigarettes.

"One left, let's share it."

He lit the cigarette and slid to a half-reclining position. He tried to appear relaxed, but his manner was nervous. He took a long haul on the cigarette and then raised it for Andrei to share. The V of their fingers overlapped. It was their second touch, and all Andrei could think was that he wanted to be in Nicolae's arms.

They stared at each other in suspense, unable to speak. The cigarette was dropped and crushed underfoot, but their fingers continued to touch, tentatively stroking and delving. Fingernails gently scraping a wrist, a thumb lightly brushing the inside of an elbow. Nicolae edged toward Andrei. Andrei could feel his heart beating through his shirt.

When they finally collapsed on the riverbank, the wanting was unrestrained. They clutched at each other, moving on the earth, twisting over the roots and branches, grabbing and pressing urgently. Their lovemaking was both smooth and rough. Dry pads of grass. Pebble-cool cheeks. Warm breath. Moist contact of tongues. Loose bunches of fabric. Knees on coarse ground. Flecks of wood. Confetti of brittle leaves. And, finally, the sinking, pleading hardness—being seized and flexed in—the sensation of both substance and evanescence at the same time. In those rapturous moments, sounds came from Andrei that he did not know. Deep, falling, hungry sounds.

When the sun set, they were nestled together under a blanket of clothes.

"I felt you watching me," Nicolae murmured. "Every time I walked into the classroom, I could feel your eyes on me." He looked at Andrei and grinned. "Did I imagine it?"

Andrei shook his head and smiled shyly. "I suppose I'm not very good at hiding things."

"No. But I'm so glad." The teasing gone from his voice. He took a deep breath and touched the back of Andrei's head.

A gentle wind swished the tops of the trees and stray leaves floated around them. A bright quarter moon hung in the sky. The stars blinked and Nicolae pointed up at them happily: "Surveillance."

A squirrel scurried by, and after a pause Andrei whispered blissfully: "Informer."

The river became theirs, their desire growing stronger with each secret meeting. When winter came, they met in an abandoned shed. A layer of gritty hay covered the floor. They lay together on a bed of woollen horse blankets. They found blocks of wood to sit on. A kerosene lamp. They stuffed burlap sacks for insulation.

In late spring, they returned to the riverside, which was blooming with new life. By early summer there was a wild bush, heavy with ruby berries. There were patches of columbine, edelweiss, and ragged clusters of yellow poppy. One afternoon, as they were lying by the river following a short hike, Nicolae's body erupted in hives. Raised white lumps that started at his neck. They became redder and angrier the more he scratched.

In an effort to soothe him, Andrei pulled up Nicolae's T-shirt and blew on the welts criss-crossing his back. Nicolae yelped. A spidery sensation formed a whorl across his shoulder blades. A blazing itch ran down his sides, then along his legs, down his calves. Placing the toe of his right foot against the heel of the left, Nicolae pushed the shoe off. A band of pink bumps circled his ankle.

Andrei set off to find a clearing away from the river.

He found a spot a few metres away and returned with Nicolae. "Lie here," he said finally, and patted the space beside him. He had stripped down to his underwear. His clothes were spread evenly on the ground. Nicolae lay down on the mat of clothes, slowly peeled off his own shirt, then pants, careful not to scratch himself. Once he was undressed he rested with his arms away from his body. The air was sluggish. He attempted to keep perfectly still, to direct his mind away from the creeping agony of his skin. He stretched his limbs, focusing on the forest smells. He stayed this way for several minutes, then gave up.

His skin was shrieking with discomfort. In surrender, he grunted and rolled on top of Andrei.

"Please," he groaned in Andrei's ear, "do something . . . I'm desperate!" He took Andrei's earlobe in his teeth. The sun slanted through the trees.

Andrei gripped Nicolae's buttocks, clamped his feet onto Nicolae's calves. They made love in quick motions. The trick was to be firm. No light, feathery touches. No aggravating caresses. Nicolae's penis was unwelted, which made them laugh.

Later that afternoon at Andrei's house, they sat in a concealed corner of the garden. Andrei had caked Nicolae's torso and limbs with a soothing mud paste, and as they waited for the mixture to stiffen and set, Andrei held a raw-potato compress against Nicolae's neck and jawbone. He put it near his hairline and patted it gently down to his shoulder. Nicolae moaned in gratitude as the rash subsided, the welts began sinking. Andrei picked up a Thermos of water with his free hand and took a swig. He passed it to Nicolae, who tipped it toward his mouth. A stream of liquid spilled down Nicolae's neck to his mud-caked chest, leaving a trail of beige slickness. With the

Thermos now gripped between his knees, Nicolae reached back and patted around for Andrei, mud-stiff arms fumbling for contact. Andrei squeezed the potato cloth in his hand and placed it on the ground. He inched forward and held Nicolae from behind. As he eased his hands across Nicolae's stomach and down into his pants, he heard the click of a shutter hinge, but chose to ignore it.

The dry mud cracked. Nicolae's back resembled that of a crocodile. Almost gleefully they found that the mud fell away with the rub of their bodies, shedding debris all around them. Andrei was able to sponge away the last crusts, and by evening the rash had disappeared. Nicolae dressed with a sigh of relief, pausing every now and then to pass his fingers over his new, sloughed skin, touching the round strawberry birthmark under his left collarbone.

The next time they met they avoided the riverbank and pushed deeper into the woods, until they reached a patch of defoliated land near a wind-toppled tree. It was a perfect spot, entirely secluded. They lay down together. Around them was the nutty aroma of beech. Fractions of light percolated through the canopy, leaving dappled shadows on the ground.

In time their love for each other became more reckless and unguarded. They became bolder, began meeting openly, oblivious to the dangers of being seen. Their intimacy would have been obvious to anyone. Nicolae absentmindedly tucking his hand into the sleeve of Andrei's shirt. Andrei picking an eyelash from Nicolae's cheek. A head resting on a shoulder. Fingers massaging the nape of a neck.

It was just a matter of time before they made a mistake.

On one occasion, Andrei's mother was standing by her window, tending to some flower pots. Andrei and Nicolae were setting up a ladder below, preparing to clean the eavestroughs. Andrei slipped the whisk broom into his back pocket, then donned a pair of heavy work gloves. Before he mounted the ladder he leaned over and brushed his lips against Nicolae's neck. It happened in a split second, but he heard something clatter against the window above. When Andrei looked up, he saw his mother stepping back into her room, the quick closing of a shutter.

When she peered out again, Andrei was halfway up the ladder. Nicolae was at the bottom holding on firmly. Andrei's mother nodded, dipped the rag she was holding into a bowl of water and began to scrub the plant leaves.

From that afternoon on, Andrei noticed that his mother hummed while she worked. An acoustic amulet: to make him aware of her presence, to spare herself any future surprises.

When Andrei was in grade school, rumour spread among his classmates that the science teacher was a pederast. Though never substantiated, the rumour stuck to the teacher like a foul stench. Obscene graffiti appeared on the blackboard. Vicious, threatening notes were left on his desk. Eventually the climate became so hostile that he was transferred to another school. Years later, another rumour circulated that the teacher had been picked up by the Securitate and thrown into prison in a campaign to rid the country of sodomites.

What mattered was not the substance of the original rumour, which could have attached itself to anyone, but the reaction to it. The children could not help noticing that the teachers were shamelessly silent while their colleague suffered all manner of harassment, governed by the ineradicable belief that they were serving their students well. To build a single-minded nation, lessons needed to be imparted, punishment dispensed. Without much said, the silence of their teachers conditioned the children.

Lesson #1: The Perils of Wayward Desire

Lesson #2: Sodomy as Treason

The boys learned their lessons quickly. Years before their first sexual experiments, they understood that to be gay was to be morally deficient—and horribly treated.

The lesson was so powerful that the first time Andrei was called a faggot, he experienced a surge of revulsion. A student he hardly knew—they had been on the same swim team as children—punctuated the epithet by spitting on Andrei's desk on his way out of the class. A white bubbly patch stared back at him like a wrathful eye. Yet it was not that which wrenched his stomach. Disgust was wiped away with his handkerchief, but what remained was a feeling of self-loathing. He fought against it, yet he could feel the hatred entering his heart, lodging there.

Wherever he went, he sensed people staring, gangs of prying eyes and busy minds that concocted fantasies about his depravity. The village always seethed with gossip of some kind or other, but now he was the *cause célèbre*, and in his dreams his persecutors were constantly waiting in ambush.

The first, tentative winds of change were beginning to blow through the cities and towns of Romania. One could hear rumbles of dissatisfaction by eavesdropping by the market stalls, in the factories, on the street. It was obvious that the country was overwrought and angry, and in this climate, fearful of authority despite the poverty and corruption, people turned on one another.

The first rumour was tame. That Andrei had brought Nicolae gifts: a bag of Hungarian sweets, a bottle of homemade plum brandy.

But they became more sinister as the fall of 1983 wore on:

That Nicolae collected postcards of naked boys . . .

That the two friends were peddling contraband condoms . . .

That they carried a disease . . .

Andrei played the role of a disgraced man, though it was not entirely an act. He kept silent around strangers. He was not proud of himself for bending to the humiliation. A braver man would have extended his arms and pushed all obstacles aside. A bolder man would have rejected the fear that had overtaken the town—crackling fear that ignited into open cruelty at the slightest inducement.

But Andrei was not a brave or bold man. At least not in his own estimation. The last thing he wanted was to call more attention to himself. After some months of this, as winter came, he sought to distract attention by avoiding Nicolae in public—not realizing it was too late. By now his love for Nicolae adhered to him as totally as his own skin. It was impossible to shed.

Then rumour had it that the Securitate was coming for them.

Nicolae was summoned for a series of interrogations in late February of 1984. They didn't meet again until several weeks later. During those lonely weeks, whenever Andrei saw Nicolae in class or on the street, his lover was barely recognizable. He had the appearance of a man who had just emerged from years of darkness into an overlit world. The impression he gave up close was even more disconcerting. He had lost so much weight that his clothes now sagged loosely on his thin frame. But more disturbing were Nicolae's eyes. They wouldn't rest: they twitched nervously around his chalk white face as if tracking an enemy. Andrei took on Nicolae's torment as well, blaming himself for not being more protective.

The next time they made love was joyless. It was sex for consolation, not pleasure. Andrei touched Nicolae tentatively, as though Nicolae's pale body were lined with tiny bruises and contusions that required delicate handling. He held back tears as Nicolae moulded himself child-like against him. Every rustle of wind sent them into high alert.

Andrei leaned nearer, put his face into Nicolae's neck. "They'll soon tire of us, you'll see. Just hang on," he whispered. "Tomorrow, in a week, in a month . . . life will get easier."

They drew up a wish list full of sumptuous and mundane things: an apartment of their own, a refrigerator, a stereo, delicious cakes and tender cuts of fresh meat.

They began to speak in a language of glowing prospects, open dreams, luminous possibilities—the language of the persecuted and oppressed, for whom happiness denied defines their lives. Tomorrow's people.

And so time passed for them, fed by imagination.

Eighteen

I treasure the photograph taken of me and my mother a year ago. Though I have always preferred stealth shots to posed portraits, I have come to see that life is too short to wait for candid moments. My criteria for album-worthiness has relaxed considerably with my mother's illness. I now take what I can get (her clear eyes, her engaged grin) and do not dwell on imperfections (in this case a beige blur in the corner, where Roy Ishii's finger accidentally covered the shutter).

I remember that the basement of Grace Church, which provided temporary shelter to the evacuated residents of Sakura, was simple and uncluttered. The furniture, what little there was of it, was clean and utilitarian. The walls were white. Near where my mother sat there was a tall bookcase, filled with Christian books. As we waited to hear what arrangements were being made for the night, I stood up to browse through them. Among a row of dark blue Bibles was a book titled

Object Lessons for Young People's Worship. The cover showed Christ surrounded by small children. I opened it to the first page.

> *Don't forget: a good object lesson is divine. There's no better*
> *way to impart a lasting moral lesson. Just remember Jesus*
> *with the mustard seed or Jesus with the fish and loaves and*
> *follow his example with interactive, point-making object*
> *lessons designed for young worshippers.*

The book contained fifty-two object lessons, one for every week of the year, based on texts from every book in the New Testament. I scanned the contents list—eggs, umbrella, lightbulb, pencil, et cetera—and randomly flipped to a page near the middle of the book.

T-shirt Label Lesson
Props: a T-shirt, scissors
(Remove label while explaining to the children)

> *Here is a label that lets us know what kind of T-shirt we*
> *have purchased. It tells us where it was made, what it was*
> *made from. On occasion, you may find that people place*
> *labels on those around them. They may label people with*
> *names like dumb, dirty or criminal. Such name-calling has*
> *no place among those who follow the light of the Lord, our*
> *Saviour . . .*

As I stood by the bookcase, I glanced over at my mother. She looked rumpled and tired. Pieces of hair kept falling out of her bun. Her lips were chapped and pale. I went to get her another orange drink box and left her with the book. When I returned, it was still closed in her lap.

My mother didn't need the book. She had her own object lessons—non-religious, perhaps, but no less wise, if she could articulate them:

1. There is a comfort and constancy in objects. If you buy a toaster oven, you know you won't go down to the kitchen the next morning and find it has transformed itself into a blender.
2. Collecting objects teaches patience and perseverance. A collection is a step-by-step endeavour.
3. Objects can be multi-seasonal. An umbrella will keep the sun off when you're hot and keep you dry when it rains.
4. Objects are discrete. It is usually possible to tell where one thing ends and another begins.

Half an hour later, the book was back on its shelf and I was sitting cross-legged in a chair, looking at my mother, who was removing her necklaces one by one. Someone had recently given Roy Ishii a new camera and he was taking the opportunity to test it out. He walked by, then stopped and crouched.

"How about a picture," he said, squinting one eye and raising the camera to the other one.

I uncrossed my legs. My mother raised her index finger, gesturing for him to wait a moment, and proceeded to replace the necklaces. She composed herself slowly, forming her picture face. I noticed that Roy's thighs had begun to tremble from squatting.

"Say 'chee-zu,'" Roy said.

I reached up to fix the collar of my shirt.

The shutter clicked.

"Picture perfect. You both look lovely," he said, standing, ready to move on to his next subjects.

As I watched other people put on their picture faces, I wondered what our pose had conveyed. How easy it would be to adjust the mood. I tried to imagine a different picture—one with our heads touching, or my arm around her shoulder, or her face turned toward mine—but the images didn't cohere.

Andrei had only two photographs of himself and Nicolae together. Back in Romania, they had been taped to the inside of his closet door. Once they made the decision to escape, he had taken them down and set them aside, with the hope of preserving them for the journey. In the first picture, they are standing in a garden. Andrei is grinning widely at Nicolae, his head turned in profile, as if unaware of the photographer (Andrei's mother). The second one is an overexposed photo taken on a breezy summer day. They are standing shoulder to shoulder in the grass, both of them smiling up at a camera held in Nicolae's outstretched hand. Their hair, lifted by the wind, covers the sun, creating a blurry halo of light above their heads.

I knew this second photograph well. The photos did end up travelling with Andrei. Taped to his leg in a waterproof pouch, they survived his swim across the oily Bosporus and the weeks he spent in Turkey, miraculously arriving in Canada with very little damage—just a few folded corners and a bit of buckling easily corrected by an iron. That first afternoon that I visited Andrei's apartment, he retrieved the second photo from his desk. His eyes began to moisten as he held it out for me to see. He blinked back tears.

"It says something different now," he said, pointing to the light above Nicolae's head. A vision of afterlife. Nicolae, an angel in heaven.

After Andrei disappeared, I found myself remembering that picture. I hoped I would see it again; perhaps Andrei had left it in his apartment. I wanted a chance to pore over it for clues, any sign of their disengagement. In photos of my parents before their separation, the signs are there: the distance between their bodies, their coaxed smiles, the awkward bend of an arm placed around a shoulder. In the way they look distracted, dutiful, bored, I know they are already half-way gone. If one looks carefully at a photograph, there is usually some intimation of the future.

Andrei and Nicolae. Nicolae and Andrei. How fragile the bonds of intimacy if not daily renewed. What, in the end, did Andrei retain of his friend and former lover beyond a couple of photographs?

By the time Andrei reached Canada, many new images crowded out his memory of Nicolae. Nicolae's presence needed to be reinvigorated. Nurtured and revived. Andrei began telling me things about him, personal details as well as extraneous asides that surprised me. How Nicolae liked to drink but always excused himself before he became too sloppy or sentimental. How he disliked most sports but enjoyed walking, preferred night over day, was fascinated by the idea of faith but detested religion. How he collected vintage postcards but showed no interest in photographs of places or people he knew. He told me about Nicolae's love of chess and his inability not to gloat when he won. How Nicolae always signed his letters with a cartoon rather than his name.

One afternoon when Andrei and I were alone in the kitchen at work sharing lunch, I decided to ask a question that had been weighing on my mind. It had occurred to me that I was the only one who knew about Nicolae and Andrei and their relationship. If others knew, I thought, perhaps I would feel less accountable, less responsible. I feared that I was not a wise enough confidante. Maybe I was seeking reassurance.

I asked, "Have you shared this with anyone else? Am I the only person you've told about Nicolae?"

For a moment, Andrei said nothing. He ran a hand over his bristly jaw. Then he smiled uncomfortably. He finally answered, his voice subdued.

"I told my fiancée."

THREE MONTHS BEFORE HIS escape from Romania, Andrei was betrothed to a woman from his village. It took everyone by surprise. No one expected it.

It was his brother Eli's idea.

One evening shortly after Nicolae had been summoned by the Securitate, Andrei's brother slipped into his room. Andrei was lying on his mattress drawing in his sketchbook, making tiny notes in the margin. Eli stood by the bed and looked at his brother intently.

"I'm going to put this as bluntly as possible because we're brothers and I don't think it will help matters to be vague or polite about it." He sat down on the bed. "Everyone's talking about you and Nicolae."

Andrei kept sketching, pressing harder, carving the page with his pencil. Eli continued.

"I've known you two were very close, but now everyone else seems to know. Can't you be more careful?" His voice was direct but kind.

Warmed by his brother's tone, Andrei closed his sketchbook and looked up. "I wish they'd just leave us alone. What harm do we do anybody? It feels like we're being hunted."

"That's just it. You *are* being hunted. It's time to create a diversion," Eli said.

"But how?"

"Stop acting like a target. I promise in a few months they'll forget about you. You just need to fit in a bit more."

"Just tell me, how?"

Eli considered Andrei for a moment. "Listen. There is a girl I know . . ."

When he had finished telling Andrei about Ileana, he touched him lightly on the arm. "Don't worry, we'll turn things around. You'll see."

The significance of what Eli was proposing didn't sink in right away. When it began to settle in Andrei's mind, he was stunned that the solution to his problems could be so straightforward, so ordinary: a very open courtship could redeem the most fallen of men in the mind of the village. He would be reinstated—a reformed citizen, a born-again patriot.

Five days after Eli's visit, Andrei agreed to meet Ileana.

She was the eldest daughter of a music teacher who played the bassoon with the Baia Mare symphonic orchestra. Ileana had inherited his sense of rhythm and ear for music. When she was only nine, she had shown an aptitude and intensity for swing guitar that had people open-mouthed with delight. At eighteen, however, her joyous enthusiasm elicited only sneers of disapproval. Whereas before people had seen a charming prodigy, now they saw a boyish young woman with a guitar perched across her splayed trouser-clad legs ("Like a whore!"), a grimace of concentration distorting her otherwise pleasant face ("So mannish!").

In truth, Ileana's face was not altogether pleasant. At least not by the usual standards. She had been born with a disfigurement. Where her lower lip relaxed into an attractive pout, the upper lip bore a severe cleft. This birth defect, however, served to rid Ileana of any pretensions of beauty, liberating her from the self-scrutiny that afflicted many of the village girls. Unlike other women her age, who were conditioned to watch themselves being watched as they walked down the street, Ileana paid little regard to her own appearance. She showed not the slightest trace of self-consciousness or, for that matter, self-doubt. Her only nod to femininity, the product of negligence rather than vanity, was a thick brush of black hair that fell to her waist on the rare occasions when it was untied.

Unlike Jenica, her voluptuous younger sister, Ileana was thin. Not just her ankles and wrists, but her hips, her chest, her shoulders. "You've got no bum," her father would say unhelpfully, adding that men liked padding on a woman. Every time she prepared to sit down at the dinner table, he would rush over with a cushion and pretend that he was trying to save the chairs from being scuffed by her bony backside.

Ileana was punished for her self-reliance and for not caring for her looks. By the age of twenty, she had gained a reputation as a *garçon manqué* who dressed like a factory boy and played music like a gypsy. She was an easy target for disdainful remarks that threatened to tar the entire family. *Magyars! Papists! Hebrew-lovers!* Even strangers knew of the denunciations, prompting a family friend to suggest a remedy: Ileana should get married as soon as possible. Given so much hysteria, nothing less than a public wedding would bring acceptance. A marriageable woman who chose to remain alone only courted trouble. Ileana's family took it upon themselves to find a husband for her. They made the announcement one evening over dinner.

The idea of giving up her freedom flooded Ileana with panic. The prospect of an arranged marriage contradicted everything she believed about independence and choice. Yet she assumed her fate calmly, going along with her parents' wishes in a dissociated manner, resolving to make the best of the situation for the sake of her family.

It was around this time that Andrei stepped into the picture.

Two outcasts: a derided tomboy and a scandalized homosexual. Their destiny was a marriage of wile and utility. With Andrei, Ileana would find a freedom she could never have with another man. With Ileana, Andrei could erase the infamy associated with his recent past.

Andrei was sure Nicolae would not regard this new arrangement as infidelity. He convinced himself that Ileana's presence could only offer benefits. Under cover of hollow matrimony, his stolen moments with Nicolae could be fuller and more frequent.

Andrei and Ileana went walking every night for two weeks. They wandered around and around the town square, arm in arm, at a slow, easy pace. They were careful to be seen. They both wanted witnesses. In the early evenings they sat on the stoop of Ileana's house. Whenever they saw a curtain shift across the street, they squashed up close like a couple caught in a private moment. They flaunted their courtship with perverse relish, exchanging bouquets of flowers, small gifts and "love" letters. They enjoyed the conspiracy, the satisfaction of a well-plotted deception.

Andrei was happy in a way, in many ways. Their engagement had not put an end to the stares or the gossip—but the tenor had changed. It was no longer the spiteful attention they had endured earlier. The peering eyes behind painted shutters seemed less hostile now. Mothers pinning their laundry in the sunlight stopped to say hello. Bony fingers wagged greetings from balconies. Children on creaking tricycles rang their bells in greeting as they passed. Of course, there were skeptics who muttered under their breath, *Condolences to the children born to such a strange couple* . . . But for the most part, believing they had influenced events, people in the village were self-congratulatory—wasn't it miracle the two had been cured!—a glimmer of victory in their eyes.

Eli was triply pleased by the engagement. Pleased that his older brother was spared the spattering of his reputation. Pleased that the family name had been redeemed. Pleased that he had been the one to help spare him. Andrei's mother was initially suspicious but she soon lost herself in the preliminaries of wedding planning. The cake design was her *coup de maître*: three tiers, topped by two ceramic figurines, feet embedded in rich butter icing. A white satin dress for the woman. A tuxedo and hat for the man. Cake sides decorated with crushed almonds and raisins. A sprinkle of cocoa.

Only Nicolae was distraught.

Nicolae considered Andrei's engagement an act of cowardice. It devastated him. He didn't accept Andrei's assurance that the relationship was a sham, that it had helped stifle the scandal. Perhaps he feared deep down that Andrei would grow to love his fiancée. With its layers of deceit, the coming wedding was too painful a subject to mention. So between them Ileana was never discussed—until one afternoon Ileana and Nicolae met. A brief encounter near the market. Andrei and Ileana had been out walking when Nicolae pulled up beside them on his bicycle. They shook hands and exchanged pleasantries for a few minutes. Chitchat about the improving weather, the cycling group that had passed through town that morning, the meagre loaves of bread at the bakery . . .

Andrei was under the false impression that the encounter had appeased Nicolae and washed away any doubts he entertained about the nature of Andrei's relationship with Ileana.

But a week later Nicolae announced that he had checked the Cernavoda ship schedules and that he was intent on leaving Romania—with or without Andrei.

With the summer wedding only a few months away, Andrei tried to convince him to reconsider. "Wait a while. Things will settle down."

They were sitting in the forest. Nicolae was petulant.

"How long do you plan to continue with her?" Nicolae asked.

"Until it's safe," said Andrei.

"Aren't you sick of it? Haven't you grown weary of your little performance?"

As Andrei looked down at his feet, something clicked. "I don't believe it." He glanced up, incredulous. "You think I've fallen in love with her."

Nicolae brushed off Andrei's words with a smirk. "Do you think people have really forgotten about you? Do you think it's that simple? That you can just choose to erase who you are?"

Andrei shook his head slowly. "But what do you want me to do?"

Nicolae was silent.

Andrei continued. "I thought you'd understand. This is for us."

At this Nicolae released a cynical laugh and, still without a word, began to pack his bag. Andrei tried to reach for him, but Nicolae turned away in a manner that said there was nothing left to discuss.

When Andrei returned home that evening, he closed his bedroom door with more force than he had intended. It shook his bedside table, causing a small lamp to wobble, and he caught it just before it fell. Having restored it, he sank down onto the floor and began to cry. Nicolae was right. He had acted out of weakness. Was he really intending to go through with this marriage?

All that mattered to him at that moment was that he wanted to be with Nicolae again. It was not too late. The courtship could be called off. There was still time.

That evening, Andrei brought out a map of Romania and spread it on his bed. He stared at the winding lines that represented rivers and roads, finding comfort in the map's simple abstractions. He looked at every notation, ran his hand from corner to corner, from the mountains to the coastline. His finger settled on a southeast point, a thumbnail distance from Constanta. He began to trace the route.

Drained by the day's emotions, he felt his mind shutting down. The weight of his eyelids pressing. Sleep finally overtook him. He woke up several hours later to the sound of Eli coming home, the noise of a screen door squealing on a rusty hinge. His eyes sprang open. The map was crumpled beside his head. He felt paper creases on his cheek. He rolled over in bed but couldn't fall back to sleep. As the house became quiet, he began to consider Ileana. The more he thought about leaving her, the more ashamed he felt. For the rest of the night, he slept poorly, turning from side to side, from Nicolae to Ileana and back again.

The next day, Andrei waited for Ileana by a fountain in the main square. He sat on a stone bench facing the dry basin. On the side of the fountain someone had painted *For whom do we suffer?* The faint grey words peered through a cloud of whitewash. The fountain had been out of commission for five years, turned off as a symbol of the new austerity; now it was just an ornament to bureaucracy. Where once water had cascaded down, there was cracked ceramic and bits of trash.

When Ileana arrived, she shouted out in a friendly voice. Her hammock bag, slung on one shoulder, bumped against her thigh with her quick steps. It was only as she drew nearer that she hesitated. Seeing Andrei's solemn look, she sat down warily, still short of breath.

Over the course of the next hour Andrei confessed everything to her. There was a look of surprise on her face, then dismay. For a time, after he finished, she kept her head lowered, nodding ever so slightly as if pondering each part of a confusing puzzle. When she raised her head again her eyes were red. A vein flared at her temple. She seemed about to cry.

"Andrei. Please forgive me," she said, reaching for his hand. The compassion on her face at that moment was overwhelming.

He looked at her suspiciously. "I don't understand."

"It's all my fault. What a mess." She shook her head. "Eli said it was over between you and Nicolae. He said you were just friends. Oh no! Nicolae must just despise me."

Andrei was totally confounded by her reaction and it took him a moment to respond. "He doesn't despise you. Anyway, you're the one who should despise us—or at least me. How can I marry you now that I have plans to leave?"

"Yes—now all the old problems are back." Then, as the meaning of what Andrei had said finally sunk in, she groaned. "Now I'm back where I started." She raised her hand to her temple. "Please, Andrei," she pleaded. "You have to help me."

All afternoon, they sat on the stone bench and plotted. Ileana folded her arms into the body of her jacket for warmth. Andrei gave her his scarf to wear. They considered their situation from every conceivable angle. They resolved that as wrenching as their predicament was, it could be turned in their favour. By the time Andrei left the square, kissing Ileana on the cheek, they had agreed on a course of action. They had a compact. Another conspiracy.

Nineteen

The quota change was announced on state radio. It was squeezed between a story about the construction of a massive new government building in Bucharest, to be called the Palace of the People, and news about the Olympic team tryouts. Before the broadcast came to an end, the news reader recapped: The former quota of four children for every woman had been raised to five.

"This is unbelievable," Ileana said, pointing at the radio in Andrei's kitchen.

"Idiot counters," Andrei muttered. "They're turning us into a nation of numbers. Lightbulbs in the house. Loaves of bread on the table. Potatoes in the pantry. Litres in the gas tank."

"Five babies." She shook her head incredulously.

"It's the babies who should be rationed. The last thing this country needs is another child to—"

"Andrei!" Ileana flinched.

Andrei had not meant to sound hard-hearted. To his mind, the callousness lay with the authorities, and the unconscionable outcome of its campaign for population growth. Row upon row of metal cribs. There were more children than there was love to go around. Concrete warehouses throughout the country were teeming with jittery orphans who rocked like mechanical toys; children who cried for mothers until they were hoarse, and then stopped crying; children who lay on urine-soaked cots; bright beautiful children tethered by limb to furniture; silent, staring children hiding under a jumble of blankets.

The orphanages threatened to erase all the ingredients that made one human. Such was the legacy of the long aisles of babies treated as undesired goods.

One day Andrei took Ileana to the hidden clearing in the forest. The ground still smelled of spring. There were droplets of moisture on the leaves. "Right here. Shall we lie down?" Andrei placed a bed of clothes over the ground, a faded canvas jacket beside a grubby pullover beside a flannel shirt. This makeshift arrangement cloaked Andrei's secret: the imprint of other bodies pressed into moss.

The moisture seeped through the clothes into their skin. The hairs on Andrei's neck rose when a deer bounded across the forest floor only a few metres from where they were lying.

Their mutual desperation brought a tenderness. They lay side by side. He explored her with his fingers, *Tell me if you mind.* She moved slightly and pulled down her pants. His hand moved to her hip. *May I?* She had the body of a soft boy. Flat planes, opulent moments. *Is this okay?*

Her arms around him. Fingers tracing his spine. Andrei knew he was the first man to brush himself against her breasts. He touched his lips to the cleft near her mouth. Ileana rolled on top. He held her shoulders. She rocked on top of him, her hips pushing slowly, back and forth. She leaned forward. A string of tiny red beads hanging from her neck rested on his chest.

They moved, awkwardly, their every gesture strange in the fumble of first lovemaking. Neither had a claim on the other. But they released each other, and their feelings lifted, cleansed like a fresh wind.

The silence afterwards was not an embarrassed one. They relaxed into the earth. The blue sky darkened around them. Ileana's breathing was so deep and regular, Andrei thought she might be sleeping. But then he saw her open eyes gazing upwards. The wind was warm. She sat up, lifted her hair and retied it gently.

What startled Andrei was the strength of his emotions after the fact. A raw affection toward Ileana, a genuine sense of excitement at the prospect of becoming a father or, at least, a father figure. He thought it was cut and dried—that his feelings would conform to his intentions. He assumed he was in control of his own fate. What he discovered was that there were the mechanics of the matter and then there was something more.

"Come here," he murmured.

As he reached to embrace her, their hands bumped and their arms moved at different angles. Flustered, Andrei shook his arms in playful frustration and pretended to hug the air. She laughed. They both blushed.

On the walk home, she threaded her arm through his.

Agreeing to get Ileana pregnant was the last sentimental thing Andrei did before leaving his country. Otherwise, his days were spent going over logistics, studying maps, deciding what to take.

"Listen," he told Ileana one evening after they had been walking. "I want you to take my room. I'll tidy up everything, make it beautiful for you and the baby. There's a closet, some shelves, a big window with a tree just outside so it's nice and cool in the summer. I want you to say yes. Say you'll move into my house."

Ileana agreed.

The first thing Ileana did when she found out that she was pregnant was crop her hair. It was an impulsive gesture. People stared at her bristly head with disapproval. But once it was known that she was a woman with child she was granted immunity.

When Ileana was eleven weeks pregnant, she moved into his room. Those last nights before Andrei left, he busied himself making her comfortable. He built a bassinet and he altered his old trousers so they would fit her in the coming months. He cleared a shelf and prepared it with strips of fabric, a bottle of olive oil and a jar of talcum powder.

The last thing he did was slip a note inside Ileana's coat pocket while she was sleeping. The note was for his mother.

It took Andrei's mother many weeks to accept the fact that her son was not coming home. Despite the goodbye note, she behaved as though she expected him to walk through the door at any moment. At least that's what Andrei gathered from Ileana's first letter, every bland, censor-evading word subject to his scrutiny, his emotional telepathy. ("Your mother has been extremely busy with housework for two months. She wakes up in the morning and throws herself into her chores.") She spent hours restitching the seams of Ileana's wedding dress as if to reorder events. She ironed napkins and polished cutlery for a reception that would never happen. She trimmed the threads of her curtains. She mended a cushion cover that had been in storage for years. She oiled the hinge of the screen door. She noticed that the door to the hallway closet was creaking, so she oiled that, too.

Quickly the days sped by—one day, another day, a week, a month—

until gradually, through a process of sewing up all the ragged things, shining all the tarnished things and repairing all the broken things, she seemed at peace with herself. ("This afternoon, I came home as your mother was bundling up to leave the house. It's Sunday. The shop is closed. I asked her where she was going and she shrugged. 'For a walk,' she said. 'There's nothing more I can do.'")

Six months after Andrei's departure, the baby was born. Andrei never saw the baby nurse at Ileana's breast. He never saw him roll or crawl, toddle or walk. Ileana got her independence. She was spared the harassments. Because she was bound to a man who had left, because she lived in the home of her fiancé, she was not pressured to marry. It was only a partial freedom, but it was enough. ("I can walk through town with a sense of peace—I'm happy.") It was not the rosy euphoria of maternity, just a feeling that she had found a pocket of air.

Ileana carried the baby in a sling fashioned from a folded bedsheet. When people called Andrei a deserter, she never uttered a word against him. She worked in the tailor shop during the day and she played her guitar at night. Between these activities, Ileana dedicated herself to making her son, Mihai, feel wanted. And he was. For Andrei's mother, the baby was an unanticipated gift. She bathed him, wrapped him in pieces of clean old cloth and treasured his newness, believing that some ancient dimension of the family she had lost might endure through him.

According to Ileana, the baby had black hair, twiggy legs and skinny fingers that looked exactly like Andrei's.

I REMEMBER WHEN ANDREI relayed this information to me in the fall. There was a mixture of pride and something else, yearning perhaps, in his voice. It took me by surprise because I had never seen him in a paternal light. It is only now that I wonder if the baby's birth—the result of a pragmatic sperm donorship—and Ileana's reports on their son's progress had a more significant effect on Andrei than he let on. Did he want something more than a commitment-free fatherhood? Did he long to meet his son enough to be pulled back to Romania?

The other night I watched a man and his son as I was riding the bus home from Sakura. The bus was almost empty and they were sitting in a row near the front, sharing earphones, listening to music on a Walkman. I watched, studying the shape of the man's head, observing how his hair curled over his jacket collar just like Andrei's. A few minutes passed and I noticed the young child remove his earphones and lift his face, then ask a question. Still gazing ahead, the man nodded. The child asked another question, and at this point the man leaned toward him and began slowly and tenderly stroking his hair. I could not keep my eyes off them.

After a few more blocks the man reached up and pulled the yellow cord, signalling a stop request to the driver. When the bus stopped, they stood up, shuffled into the aisle and made their way toward the front exit. I pressed my forehead to the window and continued watching them get off, my warm breath fogging the glass.

Long after they had disappeared from view, the idea that the man and the child were somehow linked to Andrei and his son stayed with me: a notion that I had been given a message about Andrei's existence and fate. As the bus continued its course toward the station, images began to form in my mind. A young boy having his hair combed by his mother. An older woman chopping vegetables from the garden at the table. A cooking pot full of soup steaming on the stove.

And then another image: an early winter afternoon, the clouds advancing unhurriedly in the sky, a man's shadow moving at long last up a winding dirt road between two fields. As he passes a small dairy farm, he recalls the unevenly tilted shoulders of the woman who sells milk; the ducklike waddle of the woman's brother, the town's postman. In the distance he sees a house with light yellow trim and large arched windows. A small face above a flower box.

THE SUMMER OF 1984, when Andrei arrived in Toronto, everyone was watching the Summer Olympics in Los Angeles on TV. The Soviets had boycotted the games, ordering all of their satellite states to do the same. Romania openly defied Moscow, becoming the only Warsaw Pact country to send their athletes to the games. In the absence of the Soviet competitors, an eighteen-year-old Romanian gymnast by the name of Kati Szabó rose to the top, winning four gold medals.

On the day of the final competition, Andrei ventured a few blocks from the settlement house to a Portuguese coffee bar called Milky Rose. He had noticed the television mounted above the bar and walked in. The gymnasts on the screen wore white leotards with red, gold and blue stripes running down the sides. They had matching ribbons in their hair and delicate-boned limbs. From the back of the bar came the harsh *clacking* of dominoes hitting a table.

The refrigerator cool of the place was a sharp contrast to the humidity outside. At the front table sat two middle-aged men in construction clothes, both staring at the mute television. Beside them sat a younger man reading a newspaper, taking short slugs of Coke from a bottle. Andrei made his way to the counter and ordered a sandwich and a latte from a man with thick grey hair. As the man steamed some milk, he turned his head toward Andrei.

"My son goes nuts over the track-and-field competitions. He's a runner. It's all he cares about." He poured the espresso and steamed milk into a glass and set it down in front of Andrei.

Andrei dropped two sugar cubes into the coffee and stirred, then leaned his elbows on the bar. In the corner, a man was punching the pay phone to try to get his quarter back.

"Hey, strongman. Ease up," the man at the counter shouted.

"Yeah, yeah, Manuel. All right."

A storm was hatching and the sky darkened. Cyclists and mothers with plastic-covered strollers hurried by the window. There was a crack of thunder. Manuel turned on the overhead lights, which pulsed a discontinuous and irregular tempo. Outside, the rain became lavish. Inside, the gymnasts twirled soundlessly across the screen.

At the end of each routine, Andrei watched the girls huddle with their coaches as the scores appeared on the board. He read their bodies. Ecstatic hugs and high-fives, or arms flopped at their sides in disappointment. Tears of triumph or defeat. Girls whose entire equilibrium depended on one thing: winning. He held his breath for them. He thought of asking Manuel to turn up the volume but realized that it didn't matter. Their movements were synchronized to the sound of the cappuccino machine. Hums and groans. Sudden blasts of air. The loud *thith* of milk being frothed.

"Your country?" Manuel asked, pointing at the Romanian leotards.

Andrei nodded, spinning slowly on the vinyl stool. Manuel turned off the cappuccino machine, a gesture of respect. He reached up to the television set and jacked up the volume.

Manuel walked around to the other side of the bar, a can of ginger ale in hand. He sat down beside Andrei. Together they watched one of the most dramatic duels in modern Olympic history: Szabó going head to head with a pixieish Mary Lou Retton for the all-around title.

Andrei wasn't a heavy smoker, but that afternoon he lit up one cigarette after another. Manuel let out a small gasp when Szabó missed a relatively simple turn on the high bar and tumbled to the floor. Looking genuinely tense, he went around to the fridge and brought back two bottles of beer. He popped the caps, slid one bottle over to Andrei.

The final vault portion of the competition lasted a nail-biting thirty seconds. All the men in the Milky Rose had risen from their seats and were now sitting along the edge of the Formica bar, eyes fixed to the screen. Retton was still trailing by five one-hundredths of a point. She needed another 10 in the vault to win. The stadium fell quiet. Retton stepped to the mat, eyes centred on the pommel horse, and began her run. She smacked the horse with both hands, twirling over it and sticking her landing—feet hitting the floor and staying there. She knew right away, and stretched her arms in victory.

Andrei grimaced in disappointment, slapping the counter with his hand, surprised that it mattered, surprised at the primal connection to Romania he felt at that moment.

Sarah was also watching the Olympics on an old black-and-white television screen, along with Eli and Ileana. Unlike her son, she was feeling no particular loyalty to her country. What she was focused on were the team uniforms. It was not the colours she studied, because her monitor didn't permit her to see any. What she was studying were the insignias—all the crests, the letters and patterns, the shoulder stripes, the stars and the hoops.

A young woman was doing a floor routine. Her featherweight body tumbled past, performing aerial flips, her arms tucked, then extended like bird wings. She flowed with whirling, gleaming energy. It was only when the girl stopped, back arched, arms in the air, that Sarah deciphered the writing on her chest: white letters knocked out of a dark bodysuit spelling CANADA.

Sarah felt an uneasiness. The word had jarred something in her, something unrelated to Andrei. Her brain tried to recall when she had heard it before, in some other context. Then she remembered. The gates of memory opened. Her mind was suddenly filled with images. And they all related to a place called Canada.

She didn't share these memories with Eli or Ileana. Instead, she excused herself and went to her bedroom, where she composed a letter to Andrei, a letter she carried for several weeks, until one day she passed it to a map-toting scholar she encountered outside the town's abandoned church. Following a brief mime of an exchange, the man assured her he would post the letter once he returned to Cambridge, England.

The letter arrived two weeks later. After that, Andrei could never see the word CANADA without thinking about it.

Twenty

One morning close to Christmas, a particularly depressing note arrived at my desk from a mother in Kamloops, British Columbia, who was "frantically anxious" to trace a family heirloom, a "modest" jade pendant necklace she had sent as a reconciliation gift to her estranged daughter in Boston. The handwriting was barely decipherable in parts. One could see from the shaky lines and clots of ink that she was old and possibly suffering from mild Parkinson's. She divulged in the letter that her husband had recently died and her daughter, who had run away from home at an early age, was now her only living kin.

Her daughter would "surely have sent a letter or note" to her "ailing mother" if the gift had been securely delivered. Perhaps the present had "burst open" along the way, in which case would we kindly search for the lost necklace, which had originally come all the way from Singapore?

Feeling low in spirits, I reached my hand deep in the box labelled JEWELLERY and confirmed what I already suspected. No necklace. I refolded the letter and placed it in a folder of correspondence to be answered later. I wondered how many mothers, at that very moment, were writing letters of appeal to their disaffected children.

Warren didn't come to work the next day. He was already on his way to Sudbury to visit his family. The rest of us finished up at noon to allow everyone time to join their relatives. I spent the morning sorting through holiday greeting portraits.

I picked out the glamour shots. There were a half dozen of these portrait studio creations. I lined them up side by side on my desk. The women all bore a certain similarity. Salon-swept hair, unnaturally tilted heads. The soft-focus lens had melted away any worry lines and blemishes. In one shot, a woman gazed wistfully off into the distance, holding a rose to her cheek. A few had fantasy backdrops—palm trees in an orange haze, a star-speckled night sky. These images were both baffling and fascinating to me. The women they showed were not evidently wealthy. (The rich did not require cardboard-framed testaments to their glamour. The rich exercised a sort of blithe informality by wearing Lacoste shirts and chinos in their Christmas portraits.) Who knew what these women really spent their lives doing? From the notes attached, I saw that several of the portraits were directed overseas, to the Philippines, Colombia, Portugal.

Making use of my rudimentary Spanish, I discerned that two of the notes contained elements typical of letters from recent immigrants and migrant workers. A chronicle of status symbols of a "better" life (newly acquired televisions, appliances, suitors, friends), these letters aggrandized so as to settle any worries and doubts back home. Seen in this light, the glamour photos felt valiant, like pictorial embellishments, wishful more than boastful, gracious more than vain.

Paolo was working until 6 p.m., so when the mail office closed at noon, I decided to head over to Sakura for a visit. I picked up a coffee on the way, to perk up, and found myself in a mall full of desperate and impatient shoppers. Sweating in my coat, I watched men hovering furtively in the lingerie store, picking through complicated lace undergarments; women plucking stocking stuffers from bins and elbowing their way to the front of the checkout counter. Even the utilitarian shops—the shoesmith and the vitamin supplements stand—seemed to beg for a last-minute seasonal purchase. I bought a pack of cinnamon gum and a small notepad at the drugstore and continued on my way.

When I arrived at Sakura, the residents were clustered around the television eating pieces of cake with toothpicks. A sugared satisfaction could be seen on their faces. But my mother's face was not among them. I assumed that she was in her room, and took a moment to sit with Gloria, who was off to the side in a wheelchair, holding an untouched plate of cake on her lap. Her grey hair was newly cropped. I was shocked by her gauntness, by how much she seemed to have dwindled in only a few weeks, but I was careful not to let it show on my face. I kissed her on the cheek and promised myself that next time I would bring her some thread or wool, something to embroider or knit, something to occupy her fingers. A substitute for the quilt, now that it was completed. She needed busy hands to work away the worries in her head.

Just as I was about to leave, I remembered the notepad in my bag and pulled it out. I removed the plate of cake from her lap and set it on the table.

"Here, Gloria." I handed her the notepad along with a pen. "I thought you might like this."

As I walked toward the elevator, I stumbled into Roy Ishii. He was wearing a green sweatshirt and short red scarf, which he had attempted to toss over one shoulder.

"It's beautiful, isn't it?" He stopped at the window, rested a hand against the glass, pointed at the slow-falling snow.

"Yes."

"The barometer is rising. There's a warm front coming in from the Gulf of Mexico."

"Sounds promising."

"Are you going to see your mum?"

I nodded and he dug into his pocket. "Here. Give her this from me."

He handed me a roll of butterscotch candy and ambled away, his mouth pursed into a whistle—a pretty slip of a melody lingering in my ears. Through the window, I could see that the snowflakes were melting before they amassed, disappearing on the branches, sliding off the cars in the lot. I watched Roy as he made his way down the hall, then rounded the corner to the common area. How perfectly the basic criteria of weather paralleled the highs and lows of daily existence. There could be overnight changes, spectacular shifts in clouds and air currents, sudden movements from murk to brilliance.

Sakura, however, bore no real notion of seasons or time. The same controlled temperature existed all year around. It could be July or February, it always felt the same.

The rooms were small, but each was bravely decorated with keepsakes and personal photographs—modest or elaborate attempts to individualize that helped stave off the air of institutional uniformity and provided a buttress for those with memory impairments. The paintings that lined the corridors were bold and bright: realistic portrayals of nature and animals—a dog springing through a meadow of flowers, an apple orchard—spaced at regular intervals to encourage movement. Easy to look at, nothing abstract or geometric or patterned all over; nothing to swallow up the mind. The wide, well-lit hallways, designed as a circular walking path, led to carefully spaced sitting areas. Those with wandering tendencies could shuffle from one site of comfort to another. They would never experience the frustration of a dead end; their self-esteem was boosted by the fact that every pathway had an achievable destination.

A framed photo of my mother as a young woman hung on her door. It was a memory aid recommended by the in-house therapist. We had selected it together, she and I, from a slew of images, knowing in the back of our minds that we had chosen a picture that separated us, or rather, eliminated me. It captured her life before I was born.

Every time I stepped up to that photograph I was reminded of our differences. At my age, my mother had lustrous black hair and pert little breasts that created tiny tents in the front of her sleeveless mock turtleneck. She wore white hip-hugging slacks and, looped on her arm, right below the crease of her elbow, she carried a small half-moon purse. Her hair was cut in an immaculate bob, perfectly rounded ends creating a Cleopatra silhouette. A razor tidied up the neckline. She wore sleek leather pumps that gave her blisters and eventually bunions. She was beautiful.

What happened to that purse? How many had she owned in her lifetime?

I thought of all those old purses, filled to the top with personal matter (lipsticks, tissue packs, metal compacts), satin linings stained with ink and powder so embedded it could not be shaken out. With each new purse, she took what pleased her from the old one and left the rest: a fresh start, a chance to reorganize life until the jumble began again.

I tapped on the open door and entered slowly. My mother was sitting in a chair in her housecoat, opening and closing the snap of her latest purse, an item for which she showed almost unlimited love. This one was soft black leather and had lots of compartments, some with zippers. Watching her, I felt as if an entire day could pass in the emptying, sorting and filling of the purse. Some days it was as flat as an envelope, other days its contours bulged until the seams strained to the point of popping. Today, the purse was flat.

One thing had remained consistent since my childhood: she was the only one allowed to rummage inside. Everything else was up for grabs, but her purse—that was hers; something never to be surrendered to curious, acquisitive kin. It was a pathetic container for something as uncontainable as a life, but for my mother, a purse was a palace.

Her hair was tied back in a loose ponytail, and from its limpness I could see that it hadn't been washed for several days. She looked up as I approached. Her face softened in recognition. I breathed a small sigh of relief. I was still on the side of the remembered.

Snap. She closed the purse.

"Naiko," she said. "*Kochira oide.* Come closer. I have something important to ask you." She wriggled her feet into a pair of sage green slippers. I walked toward her and sat down on the bed.

What she said next was disconcerting.

"Cremated?" I repeated. Part whisper, part choke.

"Yes. I think that's what I'd prefer."

"Okay. But do we need to have this conversation right now? It's a bit early, no? I mean, you're not dying or anything."

"Of course, there's time. But I've been thinking."

"Yes?"

"Will you keep me?"

"What do you mean 'keep you'?"

"The urn. My ashes. I don't think I want to be tossed all over the place. And, frankly, I'm not sure that Kana would want the responsibility."

Flustered, I tried to compose an appropriate reply, but my mother had trailed off and was now talking about something else. A banquet dinner. A seasonal talent show. Holiday activities skilfully organized to prevent the residents from feeling alone. As I watched my mother twirl the strap of her purse, I fell into my own solitude. A few seconds passed.

I tried to conceal my dejection by offering to cut her hair. She refused at first. I told her that we could dye it, and that she could save the bits of hair we cut. In the end she agreed.

"The ends are dry anyway," she said.

A few of the women on my mother's floor had perms. Mary Kawamata's hair was so overprocessed you could see the light shine through it. It looked like candy floss, sitting lightly on her head as if it was not joined to her scalp. Mary spent her days drawing rotting fruit and vegetables. *Nature morte*, she called it. Most mornings, her eyebrows were plucked and powdered away and replaced with carefully pencilled arches. My mother avoided the Asian "afro." Her one chemical concession was hair dye: every few weeks, I helped her comb her white roots with black Clairol.

"Let's run a bath," I said after I had finished cutting her hair in the bathroom. My voice bounced off the tiles.

As the bath filled, a lavender mist invaded the room. The mirror clouded. My mother's hair was piled up in a towel. Hair bits stuck to her moist neck.

I waited for her in her room while she made her way through jars of face and body cream. Today, her room was a store of bright and beautiful things: colourful spools of thread lined on a shelf, bottle caps in a Mason jar, necklaces on a small wooden rack. Things in their proper place.

My mother was still in the bathroom when Setsuko arrived with the afternoon mail. Setsuko was a visiting student from Japan who hid her feet in heavy walking shoes. She wore sparkly blue eyeshadow, pink lipstick and an alpine ski hat. The residents depended on her. Between twelve o'clock and four o'clock there were other people and activities they depended on, but at four-thirty, they relied on the girl with the hat.

"Ayumi-san? Ayumi-san?" Setsuko peeked into the room, steadying a basket of letters in her arms. "*Ara*. Naiko-san. *Konichiwa*. I have something for your mother." She *clip-clopped* into the room.

My mother bolted out of the bathroom and snatched a postcard from Setsuko's hands. I smiled apologetically. My mother had lost her sense of courtesy—she no longer insisted that someone else take the most comfortable seat or the largest portion.

She studied the postcard with a knobby, arthritic finger, then held it to her chest like some hard-won prize.

"It's from my daughter," she announced to Setsuko. Then added for clarity, "The other one." Setsuko nodded politely, backing toward the door. "*Asoko*," my mother said, and pointed at a photograph on her dresser. *There she is*, as if Kana were actually present in the frame, living behind a bevelled cardboard mat. (Trust Kana to send a promotional photograph of herself.)

When my mother had finished poring over the card, she handed it to me to read. Postmarked from Prague, it had haste and artificial cheer written all over it. This pathetic little token, with its loopy, over-large script, filled me with spite. I wanted to rip it up and stomp on the pieces. At that moment, I hated Kana—for cheating, for always taking the shortcut. And yet my mother responded like a cat being fed, almost purring, virtually swishing her tail with delight.

My mother's hair was drying in waves. She looked wild and alert. Some glimmer in her at that moment moved me to tell her about Andrei's disappearance.

"You mean you've lost him?"

I immediately regretted mentioning it. "Yes. Well, no. Not exactly 'lost him.'"

"There was no note? No phone call?"

I shook my head. "He's disappeared before, but never like this—Hey, don't look so upset, Mum." I pulled out a chair and pointed for her to sit down. "Listen, I don't want you to take this on. He'll turn up, don't worry."

"Yes. He'll turn up. But if you want, I'd be happy to help you look for him. I mean, I did like him when he came to visit last week."

That was two months ago, I corrected her silently.

"I can help, Nai-chan," she said.

"Thanks, Mum. I'll bear that in mind. Now let's finish drying your hair before you catch a cold."

She sat in front of her dresser while I gently rubbed her head with a towel, my hands moving in small circles from the top to the sides. She smelled of apple shampoo. I glanced at her briefly in the mirror, and she smiled with an expression of sympathetic support. Then a thought seemed to occur to her. Her voice took on a musing quality.

"What about your office?"

"What about it?"

"Have you checked there?"

"Yes."

"Your place?"

"Yes. Mum," I said firmly, "we're talking about a person. Not a set of keys."

She turned away for a moment, perhaps stung by my words or perhaps waylaid in her thoughts by all the keys she had lost over the course of her life—those she'd left in bicycle locks or sitting on restaurant tables.

"You're right. He'll turn up. What's important, Nai-chan—" She paused. "What's important is that you have good, close friends. You should consider yourself fortunate." She smiled.

"Thanks, Mum."

I realized my fingers were still covered in bits of my mother's hair. I rubbed them off on the towel and began paring her nails.

I was halfway down the hallway on my way out when I heard a scream coming from Gloria's room. As I rushed toward the door, I could hear crying.

"G-g-o a-away," Gloria was repeating between sobs.

Two attendants were huddled inside the entrance. Behind them, a nurse was trying to prevent Gloria from thrashing around in her wheelchair. Every time she touched her, Gloria started screaming again.

"What's going on?" I demanded. I noticed a burning smell in the room.

One of the attendants turned around. "She just tried to set fire to her room," he said, pointing at a singed curtain hem. "We're moving her upstairs, where she'll be more secure."

I knew that "upstairs" meant the restricted ward—living under lock and key with full-time attendants.

Recognizing my voice, Gloria looked up, her skin blotchy from crying. The wide neck of her sweater had slid down her arm to reveal a bony shoulder. The nurse took advantage of my arrival to slip a sedative between Gloria's parted lips.

"This will make you feel yourself again," the nurse said, and handed a cup of water to Gloria, who, in her distraction, dutifully swallowed.

"May I come in and be with her for a moment?" I asked.

The nurse nodded and stepped back toward the window. The attendants moved aside, allowing me to pass.

I crouched by Gloria, lifted her sweater back on to her shoulder and held her shaking hands.

"They're sending me away," she whimpered.

"No, Gloria, not away, just upstairs."

Her fingers curled around mine. Her breathing was becoming more even and regular. She glanced at the nurse and attendants, then lowered her head toward mine. "I'm going to take notes," she whispered, looking down at the notepad I had given her, which was tucked beside her right thigh. "Just like you told me to do."

I studied her face—the sedative was starting to work, her eyes were becoming soft and less focused. They said, *nothing matters.*

"That's right," I whispered back. "Write it all down."

I returned to my mother's room feeling shaken, to see if she was all right. I was worried that she might have overheard the screaming down the hall. The door was slightly ajar, but when I peeked in, she seemed fine, obliviously wrapping a small mirror in a handkerchief. It was only after I sat down beside her on the bed that I noticed the clenching in her jaw.

She rested the mirror in her lap and turned to me.

"Naiko, suppose I wanted to leave here one day—could I?"

"Yes," I replied without hesitation.

She tilted her head, lifted her shoulder to her cheek almost bashfully, then relaxed her shoulder and said, "Good."

When I left Sakura that afternoon at five o'clock it was with relief that my mother was continuing her sorting. My visits interrupt her, but the minute I am out the door, her fingers begin roaming. She is in a state of constant bonding and rediscovery, experiencing her world of possessions as a bottomless source of curiosity. On any given evening, some item begging her attention may distract her even from her dinner. Several times she will fail to hear her name being called to the dining room, her entire being focused on the burgundy lining of a wallet, the sleek curve of a shoehorn, the smooth-running drawer of a night table.

Wet snow was dumping down. I boarded the bus for home, glad for the warmth, and untied the soggy scarf around my neck. I sat toward the back, watching the slush slip down the oily windows, feeling a thread of cold air coming through a gap in the glass. A man with a grey beard was reflected in the window ahead of me. I removed my gloves and folded them into my pocket. The bus went up a hill and stopped. A teenage girl boarded, carrying several bags of takeout chicken. She shuffled down the aisle toward me, blue eyes peering, and stood over my knapsack until I moved it and let her plop her dinner onto the seat. My stomach growled at the smell of grease and spice.

When we arrived at the subway station, I joined a crush of people waiting on the concrete platform for the southbound bus. A man crouched against a pillar was selling individual roses from a white plastic bucket. The illuminated poster above his head advertised a romantic beach vacation to Mexico with a company called Carousel. The woman in front of me was reading Matthew 25:40 in her leather-bound Bible.

Soon people were rushing past me. I studied their faces, looking for Andrei among the younger men walking toward me. A tall man with a wool coat and fur earmuffs, a shorter man with owlish eyes peeking out from a down hooded jacket . . . I was momentarily distracted by a boy waving his arms excitedly at a woman stepping off the escalator behind me. The ear flaps of his hat bounced up and down as he ran to her. I turned to watch them, and when I turned back, the platform was densely packed. I tucked my chin into the cowl of my black sweater to ward off the wind. Just then the bus pulled up, the windshield wipers swooshing across the window.

At home, a small stack of mail was waiting. I had been hoping for several months for a thin grey envelope addressed to me—the kind my father used—but no envelope had arrived. When I turned sixteen, my father had sent me the first of his grey envelopes. Inside was a birthday cheque and a letter telling me to *find something you love doing so much that it becomes your bedrock*. (Naturally, a geography metaphor. The subtext: You can't count on human relationships.) It was close to a year since I had last seen my father, so I counted on these letters to stay connected. Instead, I found a heating bill, Christmas cards and another postcard from Kana. This one was a shot of Wenceslas Square in the centre of Prague. An imposing equestrian statue stood in front of a bulky dome-capped building. The message was short.

> N: *Election in less that two weeks! I will file my story as soon as the results are in. Hope to be home soon! Kana. P.S. The rest of the team is off to Romania to cover the unrest there. The harassment of a dissident Hungarian priest in Timisoara has touched off mass protests. The whole region is on fire!!!*

The windows were all closed, but my limbs felt as though an icy draft had suddenly entered the room. I thought about what Kana had once said to me about keeping on top of world events. A postscript she had sent from Libya . . . or was it Lebanon? *P.S. We are witnesses to the march of history!* or some such grandiose declaration. I had never felt so cut off as when I read those words. World affairs always seemed inflated when communicated by my self-important sister.

This was not her world. Nor her history.

I called Paolo just as he was leaving work and asked him to pick up an evening edition on his way over. He arrived with three newspapers, by which time I was already planted in front of the television watching the news.

The report on Romania was both vivid and unreal to me. I tried to concentrate on the reporter's words.

The Central Post Office has been occupied.

The television and radio stations are in the hands of the rebels.

There has been a coup.

But it was the images that stunned me. I realized that I had never before seen a picture of Andrei's country. I had never heard the sounds of Romania. Everything looked so distinctly un-Canadian. The bloated square buildings and oversized streets, the faces of the people, the grey forests of construction equipment, everything so drab.

The footage was perhaps a day old, and what it showed was undeniable: the breakdown of command, the collapse of tyranny.

Twenty-one

$\mathcal{A}$ massive crowd is gathered beneath the low balcony of the Central Committee Building in Bucharest. The dictator in a fur hat is reading from a prepared speech when suddenly, a few minutes into his address, a single shout of "Ti-mi-soara! Murderer!" rises from the back of the crowd, followed by several boos.

The dictator falters, surprise and uncertainty passing across his face. Urged on by his wife, he attempts to continue his speech. Again there are shouts and more boos. Realizing his hold on the crowd is lost, he stops again and begins to wave. Confusion spreads on the balcony while the dictator and his wife, who are still being filmed, consult with their attendants and several members of the Political Executive Council about what to do next. Finally, they are ushered inside the palace. The camera is switched off.

Three minutes later, the broadcast resumes to prerecorded cheers and applause. Visibly shaken, the dictator has returned to the balcony to finish his speech. This time the crowd bursts into jeers and whistles. No longer cowed, it chants: *Down with Ceausescu!* As the shouting rises, the image shakes and distorts. The screen becomes a field of red.

The recorded picture again returns, revealing the sky toward which the cameraman has aimed his camera, as he has been told to do should anything disturb the demonstration. There are intermittent images of the dictator calling for calm. At one point the camera moves away from the balcony and sweeps across the crowd to locate the source of the disruption. Then, training remembered, the cameraman swings back to the balcony. By this point, the dictator and his wife are gone.

Books and papers are spilling out of buildings. Students are fighting with riot police in armoured vests. Cars are overturned. Images of the dictator are burning in the streets. Tear gas has been fired into the Piata Universitatii, where more demonstrators increasingly gather, ignoring the presence of guns and tanks.

Throughout the night, police, Securitate and the army sporadically fire on the crowds, but the people return in even greater numbers the next morning. But the most stunning image comes from outside the University of Bucharest, where students, sitting on each other's shoulders, are hanging paper cut-outs of pears on the poplar trees. For the dictator this is a symbol of impossibility.

The image expresses to the world that reform is coming.

Everyone with a television watched the news that night but noticed different details.

I noticed the way Elena Ceausescu held her hands: first resting them confidently on the balcony, then pulling them back, holding them against her diaphragm in a tight clasp. The more the crowd jeered, the more ordinary she appeared. Like a woman waiting for a bus.

Roy Ishii noticed the light jackets and open coats worn by the crowd. He deduced from their apparel that it was an unseasonably mild day, with a springlike temperature unusual for December. And he was right.

My mother noticed a man in the crowd with long silvery hair who reminded her of someone she once knew—a painter she had dated many years before.

Kana noticed acutely that her coverage of the presidential elections in Czechoslovakia had been supplanted.

Paolo noticed a trampled evergreen medallion off to the side on the square, a low-growing topiary portrait of Ceausescu above the words THE EPOCH OF LIGHT.

But all of us noticed them flee—the dictator in a black hat, his wife trailing after, running along the roof of the Central Committee Building toward a helicopter.

He and She. Each carried a bag.

The minute I spotted them I wondered what these bags contained. Were they laden with booty from the palace? Did they contain their most cherished items? Or simply the most expensive? It was hard to fathom. What would have meant most to them, when they had held—seized—whatever they had wished?

Paolo and I watched the television screen that weekend until our eyes hurt. At about eleven o'clock on Christmas Eve, long after the news reports had ended, we pulled out the couch and smoked a bit of pot. Neither of us had the energy to do anything after that, so Paolo flipped between *The Sound of Music* and *Miracle on 34th Street*. I didn't really pay attention to either one. We had strung up coloured Christmas lights, and they flickered by the window, breaking the dark with a flashing rhythm. I watched them for a while, feeling a brief dope-induced swell of empathy for the weakest light, but mostly my mind just floated.

I kept seeing the wince on Ceausescu's face when the crowd started booing, when he experienced exactly what so many of his subjects had—the flinching of the victim waiting to be hit.

I heard Maria, the cheerful governess, singing about raindrops on roses. When I looked at the TV screen, she was flitting around her bedroom, praising the virtues of those simple delights that helped make her life so gallingly effervescent. What were my favourite things?

It occurred to me at that moment that I owned seven black turtlenecks.

The last thing I remember before drifting off around two (Paolo already asleep beside me) was the nuns alerting the von Trapp family to flee the abbey, as the Nazis were approaching.

On Christmas Day I woke up at half past six to hear the thump of a tree branch hitting the living-room window. It was still dark and the Christmas lights were flashing ominously. I had a premonition at that instant that something had happened. Maybe a vase had broken in my mother's room, triangles of phthalo green crockery littering the floor. Maybe Gloria had escaped again. There was a perceptible change in the air, the sort of fluctuation in pressure that precedes a thunderstorm. My skin was tingling.

I held my breath and waited. Nothing happened. I looked over and saw that Paolo was still sleeping, curled up on his side. His bare torso was exposed, and I saw the undulation of ribs under his skin, dark oblong nipples at either side of a small patch of hair. He looked beautiful. It brought me a moment's sadness to see him so far away in sleep.

The television was on, though Paolo had risen at some point and turned down the volume. I stayed on the bed for a while longer. The refrigerator buzzed. The clock ticked. I lay there and waited, but the sense of foreboding wouldn't go away. Finally, stretching out my hands, I leaned over and groped along the floor for the television converter, changed the channel and turned up the volume. The headline news told me Ceausescu had been executed.

All my possessions for a moment in time.

Queen Elizabeth I on her deathbed in 1603

Part Four

CEAUSESCU'S THINGS

A small moon rock (gift of President Nixon)

A 1975 Buick limousine (also from Nixon)

A 1974 Hillman (gift of the Shah of Iran)

Sequined slippers (gift of President Mobutu of Zaire)

A desk clock (gift of Soviet leader Brezhnev)

Mother-of-pearl pen set (gift of Philippine president Marcos)

A yacht (gift of King Hussein of Jordan)

25 marble and gold-plated mansions

1,000 bottles of wine, champagne and cognac

113 taxidermic animals

2 Goya etchings (possibly from *Los Caprichos* series)

A silver replica of Pakistan's Lahore Palace

Peruvian ceremonial daggers

A painting of peasants mowing

A wooden chess set (gift of Russian chess champion Anatoly
   Karpov)

9,000 suits (one for every day of his almost quarter-century rule)

Twenty-two

It was Boxing Day. My mother was staying with me for two nights and we had spent most of her visit so far on the couch, our gaze riveted to the television set. Our unwrapped Christmas presents were piled in a corner. My mother never stopped playing with her purse. *Click-click-click* went the large magnetic snap. Paolo made runs to the kitchen to fix us plates of leftover turkey. Without openly stating it, those close to me understood that my friendship with Andrei connected Romania to all of us. Even my mother seemed to accept my silent concentration.

A student outside the Intercontinental Hotel in Bucharest was talking to the camera. The building behind him was riddled with bullet holes. "The dictator wanted us to bury our dreams," said the student. "That's never possible."

Every now and then my mother would point her finger at the screen and say, "Is that . . . ?" or "I think . . ."

Her theory was that since Communism had forced Andrei to leave Romania, he had been drawn back home once it was clear that Communism was collapsing. There was something in the way she said "Communism is collapsing" that made me picture the Wicked Witch of the West dissolving into a steaming puddle.

For my mother, Communism meant only one thing, the loss of property, and so revolt was the only possible solution. "We forget how lucky we are," she said. "Just imagine." She shuddered. *Click-click.* The contents of her purse were now spread out on the coffee table in front of her: three hair combs, medicated eyedrops, and a sandwich bag containing store receipts and what looked to be her gold wedding band.

I petted Miko. He purred loudly, then curled up in my lap and went to sleep, his face buried under his paw.

At 6 p.m., when the news began, Paolo raised the TV volume. On the screen we saw a montage of the day's events, combined with flashback shots: a sea of people flowing into the centre of Bucharest, hundreds of candles burning in the snow at the martyr's shrine, demonstrators sitting on tanks waving tricolour flags alongside rebel soldiers, and the now iconic image of the Ceausescus' bullet-ridden corpses. Queen Elizabeth had repealed an honorary knighthood she had conferred on Ceausescu a few years earlier. Foreign statesmen who had once travelled with Ceausescu by motorcade were now referring to him as a despot. For so long, the outside world had chosen to see Romania as a semi-free Soviet satellite. Suddenly the true face of tyranny was revealed.

We had heard from Kana in Prague earlier that day about growing suspicions that the Romanian revolution was not a revolution at all but a *coup d'état*, that the events had been staged by Party insiders who were waiting to install another Communist junta. That seemed like big news, and we kept waiting for it to be mentioned on the television—but not a word was said.

What we saw instead was a segment about the arrival of imported goods in Bucharest on Christmas Day. The segment began at Otopeni airport, where a small group of people had been camping out on the Tarmac. One woman was lying on her back, staring at the sky. She was bundled in blankets, ashen-faced from exhaustion. A man was huddled with a young boy under a patched tent. Like members of the resistance, they had been waiting for three days for an airlift bounty of glistening American goods. They had imagined it so often, and now it was their turn: America's intoxicating promise of material deliverance!

The planes never arrived.

There was nothing up there but cloud and snow. What arrived instead—and here the story moved to the centre of Bucharest—was a herd of trucks loaded with smaller favours—bottles of beer, cartons of Kent cigarettes, packets of coffee, cans of cola, cheap consumables. Against the grey riot-torn streets, the colours alone—streaks of red, white, bright blue, yellow—were electric, a spree of capitalist opulence.

The goods that arrived next were the promised products, not desperately needed and still-rationed items like bread, sugar, meat and petrol, but pleasure items. Imported drugstore cosmetics, digital watches and transistor radios. Inexpensive, usable rubble. I sorted through this kind of stuff every day.

Next came the religious tracts. Operation Grace: one hundred thousand Bibles and thirteen million gospel pamphlets distributed to "needy families" to help "sweeten the bitterness."

The Western cameras couldn't get enough of it: the kids running around as if it was Christmas (which it was); the driver tossing handfuls of candy into the air; a teenage girl staring at a photo she had just

been given of a Hollywood actor; a small boy holding a bar of chocolate up to his nose as if it had to be squeezed and sniffed for a while
to be truly believed.

At one point I thought I actually spotted Andrei near a makeshift
retail kiosk. There was something familiar about the way he gripped
the strap of his shoulder bag. But when the camera moved in closer,
I saw I was mistaken. The man's face was waxy and pale, anemic. He
had an untrimmed beard and dirty, matted hair. He looked as though
he had been standing at that corner for centuries. It was certainly not
Andrei.

By 10 p.m., the action in the streets began petering out. The same
footage was being recycled. The news graphic now showed a toppled
statue of the dictator above the title "Transition: After the Revolution."
It was a new chapter. Suddenly the reporters wanted to know about
the future of the country. They were plucking out experts from this
and that university, a slew of scholars with presumably enlightening
things to say.

One man, who was identified somewhat ambiguously as a "soci-
ologist of transition," talked about the fact that Romania was a new
growth market for the home-security industry. "As people start to
acquire more things, they'll want to protect their homes. They'll need
better locks, intercoms, alarms, insurance plans."

Paolo snorted and raised his glass into the air. "Here's to a better
life."

A woman, a psychology professor who had spent time in the Balkans,
talked about the power of the secret police, its system of informers
creating betrayal even among family members. Her eyes were ringed
with dark liner, which gave her a Gothic quality.

"Scarred," she said. "The people are scarred."

"Emotionally scarred," the reporter clarified.

"Deeply, deeply scarred. The bonds of trust were broken and now they must be restored," she continued. Her face became drawn and pensive. "The trappings of terror have gone, but bits of it are still embedded in the collective psyche." She placed her finger on her forehead. "It will take time to rid the Securitate from people's minds."

My mother, who had donned a heavy quilted jacket even though the apartment was warm, was resting her hands in the mouth of her purse. She was concentrating on the faces on the screen.

An expatriate Czech author was asked to comment on "the four lost decades" of Communism. As soon as the reporter asked the question, the writer sneered. He held his pen aloft between his fingertips as if about to throw a poison dart. His other arm was slung over the back of his chair. Behind him a studio screen showed a night view of Bucharest. When he spoke, his voice undulated like a preacher's.

"This period of transition cannot erase everything that happened before. Lost decades!" he scoffed. "To suggest that those years were a black hole is a scandalous negation! No matter how difficult it was, no one wants their past reduced to a zero."

"I see—" said the reporter.

"Yes, you will see," the writer continued. "Give them time and the people will create their own stories about those so-called lost decades: they'll find excuses, they'll find heroes, they'll find answers, they'll even find nostalgia!" And then he began to chuckle, amused at the thought, and the reporter laughed nervously along with him.

That Christmas, the attention of the world was gripped by the collapse of Eastern Europe. The jangling of keys carried by crowds in the streets of Prague, the *tock-tock-tock* of people removing pieces from the Berlin Wall, the resounding boom of gunfire in the streets of Bucharest—a symphony of change.

I wondered if Andrei was part of it.

Twenty-three

When Warren returned to work on the twenty-seventh of December, he came directly over to greet me with a tin of almond florentines that his sister had made. After a few minutes, he moved to his desk and began his morning ritual, adjusting his suspension chair, tinkering with his pens and arranging his ledger, just as Andrei had done when settling in each day. As he busied himself, I continued to stare into space, not yet motivated to commence work. Sensing my distraction, Warren swivelled his chair toward me, his way of saying, *we can talk if you feel like it.* He continued to face me as he shuffled through a stack of packages, silently counting to himself.

When he reached the bottom, he set them aside, glanced at the top one and said, "Is it my imagination, or are we seeing more mail from Eastern Europe lately?"

"I hadn't noticed," I replied.

Warren plucked at a staticky piece of cellophane that was stuck to the surface of his desk. "There'll be a flood of mail within a few weeks. Now that the gates are opening." Then he looked up, a more serious expression on his face. "I assume you've been watching the news?"

I nodded.

He continued. "First a flood of letters, then a flood of people following their letters. Then we'll see how the West feels about the fall of Communism."

The stakes had changed for Western governments and individuals who prided themselves on their broad-mindedness. While the defection of an Olympic gymnast was easy to cheer for, the arrival of masses of asylum-seekers was quite a different test of liberalism.

"Don't be so sure they'll want to leave," I said. "After all they've been through and fought for, they may want to stick around and see how things turn out. Their letters might even be calling their relatives home."

I knew from my years at the mail office that the mail arriving in the early moments of political transition was unpredictable. The first parcels arriving from Argentina, Bolivia, Brazil, Chile and Uruguay, after their dictators fell, had surprised me. Of course some of these ended up in the UMO, their recipients having disappeared into the stream of North American life. How did people express their newborn and uncensored freedom? By sending care packages to their relatives in Canada, it seemed—cardboard boxes sealed with tape and tied with cord.

I had learned from these gifts that satisfying a hunger for North American things was not the only way of expressing freedom. When families "back home" sent packages of goods—bags of sweets, recent photographs, bolts of brightly patterned fabric, bars of soap—it was their way of regaining their dignity. They were reversing the flow of giving. After years of repression and hardship, generosity was liberty.

Paolo and I went for a long walk that night after work. We ended up at a pub toward 8 p.m. It was right next to a store called Liquidation World. The pub sign was an imitation tin plaque, dark green letters embossed against a mustard-yellow background. The interior was a mixture of old and new. Old in style: cozy nooks, a fireplace next to a massive handcrafted bar. New in attitude: electronic music, a complicated fusion menu. We sat in a cushioned booth by a window overlooking the parking lot.

Paolo ordered a beer for himself and a glass of wine for me and said, "So?"

"I've never noticed this place before," I said.

"You mentioned when we were walking that you wanted to tell me something about Andrei."

"Yes." I rolled up my napkin tightly on the table and watched it slowly uncurl.

In the past, every time I had reached this part of Andrei's story, I felt in my mind as though I were standing on a bridge over a dark pit. For months I had believed—somehow needed to believe—that Nicolae and Andrei had a perfect relationship, one that would have survived all adversity.

Was it possible for a person to be open and closed at the same time? I was realizing that though Andrei had shared many things about himself, there had been other aspects he hid, that perhaps he couldn't admit even to himself.

"I'm not sure but sometimes I wonder . . ."

"What, Naiko?" Paolo said. "What do you wonder?"

IT WAS A HOT afternoon in late spring, a few weeks before their defection. Andrei was leaning against the sloped riverbank. Nicolae was squatting a few metres away, building a pagoda of rocks and stones. The sun was so harsh and bright that a row of gulls had retreated to a sliver of shadow near a jutting tree trunk, yellow eyes scanning the water for food.

"I should head home soon," Andrei announced, shielding his eyes from the brightness.

Nicolae looked up. "Already? But it's hardly been an hour. Can't you stay a bit longer?"

"I need shade. This heat makes me dizzy." He pulled the fabric of his shirt away from him and began flapping it to create a breeze.

"Go find a place up there," Nicolae said, indicating a hill. "I'll join you in a minute."

Andrei trudged up and found a shady spot under a tree. He lay down and closed his eyes. He was drifting into sleep when he heard a loud splash. Then another. And another. Andrei opened his eyes. Nicolae was lobbing rocks into the water.

But Andrei also saw what seemed to be a cloudburst of wings beating in distress, a score of gulls circling maniacally overhead. He squinted into the sun. Every now and then, one of the birds dived toward the ground. Their cries pierced the air. He sat up and called out to Nicolae, but there was no answer.

He hurried back toward the river to find the source of the commotion. As he approached he saw an injured gull trying to uncurl its head from its torso. There was a gash of blood on its side, and a violent tremor passed from its gullet to its legs. Andrei observed with horror as it made a shuddering attempt at flight, one wing dragging, a blind crash into the sloped riverbank; its beak speared the ground, its body flipped, this way and that, convulsing, its neck twisting from the effort.

"No! Stop," Andrei cried, scrambling toward Nicolae.

Nicolae turned to him, hand still gripping a rock, his whole body flexed and dangerous. He glanced at Andrei's frightened expression with amusement and started to laugh.

Andrei grabbed Nicolae firmly by the shoulders. "Stop." He pointed at the bird as it gave a final twitch and died.

Nicolae paused, then pitched the rock into the river.

"What's wrong with you?" Andrei hissed.

"It's just a stupid bird. It was an accident." The stony expression on Nicolae's face was unbearable to Andrei.

The water now flowed placidly, unruffled in the still air. Beside them the bird lay dead. The circle overhead had widened and the cries were fading.

Andrei felt uncertain now. He had been horrified, but had he over-reacted? He touched Nicolae on the shoulder, a tentative caress. He felt Nicolae stiffen, removed his hand.

"I'd better get going," Andrei said.

He was turning to leave when Nicolae's voice pleaded, "No—don't go. I didn't mean it." His face crumpled. In a second, they were in each other's arms. "Oh, Andrei, I can't explain it," he whispered, tears on his cheeks. "That wasn't me."

"Don't think about it anymore," Andrei said.

But as Andrei held Nicolae, something inside him grew numb.

"Are you all right?" Nicolae asked on the walk back through the woods.

"Yes. Just tired," Andrei replied.

"I'm sorry about what happened," Nicolae said, and reached for Andrei's hand just as they arrived at the edge of the woods.

Andrei pulled his hand away and glanced nervously around. "Not here. Have you lost your mind?" he whispered in irritation.

They walked on together in silence.

Andrei was superstitious. The dead bird haunted him. He believed it was unlucky to have a fight so close to their departure. He worried that they were cursed after the incident.

Ten days after the episode with the seagull, Andrei and Nicolae left Romania by car. The journey to Cernavoda took two days. Most of it was spent in silence, but they found ways of explaining it, ways of bearing it.

They'd need their energy, Andrei said, for the effort ahead.

Nicolae, hunched in the car seat, said he was nervous. "My stomach won't stop jumping."

Andrei told him to close his eyes and try to relax. "Once you're in the water, remember not to thrash. Pace yourself, let the waves carry you whenever you can."

Their final embrace took place on the deck of the ship, under a suspended, canvas-covered lifeboat.

Andrei blew up a plastic bag containing a few keepsakes so that it would float during the swim. He tied a tight knot at the top of the bag and attached it to his swimming trunks. The plastic pouch containing his birth certificate and several photographs was taped to his thigh. They had planned the entry carefully. Nicolae had wrapped a long rope around the ballast. He would lower himself first, holding on to the rope, pushing away from the ship so as not to get caught in the propeller. Andrei would count thirty seconds, then follow. Their plan was to swim parallel to the freighter until it was some distance away and then call to each other.

Nicolae wore a snorkelling mask. Andrei wore marine goggles.

In the water, Andrei set out steadily, beginning with front crawl and changing to a side stroke that made it easier to avoid the water cresting from the ship. Once the ship had passed, he listened for the soft splashing that would help him locate Nicolae. Hearing it, he called out. Nothing. He shouted louder, but there was no reply.

After a few more tries, Andrei gave up, assuming that Nicolae was out of earshot. He began to swim at a slower pace, trying to contain his worries. An hour or so passed, and he stopped swimming and lifted his head high above the surface. He treaded water and called out to Nicolae again, feeling his precious store of energy draining away with each new effort. He heard splashing, but it could have been the waves or the wake of some ship. He thought he heard Nicolae shouting quite near to him in the darkness, but it might have been the blood pounding in his ears. He continued with a sluggish breaststroke and began praying for morning light to come.

At roughly one and a half hours, already half the time they had expected it to take from ship to land, Andrei abandoned the plastic bag. With a firm tug he ripped it from his swimsuit, relieved to no longer be towing its weight. His father's handkerchief, a pendant belonging to his mother grazed the water, then sank.

He continued swimming, on his side again, chopping his way slowly along. The salt water, inhaled in large amounts, made him feel nauseous, so he closed his mouth and tried to breathe through his nose.

For a while he floated on his back to regain his strength. His legs were getting heavier and heavier. They ached with cold and exhaustion. How long had he been in the water now? They had calculated three hours from their point of entry to shore, three hours at the most. But now all seemed lost.

Where was Nicolae? Was that him splashing in the distance?

A plan had been set. All they had to do was follow it. Metre by metre, they would arrive.

At approximately two hours, nothing had definition, the world was black to the horizon. His ears throbbed. He felt a humming, then a harsh whine, then a deep drilling pain boring through his head.

At three hours, he saw angels falling into the sea. He saw an image from his childhood. He recalled a violin his father had bought him when he was ten. He remembered that one day when a neighbour had come over to fix the kitchen stove, he had spotted the instrument on a shelf and asked to borrow it. With his father's permission, Andrei had lent it to him, and then forgotten about it. His father had fallen ill. There was no music in the house for many months. Years later when he looked for the violin he could not find it. He had no recollection of where he had last seen it. The mystery of the missing instrument had gone unsolved. Now, almost twenty years later and struggling for consciousness, Andrei found it again.

At three hours and many more minutes, he died. He believed he was dead. He floated on his back like a corpse.

After an interval of darkness, he saw light appear on the horizon, then a scroll of mountains.

The last stretch seemed to take the longest. Andrei's arms were now slack, and as he moved toward the shore he inhaled more water.

And then came a beautifully tranquil moment, a sensation of weightlessness, a feeling of being lifted and lifted. He let the tide carry him onto the shore, riding his exhaustion and at last closing his eyes.

"HE SAID TO ME, 'If only I hadn't gone in first. I was the stronger swimmer. Nicolae couldn't keep up.'

"I said, 'But I thought he jumped first.'

"He looked a bit confused. Then he said, 'You're right. He did.'"

Paolo, who had been looking out the window, turned to me and asked, "And what did you say?"

"About what?"

"When Andrei corrected himself, you must have said something."

I shook my head. "I just let it go."

"But you started to have doubts."

"Yes. But I didn't feel I had the right to demand anything of him; his experience was too painful. Besides, he never told me his story all at once. It was always in snatches, small details passed on here and there."

But my doubts increasingly weighed on me. And as the doubts persisted, I felt my faith wavering. I knew Andrei as someone who could remember most things exactly; often I'd seen him pause to correct himself on some minor detail. Now I kept asking myself, *How could this man not get the basic elements of his own story right?* Whenever he tried to narrow in on what had really happened in the water, the story changed.

More important, why did he keep moving ahead in the water when he lost track of Nicolae? He said he shouted, but why didn't he keep shouting? Why didn't he wait for a response? How hard had he tried?

My mind spun trying to think it through.

Why hadn't I pressed him further?

"That night he told me about the bird," I said to Paolo, "later I had an awful thought. What if he had wanted to lose Nicolae all along? What if it wasn't an accident?"

Paolo was hunched forward, his elbows resting on the table. "But you said they were in love," he said. "Besides, why would he have shared his story with you if he had something like that to hide?"

I nodded in agreement. It made no sense. Unless Andrei needed to atone.

In which case, why did I feel guilty? With Andrei's story ringing in my head, why this nagging feeling that I was the one who had fallen short?

I pictured the night. The freighter pitching on the water as it moved through the Black Sea, east toward Istanbul. I saw Nicolae huddled on the deck, frozen with indecision. What lay ahead for him? What really happened in the water, in those hours between the ship and the shore?

I imagined that Andrei abandoned Nicolae in the water.

I imagined that Nicolae, numb with fear, decided not to join Andrei. He never made the jump.

I imagined that he decided he would rather die than face an unknown future.

I imagined that Nicolae slipped, hit his head as he entered the water.

He became tangled in a drifting net . . .

He suffered a leg cramp . . .

He encountered a forceful current that suctioned him straight down under the sea, water flooding his lungs . . .

As for Andrei, I imagined that he waited, paused for a minute before continuing, survival instinct the prevailing desire.

Then there was the darkest scenario.

Andrei, who longed after so many lost things, who was filled with fear and uncertainty, who had left behind the family he adored, who believed the disintegration of a relationship beset by misfortune was inevitable, who had once used the Romanian word *curaj* ("I lack courage") when asked to describe his weakest quality, who didn't trust what was on the other side of the water—I imagined that he had decided to desert the man he loved, simply because he could not contemplate starting again with Nicolae in another place.

I have known people to break away from those they claim to love simply because they distrust the idea of second chances. It is a kind of defection.

Twenty-four

There were five trawlers lining the Turkish shore. Metin was busying himself with the nets, pulling them one by one from a pile to examine them for holes. The torn ones he folded up to take back to his wife for mending.

His dog was barking farther down the beach. He raised his head to look along the shoreline. His eyes fixed on a point in the distance: a figure huddled near a rock. He hesitated, briefly held back by the thought of so much work still to be done, then he dropped the nets and made his way across the beach, his stride slowed by sand.

The man he encountered appeared dead. The dog sniffed the man's face and nudged his waist. Metin took his pulse: it was sluggish. The man's skin was cool. Metin knew that it was important to get the body moving, to increase the blood flow to the man's brain. He couldn't be allowed to stay asleep. After a few unsuccessful efforts, Metin managed to wake him.

Andrei wanted to say something to reassure the man floating over him, but his words were slurred. His own voice sounded to him unearthly. He reached out his hand clumsily, missing the man's shoulder, swatting the side of his head instead. As the man leaned in, Andrei tried to think of something to say in Turkish, but no words came. Finally he settled on a word from another language.

Andrei repeated the word several times before he was understood. On the fourth and slowest try, the man's face softened and he began to laugh.

"*Ami.*"

The dog trotted around them in a circle.

"Where are you from?" Metin asked, once they were using passable French.

"Romania," Andrei replied twice. The second time, he was understood.

Metin frowned. Life had taught him not to ask too many questions.

Andrei moved into Metin's house for a week. His bed was made up in a yellow guest room. Bit by bit he regained his strength. The polluted water in which he had swum passed through him, and for several days he experienced stomach cramps followed by bouts of vomiting and diarrhea. Metin's wife devoted herself to getting him back on his feet again.

"You are too skinny," she chided. "I'll make you meaty again." She knew maybe a hundred words of French. She covered him in blankets. "Rest now. No talk. Just close your eyes."

From his bed he could vaguely see a dark brown rocking chair, a grey plastic bucket beside him on the floor, a silver cigarette case. The curtains in the room were drawn. He passed in and out of sleep.

In his waking moments, he stared at the white ceiling. Once he heard music playing on the radio—a woman, her voice trilling like a bird's, a man's voice, an earthy bass, swooping down beside her. The man's voice expanded until it pressed against his ears, filling them with a deep hum.

Metin's wife came into the room. She held out a bowl of lentil soup, piping hot, the steam fragrant. He saw that she was relieved to find him sitting, relieved to know he was on his way to recovery; soon, on his way to leaving.

Her dark eyebrows met at the bridge of her nose. Every time Andrei tried to tell her what happened, she pleated her forehead and quieted him. ("Shh. I told you I do not want details or names. Certainly no names," she repeated.) On the third day, he overheard her speaking to Metin in Turkish. They thought he was still sleeping. He tried to decipher what they were saying from the rise and fall of their voices.

As he was drifting toward sleep, he had a vision of Metin's wife standing over him, asking: "What is your name?"

Andrei dreamt of his mother as a young woman. She was lying in a hospital in faded brown pyjamas. The cots were covered with snow. Everything was spotlessly clean. He dreamt the smell of bleach and oranges on her pillowcase, the cool feel of the metal bed rail against her cheek.

"What is your name?" the Red Cross doctor asked his mother.

In his dream, the American doctor was handsome, rugged, healthy, unlike the others in the room. He was aware of his mother watching the doctor with a mixture of desire and guilt, ashamed at her quite normal thoughts when so many were still suffering, so many were dead . . .

When he was awake Andrei would hallucinate. Everywhere he looked, he saw Nicolae. Framed by a window. Coming up the stairs. Opening, then closing the bathroom door. Reading a book at the foot of the bed, then lying beside him, sharing a pillow.

Four days into his recovery, Andrei confided to Metin that he had not been alone when he left Romania. The next morning at daybreak, Metin assembled his friends and they began to search the far shore-line—but they found nothing.

At the end of Andrei's convalescence, they had a farewell dinner, and that evening he and Metin stayed up talking into the late hours.

"He must be dead. He must have drowned," Andrei said.

"How can you be so certain?" Metin replied. "You made it, didn't you? Don't you owe it to him not to give up so easily?"

"Yes. I do." Andrei instinctively lowered his head. He rested a drinking glass against his thigh and concentrated on pulling a teabag by its string, up and down through the darkening liquid.

"There are men that are found. Long after their families have given up looking. You read about these cases sometimes," Metin said.

"Then you think I should keep searching." He did not raise his head.

"It's important to keep hoping, my son. One never knows. Go," Metin said softly before taking himself to bed, "but don't give up."

Andrei spent his last two weeks in Turkey in a massive transit camp. It was crowded with other asylum-seekers waiting for their status to be determined by an adjudicator, waiting for third-country resettlement. The camp was situated at the edge of Istanbul, on a stretch of wasteland. Just a vast expanse of dirt and sky.

They slept in dormitories at night and during the day they lined up for their resettlement interviews. The officials sitting behind the desks waded through stacks of files. They were assisted by harried interpreters who rushed around as each claimant came forward with a new story and request. You could hear Romani, Arabic, Polish and Croat.

The officer who organized the queue was very friendly. He shared his cigarettes and handed out canvas hats to shield people from the sun. He spoke a bit of French. He told Andrei that his family lived in the Meandros Valley, near the river made famous for its meandering course.

"It doesn't seem to know exactly where it wants to go," he said. He didn't add *like you*, but that's what Andrei heard.

When it was Andrei's turn, he was interviewed, photographed and told to sign a form. The man at the desk placed the tip of his finger by a line marked with a pencilled cross. "Right here."

Andrei reached for the pen.

Under the question "Where would you like to be sent?" he carefully printed the word CANADA.

In his mind, Canada was a country of pristine snow mounds, perfectly paved highways and quiet cities where people paid little attention to the past; a country beckoning with promise—big enough for anonymity, wide enough for goodwill. A country that didn't close ranks.

Andrei arrived in Canada virtually empty-handed, an engineering graduate whose Northern Romanian degree was untranslatable in his new homeland. Four years later, by dint of luck, good contacts and dogged perseverance, he was working at a decent job, putting aside money every month in the hopes of one day sending it to his mother. The extent of that accomplishment was something he downplayed. "I do what I have to do," he would say, adding, "There are taxi drivers in this city who could remove brain tumours."

IN ALL THE TIME that we talked, Andrei never once indicated that his stay in Canada would be temporary. It did not occur to me that he might one day want to leave for good. But looking back I wonder if there were signs I should have deciphered.

One afternoon in June we were taking a break in the staff kitchen. I was pouring two cups of coffee, talking idly about a Spanish movie I had seen the night before, asking if there were any Romanian films he might recommend, when Andrei interrupted.

"You know, it's been so long, so unbearably long, since I spoke my language, or even heard it," he said.

His tone was so despairing, it alarmed me. The longing he expressed at that moment had claws. I put the glass coffee pot back on the burner and sat down.

"Andrei," I said tentatively, "maybe you can go back and visit one day."

"Never . . . maybe." He halted, then laughed at his reaction. "I think about it all the time. But you know how things are."

"But things could change. Look at what's happened in Poland. You must have seen it on TV."

"I've been watching the TV every chance I get. What's happening in Poland is extraordinary. But I'll tell you right now, it would never go like this in Romania."

"But if it did?"

"If it did? If it did, what a revolution that would be!"

Twenty-five

It occurs to me in hindsight that doubt was always present. Doubt is a part of everything I think and do, at the root of who I am. Doubt is the eighteen-month-old baby toddling around a coffee table, worried about letting go. Doubt is the child screeching to be taken off the skyride at Coney Island, the adolescent flatly refusing to set foot in a canoe on Lake Simcoe. (My father eventually took to calling me St. Thomas after the doubting apostle who refused to believe in the Resurrection until he could be persuaded by pressing his hand into Christ's wounded side.)

For a while, my doubt was centred on my merit as a listener and as a friend. Then, rightly or not, there came a time when it shifted to Andrei. I began to question the accuracy of his story. A tangled web, it now seemed, with so little tangible to hold on to. Those closest to him—Nicolae, his mother and brother—remained unknown to me.

Yet what I took from the story of St. Thomas was that you didn't need to plunge your hands into something to make it real. All you needed was faith and trust. So I continued to listen, hands by my sides, trying not to judge his version of events, even when it felt as if I was being led over very shaky ground. (Was the Ileana chapter of his story true—that they were engaged, that she was pregnant? If Nicolae was a slow swimmer, why didn't Andrei swim alongside him instead of heading independently for the shore?) Questions arose but I learned to deflect them. If I were to forfeit his account of what happened, what would replace it? And what would be left of our relationship?

Not once did I feel that Andrei was consciously deceiving me. I knew he wasn't a liar. He didn't even have a lively imagination. What seems more plausible is that he recounted different versions of certain events because he honestly couldn't commit to one.

Life is unpredictable. There are moments when everything seems to break down around us. And there are moments when everything snaps into place so perfectly that it seems like a miracle. Yet when we look back, much of what we have experienced seems unclear. Even the most important moments—the incomparable lows, the unsurpassed highs—blend together inexplicably.

I resurrect the past by relying on the physical world-documents in my possession, photos in my album, my old high-school yearbook, my teenage journals. Prompted by these objects, I can tell you, for example, that I travelled to England when I was seven and stayed for over a month, breaking my foot the last week; that I spent two summers working as an assistant carnie at the Canadian National Exhibition (the ring toss one year, the wheel of fortune the next); that I wore a strapless midnight blue dress to my high-school prom; that my best friend in grade eleven had the same name as Andrei's mother, Sarah. Left to my own devices, I remember very little. My mind is lax. I need these memory magnets.

Andrei was driven from his country and, aside from a few photographs, his stories were the only possessions left to him. No wonder he handled them so often, eventually reshaping them. There were the solid, unchanging things: the river, the moon, the freighter, the tips of the waves. And there were the indefinite things: the things weighed by his conscience and by his heart.

I believe now that wherever Andrei is, there are events he will reexamine for as long as he lives, there are choices for which he may seek forgiveness, there are thoughts that will awaken him in the middle of the night. I cannot change that, not now. If I retain a share of guilt it is over "what if"—what if I had been a better friend . . . what if he had found a more open, perceptive audience in me . . . what if I had been willing to face the burden of complete disclosure . . .

I know that, in some people's eyes, a story cannot be true and false at the same time. For some, the distinction between the probable and the possible, the contrast between what Andrei knew and what he hoped, is of no account. In a culture of absolute verdicts, all that matters is the final outcome.

A fresh supply of stationery sits on my desk. It includes a new book of adhesive labels. Postal instructions in Day-Glo colours.

> Do not open. Read carefully before using.
> Place stamp here. Reproduction strictly prohibited.
> Do not bend. Fragile. Not transferable. Do not write
> below this line. Return to sender.

I stare at the bright instruction labels.

Every personal story should be stickered with words of notice, a thousand red flags and caveats.

Twenty-six

$\mathcal{P}$aolo and I detoured through a park on our way home from the restaurant. Before we entered the house, we stopped to bang the snow off our boots. I was just about to unlock the door and go in when Paolo took hold of the sleeve of my coat.

"Wait," he said.

I turned around, still clasping the key in my hand.

"I want you to know. After all you've told me, it's not the missing I feel sorry for. The ones who have my sympathy are the people who have to keep on going. All that uncertainty, waiting for some conclusion. It's too painful."

Although I sensed his words were meant to comfort me I shrugged my shoulders and said, "Maybe the trick is to just let go."

"Maybe," he said softly.

Our eyes met for a moment, but before anything more could pass between us, I turned toward the door. Looking at him right then made me feel like crying.

I knew that there was one last step I had to take. I knew I had to visit Andrei's apartment. I fantasized about finding a piece of paper on which he might have drafted a farewell. However irrational, I felt stung that there had been no parting words. No formality, not even a utilitarian memo. I would have settled for anything.

There were four days left till his lease expired.

I was alone the next evening. It was Thursday and Paolo had plans to visit a friend who was leaving for Europe the next day.

"Let's go on a trip," he said as he was getting dressed to leave.

"When? Where to?"

"I don't know. We've never travelled anywhere together before."

"How about Argentina? I bet we could find a cheap flight. What about Buenos Aires?"

"Buenos Aires. Where's that?"

"Quit joking, Paolo. Don't you want to show me where you grew up? I have no image of it at all. What's it like there? Is it hot? Is it green?"

"Hot, yes. Green, no." He laughed. "It's more grey and brown."

"No trees or wildlife?"

"Not really in Buenos Aires. There are parks. But if you want real wildlife, you go to Iguazu—that's a day's drive away. Buenos Aires has a different kind of jungle atmosphere."

After he left, I made a simple dinner of melted cheese on toast, then sat down at my desk with a pen and paper. I opened the drawer and pulled out a small velvet box.

I began a letter to Kana on my best paper, then moved to the floor to write, finding a book to press against. I wrote neatly, in blue pen.

Dear Kana,

Seeing that you won't be back in time, I have enclosed a present for your birthday. A ring box. Recognize it? Look inside. Remember the black opal? You once said it was your favourite.

I came across it when we were packing for Mummy's move to Sakura. It was inside her wardrobe in a tangle of jewellery. It seemed a good time to help her by removing a few things. Some of the stuff I gave away. Some of it ended up outside with the garbage. But I asked Mum if I could hang on to a few items.

I'm sending you the ring because I thought you might want to keep it. You were right to like it so much. It's beautiful. I slipped it on my finger tonight and noticed that if you hold the stone up to the light, you can see flecks of blue and green. I had always thought it was just one colour.

By now you're probably preparing to move on to another assignment, so I am hoping that this package reaches you in time. Maybe drop me a line when it arrives.

Love, Naiko

p.s. I know you're very busy, but Mummy really looks forward to receiving your postcards. Could you try to write her more regularly? It would mean a lot to her.

December 29. Doreen removed the box of Andrei's belongings from the kitchen cupboard in which it had been stored. The manager had asked her to sort through it all one last time. Every item was laid out and examined, an exercise that took place on a table in the staff kitchen. My nosy co-workers made up excuses to look in on her. I tried not to hate them, their smug, vulturish presence.

Baba observed the proceedings from a distance, consciously separating himself from their curiosity. I felt grateful for this small courtesy, but at the same time he flustered me. I could sense him studying me from under his compassion—furrowed brow, a mix of sympathy and bafflement that said, *Poor poor Naiko. She never could let go.* When he looked at me like that, I felt like crawling away. Pity has a shrinking effect. Warren, on the other hand, kept me afloat with his good humour. Every now and then he raised his eyebrow or winked extravagantly from his desk.

Doreen packed a few items into Ziploc bags: a digital watch, a pair of reading glasses, a set of keys, a roll of subway tokens, a miniature chess set. "I've left the clothing behind," she said to the manager when she finished. "Do you want me to get rid of it?"

She put the Ziploc bags down on a table in the middle of the office and excused herself to take a phone call. I noticed from where I sat that Andrei's notebook wasn't among the belongings she had so carefully set aside. It seemed strange that she would have overlooked it; then I remembered, with a mixture of guilt and glee, that the notebook was in my desk drawer, where I had left it several days before. My fingers pushed the drawer closed so that its contents vanished from view.

With the manager's permission, I adopted the clothes that had been left behind, packing the items back into a cardboard box. It occurred to me that I should take just one thing—for the sake of appearances, propriety and such—but I could not decide, so I took everything. I carted it all home. Andrei's moth-eaten blue sweater, his raincoat and a pair of old boots, the tongues sagging over slack laces. I transferred it all to a big green Rubbermaid box in my hallway closet.

The notebook was a different story. I began to carry it with me wherever I went. I brought it out when I was alone. I soaked up every page, every notation and drawing, always encountering something new. I read the newspaper clippings tucked between the pages, stretching the task over hours, drawn in by the details but no longer looking for clues. I was completely absorbed in it, but absorbed in the manner of a child enjoying random discoveries—the pleasure of a pastime without lofty purpose. I raced through meals, skipped after-dinner walks and movies on television so that I could return to the notebook. Paolo would just give me a look, a silent, *Oh no. Here we go again.*

Without the notebook there were moments when I might have doubted Andrei's existence or questioned my own sanity. I remember coming across a cheaply printed postcard of Bucharest sandwiched between two pages. The image was faded, but it showed the main boulevard, roads wide enough to host motorcades. I touched it and the ink left a smudge on my fingers. See? I remember thinking. Real ink.

I knew that the notebook and its contents were not mine to keep. I was preparing to let them go. I knew that one day soon I would put these things in a package and send them off, *To: Andrei Dinescu c/o Northern Romania.* (Might there be someone like me in a Romanian mail recovery office who would search for him?)

I also knew that when I sent this package it would include something else; something of mine. My sense of self had not perished, after all. But what would it include? I looked down at my hand—a silver ring, a present from Paolo . . . No, not that. I glanced around my apartment, and on the bottom of my bookshelf, I spotted the object.

A pre–Second World War atlas. It was given to me by my father as a high-school graduation present. When Kana graduated, she was given his old field binoculars. (Did he give any thought to who got what? It's strange how things turned out: she is the one who travels, and I am the one who looks.) I lifted up the atlas. When I cracked open the enormous pages, I smelled dust and stale tobacco. Many of the countries were now non-existent or had changed names. Ceylon. Rhodesia. Countries marked with bold, well-spaced letters. There were light yellow islands and pastel green territories. Romania was pale pink. It showed lines of dashes running along the crest of the Carpathian Mountains. A red line for the Tisza River. A broken line where Romania met Hungary, indicating that the border was under dispute. I let the pages fan through my fingers. I caught glimpses of ultramarine ocean.

Yes. I would send the atlas and with it a note. And in doing so, I would complete the loop. I would become both sender and receiver. I would keep things moving. I would exist.

Life is beginning. I now break into my hoard of life.

From *The Waves* by Virginia Woolf

Part Five

MY THINGS

Andrei's sketchbook
His boots
His sweater
His pen
His plant
His roll of mints
His extra pair of eyeglasses
His brass belt buckle
A silver ring (from Paolo)
A world atlas (from my father)

PAOLO'S THINGS

1 nylon knapsack
1 toothbrush
1 disposable razor
1 box of condoms
3 pairs of underwear
2 pairs of socks
4 oz. bottle of Maalox
1 bottle of Gaugho Green
   hot sauce

Twenty-seven

On the Sunday morning of New Year's Eve, Andrei's rent expired. I made my way to his apartment at 1478 Lakeview Avenue. As I got off the streetcar, I could see the flat-roofed, brick building up ahead. The wind was raking old candy wrappers and bits of garbage around the iron-gated courtyard. A sun-faded sign announcing VACANCIES had been nailed permanently to the front door, suggesting something about the turnover rate.

The building caretaker met me as arranged in the lobby. He was a big man with a big voice, thinning grey hair and wide blue eyes. From the minute we met, he made it clear that this was not a social visit. He had the officious manner of a sergeant and he spoke as though he were reading from an army drill. He told me I was to clear out all of Andrei's personal effects before evening. The police had told him Andrei's stuff was still there. A new tenant was arriving the next day. Everything that was left behind would be sold or put in the dumpster.

I guess I was too quiet for his liking, because when he finished, he stared at me and said, very slowly, "Do you understand?"

"Yes," I said, tucking both hands into my coat pockets, squeezing my wool gloves, feeling like a chastised schoolchild.

He dangled his keys for a second, considering me, and then said, "You his girlfriend, or what?"

"No, just a friend," I replied casually. But the second the words were out I felt panic. Why had I corrected him? What if being "just a friend" wasn't enough to open the door to Andrei's apartment?

I breathed a sigh of relief when he turned toward the stairs and gestured for me to follow him. "Just remember, you need to be out by six. No later. I have plans this evening."

We lumbered in silence up six flights of stairs. Andrei's place was at the end of a long, dim hallway that was more lurid than I remembered from my last visit. A damp-looking ochre carpet abutted a brown runner. The burgundy walls were flecked with flowers the shade of tomato gravy. Andrei's door was painted green, with the number 12 in black.

I waited while the caretaker searched for the right key. A ragga floated from apartment 9. I could hear the voice of a man talking into a telephone in another. There was laughter from a television, the hiccuped sobbing of a child, the clatter of plates.

After some fumbling, the caretaker turned to me and said, "I brought the wrong set of keys. Wait here. I'll be right back."

Leaning against the door, chewing my thumbnail, I waited. I noticed that the lower keyhole was one of those old-fashioned slots and suppressed the urge to crouch down and peer inside.

Soft whistling came from apartment 10. A woman washing dishes, sloshing pans in suds in the sink. I liked the sounds. I liked the way the tenants' diverse activities were accoustically interwoven. As my eyes adjusted to the poorly lit corridor, I began to notice dirt in every corner. The wallpaper, on closer inspection, had as many stains as flowers. Magic Marker, bike grease, even bootprints stamped its surface. No amount of blotting, rubbing and rinsing could ever make it clean again.

The caretaker returned after five minutes. When he opened the door, I slipped inside and found myself in near darkness. The caretaker fumbled along the wall next to the door frame and flicked the switch. Then he left me, firmly closing the door behind him.

The room was quite different now. There was little evidence of the casual and comfortable clutter I had come to associate with Andrei. Someone had cleaned and stacked the dishes by the sink, had even tidied the bookshelves. In the bedroom, the bed was perfectly made. It was impossible to tell how much time had elapsed since Andrei left. An old suede jacket hung on an otherwise empty coat tree. A plaid umbrella was propped in the corner.

I sat on the couch and scanned the room again, looking for some breach in the facade, wondering where to begin. Even among the familiar contents, I was unnerved by the stillness of the apartment. I had always imagined that I would find it in disarray—a room befitting the drama of a sudden disappearance, strewn with broken plates, spilled liquor bottles, a messy sprawl of clothes and papers. I was looking for signs of emotional rampage. I wasn't prepared for the tidiness. There was something mausoleum-like about it.

I opened the window and within a few minutes a pigeon had settled on the ledge. I went to the kitchen and found some stale cereal, which I laid out in a line. The pigeon finished its meal and began pecking at its feathers. Noticing its tiny rib cage contract and expand, I felt a sudden protectiveness. I leaned forward, thinking I might try to touch it, but my movement prompted the bird to swoop off the ledge. I watched it drop, then rise again, the white undersides of its wings visible as it flew away. I closed the window.

I was sitting on the couch again when there was a knock at the door. My heart stopped. I steadied my breathing and went to open it. The caretaker had returned with a few green garbage bags and an empty cardboard box. It was possible that he was apologizing for his earlier brusqueness, or perhaps he was rewarding me for my good manners. I thanked him quickly and closed the door, hung up my coat and returned to the living room, relieved to be alone again.

The question of where to begin resolved itself immediately. My eyes gravitated to the corner of the room. A patch of white. Andrei's desk was almost bare: a sharpened pencil, a pad of paper on the recently painted surface. It looked expectant. I walked across the floor and began to prise open the heavy drawers.

The first thing I came across was a bundle of letters, all written in Romanian on heavy unbleached paper: letters, I assumed, from Andrei's mother. The sturdy envelopes were scuffed from handling and sealed on the left side with brown censor tape. I opened them all. I was able to see that most of the letters were short, a paragraph or two long, and heavily censored. But there was one that stood apart. The handwriting and signature were the same as the others, but this time the words flowed across several pages without interruption. Not a single word was blacked out. Perplexed, I studied the undamaged envelope and discovered the reason for its preservation: a British stamp. This had to be the letter Andrei's mother had managed to smuggle out of the country.

The next thing I found, just under the bundle of letters, was a manila pouch containing a small stack of photographs. I thumbed through them quickly, then put them on top of the desk alongside the letters and a shopping list bordered with Andrei's intricate doodles. I planned to keep these things. Everything else—the old receipts and bank statements, the paper clips, pencil stubs, near-finished rolls of tape—went into the garbage bag. I was well into the second drawer when I came across a folder containing forms and papers relating to a pending citizenship application. My chest tightened with dread. Had Andrei been planning to stay, then decided to kill himself? The thought was more than I could bear. I grabbed the shopping list I had placed on the desk and read through its mundane contents for comfort: cigarettes, milk, frozen peas, hamburger, toothpaste . . .

I should have been braced for anything, but even now the memory of what I found next is a body blow. I was sifting through the bottom drawer when I found them. There, under a pile of Romanian magazines, was the second batch of letters we had written together in July—envelopes we had addressed to embassies and consulates inquiring about Nicolae's whereabouts, all carefully typed. I was baffled. The envelopes were still sealed and unsent. I slid a finger into the fold of one envelope and tore it open, being careful not to rip the stationery. Inside was a letter we had composed to the Turkish consulate. My heart sank.

I moved back to the couch, spread the photos, papers and letters out in front of me, and began leafing through it all, piece by piece. I examined each photo. They were a variety of sizes, some in colour, others in black and white. Most of them were dated after Andrei's arrival in Canada. Photos taken during a field trip with his ESL class. A snapshot of Baba and his wife sitting on an outdoor sculpture by Henry Moore. But the one that captured my attention was the small snapshot of Nicolae and Andrei standing in the grass. As far as I could tell, it was the only Romanian photo left in the apartment, which led me to believe that it had been somehow overlooked in Andrei's hurry to leave. The first time Andrei showed it to me, I had remarked on how happy they looked. There was no hint of tension or distance.

I put the picture back in the envelope with the others and picked up a brown folder. It was full of photocopied newspaper articles reporting on missing men, some accompanied by photographs or police sketches. I knew the contents of these articles from months before; rereading them would only deepen my depression.

I held the folder on my lap, sitting perfectly still, staring into space as the minutes passed. Finally, I shifted in my seat, maybe I crossed my legs. In either case, the slight adjustment caused the folder to tilt. The contents started to cascade to the floor. It took me a second to right the folder but by then it was too late. The pages were scattered at my feet—a small but fateful mishap, for my clumsiness had its rewards. Among the papers that fell was a half-finished letter addressed to me. It was composed on a sheet of bond paper. A slippery piece of fax paper was folded up inside of it.

I read the letter first.

December 5, 1989

My dear friend Naiko,

Forgive me for not expressing myself earlier. Every time I thought of calling or writing, I do not know how to explain myself and when I try to find the word, I start to feel very bad about putting you in this place.

I feel shamefaced. Was it wrong to get you involved?

I am not proud of myself for running off without saying goodbye. It is becoming a poor habit.

I have found out about Nicolae. Now I know I will never

see him again. I feel terrible sadness. Yet for me, knowing
what happened is also a ~~releaf~~ release. Perhaps I can put it
all behind me—it is over.
Thank you for your friendship. I always felt that you were

The letter stopped there.

I read it several times. Then I put it down. It revealed nothing of what he had discovered about Nicolae. I unfolded the fax. A newspaper clipping had been copied and transmitted to Andrei by a librarian at the *Turkish Daily News*; a single column of text no more than five centimetres in length accompanied by a blotchy police sketch. It was taken from the English edition of the newspaper.

Man's body pulled from Istanbul harbor. The man, mid-
twenties, with light brown hair, was discovered by coast
patrol on Monday night. No identifying possessions have
been found. There were no signs of bodily injury. He is
presumed drowned. The Bureau of Missing Persons in
Turkey processes more than 20,000 cases a year.

The article was dated June 16, 1984—just around the time that Andrei had moved from Metin's house to the transit camp in Istanbul. The date had been circled in blue ink, but the rest of the column was unmarked. I read it over twice. Of all the clippings, all the other reports of drowning victims, did this one hold the clarity of truth? Was Nicolae dead? I pictured his body floating face down, white shorts glowing in the moonlight; imagined just how close he came to reaching the shore.

I continued to stare at the crude police sketch. One side of the man's face was blotted into a shadowy silhouette, his features further smudged by the dark toner. If I strained my eyes to focus it, I could make out an eerie, distorted likeness. But the reality was there was no clear resemblance. It could have been Nicolae or any one of the twenty thousand other unfortunates. I found myself fighting back tears, thinking of kinder images of Nicolae; trying to understand Andrei's state of mind on reading the clipping, his desire for finality, however terrible or questionable.

I was refolding the article when I happened to notice a line of text at the bottom right-hand corner of the fax: 18/07/1989. But there must have been some mistake; how could that date be correct? My hand began to shake and the paper slid from my fingers and drifted to the floor. July 18, 1989. The date was circling around and around in my head. If Andrei believed Nicolae was dead, why had he kept the information from me for so many months? I felt my heart thudding, my head reeling. Everything was becoming confused: my perception of the summer, my recollection of what we were talking about back then. Had it all been pretense?

I tried to remember the days we had spent writing the second group of letters and the hours we had spent poring over newspapers and contacting archives. Did he receive the fax then? If so, who was served by the act of writing those letters?

Grief swept through me.

On the table across the room, I spotted a copy of *The Waves* that I had given Andrei for his birthday. I walked over and randomly flipped to a page. "'For one moment only,' said Louis. 'Before the chain breaks, before disorder returns, see us fixed, see us displayed, see us held in a vice . . .'"

My eyes began to blur. I felt exhausted. I set the book down and went to open the window again. I stood there, blinking back tears, inhaling the cold air, watching people with their strollers and dogs, joggers huffing along in sweatsuits and scarves. A couple sauntered by holding hands. I buttoned up my cardigan and went to lie on the bed, flopping down carelessly, mussing the covers and bunching the pillows against my chest.

And then I began to cry, tears that came with great, heaving sobs, racking my whole body, stealing my breath. Uncontrollable tears. I cried until my eyes were swollen and my mouth was parched. I cried because my soul felt heavy. I cried for Nicolae. I cried for Andrei, for his loss and for whatever deeds or knowledge he had to carry in his heart. I cried for my mother. I cried for Paolo, for his endurance and patience, for all the times I had withheld my affection. And I cried for myself because Andrei had left without warning, without telling me the truth.

When the spasms subsided, I rolled onto my back and closed my eyes. As my body settled into the mattress, my fatigue overtaking me, I suddenly had a flash of what Andrei must have felt after he was revived by Metin. To pass out of one world and into another, breaking away so absolutely, was almost unfathomable.

I didn't expect to doze off, but the shock of the afternoon had taken a toll. I must have slept for several hours, for when I awoke the sky was darkening. A faded green blanket lay twisted beside me. I glanced at my watch and realized that it was half past five, almost time for me to leave.

Except for the letters, I had already decided to leave everything behind.

Among the items I carried away with me that evening was the uncensored letter Andrei had received via England from his mother. One week later, thanks to a Romanian professor I located through the University of Toronto, I held a translated copy of it in my hands. It was typed on department letterhead, the university crest so at odds with the intimacy of the words that followed.

September 1984

My dearest Andrei,

My son in Canada. Remember when we talked about whether there was anyone who knew the fate of my family during the war? I had told you that I lost track of them when I and the healthiest women of our village were separated and then sent to Ravensbrück. I must tell you now that was not entirely the truth. You see, I found out that there was a Russian girl who knew my mother at Birkenau. I met her in the Red Cross hospital after the war. Her name was Rachel, then nineteen years old. She had already been in the camp for one year when my mother arrived.

They both belonged to a women's kommando that was made to sort belongings taken from the arriving prisoners. The luggage these prisoners had so carefully packed was taken on arrival to a series of special barracks. The Nazis called these possessions "effects," and among them Rachel and my mother found extra food to survive.

It was my mother's job to open the pocketbooks of the women who arrived. One time she came across a woman's leather wallet with a photo of a student, a young man, and letters that his Austrian mother had sent in hopes of finding him—to the Gestapo, to the embassies—all returned with the stamp "Whereabouts Unknown." Seeing all this, my mother began to cry.

284

Rachel had been assigned to cut the lining out of coats to look for hidden valuables. When she noticed my mother crying, she laid down her scissors and began to comfort her. My mother cried, she told Rachel, not just from pity but also envy: death for this woman would reunite mother and child.

My mother began to work more slowly. It was as if she had made up her mind to preserve each pocketbook firmly in her memory. She would try to retain an image of each, and maybe one day she would recite these details should anyone ask. With these last belongings she would become a silent historian. She would protect their neshome. This was her tribute.

In the end, Rachel attempted to assist my mother with her sorting, but it was too late. My mother complained of pains in her hands. She became dizzy with fever and was unable to continue. By the time they took my mother away, the piles were as high as the ceiling. The barracks had become too small for all the property brought to the camps. Trains full of disinfected possessions made their way to the Reich every week. Who knows what strangers inherited these things?

Tonight, through a strange turning of memory, I was brought to remember something Rachel told me. The sorting barracks, she told me, were located in an area of Birkenau known as the personal effects camp. The Germans called them Effektenkammer. But the barracks had another nickname. They were together known as Canada. For many of the prisoners, the word earned a special meaning. It came to symbolize a place of wealth and plenty. For others, it was just a place of pillage.

*But let me share with you one final story. On the morning
that I was leaving the Red Cross hospital, Rachel called me
to her bedside to say goodbye. There was no knowing where
we would end up or if we would see each other again, but
she wanted me to know that however much time passed, she
would always remember my mother and me. My mother
had given her courage. My mother had been Rachel's only
friend. When my mother was taken away, Rachel buried
her sorrows in her work. But now the precious items found
in coat linings she threw rebelliously into the toilets—rings,
cufflinks, watches, all of it. A sabotage against the greedy
citizens of the Reich. "I made this my homage," she said. "In
memory of your mother."*

*So, yes, there was a girl who knew my mother. And now, I
have told you the story of your grandmother.*

Your loving mother

I sat on the couch in my living room holding the letter in my hand,
feeling like a voyeur from another world. Everything in my life felt
trite when set beside Sarah's story. Her life had been torn apart, her
family swept away in the torrents of war and persecution. How had
she survived loss of that magnitude? How does anybody?

I thought of Andrei's flight from his country toward what he hoped
would be the freedom to love, the plunge into the sea, the reaching
shore. I thought of him realizing that his mother had suffered so much
and never spoken of it. I thought of him resolving that Nicolae was
dead and not having the courage to tell me that's what he believed. No
wonder he slipped quietly away.

I walked over to the window and scanned the darkening rooftops.

In the distance, a red trail of light blazed against the purple dusk sky.

In the ten months Andrei spent working beside me at the Undeliverable Mail Office I had watched him approach his tasks with an unusual intensity. I had seen him study a package with a diligence that often exceeded necessity. I had seen him grin when a gift reached its destination, showing the delight of someone finding a lost friend.

There was nothing straightforward about Andrei. He found his way to the UMO along an emotional path that spanned decades and continents. For a brief time I think he found happiness in the work.

Perhaps it was his homage. Perhaps his penance.

As I lay in bed that night, the image came back to me of a young girl trudging across a white plain, chin tucked against the cold. I saw how several girls fell back in the marching column, desperate for rest, while others swept them up before they could fall and be left behind. On the edge of sleep, I saw Andrei's mother holding another girl as they marched, stamping through the snow, gripping each other as though their survival was being decided in that moment, as though they were the last of their people.

Twenty-eight

When I think of my mother's room at Sakura I always see us in the bathroom. The yellow tiled walls, the white slip-proof floor and the narrow tub with its support railing. I stir the water with my hand to test the temperature, set aside tear-free shampoo, a fresh towel. She waits on the closed toilet seat in her bathrobe, slipping it off at the last minute. She seems slight without her clothes on, with her sunken chest, a mild scoliosis of the spine.

A soapy washcloth moves along her limbs. She takes charge of the front, washing the accordion folds of her belly, lathering her empty breasts. Her skin has become loose and thin, too big for the body it contains. She lifts her arms to wash her armpits, then hands me the cloth so I can scrub her back. When I am finished I turn on the hot water to warm the cooling tub and begin to rinse her. We work in silence. She responds to my assistance like a child. She used to become rigid at my touch, but now her body is pliable. Her naked-ness doesn't embarrass us. It has become something separate from her—habitual, unerotic, chaste. Skin is the largest organ of the body. We tend to it unselfconsciously.

Beside the sink there is a wall-mounted soap dispenser (made in Cornwall, Ontario). It is placed beside a roll-towel device (made in Livonia, Michigan). Am I wrong or do these institutional accessories keep small towns in business? The soap has a medicinal smell. There is usually a gummy trail of pink liquid running down the wall, even though we almost always use our own soap. The soap I buy for my mother smells of magnolia or almond blossom or tea rose—perfumed vanity as opposed to antibacterial hygiene. Pucks of Roger & Gallet wrapped in pleated paper. It's a small, pampering difference.

After the tub has drained I mop up the remaining suds, claim my mother's stray hairs. She moves into the bedroom and dries herself with a large towel. When she's finished, she wraps the towel around herself, twisting and tucking the top corner in over her right breast, and sits down. I pull a pair of nail clippers from her bedside drawer and begin to pare and clean her toenails. The skin on the tops of her feet feels like mulberry paper. I daub them with moisturizer. I'm in charge of the unreachable parts.

As I work on her feet, she lathers cream on her face. My mother's skin is darker than mine. To the left of her nose is a large, raised beauty mark. My own face has a dimmer version of the mole, as if the stamp that created hers had run out of fresh ink. This is our correspondence. A man hitting on my mother once pointed to the symmetry of our moles and said, "I swear you could be twins." Several years ago my mole fell off. Actually, I tried to pluck a stubborn hair from it (which I now know you're not supposed to do) and accidentally scraped off the pigment. It reappeared eventually, but the whole experience was deeply unsettling.

I know one can place too much weight on the minute details of family resemblance: the fact that I have my father's ears, my mother's mole. But I also know that the signs of difference can be even more revealing. Not that these signs—my untraceable hazel eyes, for instance—are proof of independence, idiosyncratic as they may seem. I am convinced, for example, that I am "soft-spoken" not for some innate or genetic reason, but because when we were children my sister was often a screamer.

We are never wholly of our own making, or even our parents' making. We are DNA and destiny blended together. The blueprint of who we will become versus what was meant to be, redrafted by circumstance at a moment's notice.

In my mother's case, I find it difficult to distinguish nature from nurture. Like her own mother's, her face has grown angular with age. She has lost much of the facial fat that once made her look soft but sturdy. Now her cheeks are sinking and her always prominent nose seems to protrude even more, like a beak. Is it nature that pares her down, makes her look like a bird? Is it nurture that has turned her into a magpie?

On New Year's Day, as I was brushing my mother's hair, I noticed a Swiss Army knife resting on top of her wardrobe.

"Where did you get this?" I asked, examining the jelly red casing.

"That is from your father," she said, and turned away. She was *plinking* the teeth of a long-handled comb.

"Do you use it?"

She shook her head.

"Let me look."

The knife contained a generous assortment of tools, which I pulled, one by one, out of the casing.

Large blade
Small blade
Can opener
Small screwdriver
Bottle opener
Large screwdriver
Wire stripper
Awl with sewing eye
Toothpick
Tweezers
Key ring
Corkscrew
Mini screwdriver
Scissors

When I had finished and all the tools were protruding, I placed the knife on the table. It looked like a porcupine. I picked it up again, retracted the jagged spine. I could tell that the gift displeased my mother. A survivalist accessory. Further indication of her ex-husband's detachment—an instruction to fend for herself in the wilderness.

"I wonder how he is?" I said aloud, returning the knife to its place. A year had passed since my father's last visit to Toronto.

"*So da ne*," she said, musing over the hairpins in her hand. "I was just reminiscing."

"Really, Mummy? What were you reminiscing?"

She reached forward and picked up a rectangle of painted silk—another present from my father? She fluttered it for me slowly, as if demonstrating its allure. "Look," she said, playfully draping it on her head, then over her shoulders, then across her chest, around her waist . . .

I have grown accustomed to my mother's habit of veering off in the middle of a conversation. But I see patterns in her behaviour. Her digressions, so regular, by now are more comforting than alarming. For those who don't know her well, however, for those who see her only occasionally, I know the suddenness with which she tilts in and out of the present can be disturbing. I know it shakes Kana. These are a few things I've heard her say to our mother over the years:

Please, Mom. Get a grip.

Can you try to hold it together?

Listen, if you can't handle it, then we won't go/stay/leave, et cetera.

I find these statements to be funny and sad, but mostly paradoxical, because if nothing else, my mother is a gripper, a holder and a handler.

Paolo calls her the "anti-ascetic," and I think the term appropriate on a number of levels. Ascetics shed themselves of all worldly goods in order to experience divinity. Ascetics seek out truth by retreating to otherworldly places like caves, cloisters, temples or deserts.

There is no question that my mother is un-divine. Her life is not one of renunciation. There is not the tiniest notion of God in her head. She is not waiting for a bolt of spiritual inspiration. She revels in her own corporeal existence. Often, too often, her acquisitiveness arouses deep discomfort about her total lack of discernment and propriety. Yet at other times, I am astounded by her almost pious attachment to objects, her numinous touching of what she loves, like the veneration of the rosary, only more ancient, more primal. More like a prehistoric cave dweller arranging and rearranging strange assortments of pebbles and flint.

The other day I watched my mother replace the cap of her eau de toilette bottle and sort through a pile of socks until every sock had found its match, and it comforted me that her mind continues its active routine and will likely do so for as long as she lives. Her objects bear her along. They round out her emotions. They represent a life of pleasure (a ticket stub from a Placido Domingo concert, a box of matches from a favourite restaurant, trinkets from her pre-married life) or displeasure (or ambivalence: a lilac sundress purchased by her then husband/my father during their honeymoon). She holds these reminders of a mixed life in her lap without discriminating. She embraces them, thanks them. She locates virtue in repossessing the things we call garbage and junk. Her collection is a museum of her mind, and she comes by it honestly. At least no one was plundered.

The problem with Kana is that she allows herself to see the craving but not the caring. That is why she judges our mother so harshly. She examines the sheer volume of the possessions our mother has managed to cram into her small room, and detects a character flaw. She sees evidence of "a vulgar and excessive materialism." She tries to make light of the situation: "Hey, Mom. Leave it to others to save the world." But in her eyes, our mother is a warning of what happens if you don't try to escape the mind's village, its cluster of narrow roads and ambitions.

Lately, when I look at my mother I think maybe the trouble is not that she is too materialistic but that many of the rest of us in the First World are not materialistic enough. We are quick to discard one possession to chase something else more tempting. Our lives are, in essence, a cycle of acquiring and unloading. We cast off people and things to live more freely, to clear the deck for future acquisitions. Yet the objects we leave behind bear our touch, perpetuate us in different ways as we remember them, too, consciously or not. Whenever my mother says, "But I put it down right there," or "It was here just a minute ago," sculpting the air with her hands, without recalling with any precision the "it" that was "there" or "here," I know she is conjuring the missing or mislaid object by the shape of its absence.

Paolo is right. My mother is not an ascetic. An ascetic would say that truth reveals itself only when one is prepared to forget about oneself. An ascetic would say that it is difficult to let go. My mother, the anti-ascetic, would disagree. It is not hard to lose oneself. It is all too easy to fall apart and be swept away.

Andrei swivelling on his chair.

Gone.

When I was a child, I believed that if something vanished from one place it would instantly crop up in another. Maybe I thought this because of something my father said when I left my favourite Tressy doll on the streetcar. I was inconsolable, and he hugged me and said, "Don't worry, Nai-chan. Lost things travel to good places. Now another little girl somewhere in the world has your doll."

Every time the string of a balloon slipped through my fingers or a marble rolled away, I imagined a little girl named Carlyn living on a faraway island wearing my hat and mittens and a million pairs of mismatched socks, chiming, "Got it!" I could see her skipping across a heathery field in a light drizzle, clutching my doll by the arm with a huge grin on her face.

Perhaps if I had listened more carefully, I would have heard something else in my father's voice: *Don't be too possessive. Don't depend on things, or others, unduly.*

We were three days into the new year, the dawn of a new decade, when Kana called to say she was home.

"Oh no," I said when I finally registered that she meant she was back in Toronto. "That's awkward."

"Naiko!"

"I'm sorry, Kana. That sounds terrible. I'm happy that you're back.

Honestly. It's just your timing. You see, Paolo and I were planning to leave tomorrow." A small white lie. The travel agent's number was on the table in front of me. "Paolo wants to go to Buenos Aires and my manager thinks it would be a good time for me to have a break. You know, now that it's not so busy."

"But I just got in. Do you have to leave right away? I mean, you never go anywhere. Why start now?"

That peeved me.

She could tell by my silence that I wasn't amused and began to laugh nervously. "I'm sorry. I can be such a bitch."

"Look, I'm going. I've already booked the ticket," I lied again.

"I'm sure they'd let you exchange it. People do it all the time. Please stay. There's so much to catch up on. I'm bringing dinner over to Mum tonight. I want to surprise her."

"Kana—"

"I need you to come. Please?"

Always what she needed, not what I needed. She could not let me change. I also realized that she would never have any idea of the journey I had taken with Andrei. She would never know because I had no way of expressing it in words she would understand. Andrei's life and mine had merged, then separated, without a physical trace—not so much as a photograph of the two of us.

In Kana's world, events were tangible, the facts concrete. To her anything that didn't happen right before your eyes was irrelevant. It wasn't news. It was hearsay or make-believe—at best, a good story. I thought of her profession's remoteness, its pretense of neutrality; the ruthlessly compressed capsules of human life; the scrunching of tragedy into sidebars of text. What did I want her to know? Had she ever been subsumed by someone else's story the way I had? The truth was that in her own way she had. We both liked second-hand stories.

"Usually it's you who leaves, right?" I said.

"Yeah, but that's how I survive—I mean, make a living. That's my job."

"Then you understand."

"I suppose so."

But I could tell she didn't. "I'll send you a letter as soon as I get there."

"A letter?" She sounded genuinely puzzled.

"A postcard."

There was a certain pleasure in putting the receiver down. I was taking control for once. How can I prevent people from slipping away? By going away myself.

Twenty-nine

$\mathcal{M}$ore than a year has passed since I last saw Andrei. In the first months after I entered his apartment and discovered his unfinished letter to me, I was plagued by the recurring thought that I had failed both him and Nicolae. Wasn't I obligated to Nicolae's memory and Andrei's well-being to discover the truth of what had really happened that night at sea? I mulled over the muddy, unfinished account of their escape again and again, each time remembering fresh things, but never finding fresh meaning. Some nights I felt furious with Andrei for having involved me in the first place. Why had he earmarked me? Was I someone people took advantage of? I ruminated over the circumstances that had brought us together.

Yet as the months passed, I began to let Andrei go. I relinquished the house that overlooked the Carpathians. I relinquished Mihai, the baby born to Ileana; I relinquished the forest I would never visit, the freighter with its rusted hull and the settlement house in Toronto. I released it all.

It was not to forget it that I released it all. It was not to bury it, because that was not possible: there is no unplugging the power of the mind, whether tomorrow or ten years later. I simply loosened the grip of my need to possess and comprehend it. More difficult to release was the feeling of purpose his need and despair had given me.

After six months, the last of Andrei's belongings, which Doreen had stored in a locked drawer on the manager's request, were given away or destroyed. There were still so many unanswered questions, but there was also an unmistakable air of conclusion as I watched those items be dispersed.

There were times when Andrei's entire existence seemed an invention of my imagination. But some things had moved out of the realm of the imaginary. Through weeks of watching television newscasts, I had come to know Bucharest as well as I did New York or London. I could call up an image of the city that felt unnervingly real: packs of mangy and scab-covered dogs roaming through concrete courtyards; streets choked with traffic; Romanian-made Dacia cars and brand-new imports swerving around an occasional horse-drawn cart from the countryside.

Over the past year, the missionaries have marched in where the international press galloped off. The Christians have descended on Bucharest, bringing their zealous spirit and salvationist cameras to its ideological vacuum. They tour its neighbourhoods and visit its hospitals and schools. The orphans are the treasures they take home, as previous visitors would have returned with embroidered shirts and busts of Dracula. Every few weeks there are stories of solicitous Americans and Canadians who are preparing to hop on planes and take matters into their own hands. Television is filled with images of iron cribs and street orphans living in sewers.

Paolo and I did take our trip, though in the end, Paolo had a change of heart and we went to Cuba instead of Argentina. It was a repairing vacation. The sun made us mild and generous with each other. I shared a few more pieces about Andrei, but mostly we tried to find our way back to being together, just two. I had told him about Sarah's letter, but I never showed it to him. I stored the original, along with the translation, in my desk on top of a pile of my own papers. It stayed there for three months, its stiff heavy paper weighing down on the pile just as the words had weighed down on my heart. I knew the letter wasn't mine, but it also didn't feel right to keep it a secret. In the end I investigated the options and, after some consideration, sent it to a Holocaust memorial museum in Paris, the first of its kind in Europe.

Paolo and I stayed in Havana but took day trips to the Varadero Peninsula, where we lazed on the beach and did a lot of walking along the water's edge. On our last night, after strolling through Havana's Barrio Chino, we came across a restaurant coincidentally called Sakura, a small sushi bar run by an older Japanese Cuban named Eduardo Miyasaki. Over a dinner of miso and salmon maki we found out that the spry man in front of us was actually five years older than my mother, and that he had been interned along with his sons (and eleven hundred other Japanese Cubans) during the Second World War. He clearly took a shine to us, maybe seeing in our relationship some moments of his own past. I told him about my mother, an ocean away, living in the other Sakura. Just as we were about to leave, he hurried into the kitchen and presented us with a small bag of green tea from a nearby farming collective. We were so overwhelmed by his kindness that we asked if there was anything we could send him from Canada. No, no, he insisted, nothing to send. Just something to bring next time we visited: "Dried shiitake. And aspirin."

Paolo and I returned to Toronto on a blizzardy Sunday night in mid-January and I resumed work the next day. Kana, unexpectedly, was still in town. (In my absence, she had spent more time with our mother than she had since we were kids.) Back at work, to my surprise, I sank into old rhythms as though nothing had happened. And as the routine took over, I eventually began to believe nothing vital had changed at all.

In February, Baba and his wife had their twins a month early. Yasmine Belle Maloof was born first, at 5 1/4 pounds. Asaad Michel Maloof came ten minutes later, weighing just over 6 pounds and, according to Baba, announced himself with an ear-splitting squawk. They were both born with a thick mat of curly hair, which made them look uncannily like their father.

In March my father paid his yearly visit. We met up at his favourite restaurant, a French bistro in the east end of the city. I had been standing outside in my coat waiting. He showed up in a wool suit and tie, his hair noticeably whiter than the last time we had met. He looked distressingly elderly. As we made our way into the restaurant, he touched me lightly on my shoulder.

We had a quick lunch of soup and sandwiches before heading off to visit my mother. My father had rented a car, and as we caught up on recent events—my trip, his retirement—my eyes locked on his hands. I watched them as he flicked the indicator and rotated the steering wheel to the right, letting the wheel slide lightly through his fingers when the turn was complete.

I had always loved my father's hands. His body was slight but his hands were large, strong and square. They were hands that could play a piano or work a rotary saw. As a child I always wanted to hold them; longing to feel their rough texture and warmth clasping mine. But after my parents separated, this longing felt disloyal and I learned to tuck it away.

When we got to Sakura, my father pulled into a parking spot and turned off the engine. We arrived slightly ahead of schedule, so we sat there and started to talk. I rolled down my window to get some air. He told me he had been meeting up regularly with Kana, whom he referred to, in an aggravating fashion, as "our journalist *du jour*."

"We connect at airports. Heathrow and sometimes Gatwick," he said. "Our journalist *du jour* is doing great things out there in the world."

I said nothing, just sat there, glowering at the dashboard.

"Hey, why the frown?" he said.

I turned to face him. "Am I really such a failure?"

He looked shocked. "Not at all." He hesitated. "Naiko, you have to understand that sometimes I feel responsible. I imagine that things might have turned out differently if I hadn't . . ."

"No," I snapped. "No, they wouldn't have."

He rolled down his own window.

"Look. I like my job. I'm pretty good at it, too," I said. "Everything else, well, that's a different matter."

When he didn't say anything, I continued, feeling suddenly bold. "You know. Now that we're on the subject, I've always wondered why? Why all of a sudden? What happened? Did you lose 'the spark'?"

"It's complicated. We had a lot of ups and downs."

"That's it? Ups and downs? That was enough for you to just give up?"

"You were too little to understand."

"You left us alone."

"I never shut you out, Naiko. I left but I didn't reject you."

"Then why England? I mean, another town maybe I can understand. But a whole other continent?"

He rubbed his temples slowly. "At the time I thought it would be easier, I would save everyone the pain of seeing one another too often."

"It hurt anyway," I said. "It hurt more."

"Yes," he said. "I know." His tone was resigned but conclusive, as though those two words were the reparation of all his transgressions, all his failures as a father.

I felt the first stabs of a headache and put the heels of my hands over my eyes. When I removed them, everything looked blotchy and unfocused but the pain had receded. I glanced over and saw that my father was now slumped in his seat, a deflated version of himself.

I rolled up the window and took a deep, shaky breath. "Well, here we are." I smiled at him. "I realize it might not show, but I'm still glad you came."

"Me too," he said, and gave me a sad smile back.

I pointed at the clock on the dashboard: 3:03.

He patted his side pocket. "I brought your mother a charm for her bracelet. A silver lily of the valley with a pearl inside. Maybe we should go and give it to her."

I nodded.

As we walked through the front entrance, he slipped a grey envelope out of his suit pocket. I knew it contained the charm and it touched me. He didn't like extravagance, but at that moment there was something lavish about how hard he tried, when he tried.

That afternoon, as we sat in the common room at Sakura fumbling through the first moments of our reunion, my father complimenting the stack of tea biscuits my mother had prepared with Mary Yamada, my mother's stockinged feet, as she sat, brushing the floor with delight, I noticed that my hands were very similar to his. I had inherited large, strong hands—uncommon on a woman. The discovery filled me with pleasure.

While my father poured his third cup of tea, I excused myself to call Paolo and to give them time alone. On my way to the phone, I had a sudden desire to say hello to Gloria on the third floor, so I made a detour. I took the elevator up and walked down a short hallway to the ward entrance, where a nurse buzzed me in to the common area. I spotted Gloria reading a book in a secluded area by the window. An orderly was seated a metre away. Gloria was holding the book up by her chest like a plate of canapés, resting it flatly on one palm, turning the pages carefully with the other hand. I watched her in profile for a moment, then walked over.

"I filled up the notepad," she said once I had sat down.

"Shall I bring you another one?" I noticed a strange bracelet on her left arm. It looked like a white wristwatch but the face was blank.

She said, "I'd like that," then lowered the book to her lap.

I made out tiny black letters on the side of the bracelet: Wander-proof™.

"They won't let me have matches now."

I returned to the first floor, made my phone call and then walked back to the common room. When I entered, I saw my mother passing her purse to my father, who ran his fingertips lightly over the leather in a show of appreciation. When he noticed the damaged strap, he stopped and looked up.

My mother gave a little shrug and grinned at him.

He smiled and looked back down.

I glanced out the window and saw that it was growing cloudy outside.

We concluded our visit to Sakura on a friendly note. My father presented my mother with the gift he had brought. She was instantly entranced and kept shaking her wrist so that we could hear the tiny pearl tinkle inside the silver flower. Just as we were set to leave, Roy Ishii walked over and shook my hand. I was happy to see him. He had become a fixture of my visits.

"Bad *tenki, ne?*" he said, gesturing to the sky, then pointing to the matching grey stretch of corridor. "Same *iro, ne?* Exact same colour." He nodded at my father, then fished around in his pocket and handed us each a wrapped candy.

As I watched my father shuffle toward the departure gate the next morning, searching his jacket pocket for his boarding pass, a blushing smile passing across his face when he noticed my eyes on him, I felt something change inside me. He was not that father I had invented. I was not that daughter I had imagined. I wasn't pining anymore. I wasn't lonely.

I had driven with my father to the airport because it was a Sunday and because I wanted to and because he had asked. ("We have become a family of airport habitués," he drawled in a playful patrician manner.) I waited right up until the plane took off. I put my hand against the glass along with the other families and watched the Boeing 747 taxi along the runway, rise into the air and slowly disappear. I had never done that before and I found the ceremony oddly reassuring. It was a leaving ritual.

It reminded me that there can be such a thing as a good ending.

Two days after my father's visit, Paolo and I celebrated our fifth anniversary together. To surprise him, I did a little spring cleaning. I emptied out two drawers in my dresser. I cleared off a few more hangers in the hallway closet. I polished a small wooden table near the balcony window and placed a potted ivy on it so it would get just the right amount of sun. My intention was to create a space for Paolo to feel more welcome when he stayed over. Remembering how much he hated seeing good flowers go to waste, I resuscitated an old bouquet of gerbera, removing the smelly, viscous water from the glass vase, picking off the brown petals and spraying the healthy ones. I let the water run until it was cold and clear, filled the vase and added a spoonful of sugar—a trick Paolo had taught me.

After I had finished preparing the living room, I moved on to the bathroom. I had bought Paolo a fancy shaving kit and I threw out his old disposable razor. The kit came with a chrome-handled razor, a shaving brush with natural boar bristles and a stainless steel bowl filled with shaving soap. I set each item out on the bathroom shelf I had prepared for him.

To my surprise, during our dinner there was no mention of Paolo moving in. I kept waiting for him to say something, but by the time dessert arrived, I realized he wasn't going to bother. What surprised me—astonished me, really—was my disappointment.

We had left the restaurant, and as we were walking through the park near my apartment, I was talking about my day. "There were two cremation urns this morning. I don't think I've ever seen one, and all of a sudden there are two in one day. Do you think that's a bad omen? . . . Paolo?" I tapped him on the shoulder and stopped walking. "Did you hear anything I just said?"

He stopped, rubbed his palm over his neck, looked momentarily confused. "Sorry? What did you say?"

"Hey. Look at me, okay?" I grabbed his hand, clutching it.

He nodded but tried to extricate his hand.

"No. Keep holding," I said, and squeezed harder. His mouth opened from the pressure.

"Tell me something," I said. "Are you satisfied?" I was remembering the question Andrei had asked us on his first day at work.

Paolo arched an eyebrow. "Am I satisfied?"

"I'm asking if you're happy." I looked at his face, which showed he was now thinking, contemplating. "I want to know, are you fairly, spectacularly or not at all content?" I flapped his hand impatiently. "Well? Are you?"

As he considered the options, a wind lifted the snow off the ground and the air filled with blowing particles. I shivered. I don't know how long we stood there, but at some point I let go of his hand.

I felt heartbreak at Paolo's obvious uncertainty. For a moment, he looked like he wanted to walk on, but finally he turned to me, ready to speak.

"I could be," he said.

"Okay then," I said quickly. "Okay," I repeated with resolve, and clasped my hands in front of me like a jolly friar. I felt a grin spreading across my face.

When we hugged, it felt different. It felt as though I came into my body, came into the present. I am really here, I thought, nuzzling my face into the side of his neck. It was such a sense of discovery. I started giggling.

Paolo stepped back, put his index finger to his temple and made a circular motion. He whistled like a cuckoo but I didn't care if he thought I was off my rocker.

My body felt alive with heat and cold. I wrapped my arms around myself and jumped up and down, bleating, "Brrr. Brrr. Brrr."

It would have been so easy for one or both of us to have given up.

I took hold of his fingers and we walked and then ran toward home.

Thirty

*I*t is my job to distinguish between objects, to arrange things into clean boxes, sorting the similar from the dissimilar. It is the modus operandi of my working existence. It's what I do best. Every morning when Marvin arrives I must begin again.

In the anarchic bins he delivers I see the whole world, the chaos and the change. Someone in the pile may give birth tomorrow. Or die. Someone will fall in love. Or get divorced. Someone else will retire. Or move into a nursing home. Someone will leave for Mozambique. Or Florida. Eternity stretches here, in this pile of photos, keepsakes, books. What brings me to isolate this rather than that particular thing, story, person? (Why him, why you, why then, why now?)

I am not a collector or a saver by nature. But several months ago I set my own box aside. I have been chucking unclaimed pieces of silverware into it. I can see a bohemian picnic aesthetic emerging. There are forks with bent tines and butter knives with chipped bone handles. And there are spoons. Lots of spoons. Dainty ones with little engraved flowers. Tiny ones with airline logos. Tablespoons with metal bark handles. Thick weighty soup spoons with an agreeable dip. Spoons, knives, forks, never meant to be brought together, some from the dingiest of cafeterias, others from elite dining rooms—the cutlery of class. I polish each piece until it gleams in the light. I am hoping to compose a complete set in time for Christmas. It will be my present to Paolo. When I am finished, I may paint a blue band around their handles, or have them engraved with a *P*—something to stamp them as a family. Or maybe I will just leave them as they are, odd and mismatched.

I am learning more about what true and unconditional love really is.

Today something unusual happened at work, something that has happened only twice before during my nine years in mail recovery. Halfway through the morning I realized that my hamper was empty.

I might have celebrated the accomplishment, but I felt strangely lost. Had I botched things, taken too many shortcuts? I have learned I am error-prone when not fully focused. I had to work to a plan, sorting and storing, or things were as good as lost.

Before I could think any further on the matter, the clatter of Marvin arriving interrupted my thoughts. He was pushing a bucket toward me. It was full. He had several vintage concert buttons and a smiley face pinned to his open jacket, his own private message board. His T-shirt said: *This is it*, referring, I suppose, to life. A small cellophane bag of chocolate dangled from between his teeth. Christmas is coming.

And so it begins again.

Andrei once said that there are things best kept to oneself, that to share is not necessarily to give; thoughts and objects can become a burden to others or become lost in forgotten drawers. But, I say, not all things, and not for all time.

I still dream about him. I wake up feeling soft and bleary, not immediately remembering what I've dreamt, but then I know. It's the birds that tip me off. I hear the *whoosh* of their wings in my head and I know he's still with me.

For all its dangers, I still put faith in constancy; such is the core of human nature, I think. Every day when I open the door to my apartment (yes, my apartment, I still live alone) and venture into the world, there are habits of seeking, reaching, testing, retracting that endure. As a geographer's daughter, I am aware that the ground on which I stand will shift but I trust that it will endure, and that on it things will grow and walk and stomp and live. I know that there will be days when nothing lines up and other days filled with amazing moments of consonance. I suppose that this makes me an optimist. I did not inherit my father's pessimism after all.

This morning as I rode the bus to work I thought of Kana. One day she may come home. One day she may even say, "I kind of left you holding the bag."

I watched the early December snow drift past the windows.

Somewhere in the world there is my father. Somewhere in the world there is Andrei. I think of us—them, myself—moving around the planet, each one scuffed and creased, each one overlaid with labels, scrawled with histories. I imagine that the future is where we send ourselves, not knowing when or how we'll arrive.
"Look," says a voice behind me. Then a creaking sound.

When I turn around, Warren is leaning back in his chair, a letter in his outstretched hand.

"Look at this," he says.

Acknowledgments

I feel extremely fortunate to be surrounded by a community of friends and extended family who fill my life with wisdom and humour on a daily basis. Many thanks to Jude Binder, Brett Burlock, Terence Dick, Mario DiPaolantonio, Brenda Joy Lem, Avi Lewis, Kelly O'Brien, Sarah Rosensweet, Sugie Shimizu, Frank Venezia, Megan Wells and the Maclears of Sussex (especially Andrew, Robin and Ingrid), all of whom kept me company throughout the writing of this book, and many of whom read earlier versions of the manuscript and offered significant insights. This book would truly not have been possible without the presence of four guardian angels: Eliza Beth Burroughs, Naomi Binder Wall, Nancy Friedland and Naomi Klein.

Several of the events that take place in Romania, while fictional-ized, are loosely structured around actual historical events. For help in limning background details, I wish to acknowledge the following books and authors: *Out of Romania* by Dan Antal, *The Hole in the Flag: A Romanian Exile's Story of Return and Revolution* by Andrei Codrescu, *The Appointment* by Herta Muller, *Exit into History* and "Obsessed with Words" by Eva Hoffman, *The Seamstress* by Sara Tuvel Bernstein, *The Return* by Petru Popescu. Of the other works that have informed this novel, I would especially like to mention the following: Eleanor Cooney's *Death in Slow Motion* and Thomas DeBaggio's *Losing My Mind*, two powerful chronicles of Alzheimer's disease; Audrey Kobayashi's *Memories of Our Past: A Brief History & Walking Tour of Powell Street*, a reconstruction of Vancouver's pre-war Japanese Canadian community; and Stephen Andrews' *Facsimile*, a haunting series of portraits drawn from faxed obituary photos.

Speaking in the Air by John Durham Peters, "Remembering the Dead" by James H. Bruns, "Lost in the Mail" by Jonathan Franzen and Paul Tough's radio segment "Other People's Mail" on *This American Life* provided helpful particulars on mail recovery. *Let the Children Come* by Robert B. Lantz introduced me to the Christian practice of object lessons. The "Czech author" mentioned on page 245 is based on Milan Kundera, who wrote about the "lost years" of Communism in his book *Testaments Betrayed: An Essay in Nine Parts* (HarperCollins, 1993: p. 225).

The image of Rachel throwing valuables into the latrines at Auschwitz-Birkenau on page 286 was inspired by Chavka Raban-Folman's testimony "The Liaison Agent" in *Women in the Holocaust*, eds. Jehoshua Eibeshitz and Anna Eilenberg-Eibeshitz.

For those interested in an inside view of the fall of the Ceausescu regime, I highly recommend *Videograms of a Revolution*, Harun Farocki and Andrei Ujica's fascinating video essay covering the events of 1989.

I am profoundly thankful to George Foussias, Marvin Waxman and Marvin Wiesenthal for their support; to Horia Albu and artist-curator Mona Filip for sharing thoughts and memories about their former homeland, Romania; and to Hiromi Goto, Karen Hanson, Elisabeth Harvor and the Humber School of Writing, Kerri Sakamoto, M. NourbeSe Philip, Martha Baillie and Lorissa Sengara for providing literary mentorship over the years.

I am also appreciative of the Japan Foundation Library, the Gladstone Hotel, and the wonderful caregivers at Queen Street Childcare Centre and Givins-Shaw School and Daycare for their respective gifts of writing space and writing time.

My deepest gratitude to:

The Canada Council for the Arts, the Ontario Arts Council and the Toronto Arts Council, for foundational support.

The amazing team at HarperCollins Canada, particularly Kate Cassaday, Debbie Gaudet, Sharon Kish, Allyson Latta, Nita Pronovost and Noelle Zitzer for showing true dedication.

Nicole Winstanley, for expressing steady faith.

Jackie Kaiser, a model of kindness, for guiding this book to print with such commitment and flair.

Phyllis Bruce, for performing great feats of literary and human magic.

Finally and foremost, I offer a toast to my loving family—and in particular:

My parents, Mariko and Michael Maclear.

David Wall, my soulmate.

Yoshi and Mika, our two beautiful boys.

This is for you.

About the author

About the book

Ideas,
interviews
& features

Read on

Author Biography

KYO MACLEAR was born in London, England, in 1970. At age three, she enjoyed a brief theatrical career in *The King and I* at the Adelphi Theatre on the Strand. "I had the loudest voice at the audition," she says. "My only line was 'I believe in snow.' It was a visionary sentiment." A year later, in the midst of "a very snowy winter," she and her parents moved to Toronto, Canada.

Maclear graduated from the University of Toronto with an undergraduate degree in fine art and art history, and a graduate degree in cultural studies. She spent many years writing creative non-fiction, short prose and poetry before taking the plunge into novel writing with *The Letter Opener* (2007). She has compared the process of crafting a novel to "a high-wire act," adding that "sometimes it's best to keep going and not look down."

Her earliest writing began with her active involvement in the anti-apartheid movement. "I used to write and illustrate our group's literature. It was very declarative, zealous writing. The challenge was to use language to *literally* move people." She says that her subsequent magazine writing took place in fits and starts between university sessions and job contracts. She was on an academic path through her mid-twenties (much to the chagrin of her parents—who formed a "less school is the best school" lobby once they discovered she was not on her way to becoming a lawyer or an orthodontist). In fact, she was all set to start a PhD when she decided she needed to leave the academic world because she cared about writing and language too much. "I wanted to explore literary subjects

Kyo Maclear

2

and knew I couldn't do that and remain under the blanket of academia. . . . At some point, I heard a writer give a talk in which he advised writers to forgo narrative shortcuts and enjoy 'the scenic route,' and that's what I've tried to do ever since—be less rushed, be more perceptually and emotionally open."

In 1997, she received a Banff Arts Journalism Fellowship under chair Michael Ignatieff, and in 2003, she took part in the Humber School for Writers' creative writing correspondence program, under mentor Elisabeth Harvor.

One of Maclear's great pleasures over the years has been writing about the visual arts for such publications as *Canadian Art, Saturday Night* and *Toronto Life.* "Writing about art, like writing about music or food, is an exercise in perseverance and humility. One can circle the subject forever and still never capture its essence. What often matters most in art are the aspects that cannot be explained. I have found perseverance and humility to be equally important traits in the development of fiction. When I write, I sometimes feel like a Victorian collector chasing my own version of a butterfly, trying to net the inexpressible."

Maclear garnered a nomination for a National Magazine Award in 2001 for her essay "Pictures at an Execution," which appeared in *Saturday Night.* Three years later, she was shortlisted for *This Magazine*'s Great Literary Hunt. Her graduate thesis, *Beclouded Visions: Hiroshima–Nagasaki and the Art of Witness*, was subsequently published by State University of New York Press (1999). Maclear is also the co-author of *Private Investigators: Undercover in Public Space* ▶

     ❝ When I write, I sometimes feel like a Victorian collector chasing my own version of a butterfly, trying to net the inexpressible. **❞**

(Banff Centre Press, 1999), co-editor of *Life Style*, by Bruce Mau (Phaidon, 2000), and former editor of *Mix* magazine.

In addition to writing, Maclear works as an editor and has illustrated one children's book, and numerous book and CD covers. She lives in Toronto with singer and composer David Wall and their two children. Maclear is currently writing her second novel, for which the Ontario Arts Council awarded her a Chalmers Arts Fellowship.

About the author

4

Inside *The Letter Opener*

Much of *The Letter Opener* takes place in the Undeliverable Mail Office, a warehouse that resembles a giant pawnshop. What research did you undertake to render the details and feel of this unusual place?

I have never worked in a post office, though I sometimes think that being a letter carrier would suit my temperament—I like walking; I like solitude. I was originally drawn to the symbolism of the setting, the psychological and historical richness of an Undeliverable Mail Office.

Once I determined that the story would be set there, I made arrangements to visit an actual mail recovery centre in Mississauga and spent an afternoon observing the detective-manner of the employees, the serried rows of objects, the buckets of errant mail. Something about the place spoke to me on a gut level. Its attempt at order. Its massiveness. Yet also its humanness.

Beyond conducting that research visit, I also read what I could find on dead-letter offices, which, surprisingly, wasn't very much. I reread Herman Melville's classic story "Bartleby the Scrivener" (the despondent Bartleby was said to have once been employed as a dead-letter office clerk). But mostly, I embellished by drawing on other mausoleum-like places I have known. Antique emporiums. Library archives. The Musée de Cluny in Paris. It's a kind of obvious necrophilia, I suppose, but I do find something numinous in the experience of being among aged and ancient objects. ▶

> It's a kind of obvious necrophilia, I suppose, but I do find something numinous in the experience of being among aged and ancient objects.

Inside *The Letter Opener* (*continued*)

One is reminded when reading your novel that everyday objects and personal effects have significance as touchstones for memories, and even as talismans. What objects, lost or found, personal or public, hold meaning for you?

Strangely, I grew up in a family of few heirlooms. I think that part of this can be attributed to the fact that both of my parents came from families of modest means and grew up in the tumult of the Second World War. I also have a theory that when my parents decided to leave their cultures of origin, they made a resolution to travel lightly—hoping to experience the tabula rasa effect of resettlement.

Once they arrived in Canada, it was quite a different story. By the mid-1970s, my parents entered a period of rapid accumulation. My mother, who started an art gallery, collected Japanese prints, and later, antiques; and my father, who was travelling constantly as a journalist, collected, along with stories, handcrafted objects from around the world. The benefit of having grown up in such an eclectic home is that I was often surrounded by the most incredible and eccentric objects—yet, oddly, few of those items stand out in my memory today. I think what I carry from my childhood is the gestalt of a house crammed with beautiful things, which is probably why I'm drawn to flea markets and why I'll never be a minimalist. My idea of heaven is a souk on a warm afternoon.

My children both have "loveys"—or what psychologists sometimes refer to as "security"

❝ My idea of heaven is a souk on a warm afternoon. ❞

6

or "transitional" objects. My transitional objects are books. I'm a sucker for beautiful monographs and chapbooks with interesting images and typography. But I have to say that the books that mean the most to me are the ones that were given to me by close friends and family. They don't substitute for the people I love, but they have, on occasion, kept me company and given me tangible comfort.

Your novel features Andrei, a Romanian refugee. What moved you to write about the immigrant experience?

I grew up in Toronto, but I was born in England to a British father and a Japanese mother. When we came to Canada, we were all new immigrants with no real ties to our new home. Fortunately, my father had a job placement with the CBC, which provided a comfortable cushion for our landing. In that sense, we did not have the typical immigrant experience. We did not face many of the uncertainties and hardscrabble realities of life in a foreign land.

That said, the thing about being of mixed-race ancestry, I've realized, is that one never fully "arrives" or becomes "settled" in the traditional sense. A hybrid house is a compression of influence, a constant negotiation of language and custom. When you're a person of mixed descent, words such as *roots* and *homeland* are immediately denaturalized.

Growing up in the 1970s and 1980s in Canada, and spending summers in Japan, I often felt as though I was on the outside looking in. Depending on the context, that feeling can be fairly painful and isolating. ▶

> The thing about being of mixed-race ancestry ... is that one never fully 'arrives' or becomes 'settled' in the traditional sense.

7

Inside *The Letter Opener* (*continued*)

But, as it turns out, inhabiting a cultural boundary is actually good for writers. It means being constantly on your toes, in a state of perpetual observation. I think this vantage point has been formative in drawing me to the stories and experiences of people who feel they don't quite belong or feel they belong in many places at once—those who stand outside national narratives by virtue of who they are.

In *The Letter Opener*, I derived a certain pleasure from playing with racial expectations through the characters of Andrei and Naiko, in terms of who typically gets cast in the role of "the immigrant" and who tends to fit the profile of "the Canadian." It was clear from the beginning that I wanted to avoid a simplifying saviour motif—the notion that an immigrant arrives to an open and rescuing embrace. My intention was to explore an empathetic relationship between the two characters, not a flawless one.

Your protagonist, Naiko, struggles to deal with her mother's declining cognitive abilities as a result of Alzheimer's. What are your thoughts on memory and how it defines us?

Let me say here that I have no direct experience with Alzheimer's in my family, but having watched families undergo the ordeal, I feel I have gained a few limited insights.

I don't think it is overstating matters to say that memory is what gives us our identity. We rely on memories for a sense of continuity. When a memory is revised or missing, our

> **Memory is what gives us our identity.**

self-perception can be affected in ways that may leave us feeling lost, upset or angry. Think about how unhinging it is to forget the name of a person in your personal photo album or school yearbook, especially someone with whom you were once on intimate terms. Then imagine that you are the one being forgotten, that your mother is quizzing you, asking, "How are we related again?" What happens when a relationship is irretrievably altered by memory loss—say, through dementia or emotional amnesia?

There is a kind of doubling that occurs in the novel between Naiko's mother and Andrei; both feel they are losing a foothold in worlds they once knew deeply. The way Naiko's mother reacts to this sense of flux and uncertainty is to grab hold of the material world. She becomes a hoarder. Rather than see her response through the medical lens of "obsession," I try to humanize it by setting her behaviour in a wider context and by showing that there can be moments of grace, humour and intense connection even in the midst of a devastating memory illness. I also wanted to explore this idea of "letting go" and whether there are times when forgetting is a necessary and even a healthy condition of life.

What place, if any, does the old-fashioned letter have in this electronic age?

I grew up writing letters because it was expected of me. All of our relatives were in other countries, and it fell upon me to keep in touch. I have since learned that many immigrant families delegate this job of keeping in touch to the children of the house. ▶

" Forgetting is a necessary and even a healthy condition of life. "

Now that many of my relatives have e-mail accounts, my list of traditional pen pals has dwindled to two—a step-grandmother living in Brighton, England, and a friend in Toronto with whom I continue an erratic but satisfying correspondence.

My six-year-old son recently cottoned on to the whole letter-writing idea. To him, dropping an envelope in a red-and-blue box and having it appear two days later in your home mailbox is a kind of magic—on par with pulling rabbits from hats. When I see his excitement, a part of me thinks, *How quaint.* You see, my son still doesn't know that letters are "old-fashioned." He has no idea that letters have become the ascot or bowler hat of communication media, that to partake of a dying trend is to be ascribed with an aura of outmodedness and—worse!—affectation. Because I have a sentimental streak, I sometimes wonder if either of my children will ever have the opportunity to send a handwritten love letter without feeling pompous or ironic. I feel fortunate that I was born early enough to have had the experience of conducting deep friendships and romances by surface mail. I'll never forget the experience of receiving a letter from my husband-to-be when I was staying for a time with an uncle in Mallorca. Nothing can replace the tactile significance of holding and reading a letter sent by someone you desire.

Having said all this, letter writing is still the primary means of written communication for many of the world's people. Such is the unevenness of technological "progress" that

> **Nothing can replace the tactile significance of holding and reading a letter sent by someone you desire.**

a BlackBerry still holds the connotation of exotic fruit in most global communities. Even at my son's downtown Toronto school, at least a third of the families are without e-mail access.

In my novel, I wanted to give form to the idea that people live in different "nows." By dint of geography, history, trauma or good fortune, they may be worlds and decades removed from one another. A teenager in Fallujah and a teenager in Tulsa may wear identical Nike t-shirts but in every other respect be completely out of sync.

So for me, the questions become: What stories are being left behind or are not finding a listener simply because they don't fit a familiar form or idiom? What qualities of social interaction are lost when a medium—such as letter writing—fades in significance? If Canada is a kind of meta-version of the Undeliverable Mail Office, what letters and people aren't finding a proper home?

In some respects, *The Letter Opener* is an allegory of disconnection and connection: it is about friends who never write back and strangers who choose to listen.

—To listen to a HarperCollins Canada Prosecast interview with the author and hear her read from The Letter Opener, *visit* **www.foursevens.com/prosecast** *and scroll down to "Kyo Maclear."*

&

> If Canada is a kind of meta-version of the Undeliverable Mail Office, what letters and people aren't finding a proper home?

On Postal Phantoms and Becoming Corrupted

Shortly after The Letter Opener *was published, I was invited to give a talk to a large group of book devotees about the inspiration for the story. Given that the novel was incubated in my household letterbox, I thought I'd prepare for the talk by collecting a week's worth of mail as an exercise in inventory.*

Well, here's my stack, more or less: A few bills, bank statements, membership renewals, postcards, gallery announcements . . . and a well-timed arts grant.

There are times when my mail is less uniform, less boring.

Every now and then, something unexpected or unusual arrives. A letter from a childhood friend whose big, loopy handwriting appears to have remained the same since fifth grade. A large manila envelope containing half a quilt, *literally* a quilt cut in half, sent from an offbeat writer/acquaintance living in British Columbia.

Not only this week but many weeks, I receive mail addressed to a certain Mr. Szabo. Mr. Szabo is our family's postal phantom. I should think every house has one. Over the past few years, we have seen at least a hundred letters addressed to Mr. Szabo—a man who, for whatever reason, never got around to having his mail redirected.

Because I have moved countless times over the course of three decades, and because I scrimp and only ever pay for several months of mail forwarding, it is highly possible that

> " Mr. Szabo is our family's postal phantom. I should think every house has one. "

12

I am someone else's postal phantom. It is probable, in fact, that there are envelopes addressed to Kyo Maclear regularly mingling with Canadian Tire flyers or "2 for 1" pizza coupons in recycling bins around downtown Toronto.

In my efforts to be a good citizen, I am fairly consistent about returning Mr. Szabo's mail. I leave it for the mail carrier or drop it in a postbox with the words *MOVED* or *INCORRECT ADDRESS* scrawled on the front. I consider this a small act of resuscitation. I don't like the idea of my mailbox being an end point. I believe every letter deserves a fair chance at survival.

A few years ago, Mr. Szabo's mail prompted me to start thinking about other unsolicited arrivals. I found myself wondering: What if I were suddenly to receive someone else's mail in my box—a parcel so tempting and irresistible that it set off all my prying urges, triggered all the habits of voyeurism I have cultivated through countless years of reading *People* magazine, watching reality TV and whatnot? What if, upon receiving such a parcel, I simply could not resist "coaxing" it open? But then, what if upon opening it I were to discover that it was not what I thought or expected at all? It was not a love letter. Or a prize announcement. Or a shiny new bauble. Or a party invitation. What if this package did not conform to any of my ritualized expectations? What if—more to the point—it contained a letter asking for help or insight or, more simply, a witness.

My first novel has something to do with this world of lost and misdirected mail. It's the story of a young woman named Naiko ▶

> ❝ I don't like the idea of my mailbox being an end point. I believe every letter deserves a fair chance at survival. ❞

On Postal Phantoms and Becoming Corrupted (*continued*)

Guildford who, in her strange detective work as a mail recovery employee at a dead-letter office in Toronto, finds more mystery and more meaning in the world of lost objects than in the people around her—that is, until she meets Andrei. He is a Romanian refugee who arrived in Canada five years earlier and who works beside her in the dead-letter office. One day, he mysteriously disappears. During the short time that Naiko and Andrei are acquainted, he shares the story of his past life in communist Romania and the tale of his harrowing escape across the Bosphorus.

Naiko has led a fairly insulated existence until this point, and her initial reaction to Andrei's story and subsequent disappearance is to want to return to the secure harbour of her former life, to bury herself in familiar routines. She tries to put Andrei's story out of her mind, its enormity and otherness, its unresolved drama. But she finds that it won't budge.

What Naiko discovers is that some stories cannot be consumed and forgotten. Some letters cannot be resealed. They make demands on us.

In the 1990s, I met a man from Romania. I knew nothing about the country. I quickly racked my brain for some associations and images. I came up with very little. Transylvania. Dracula. And from the art history pocket of my mind, the name Constantin Brâncuși—really just a few simplified bits. Had I met the man today, I might have had

> Some letters cannot be sealed. They make demands of us.

a few more items to summon forth—but truthfully, not many more. The reality is that Romania (like so many other neglected "B-list" countries) rarely cracks North American headlines, unless in the context of former gulags being used in the U.S. war on terror or a village standing in for Borat's fictional hometown in Kazakhstan.

When I met this man from Romania, I knew only the barest details of the 1989 revolution and the fall of Ceausescu. I was only dimly aware of the widespread repression that preceeded the revolts and had no frame of reference for the anarchy and bloodshed that ensued. Any information I had was vague and impersonal. I could not trace a single name or story.

Perhaps the seed of this novel rests in that initial encounter with a stranger—and the embarrassment I felt at my own lack of knowledge. Perhaps most of my work is an attempt to bring what was once faraway and hazy a little bit nearer. At any rate, I found myself driven to pursue the matter. And so, I began the gradual limning of scenes and characters that up to that moment had not existed. The process was sporadic, tentative, delirious.

It turns out that characters do not appear at the mere flourish of a wand or simply because you *want* them to.

Writing is the art of bothering. Of paying attention. For me, it has been a way of entering into a conversation with the unfamiliar. I've never subscribed to the motto "Write what you know." Substitute the words *read, eat, do, be, live* for *write* and you get a sense of how restrictive and solipsistic it is as an idea. I sometimes think a more useful bit ▶

Writing is the art of bothering. Of paying attention.

On Postal Phantoms and Becoming Corrupted (*continued*)

of advice is, "Write what you *wish* or *need* to know, bearing in mind that to do so means to proceed carefully, thoughtfully."

I like to think that fiction—as opposed to journalism—opens a particular ethical window onto the world. One thing a novel can do, which newspaper articles can't always do, is *particularize*. By focusing on the anecdotal, novels can take a big narrative—such as post-war communism in Romania—and make it feel less epic and anonymous. It can, for instance, take one man's personal unhappiness and give it depth and grit, and, in so doing, lift it out of the vast and (sadly) more impenetrable context of collective despair. It may move us to care about a stranger—such as a Mr. Szabo or a man from Romania—with whom we seem, at first, to share nothing in common. For me, that's what makes a book worth reading—and writing.

We spend most of our time shut in our homes, our cars, at work. How many of us regularly (or *ever*) experience what Naiko does in this novel, a chance encounter that pushes her outside of her comfort zone, that opens a door to the unknown?

I wrote *The Letter Opener* because I was compelled to pursue a conversation that had been left unfinished in my mind. The novel was driven by fragments. It was incited by questions as basic as *Who is Mr. Szabo? Why should I care about Romania? Where do dead letters go?* Having arrived at this point, I can tell you that the answer to that last question was by far the easiest to obtain.

> ❝ I've never subscribed to the motto 'Write what you know.' ❞

It turns out that the work of mail recovery and the work of writing bear certain resemblances. I discovered this unexpected kinship when I journeyed to the suburbs of Toronto and paid a visit to Canada Post's Undeliverable Mail Office.

The scene was instantly familiar: the hunched posture of the staff, the inadequate lighting, the endless labour of sorting and redirecting—the penchant for dark, comfy clothes. I recognized other commonalities, too: how difficult it can be to proceed according to plan, how very easy it is to get distracted or detained.

I noted how both mail recovery and writing require wading through mounds of stuff—the flotsam of wayward parcels, the dross of initial ideas. Both involve zeroing in on the specific, the beauty or the outrage of the particular.

"What have you seen? Tell me the most moving thing," I'd ask, and the response: *A suicide note.*

"Tell me the strangest thing," I'd ask again, and the answer: *A prosthetic leg. The skull of a goose.*

What's the hardest thing about your job?
Countless letters are shredded.
And the best thing?
Countless letters are successfully redirected.

Our world is not moving closer. In reality, we are pulling apart like tectonic plates. These letters we write to each other, these stories we tell, crossing oceans and generations, sometimes cropping up in strangers' mailboxes, move against the grain of cultural isolationism. These tales of bittersweet globalism speak to our interdependence. ▶

"" Both mail recovery and writing . . . involve zeroing in on the specific, the beauty or the outrage of the particular. ""

On Postal Phantoms and Becoming Corrupted (*continued*)

As Tony Kushner put it so simply and so beautifully in the opening monologue to his play *Homebody/Kabul*, "Ours is a time of connection. The private, and we must accept this, the private is gone. All must be touched. All touch corrupts. All must be corrupted."

—*Adapted from a talk presented at the Ben McNally/*Globe and Mail *Books & Brunch, Spring 2007.*

Indelible Ink (My Most Memorable Letter)

A. was the kind of person who attracted devotees. His warmth made the shy feel unshy, the awkward feel less so. He had a fully formed look (call it "Brainy New Wave"), which showed that he took pleasure in appearances, even if he didn't seem to care how he was seen by others. While many of us in grade nine were splintering off into cliques and subsets, he was fluid and global in his friendships. I swooned over him for a full year—and I know I wasn't alone. He could make black jeans, a plaid shirt and suspenders look really good.

Summer holidays had just begun when he died unexpectedly. He was in Botswana on an expedition with his anthropologist father. Their vehicle overturned on a remote bush road. Two days after I heard the news, I was banished to Japan (or so it felt at the time). The truth was that I was travelling to Tokyo with my mother to visit family, but it meant that I missed A.'s memorial service and with it, the opportunity to mourn among friends.

That summer was a lonely and painful one, probably the worst I've ever experienced. There was one saving grace: J., a friend of mine and a childhood friend of A.'s, was spending the summer with his parents in Paris. Our sense of exile created a kinship between us. J. kept me afloat by sending me entertaining letters and mixed cassettes of "synthpop" by Jean Michel Jarre and The Art of Noise, the music creating a melancholy and otherworldy mist that floated over my days and nights. ▶

> ❝ I swooned over him for a full year—and I know I wasn't alone. He could make black jeans, a plaid shirt and suspenders look really good. ❞

Indelible Ink (*continued*)

J. and I didn't discuss A. much, but we were both aware of each other's grief, and this was comforting. We were fifteen. Losing A. was the saddest thing that had ever happened to us.

A week before I was set to return home, my father called from Toronto.

"There is a letter here for you."

"Who's it from?"

"I'm not sure. I think maybe that boy…"

"When did it arrive?"

"I've been very busy these past few weeks." (He had a deft way of deflecting my questions.)

"Is it a long letter?"

"I'm really looking forward to seeing you," he said with a cheerful tone of finality.

The letter had been waiting for me for nearly two months. My father later claimed he believed that if I had read it while still in Japan, it would have upset me "unnecessarily." He wanted to protect me. He talked about the letter as though it were written with a poison pen.

Even though I'd been forewarned, returning home and seeing the envelope lying there on my bedspread was surreal. The handwriting was recognizable. I remember thinking, *A letter from a dead person? Is this some sort of cruel hoax?*

I carried the envelope around for a full day before opening it, and later, curled up on the sofa, I opened it with the sort of precision one might use when defusing a bomb, nail scissors moving slowly and surgically along the edge. A.'s death had robbed me of a certain spontaneity. I was conscious of posterity.

> ❝ He talked about the letter as though it were written with a poison pen. ❞

20

He began with greetings in Setswana, *Herero* and *!Kung*, and in the body of the letter, his writing displayed all the twisted elements one might expect from a fifteen-year-old boy. (He describes drinking beer from vending machines in Amsterdam one moment, then watching *Mr. Dressup* in Afrikaans in Johannesburg the next.) The letter is funny and hormonal, thumbprints and scribbles and contradictory emotions all muddle together on the page. In the middle of an intimate confession, he breaks into a completely unrelated comic-strip fantasy about a character named "New Wave Dave," who transforms into a superhero named "Pot Man."

I remember the relief of reaching the end of the letter without shattering into a thousand pieces. And I remember reading it again, and again, foraging, feeling lustful and hungry, and engaging in magical thinking. *How can he be dead? We have plans! There are concerts to see!*

The letter wasn't one that allowed me to wallow in sadness, because it was so pulsing and real. It was caring without being careful—not a sentence felt calibrated or considered. I don't think I've ever been so playfully and fearlessly addressed. Without knowing it, A. set the romantic standard for years to come.

Midway through his letter, A. describes a trip he is about to take by truck, "about a 400-mile drive down a dirt road." A hand-drawn map of Botswana shows the route with a broken line beginning in the capital city of Gaborone and ending in Dobe ("our destination"). Two stops are marked along the way. One is ▶

❝ The letter wasn't one that allowed me to wallow in sadness, because it was so pulsing and real. ❞

Indelible Ink (*continued*)

Francistown. The other is Maun. Beside the dot for Maun, there is a sentence: *You're sending letters here. You are sending letters, aren't you?*

It makes me happy knowing that he wanted me to write. I know I would have. Although I wasn't sure at the time, I now believe this was a love letter—not the kind that makes you feel prettier, happier, skinnier, but the kind that makes you feel more alive. It's shockingly life-affirming.

I rarely talk about A. anymore. I feel morbid when I do, as if I'm trying to impress. ("Want to hear the story of my first love?") Most adults can't accept this level of gravity in everyday conversation without discomfort. But when I reread his letter, as I sometimes do, it still surprises me; none of the energy has drained away. Some letters are great. Only a few are indelible. This one from a friend who died, this one from someplace else still reminds me: *There is no such thing as feeling or living too much.*

❝ Some letters are great. Only a few are indelible. **❞**

ﾟ

Postcard Art

The postcards that follow were created to mark the launch of *The Letter Opener*. They are mementoes of characters and scenes in the book, and were made by layering simple ink drawings, gouache, stamps and postmarks. (For the envelopes, I used recycled "dead letters," purchased at John H. Talman Ltd.'s philatelic store in downtown Toronto.)

The illustrations are meant to evoke parts of the story in the way a tourist card might use a palm tree to symbolize a Caribbean country—that is, they reduce as much as they reveal.

I like collage because it appeals to my sense of memory and the way it is always a matter of partial details rather than complete vistas. Every book written is a letter in search of a recipient. Some days, when the winds are just right, a book, like a letter, will travel across oceans and deserts straight to a sympathetic stranger's door. ▶

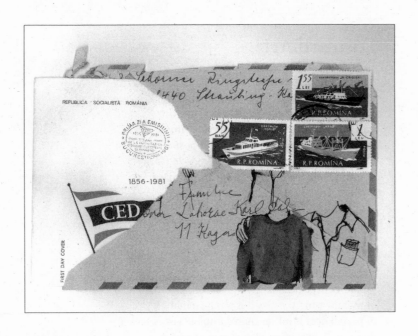

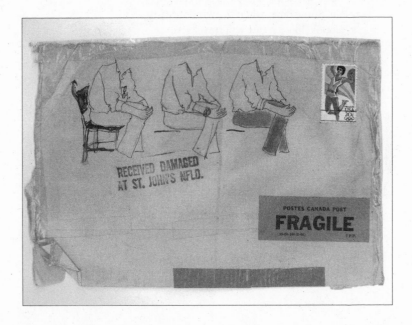

Letters, Lost and Found

Contrary to popular belief, the promise "Neither snow nor rain nor heat nor gloom of night stays these couriers from the swift completion of their appointed rounds" is not the official motto of the U.S. Postal Service, though it is displayed on the post office in New York City. The words are those of Greek historian Herodotus, writing 2,500 years ago. He was describing the Persians who delivered mail by horseback.

Mail delivery has come a long way since then, but we continue to be frustrated by letters lost, and delighted and fascinated by letters found. Here are some examples:

• One of the world's greatest collections of historical letters was discovered in June 2007 in a filing cabinet tucked away in the basement laundry room of a villa in Lausanne, Switzerland. Amassed by private collector Albin Schram, the stash comprised almost 1,000 documents penned by great monarchs, scientists, authors, painters, philosophers and musicians from the fifteenth to the twentieth century in almost every European language. One of the finds, a letter from Napoleon to his future wife, Josephine, later sold at auction in England for the equivalent of US$556,000.

• Prior to the First World War, knowing how skilled clerks in the U.S. dead-letter office were at finding people, friends and relatives sometimes turned to that office for help. According to the Smithsonian's National Postal Museum, one woman who had not heard from her son in 13 years mailed a letter addressed to "Mr. James Gunn, Power-Loom Shuttle Maker, Mass., America." Using the meagre information provided, the dead-letter clerks tracked down Gunn, who was living in Lowell, Massachusetts. Mrs. Gunn and her son were soon exchanging letters regularly.

• A Malaysian mail carrier kept 21,000 letters undelivered for up to four years. A 49-year-old post-office worker in South Yorkshire was arrested after 50,000 undelivered letters were discovered. And here in Canada, in May 2006, police charged a former mail carrier in Winnipeg with theft when they found in her home numerous bags of mail and parcels that were to have been delivered between October 2005 and February 2006.

• In July 2007, a postcard sent from Queensland, Australia, in 1889 showed up at its destination in Aberdeen, Scotland, after spending more than a century lost in the Australian postal system.

• Some of the oldest letters in existence, those of Pliny the Younger (*circa* 61 AD to 113 AD) of Ancient Rome, were not discovered until the sixteenth century.

• New Zealand scholar Constance Mews was reading a fifteenth-century volume intended to teach people how to write well when she discovered that sample letters "from two lovers" matched the story and writing style of famous twelfth-century lovers Abelard and Heloise. Though scholars still debate the authenticity of the letters, Mews published ▶

Letters, Lost and Found (*continued*)

them in 1999 as *The Lost Letters of Abelard and Heloise.*

• The Toronto-area Undeliverable Mail Office of Canada Post processes more than five million pieces of mail annually—not counting 55,000 sets of keys (car, house, hotel) and more than 50,000 photos. The office says that it returns items to customers in 92 percent of cases.

• In October 2007, a rewiring project at Arts and Crafts designer William Morris's home, Red House in Bexleyheath, South East London, led to the discovery of a letter under the floorboards that had lain undisturbed for 140 years. Dated 1864, the letter was from architect Philip Webb to his friend Morris.

• British author Anthony Trollope (1815–1882) wrote his earliest novels while working as a postman, occasionally dipping into the lost-letter box for ideas.

• The U.S. dead-letter office used to handle sums of people's money, and occasionally jewels, so in the early twentieth century, the office preferred to hire retired clergy, whom they felt could be trusted with valuables. Women were employed there for a different reason. Postal officials believed they had better analytical abilities than men and were there-fore better at deciphering confusing addresses.

• Major John McCrae's letter of May 13, 1915, to Dr. Charles Martin, found in the summer of 2002, contained the soldier-poet's "best and most concise account" of the battle that gave rise to his poem "In Flanders Fields." The letter was included in a packet of war letters to and from McGill University medical personnel. It was discovered in Yale University's collection of papers from American neurosurgeon Harvey Cushing.

❧

Further Reading

***Asservate,* by Naomi Tereza Salmon**
In 1989, photo-based artist Naomi Tereza
Salmon was commissioned to photograph
personal relics preserved at Auschwitz in
Poland, Buchenwald in Germany and Yad
Vashem in Jerusalem. As she writes in the
introduction, "The things themselves were
mostly fragments veiled in silence. . . . All
that was certain about these things was
that they had once belonged to people and
had meant something to those who had
found and kept them: as last signs, as traces
of memory, as relics, monuments, echoes,
lamentations and accusations—as evidence
of the crimes."

I was given this book by my agent after the
publication of my novel and was sobered and
moved by the inventory of objects included
in the book's pages. All had been, at one time,
personal possessions. All had been confis-
cated as booty by the murderers. Isolated and
meticulously photographed against a white
field, each individual comb, toothbrush,
rusted razor conjures a specific absence.
(Who combed her hair at Auschwitz? Who
groomed his beard with that razor?) As Naiko
observes in *The Letter Opener*, one of the most
poignant aspects of inanimate objects is their
longevity. They endure, and we do not; they
are unspeaking witnesses who can never tell
us where they have been and what (horrors)
they have seen.

***FOUND* magazine**
I am a voyeur. Most writers are. If I saw a
letter lying open on the ground, my tendency

would be to read it before attempting to return it. I am not necessarily proud of my inquisitiveness, but I also don't think I'm an exception. We live in an exceedingly voyeuristic culture—a society of "letter openers." Reality television encourages us to be peeping Toms. The entertainment/biography industry trains us to snoop and pry.

When I started writing my novel, I had a notion that I wanted to explore North America's seemingly insatiable fascination with other people's lives, while showing that voyeurism, in some instances, pushes us to respond. Perhaps it is the "thinking voyeur" in me that finds itself naturally drawn to such morally dubious productions as *FOUND* magazine. *FOUND* is a treasure trove of anonymous letters, birthday cards, doodles and notes salvaged from the garbage. Each found item is printed alongside field notes from the person submitting it, explaining the location and circumstances under which the item was discovered. The contents are deeply personal, comical, heartbreaking, epic and mundane. It is a nosy person's fantasy come true, and infinitely more provocative and stirring than the tabloids.

The Pigeon, by Patrick Süskind
Patrick Süskind is best known for his novel *Perfume*, but I still prefer his follow-up, *The Pigeon*. This beautifully crafted novella tells the story of Jonathan Noel, a fifty-year-old Parisian bank guard. Traumatized by his childhood experiences during the German occupation of France, Noel is a man so terrified of change and losing control that he has attempted to fashion a life of perfect ▶

equilibrium in which every uneventful day resembles every other uneventful day. One morning, a pigeon appears in the corridor outside his one-room flat, and in shattering his predictable routine triggers a profound internal crisis. The true triumph of this book is Süskind's flair for capturing Noel's agitated state of mind as he reacts to this outwardly insignificant event and conveying the depth of Noel's social anxiety as he attempts to restore order. *The Pigeon* brilliantly accomplishes what I aspired to do in *The Letter Opener* : it tells the story of a quiet life jeopardized—and eventually enriched—by an unexpected arrival.

Yo! Yes?, by Chris Raschka

After having my first child in 2001, I was able to immerse myself in a world of children's literature. Becoming a parent also taught me a kind of in-the-trenches Zen. One of the optimum states in Zen is beginner's mind, in which the number of possibilities is endless. *Yo! Yes?* is one of the Zen-ist and zaniest books on our bookshelf. Two lonely characters, one white and one black, one withdrawn and one outgoing, meet up on a city street. One boy greets the other. ("What's up?") The other is wary. ("Not much.") The first boy perseveres. ("Why?") The other replies. ("No fun.") The first one keeps trying. ("Oh?") The other shrugs. ("No friends.")

They continue to talk and eventually become friends. (It could serve as a precursor to the relationship between Naiko and

Andrei in my novel.) The entire drama unfolds in just 19 words and compresses the whole gamut of emotion—shyness, fear, curiosity, pleasure. Raschka gives new definition to literary elegance and economy, and I admire him greatly.

The works of Ryszard Kapúsciński

I have read a great deal of Ryszard Kapúsciński since his death in January 2007. Kapúsciński began his career as Poland's first foreign news correspondent and went on to write such classics as *Another Day of Life, Shah of Shahs* and *The Soccer War.*

He travelled all over the world and witnessed countless wars, coups and revolutions, keeping two notebooks with him at all times: one for recording facts necessary to file stories for his news agency job, the other for jotting down experiences that he felt were incommunicable but which eventually developed into the literary reportage for which he became best known. He is a peerless writer whose sometimes harrowing experiences were matched by immense literary talent and even greater compassion. He is a model of internationalism and provides a glimpse of what a global village could look like if we were only less anxious and more gently curious.

❦

Web Detective

www.nickbantock.com
Canadian artist and author Nick Bantock is
well-known for having popularized collage
and for his Griffin & Sabine books, which
tell stories through letters that the reader
pulls from envelopes. Click on "Art for Sale,"
then "Mail Art" to see examples of his lost-
letter works.

**www.nytimes.com/2005/09/04/books/
review/04DONADIO.html**
"Literary Letters, Lost in Cyberspace," by
Rachel Donadio of *The New York Times*,
explores the challenge the proliferation of
e-mail over letters presents to biographers
and cultural historians.

**www.civilization.ca/cpm/chrono/
chs1506e.html**
For the rules of letter writing observed
during colonial times, visit "A Chronology
of Canadian Postal History," and under the
heading "1704," click on "The Art of Letter
Writing."

**www.theromantic.com/LoveLetters/
main.htm**
Read love letters by some of history's most
famous personalities, including Beethoven,
Charlotte Brontë, Lord Byron and Voltaire.

www.civilization.ca/cpm/npmceng.html
The Canadian Postal Museum's website
features visuals of some of its historic
artifacts. Click on "Treasures Gallery" and
then "Airmail Letters" to read about missives

carried by balloon—the first attempts at airmail—during the Paris siege of 1871.

http://ancienthistory.about.com/library/bl/bl_text_plinyltrs2_intro.htm
The letters of Pliny the Younger (*circa* 61 AD to AD 113), lawyer, writer and philosopher of Ancient Rome, are some of the oldest in existence. This essay on Pliny, by John B. Firth, is accompanied by links to the text of some of Pliny's letters.

www.canadianletters.ca/about.html
The Canadian Letters & Images Project, begun in 2000, is an online archive of the Canadian war experience, with visuals and text of letters dating from the late 1800s.

www.foundmagazine.com
Established in June 2001, *FOUND* magazine is devoted to the "strange, hilarious and heartbreaking stuff that people've picked up," including lost letters.

http://farm1.static.flickr.com/178/402172497_4079299384.jpg
Created by M&C Saatchi, Melbourne, this striking ad for the *Australia Post* says it all.

❧